IDENTITY

ANTHONY JOSEPH

A KYLER SCOTT NOVEL

Identity is a work of fiction. Names, characters, places and incidents either are the product of the author's imagination or are used fictitiously. Any resemblance to actual persons, living or dead, events, or locales is entirely coincidental.

2013 Anthony Schubert Publishing

Cover design: David Eyman
Cover illustration: David Eyman
Back Cover Photo: Birdie Thompson

TO MY AMAZING WIFE, SHANTI...

Without you, there is little chance I would have had the inspiration and resolve to write this book. Thank you for helping me believe that we can achieve great things in life. You are the love of my life. I cherish sharing every moment we have, the good and the bad. I hope I can inspire you half as much as you've inspired me.

ACKNOWLEDGMENTS

I was driven to the write this book, in part, because of the inspirational beauty and majestic nature of my favorite city in the world, Florence, Italy. I feel that I owe it a debt of gratitude. Anyone that has walked amongst its renaissance buildings, conversed with its people, tasted its food and wine and watched it come to life with the glow of night knows the power of this place. I understand, with totality, why lovers and artists alike have been drawn there and have been affected greatly by the passion that it inspires in them. A city, however beautiful, cannot write nor edit a book. For that, I want to acknowledge the people in my life that helped steer me in the right direction, encouraged me to forge ahead and brought me to reality for what was good as well as what needed…work. With that, thank you Shanti Lowry for your remarkable insight and vision to help make a story great. Thank you to Vicky Krick, Tim Krick, Jane Lowry, Miles Lowry, Elena Welsh, Michael Pickard, Chioke Dmachi, Birdie Thompson, Eric VonFeldt, Brianna Miller, Dan LaPratt, Jamie Drew, James Drew, Danny and Violeta Bobadilla, Brian and Katie Galligan, Ben Vancura, Stacy Bradford, Jason, Flaherty, Michael McKiddy, Harli Ames, Kate Ammouchi and Scotch Ellis Loring for your support, love and friendship during this process. You are the pieces of my life that make it all mean something. Special thanks as well to Dave Eyman for your wonderful creative talent. I'm lucky to have a gifted friend like you that loves what he does. Thank you to Ned Lowry for connecting me with some great information to include in this story. And thank you to my parents, Dave and Laura, for birthing me. That was a big one. Thank you for helping me grow up to be the person I try to be. With the combined talent and influence from all of these wonderful people toward this book, you are bound to love it. If not, I blame it all on them and I'll have to re-think this whole situation. So…for their sake, do your best to enjoy… Identity!

Chapter 1

Scott Cruz looked in the rearview mirror only to find three black BMWs following him at full speed. He looked down at the gauge of his stolen Ferrari Enzo which confirmed what he already knew. He was flying down Lungarmo Torrigiani at warp speed.

Florence, Italy. One-way street hell. Thank God he knew the city but this was going to be interesting.

He slammed the clutch and launched into fourth gear, propelling the work of art forward, creating a bit of distance between him and his assailants. Quickly assessing his surroundings, Scott realized he had to find coverage quickly. Lucky for him, Florence had plenty of that. With a blink of an eye and skill that had been honed through years of professional driving, he downshifted and cut down Rampa delle Coste, its buildings seeming to hug the vehicle closer the faster he went. He narrowly missed a passing scooter by inches. The driver yelled something at him in Italian. What, he wasn't sure but guessed it wasn't "Bonjorno!"

Cruz cut the corner again, down Via del Bardi, downshifted and barely squeezed through another impossibly tight opening. He finally turned down Via dei Guicciardini, a wide street by Florence standards, giving him a chance to let the Enzo stretch its V12 651hp legs. In a matter of seconds, he was pushing eighty miles per hour.

A quick glance again at the rear view mirror told him that his followers were already struggling to keep up. They had just made the turn and were a couple blocks back. Just a bit more weaving through the city and into an area he knew he could get lost in. He just had to get there.

Cruz finally found Via dei Velluti, tested the famed F1 gearbox paddle shifters, popped into second gear, and headed right knowing it would take him back toward the bridge. Just another right on Via Maggio and bam! Daylight. The bridge. Ponte a Santa Trinita was just a few blocks ahead.

Quickly accelerating again, Scott screamed towards it, saw the red light ahead and made a choice to go for it. He gunned it and flew through the light and onto the bridge, barely splitting two Fiats coming from both directions. Another split second and the Enzo would have been toast.

He smiled after another mirror check. His trailers weren't as bold. They paused at the light, honking their horns trying to get the cross traffic to let them pass. He had gained some very valuable seconds.

Crossing the bridge, he took another hard right that took him along the Arno River with the famous Ponte Vecchio, literal translation "Old Bridge," right in front of him.

Cruz weaved through the tourist traffic and cut up Via Por Santa Maria. He knew if he could get to the Piazza, the crowds would help him get lost for good. There it was. Via Vacchereccia. He slammed on the brakes bringing the car to a screaming sliding halt, drawing no shortage of attention from the crowds on the streets.

Just then, he looked ahead to see what he least expected.

"Well ain't that some shit" He said, staring ahead at the row of Polizia di Stato with their guns drawn, screams of "Alto!" coming from that general direction sending the gangling of tourists on their stroll amidst the city scattering in a panicked frenzy.

Cruz knew it…he was screwed.

"CUT! Excellent take. Hold tight while we check playback."

At that moment, Kyler Scott, aka "Scott Cruz," Hollywood Blockbuster extraordinaire, leaned back and smiled to himself knowing that it probably meant the end of a long day of shooting on the set of Fire in Florence.

As long as his long-time friend and director, Jon Christenson, liked what he saw on the footage, they would be wrapped for the day. It was day 32 of shooting in Firenze and it had definitely been a busy month.

What Kyler would never tell his friend Johnny boy was why his A-List star, his bread and butter for action-film mega stardom, was burning the candle at both ends. But heck, Kyler had done it for years. Deception had become a way of life.

Chapter 2

As it turned out, Kyler was right. That last take had been The Magic, as Jon liked to call it when a complicated, vastly spanning sequence of a scene turned out beautifully. Christ, with all of the elements at play, they were lucky at times if the damned thing turned out at all. So the catch phrase was appropriate when he thought about it. Movie making at times certainly required just a touch of magic.

Kyler Scott had been in the biz for two decades, starting as the prototypical child-star at age ten, complete with a hearty dose of teen angst and mischievous aspirations. Mission accomplished. Puberty had found him knowing the Hollywood club scene well. He knew the bouncers by name, particularly those that accepted his generous tips to look the other way as he frequented their fine establishments. The paparazzi had done what they do best, finding him in his most compromising scenarios of drinking, drugging and whoring, and putting him on display for all to see. Kyler often laughed to himself thinking how much worse it would have been for him if TMZ had been around in those early years. He also found it humorous and wildly ironic that the same public that read the gossip in horror and judgment were seemingly the first to flock to his next big studio flick. That was the way it went though, and he loved exploiting it.

He was young, impressionable and perceivably invincible. His movies regularly grossed in the hundreds of millions. The epitome of the pre-fab story of the young heartthrob high school bad-boy falls in love cliché that somehow found overwhelming success at the box office. Teenage girls (and the boys that were trying to date them) flocked to the theater en-masse.

Bigger success, bigger balls. Proverbially speaking, of course. At the prime age of seventeen, Kyler discovered the lovely Beverly Hills establishment of county lock-up when he and his good friend Johnny Walker Blue Label made his Porsche 911 the latest storefront display at Giorgio Armani on Rodeo Drive.

A decade and a half later, as he drove back to his four-star Italian hotel in the middle of one of the most beautiful cities in the world, he reflected on the irony of how his defacement of the famed Italian designer storefront had literally spun his life around. His thirty-two year old self stared back at him in the rearview mirror. A few wrinkles of life were present but the adventurous spirit shone through his eyes as fiercely as ever. They were eyes that had seen and done things that his teenage version would have wet his proverbial pants over.

He pulled out of his reverie and looked up ahead toward his destination. His daily ride to and from set was a short one. They had been allowed to set up shop for the film on the edge of the Piazza della Signoria which, like his hotel, had a caps' view of the famed Cathedral. It was also the same Piazza, or Plaza, that housed the copy of the David, complete with a fig leaf hiding his manhood as not to offend the passing women and children. He had to admit, it was a pretty sweet office. White collar America, eat your heart out. Donald Trump may have a penthouse view of Park Avenue but he had the Basilica di Santa Maria de Fiore…a four hundred-step tower that provided those brave enough to climb it with a spectacular three hundred and sixty degree view of the entire city.

His hotel, the Boscolo Astoria, sat on the opposite side of the cathedral. Prior to arriving a little over a month ago, its website had informed him that the hotel was "a rare pearl of baroque Florentine beauty." Travertine tile flooring, arched and climbing ceilings and staff with hospitality worthy of its rating. It was, indeed a traveler's Italian dream and most certainly met his A-list star façade's expectations.

That all meant little to Kyler though. His primary concern was the existence of a secure, wireless Internet connection in the privacy of his room, an amenity that he'd found was far from a sure thing. As a matter of fact, he'd discovered that to be a problem throughout Italy. The American method of Starbucks on every corner apparently hadn't found its way here yet. As a tourist, Kyler didn't mind. He didn't mind that civilization, as he knew it, got dialed back a few notches. No massive Wal-Mart with a million products he'd never need. Few drove fancy cars. Instead, most mounted scooters, flying through the streets with reckless abandon. Still others found the smallest frame they could slap two doors onto, usually bearing the name of Italy's flagship…the Fiat.

Sure, there were the smattering of Beemers, Benzes, Alpha Romeos and Audis. Those were reserved for the elite. Then, of course, there was Scott Cruz's famed Ferrari Enzo. A million dollar Italian vehicular masterpiece. Driving it off-hours was a perk Kyler had written into his Fire in Florence contract. Most assumed, Christenson included, that it was the typical prima donna act…writing in an over-the-top demand filled with pomp and circumstance. Part of the territory that comes with the current silver screen "it" guy. His reasoning, however, was one of necessity. In his experience, a fast car with uncanny elusiveness was bound to come in handy.

Above all, Kyler loved the food. No surprise there. Italy's amazing cuisine…the cibo di buongustaio…was world-renowned and it never ceased to amaze him. It was an art form that seemed to even surpass the finest Roman architecture that had survived millennia. Sure, the coliseum had stood the test of over two thousand years but it didn't warm his heart the way a plate of handmade gnocchi could. And what was a fine meal without vino? Two-buck chuck, beware. For two Euros, Kyler could find a wine that made him want to make love to the very glass that housed it.

Yes, Kyler Scott certainly had an extensive and deep-rooted love affair with la terre di amore, his land of love, but on this trip, Kyler Scott was most certainly not on holiday. And if he wasn't careful, he may not live to see it again.

Chapter 3

Kyler Scott was a physical specimen. Not imposing in stature per se. He had intentionally maintained a physique that would not stand out in a crowd. That façade hid what could only be described as six feet, one hundred and seventy pounds of terrifying tactical force. His workout regimen consisted of a six-mile run each morning followed up with a hundred pushups of varying styles, another hundred pull-ups and rounded out with a thousand menacing crunches. Some guys trained for looks, Scott trained for survival. Training that had been ingrained in him since seventeen.

*　　　　　　*　　　　　　*　　　　　　*

"Scott! You're free to go," announced the portly policeman named Stevens who had enjoyed keeping the cocky so-called-heartthrob actor in jail for the night.

Officer Jack Stevens, who was aging quite ungracefully as told by his protruding belly and receding hairline, hated young actor-types. He hated Scott with heightened vigor mostly because he was tired of seeing the cocky son of a bitch's face on every magazine on the grocery store rack.

On-screen romance heating up off-screen for Kyler Scott and Stephanie Phillips?

Kyler Scott...get his summer look without spending a fortune.

Friends fear for Scott as he's found passed out in local club bathroom.

Kyler Scott ...gay? Childhood friend tells all.

Seriously, Stevens thought, who reads that crap anyway? He'd never seen any of the kid's movies but, judging by the titles alone, he surmised he wasn't missing much. Any movie called Bonding in Boulder probably wasn't banging on the Hollywood Foreign Press's door as far as he was concerned. Unless, he thought to himself with a smile indicative of the dirty old man he'd become, it was of the skin-o-max variety!

Yes, he had concluded, Kyler Scott was just another punk teen actor whose stand as the it-guy in this town would be short-lived, only to be quickly replaced by the next pseudo-stud. Scott couldn't leave his jail quick enough.

"Lucky for you, Scott, your loving parents posted bail," Stevens barked as he slid back the door to his cell. "I hear they got a nice place for ya to get your shit together on the other side. Shame…we may not get another Oscar-winner from you for a while. So sad."

"You know, officer, you're right," retorted a still-arrogant Kyler, despite his buried fear from his stint in the slammer. "If I'm lucky, I just may end up fat, bald, old and single…just like you."

Stevens' face flushed red with fury at the little prick. If he hadn't been so anxious to get him out of his jail, he would've considered finding a reason to throw him back in for another night. Teach him a lesson. Then he remembered Kyler Scott was on his way to the land of lessons…Fishburne Military School.

"Just get the fuck out of my jail Scott," Stevens said, grabbing his scrawny frame, thrusting him in front of him and down the hallway.

They arrived at the front desk where Kyler collected his wallet, cigarettes and favorite lighter which had been in his pockets when he was hauled in just after one o' clock in the morning. All of his belongings accept, of course, the keys to the Porsche. Kyler wouldn't be seeing those for a while what with his suspended license and all.

"It's been such a pleasure enjoying your fine establishment, Officer. Let's do this again sometime. Your charm and wit is absolutely stunning," Kyler chided, flinging one more smart-ass remark before he prepared to face what he'd been dreading since about 3:00 am. That was right about when he sobered up just enough to begin imagining what his father, retired Colonel William E. Scott, would have in store for him.

William Scott would never be described as a cuddly fellow. He was also most definitely not an old man, still fierce and fit at fifty-three, despite his retired status from the military. Forced retirement was a bit strong so the United States Army elected to tell him that they strongly encouraged him to "enjoy the good life" of a post-military career. Truth be told, the Colonel had become a bit too intense, even by Army standards. In this day and age of sensitivity and precaution, not to mention public perception, towards the mistreatment of soldiers, the senior Scott's style of cadet training had created a publicity nightmare on one too many occasions. The latest backlash of a recruit crying foul after being forced to stand outside in the rain on one leg for three hours because he arrived ten minutes late to the morning run had been enough. The recruit had threatened to take the ludicrous display of discipline to the press if the Army didn't release the Colonel. They quickly obliged. They had been hammered quite a bit as of late and couldn't afford another PR debacle. Colonel William E. Scott was retired with honors after serving over thirty years in the United States Army. Needless to say, he hadn't been ready to leave and the anger of his forced supposed "good life" had left him even more bent than he'd already been.

As would be expected, Kyler both hated and feared his father equally. Troubled teen actor with Daddy issues? That's a new one.

As Kyler had expected, the Colonel was sitting military-stoic in the chair of the waiting room with his meager mother, Ellen Scott, by his side. William was staring toward the door as if waiting to launch his fury toward it the minute Kyler strode through. Kyler actually took a beat from fear when he saw his father, never having seen him this enraged...which was saying something in and of itself. The air of intimidation Colonel Scott created even caused Officer Stevens to awkwardly salute him, not sure what else to do.

"At ease Officer," the Colonel stated all-too-calmly. "Thank you for handling my son with proper discipline. I apologize for his actions but can assure you that he will be dealt with accordingly."

Had Kyler actually had anything to drink in the last six hours, he may have urinated on the spot. The Colonel shifted his piercing gaze from Officer Stevens, who, despite himself, actually felt bad for the young punk. He fixed his stare back onto Kyler, "You're coming with me young man. Now!"

Back in his Florence hotel room, Kyler steeled himself a bit at how long ago that seemed. How different the Kyler Scott of seventeen years young had been from the current man that stood before him in the mirror. His mind still waged the argument of whether he thanked or despised his father for what he'd done, for how he'd raised him. As always, he ended up somewhere in between. He wondered aloud whether his father, seeing him on the career path he ended up on, would have felt a bit of ironic pride?

Unfortunately, Kyler would never know. His father had died suddenly when he was still in Military school at the young age of fifty-five. Some said it was the stress of not knowing a career of anything other than the Army. Others attributed it to the stress he had put on his heart from all the years of intensity he'd endured as well as that which was self-inflicted. Kyler, however, couldn't help but wonder if grief had, in the end, got him. Grief and disappointment. Kyler was his only son and the Colonel had had so many hopes for him in his childhood development. Illusions of grandeur that he would follow in his father's respectable, country-serving footsteps. As he would quickly find out, these lofty expectations he'd pressed upon his son would drive him towards what he categorized as a money-grubbing, vanity-focused, self-absorbed fluff of a career. By the time Kyler hit puberty and had started to hit his stride in the industry, all Colonel Scott saw in the son he'd had such high hopes for was a soft, emotional, pansy of a boy.

A feeling that had initially begun as hurt in Kyler quickly turned to resentment and, of course rebellion. He expected his father may not understand his choice of career but, maybe unrealistically, thought the Colonel would still be proud of him. Kyler's success was quick and formidable. What father wouldn't take just a bit of pride in that?

Kyler had been wrong.

What was worse was the fact that his mother, Ellen, had been a silent but strong supporter in getting him started. An entertainment agent had approached the two when Kyler was twelve years old while they had been out shopping on the famous Melrose Street in Hollywood. In a story that followed the seemingly too-good-to-be-true strain, Kyler was literally discovered on the streets of Hollywood. The agent said he had the look and, after talking over a surreal and cliché Hollywood lunch, also had the charisma to be a star. Being under-age, all he needed was the commitment of his parents to get rolling.

Ellen jumped at the offer, seeing an opportunity for her son to follow a safer path than her husband had. Truth be told, what mother wants to see her son enter into a career that has her wondering every day if she'll get a knock on the door from a uniform, informing her that her baby boy would be returning to her in a coffin? She'd had nearly three decades of that fear already with her husband and, although she knew the Colonel would never approve of this choice of life for his son, she was definitely not going to pass it by.

Ellen spent the next year taking her son to acting classes, driving him to audition after audition, consoling him through the heartless and cold rejections and then, finally celebrating with him when one Disney show decided to give him a shot on its newest Saved By The Bell-wannabe pilot. The show itself flopped miserably. It was canned after one episode, which had to be some sort of Disney record. The one shining star of it, though, was said to be Kyler Scott. Hence, a star was born.

As Kyler's career exploded into superstardom, the Colonel refused to watch anything he appeared in. He wouldn't think of congratulating him when his first movie remained at the top of the Box Office for three weeks straight, raking in over three hundred million bucks and ensuring that the Scott family was set for life. As his resentment and brazen nature increased, Kyler didn't miss the opportunity to point out to his father that he was merely jealous. After all, in a single movie, he'd provided more for his family than the old man had in thirty years of "serving his country."

"Maybe you should have thought about serving your family instead....*sir.*"

Kyler would receive the beating of his life that evening. He had challenged everything that was tried and true in his father and the Colonel was not about to let his pussy of a son get away with that without learning a hard lesson. If he wasn't going to get it from the Army, he would get it from somewhere.

Back in the hotel, Kyler looked in the mirror again. He ran his finger along the scar just above his eyebrow that had been planted there courtesy of his father's academy ring. The Colonel had forgotten he was wearing it when he wound up for his first backhand that night an entire lifetime ago. These days, Kyler wore it as a reminder.

It was also the first of many severe injuries he'd endured. But, unlike the previous source of provocation out of a rebellious teenager with a big mouth, his recent ones came as merely part of the territory of his chosen career path. A reconstructed knee from a three-story leap out of a building in Geneva five years ago. A dislocated shoulder that found the most inconvenient times to pop out of its socket thanks to being side-swiped by a Mercedes G-Wagon in Berlin three years ago. Then there was his closest dash with death marked by a scar from a bullet wound in his left bicep courtesy of a Freedom Fighter in Tripoli a year ago. Scott couldn't help but look at it and think of how his life had come down to a matter of inches. Five or six to the right and he would have been visiting the morgue instead of being carted out on a medevac across the Mediterranean to a Sicilian Hospital.

He shook his head back to the present. After all, now was not the time for reminiscing or casting out what-if scenarios. He needed to focus. He had a busy night ahead of him.

Chapter 4

Kyler had just finished his shower and ripped through a change of clothes when his laptop rang…an occurrence he had not quite gotten used to yet.

The tech boys back home had set him up with the latest and greatest in gadgetry. His was a laptop unlike any he'd ever seen at Best Buy.

It was, first of all, virtually indestructible. He'd been told that it was Panasonic's latest offering in their military-grade Toughbook line…the type that was usually reserved for a tanker in the middle of Iraq or Afghanistan somewhere and capable of withstanding everything short of a nuclear bomb. Kyler knew it was made of some variety of magnesium alloy which could sustain a thirty-foot plunge…more than he could say for himself, that was certain. When push came to shove, it was clear the agency was more concerned with the survival of the content on the laptop than its prize agent. The machine had iPad-like touch capability, which came in handy when pulling up geospatial images for targets sent from internal intelligence. His super-geek, World of Warcraft-addicted techs had carried on to tell him that it passed every military certification imaginable, had Ft. Knox-like security protection on its hard drive and even had software that, in the event he got captured, his boys back home could remotely detonate every relevant piece of data on it.

It was his lifeblood. Being military spec, most machines hadn't been constructed with cameras. The military tended to avoid putting features on their devices that allowed someone to snapshot evidence without anyone knowing about it. For Scott though, they Pimped his Panasonic…a phrase they had proudly coined and immediately spread to the masses via their equally-dorky Twitter followers. Had Kyler not been in the film industry thereby being forced to maintain some semblance of celebrity presence to support his underlying cover, he would have gladly remained naïve to what it meant to Tweet, "Like" a post on Facebook or check in to a trendy New York Bistro. Alas, some things could not be avoided. For the greater good, he told himself.

The camera on the laptop served as his line of secure communication. The web cam, coupled with a completely private, encrypted and virtually impenetrable tunnel allowed him to communicate via video conferencing. Sort of like Skype on steroids. They had determined that with some extensive programming, they could create a firewall of protected tunneling that would make the world's greatest computer hackers' head spin. Most importantly, it was infinitely more secure than any cell phone they could give him and added the benefit of passing information visually back and forth with the boys back at Langley.

Langley, Virginia. Home of the Central Intelligence Agency. It was indeed home, in a sense, for Kyler even though most of the agents and employees there didn't even know he existed. They most definitely didn't know he was on the payroll but, then again, most wouldn't be surprised. It wasn't a stretch to imagine that the intelligence agency had many tentacles reaching far into the depths of numerous arenas. There was a reason other intelligence divisions referred to them as "Spooks."

"Agent Scott?" rang the familiar voice of Dr. Ethan Goldman. Goldman was Kyler's keeper, the man he took his marching orders from and a man that he respected immensely.

"Good…uh…afternoon, Doc" Kyler did the mental time subtraction. While it was going on nine o'clock in the evening in Florence, it was still just three in the afternoon back in Virginia.

"Another day of riveting excitement I presume, Mr. Scott? Danger on every corner for the fearless Scott Cruz?"

"Absolutely right sir. Truly, I don't know how Cruz does it."

Kyler always reveled in what had become regular banter between the two. Friends were not a luxury synonymous with the profession. Truth be told, the luxuries were few and far between.

"At any minute, craft services could let a bad piece of meat slip into my lunch. Could keep me in the bathroom for hours. And do they call this a luxury hotel? What a dump...what with its perfect service and incredible views."

"Well I suppose you'll have to endure. Keep your head up," and that would be the end of the fun. Goldman had, of course, not called to regale in the life of his Hollywood Heartthrob.

"I'm sending over a recent picture of Gianni Dimarco. Confirm receipt."

In a moment, Kyler saw the icon pop up on his screen notifying him that he had an incoming picture and clicked on it. In a flash, an image of a finely dressed Italian gentleman in his forties matriculated on his screen in a small, thumbnail version. Kyler double-clicked on the image and it quickly filled the entirety of the screen.

"Confirmed. This is our target?"

"Affirmative. We've been watching Dimarco since 2001 when he popped on our radar for suspected arms dealings shortly after 9/11."

"As did thousands of others," Kyler commented.

He'd just recently started with the agency back then and was overwhelmed immediately. Being the new guy on the farm, there was a flood of Intel coming in every hour from every direction and he couldn't begin to decipher what was real and what wasn't. The entire country was reasonably on edge and they were getting security threat tips from their allies fearing they were next on the list, internal analysts that were on high alert and, worst of all, American citizens that were determined to "nail those bastards" for the devastation the terrorists had caused. As a result, the international Watchlist database grew exponentially as had the number of analysts tasked with probing for solid evidence against this laundry list of suspected wrongdoers. As one could imagine, many of the mysteries went unsolved but those suspects remained eternally under suspicion.

Goldman agreed, "Correct on that, agent. Dimarco has always been high on the list but the worst we've been able to nail him on was a cocaine transaction in 2006. We've been letting him operate while waiting for the big fish ever since."

"And we caught something?"

"Do you know Jason Palmer?"

"The QTS nerd?" Kyler laughed at the redundancy of the description. QTS Tek was a defense sub-contractor working exclusively for the CIA and, more specifically, for the Director and they were all full-fledged nerds.

Goldman ignored the jab, "Palmer's real name is Mikhail Nikolaevich. He's a defector from Russia."

Kyler wasn't shocked by the news. Goldman had been putting international ex-patriots in his employ for as long as Scott had been around and, he was certain, long before.

"His Uncle is Andrei Ivanova who was formerly with the 8th department of the KGB Directorate S...*before* it was integrated into Directorate S."

Kyler was very familiar with what was the most important branch of the Russian KGB. Otherwise termed as the Illegal Branch, Directorate S consisted of 13 departments handling all matters of intelligence, training and deployment and is still active though now part of the Russian SVR Service. More intriguing was department 8, however, which Goldman was referring to. This department hadn't become part of Directorate S until 1976 when an international incident forced it to fall under a group that could provide more oversight to its activities. Previously, it had been an autonomous section primarily engaged in what was affectionately referred to as *wet jobs*. A nice term for murder, poisoning, sabotage and other activities that the civilized souls of their respective countries reprimanded despite the fact that most allied nations operated some similar form of black ops group to handle their government's dirty work.

"Is Ivanova with SVR now?" Kyler asked.

"Negative. He also defected. According to Palmer, his Uncle left the country over 30 years ago and never went back. Bounced around and settled down in Italy where he found his wife and they spawned a couple of offspring."

"How's he connected to Dimarco?"

"He works for him."

"Doing what exactly?"

"Well...that's where it gets interesting. Up until recently, he was a bus boy at Dimarco's five-star restaurant in Florence, Via Di Santo Spirito. According to one of our locals on the ground there though, he no longer works there."

"He could have found something more lucrative to do for Dimarco than clearing tables then..." Kyler surmised.

"A reasonable assumption except for the message Palmer received."

"Which was?"

"Palmer received a bottle of wine from Ivanova. Palmer hadn't heard from Ivanova in a decade so you can imagine his surprise when he finally does out of the blue and it's just a bottle of wine and a tiny placard that says 'from Uncle Andrei.'"

"Please tell me there was more to the message than that."

"No agent, we're all up in fucking arms over a guy we've been tracking for 12 years because of a sweet gesture from one Russian defector uncle to his nephew."

Kyler flushed red.

"Sorry sir...you were just getting to the good part..."

"Anyway..." Goldman continued. "Palmer *figured* there must be something behind the sudden communication. After a bit of examination, he peeled back the label on the bottle and there was a written message on the back that said *Villa Santini. Andrei aiding truth. Gianni Dimarco. North Korea. MASS CHAOS!*"

The hairs on the back of Kyler's neck stood up at the last bit. In the wave of 9/11 and the wars in the Middle East, many Americans tended to forget the looming danger that North Korea posed particularly when it became the latest country to join the nuclear club in 2006.

"Where was the bottle shipped from?" Kyler asked, trying to process the information into some type of theory.

"We don't know. There wasn't a return label. It wasn't sent through normal shipping methods like FedEx or UPS. Not sure how it got to Palmer."

"What is Villa Santini?"

"It's the winery the bottle came from. I'll give you one guess on who owns it."

Kyler was already nodding his head, "Dimarco."

"Bingo! You win the prize agent."

"What could a winery owned by a coke and arms dealer have to do with aiding truth and North Korea?" Kyler asked aloud, more to himself.

"That's what we need you to find out. You and Agent Langdon will work in tandem on this. We put her on a flight this morning. She landed in Florence an hour ago."

Kyler flushed briefly at the mention of his to-be-partner on the job and was immediately embarrassed. If Goldman noticed, he was kind enough not to point it out.

Trying to move past the moment quickly, Kyler asked, "What should we start with sir? How should we address the target?"

"For now, just a bit of observation. As I mentioned, Dimarco is the owner of Via Di Santo Spirito. It's a little restaurant located on the other side of the river."

Goldman sent over an image of a map while he spoke that pinpointed the restaurant's location. Kyler pinched the location to zoom in and familiarize himself with the surroundings once it hit the street-level view.

"Dimarco spends most nights there, watches over the business, mingles with the clientele…you know the routine."

"And you want me to play my Scott Cruz card and have a fabulous and lengthy dinner whilst coyly watching the comings and goings surrounding our new friend?" Kyler finished.

"Right on the money there, agent. Son of a bitch…they're wrong about you actors…there *is* a little brains to go with the brawn."

"What about Villa Santini? Can we gather some aerial intelligence for this place?" Kyler asked, referring to the drones the CIA had at their disposal.

On a fly-over conducted remotely, the drones could zero in on a location and capture a multitude of details...images, heat zone maps, geographical statistics...all with a quality and clarity that was enough to strike more than a bit of fear into the conspiracy theorists talking about Big Brother in every breath.

"We've got a UAV with infrared heading out there tomorrow morning to get some coverage. I'll have CBP analyze the data and send it over with their summations. You and Langdon will head out there after we know what we're looking at."

CBP is the Customs and Border Protection division of U.S. law enforcement responsible for aiding protection against acts of terrorism, amongst other duties. Goldman regularly turned to them for aide in gathering site intelligence.

"Sounds good sir. I'm anxious to see what we get back."

"As are we. I'll let you know when it comes in. For now we need to get to know Dimarco as much as possible. Who are his potential associates? What's his routine? Is he running any of his operation there locally? You know the drill."

Kyler nodded. "Hopefully he'll tip his hand a bit tonight. Not sure what we'll find but at least we can get the lay of the land."

"That's a start. See who his clientele is, look for anyone that may be more than just a loyal paying customer. Like I said, observe, play dumb...you know...be Scott Cruz."

Goldman added the last part from what he knew Kyler understood to be ultimate respect and jest. Ethan had known ever since the early days of Fishburne that there was something special about the young fireball. He had definitely been right in recruiting him when he did.

"The Cruz charade will be in full effect." Kyler said. "Consider it done. I'll put on my winning movie-star smile and enjoy an Italian-style meal at his fine establishment."

"Take Langdon as your date. A movie mogul of your caliber wouldn't be dining alone in one of Italy's cities of love, now would he?"

"I do believe you have a point there sir. Always thinking you are. That's why you're the boss."

"Kindly remove your lips from my ass and get out of there. Send me a full report of what you see before you start tomorrow."

"Done and done sir."

"Watch your back Scott. Don't underestimate Dimarco. He's a slippery little shit."

"Got it. Goodnight Doc."

The image of Goldman disappeared, leaving his computer's home screen with a cover picture of his latest movie poster as its background.

Kyler opted for a quick change. He threw on his custom-tailored Luigi Borelli suit, deciding against a tie as it was a bit formal for his GQ image. He fitted his ankle holster and packed his gun, a thirty-eight special, just in case. He slipped into his thousand dollar Tanino Crisci Italian shoes, did a mirror check and laughed back at his image. His seventeen-year-old self would have died to have the style and appearance of this current version. Image had been everything at that age for him. These days, the appearance was merely that…just an image. An image that served his purpose well.

Chapter 5

Gianni Dimarco was the quintessential caldo maschio italiano, equally beloved by woman from all over the world and envied by men alike…and, truth be told, beloved by his share of men as well.

Dimarco was the epitome of style and charm. Wealth did not describe the lengths to which his power extended. His reputation preceded him as a smooth talker, connoisseur of food, wine and fashion and one that carried a dizzying blend of confidence and magnetism. Careful not to appear overly arrogant while still commanding a room, he knew how to leverage his assets and it had suited him well.

The other side of his reputation was mostly rumor, speculation and hearsay. One as a charming serpent that was calm and smooth until he needed to strike. Those that were unfortunate enough to find out, discovered that his strike was indeed venomous.

At least…that was what "they" said. Most willingly and blindly accepted what they saw on the surface which was the owner of the finest establishment in Firenze and, arguably, in all of Western Europe. It had been noted in magazines, books, newspapers, travel agencies and the travel channel. Dimarco, of course, like any good business man, had been responsible for making sure his Via Di Santo Spirito appeared in these locations. It was good for business and definitely wasn't bad for his ego.

"Buona sera, Signore and Signora Amici. Benvenuti" Dimarco flashed his famous smile as he greeted the couple. They were one of his many regulars amongst the rich and famous. Some, of course rich and infamous as was the case with Armand Amici.

"Grazie. Buona sera Gianni," Amici returned, guiding his spectacular beauty of a wife towards their reserved private table in the rear of the restaurant.

As was a habit of Gianni's, he admired the man's finely appointed Caraceni suit and Salvatore Ferragamo shoes, both handmade for the business mogul. Gianni was certainly impressed, although he smiled with just a small bit of satisfaction knowing that he was sporting a Kiton K50 which meant that he was literally wearing a BMW. At about fifty thousand dollars, it was one of only fifty suits tailored by its maker.

Amici's fashionista wife was also gracefully adorned in a Roberto Cavalli dress that Gianni enjoyed admiring as she passed. The fact that she certainly took care of herself did not go unnoticed by anyone. They were one of Italy's most formidable power couples packing the perfect combination of wealth, style and regal good looks.

To Gianni, they were great for business.

Dimarco continued to make his way from table to table, showing his elite status through his ability to greet most guests in their language of choice. He was fluent in English, German, French, Spanish, Greek, and, of course, Italian. He could also get by with the basics in Mandarin and Cantonese. Mainly, he spoke the languages of his wealthiest clientele.

"How does our guest list look this evening, Aldabella?" Dimarco asked the beautifully-adorned hostess.

"Excellent sir. Full house as usual, mostly with regulars." She replied, scanning the leather-bound reservation book. "I trust you don't mind sir, but Kyler Scott's personal assistant called …you know…the actor?"

"Of course. Our Fire in Firenze action-star extraordinaire." Dimarco nodded.

"Yes sir. Well he asked if we could squeeze Mr. Scott and his date in for dinner. I assumed you would want to accommodate him so I agreed."

"But of course. What time will he be joining us? I want to be sure to welcome him personally." Dimarco asked while consulting his Bulova watch, noting the time of nine o'clock sharp. It was peak time for dinner Italy standards.

"It would appear that your timing is impeccable sir. That looks to be his car," Aldebella said while nodding toward the front window of the restaurant.

Gianni followed her gesture only to find his valet attendant walking up to the stunning Enzo that had just arrived. Emerging from the passenger side door was, at first, just legs and then a beautiful and elegant woman completed the picture. She appeared to be a mix of maybe European, Native American and possibly something else. Whatever uncertainty there was to her origins, one thing was indisputable...she was a vision of beauty and seduction. Dimarco found himself staring, which was rare for a man that certainly did not struggle finding beautiful women.

The attendant circled around to open the door for Kyler who thanked the man and eased his way comfortably next to his date. She took his arm and they strode gracefully toward the entrance. As Kyler had expected, Dimarco took quick stock of his excellent choice in attire. Dimarco's reputation had preceded him.

"Good evening, Mr. Scott. Benvenuti!" Dimarco extended a firm hand out to Kyler as they approached the hostess desk. "I am Gianni Dimarco, the owner. Welcome to Via di Santo Spirito, Signore. We are honored to have you join us this evening."

Kyler flashed his best movie-star smile and turned up the charm meter.

"Grazie Signore Dimarco. Based on what I've heard of your restaurant, I'm only sorry that it has taken me this long."

Kyler had already made a quick scan of what he could see in his peripheral, an act that undoubtedly went unnoticed by Dimarco. His training had made his observation skills uncanny and stealth. Just like a ninja, he thought, smiling at his own little joke. He had already noticed the couple in the rear, clearly up a few pegs in class then the rest of the guests. He made a bet with himself that those would be who Dimarco spent the most time with. He would be sure to keep his attention their way.

Scott, the ever-present gentlemen, immediately turned to his date to introduce her, "Mr. Dimarco, this is Grace Gannon."

Gianni gently kissed her hand and looked up, "It is a pleasure to make the acquaintance of such a beautiful woman. Bella bella madame."

"Grazie, signore," she smiled. "You are too kind indeed."

"Mr. Dimarco, I'm sure you are aware of Ms. Gannon's work. Aside from being a stunner, she is an amazingly talented musician back in the States."

"But of course, Signore." Dimarco hadn't a clue. "We of course don't get much of the music here to Firenze but her reputation is well-known to those of us with taste." He smiled, covering quickly and hoping to move past the subject.

Kyler smiled, knowing that he had been playing the restaurateur. After all, Alani Landon, currently known as Grace Gannon, was most definitely not a musician. She would be tonight though.

He made a grand gesture of looking around the restaurant. It was an act that served two purposes. The one he intended to take precedence was the indulging his host's ego of by showing how impressed he was with the restaurant.

There was every reason to be, as it happened. It was the pure essence of Italian fine dining. Scattered throughout were a red and orange array of granite stone columns, hand-carved inlets in the stoned walls with bottles of wine, travertine-tiled floors and beautiful wrought iron separating the main dining area from the bar. The finely appointed white clothed tables reflected what was undoubtedly five-star level service by the wait staff. The lights were set at a dim level, inviting patrons to enjoy a lengthy meal filled with food, wine, dessert and intimate conversation. The faint sound of Pavarotti played lightly in the background as the ultimate final touch.

The second purpose of Kyler's draw out charade of taking in the glorious ambience of the restaurant was that it gave him an opportunity to scan the rest of the patrons. His mind cross-referenced back to the images in the electronic files he had been sent at the beginning of his work. Pictures of known associates to Dimarco.

Scott had a photographic memory...one of the many perks of being an actor for as long as he had been. Memorization either becomes part of the craft or they are obsolete. Who needs an actor that can't remember his lines? He could recite facts, recall images, and remember hundreds of names. It was safe to assume that anything he received in a file got committed to memory after a couple reviews.

"Signore Dimarco, you're restaurant is absolutely beautiful. You must have many loyal customers."

"Indeed we do, sir. We are not exactly...how do you say...cheap," Gianni said with a smile and a wink. "Guests like yourself who can afford the fine dining experience we offer are few and far between. Many are the local successful business men of Firenze. We are...eh...a tight knit group as I believe you would say."

"You're English is fantastic as well. Definitely better than my Italian!"

"Grazie Grazie." Dimarco feigned humility. "Please, don't let me detain you any longer. We have your table prepared. Prego, prego."

To Kyler's delight, Dimarco guided them toward a table that was only feet from the couple he had spotted when they first walked in. If he was lucky, he may be able to pick up a bit of their conversation. He only hoped his Italian would be up to par.

Dimarco pulled out the chair for Alani first and handed her a menu. Kyler seated himself and took the menu from Gianni.

"Would you both like to start with a glass of wine, perhaps? Might I recommend our Via di Santo Spirito red wine? It is made in the Arezzo region nearby at our own winery and is traditional, bold Chianti. I believe you will enjoy it very much."

Perfect. Kyler thought to himself.

"You're wine's reputation precedes itself," Kyler replied. "We would love to start with a bottle. Grazie Signore."

"Molte bene Signore."

Gianni glided away with the graceful yet powerful walk a man of his wealth, confidence and stature demanded. Kyler watched him go and then turned his attention to his lovely date, the radiant Ms. Alani Langdon.

"That went well," he said with a smile.

"Most certainly," she agreed. "Was I beautiful and charming yet seductively mysterious?"

"A regular belladonna conundrum," he replied. "We'll have to make sure he gets a signed copy of your latest album. What was it called again?"

"Twisted and Tormented. Self-titled, of course. It was my own personal exploration album about how my poor choices in men have led me to live a life alone, accompanied only by mint chocolate chip Hagen Daas and a VHS copy of Sleepless in Seattle."

"Grammys…look out."

Kyler turned serious, "It really is great to see you, Alani. I'm glad we are working this together. All kidding aside, you look fantastic." And she did. He had never known a woman that could match her beauty and doubted he ever would. Most notable were her eyes that toggled somewhere between blue and green. They were staring back at him now and he found himself getting lost in them.

"Nice try Cruz but you're not getting me into bed."

"Can't blame a guy for trying, can you?"

"Only when it's you," the statement was only partially true but she would never let him know that. She was quite strict on her policy of not mixing personal and business. But boy…he sure didn't make it easy. She had to admit that he looked pretty good himself.

Chapter 6

About twenty kilometers away from where Kyler Scott was dining, a telephone rang in the exquisitely appointed library of an Italian mansion-turned-hotel.

"Bonjorno," the man answered and then listened.

"Yes sir," he replied. "Everything is in perfect order. We are on schedule and have not sensed any surveillance or suspicion."

"Excellent," the voice on the other end replied. "You are my most trusted confident Vitale. Notify me immediately if there is any change."

"Grazie, Signore. Thank you," Vitale answered, gesturing his thanks to the telephone that could not see him. "You're trust will not go unwarranted. We will execute the plan to perfection."

They said their goodbyes and Vitale replaced the receiver, smiling with pride and ease. Vitale Baldacci was a tall, slender man in his early forties though his hair was full and jet-black. He sat down in the leather chair at the grand desk of the elaborate library and lit a long cigarette, dragging the smoke deep into his lungs. He took a small sip from his glass of scotch. It was not just any scotch. It was a bottle of Macallan's fine and rare collection circa 1939. The bottle carried a hefty price tag of over ten thousand dollars. He laughed to himself realizing that, in his ounce and a half glass, served "neat," he was consuming over six hundred dollars of fine liquor.

Vitale certainly loved his scotch but he was saving his prize possession, another offering from the same brand dated back to

1926. That one demanded a street price of over thirty-five thousand dollars and would be reserved for when the deal he had put his caller at ease about came to its final fruition. He would pour a glass and savor his new level of achieved wealth.

The library sat on the ground floor of Villa Santini, one of Italy's finest hotel establishments. Villa Santini, as its website proclaimed, combined a five-star hotel with the beautiful landscapes of its own acreage of the famed Chianti Classico vineyards. It was a wine snob tourist's dream. A single location that provided the experience of touring beautiful and expansive vineyards, learning how the wine was converted from simple grapes to complex blends of refined wine and then finally tasting the matured versions of said wine. For dinner, guests would take in an Italian cuisine of the finest variety and then retreat to what could only be described as five-star euphoria in accommodations.

It was beautiful, refined and elite and Vitale was its Maestro. He did not own the hotel but he was its Godfather and kept the business thriving. It was a job that, as could be seen by his taste in liquor, he was compensated very well for.

Yes, business was definitely good, he thought.

A knock came at the door of the library, "Mr. Baldacci?"

"Come in," Vitale answered.

A beautiful Italian woman in her twenties with smooth, dark features entered. "All of the guests appear to be down for the night."

"Molte Bene, Carmen." He nodded. "Anything of note?"

"A few odd requests from some of our more interesting guests but we were able to accommodate. The Americans that arrived yesterday asked if there was a Starbucks nearby for tomorrow." Carmen said with no attempt to hide her contempt.

Baldacci scoffed, "Hmm...Americans. No taste."

"I informed them that there was a fine espresso bar down the road that would give them what they need. They weren't pleased but said they 'guessed it would have to do.'"

"Fine then. Anything else?"

"Well, yes, actually," she hesitated.

"What is it?"

"There was a call from another American claiming he was an agent for the American actor, Kyler Scott. You know…the one making the movie in Firenze?"

"Yes, I know him."

"His agent asked if he could make a reservation for this weekend. It is for him and a guest."

Baldacci saw where this was going, "And I'm guessing we are *full* this weekend and you are wondering if we could make room for Mr. Scott?"

"Yes sir." She replied. "I looked at our guest list and we have a reservation for some first-time guests coming from Venice. Shall I make the change?"

Vitale thought for a moment. They could always use the press of having highly visible guests at the hotel. They could even take a few pictures with the American actor and add it to their website. With Mr. Scott's popularity, they could even raise the price of one of the rooms and advertise that it had been the very same room occupied by an award-winning American actor. He knew the award-winning was a stretch but ambiguity would work in this case.

Baldacci had decided. "Yes, make the call. Contact the incoming guests, apologize deeply for the inconvenience and promise them a complementary dinner and bottle of wine for whenever they are able to reschedule their stay."

"Yes sir. I will call them and the American agent first thing in the morning."

"Will that be all?"

"Yes sir. Good night, sir." She replied and left as elegantly as she had arrived, closing the door behind her.

Yes, Vitale thought to himself, business was very good.

It was late September. For most, it was when the winter coats whipped out of the closet. When, back in the States, the Midwest region starting saying goodbye to warmth and prepped for warming up their cars before even thinking of driving anywhere. In the Rocky Mountain regions, they prepared for the snow storms to come, being fully equipped with food and water for the more substantial versions which would confine them to their homes for days on end. Across the pond, the England and Ireland regions settled into rainy weather and wished the sun a sad so long. For Villa Santini, though, it was new life. It was wine harvest season and the vineyards and the cellars were alive.

The staff spent their days catering to the guests by offering packages, at a premium of course, to spend a day in the vineyards picking grapes that would be used to stamp out the lovely juices that would be cultivated, cured and stored for future enjoyment at restaurants, bars and homes around the world. It was a sweet deal for the winery...they not only pulled in assistance with picking the grapes but got those doing so to actually pay to do it. Temp agencies across the nation take note!

Everything was done on-site. The grapes were brought into what could effectively be described as a warehouse. They were dropped into a glorified hole in the ground where the guests would then jump in and have their very own I Love Lucy moment of prancing around the grapes, feeling part of the grand ole process.

Baldacci sat back in his chair in the library. In so many ways, it was a regular harvest season. Bottling up wine, shipping the existing bottles out that had been maturing in the cellar over time. But this harvest would be like none previous. This year, many bottles would carry an extra element that would prove more profitable than any Chianti the winery had ever produced.

Things were going perfectly to plan.

Chapter 7

Kyler perused the menu with significant distraction. Between keeping a discreet eye on his surroundings and his gaze constantly being drawn back to Alani, he had absolutely no idea what he was going to order. He took a sip from the wine they had ordered which proved not to disappoint. Its excellence was unsurpassed and Kyler had tasted his share of wine.

Gianni Dimarco, meanwhile, did not stay still. The restaurant, in its intimate style, had no more than twenty-five tables but he clearly made sure to visit each. He hadn't yet returned to the couple adjacent to Kyler's table but he was certain that would be coming soon.

"So, Mr. Scott, how is the movie coming along?" Alani asked.

"Well, when you are as talented as I am, it makes the process so much easier," Kyler responded with no shortage of sarcasm.

"Ah yes…amazing that you've been overlooked by the critics for so long," Alani replied.

"I'm glad you see it that way. Some people just don't understand what true art is."

To Kyler, Alani was an anomaly. He knew her to be around thirty years old, although her exact age was foggy and there was no chance in hell that he was about to ask. Being brilliant, talented and stunningly beautiful, he wondered how she remained single. If he truly thought about it, it was probably for the same reasons he was. The career didn't lend itself well to relationships.

While there had always been a sexual tension between them, they had only crossed into the realm of acting on it once. It had been on a job in Barcelona on a night that involved a bit too much wine coupled with a room with a fantastic view of the city. One thing had easily led to another and they found themselves waking up naked in bed next to each other the following morning.

Discretion was the name of the game in this business though and if it appeared that Alani was anything more than just another date for the famous Kyler Scott on a night on the town for a man-whore movie star, much of his persona would be pierced. They had decided at that time that it would have to be the only time they crossed that line.

That decision only made their draw to each other that much more difficult to ignore.

"Who's the love interest this time?" Alani asked, doing her best to hide her deep-rooted jealousy.

"Veronica Stone is tasked with wooing Scott Cruz this time" Kyler responded hoping that would be the end of it.

Alani nearly choked on her wine, "Really? Wasn't her last appearance some glorified soft-porn movie?"

"Uh…you know…I'm not sure," Kyler lied. "I don't really keep up with any of my colleagues' careers. You know, not much time in our business." he fumbled, pointing back and forth between Alani and himself.

"Oh really? So you're trying to tell me that the famed Kyler Scott, Mr. Hollywood Playboy, isn't the least bit interested in Ms. Double-D's Stone?"

"Double –D's? Huh. I hadn't noticed," Kyler lied again while recalling their scene together from just a few days prior. It was the climactic love scene that presented Ms. Stone with her opportunity to flaunt what she had clearly been cast for. Jon Christenson made no attempt to hide nor did he feel any shame for the fact that he'd hired her for her famously voluptuous assets. Assets that Christenson knew were part of the typical draw for his predominantly male audience.

"Ok, Kyler, I'll play along. You are completely innocent and oblivious on the subject."

"Completely."

"Moving on then."

"Gladly."

"So what do you know about Mr. Dimarco?" as she asked the question, she did a quick scan to make sure Gianni was out of earshot. Dimarco was talking to a young but wealthy-looking couple that had just entered.

"Probably about as much as you do," he answered and began to rattle off what he'd gathered on the man thus far. He knew that Goldman had briefed Langdon already so he elected to highlight the bits he'd been able to gather on Dimarco that weren't in the docket.

"I know he's amongst the wealthiest men in Italy right now. In his forties although vibrant and youthful as we see first-hand. He's got an extraordinary and well-known affection for clothing and all things stylish…particularly those of the expensive variety. And he's built up quite an enterprise including this restaurant, another in Rome, another in Sicily, a clothing store in Milan and the famed Villa Santini hotel slash winery not far from here."

"Villa Santini," she repeated. "That's where we're headed this weekend, right."

"Right. My agent, Phillip Schumacher, was able to make us a reservation there. No easy task from what I understand. I got a text from him just a few minutes ago saying it was all set."

They both paused momentarily knowing that would mean a considerable amount of restraint would be in order. A weekend spent in one of Italy's most romantic hotels meant for couples to go and spend their days picking grapes and tasting wine and their nights being heroes in the bedroom. It would be very difficult to keep to their commitment.

"Ok," she continued. "What else?"

"Well, then there's his street reputation…"

"Of a high-class thug of the most dangerous variety?"

"That'd be the one."

"If half of the stories are true, I can see how he'd be as feared as he seems to be."

Kyler nodded his head. "I heard that someone had tried to put a restaurant in about two blocks from here. The owner hired one of Italy's best chefs. He pulled out all the stops, invested his life savings in building the restaurant. Granite this, marble that. Paid thousands on importing wines from all over Italy and Spain. And then paid even more to advertise leading up to its grand opening...the big inaugurazione."

Kyler took a sip of his wine and then continued.

"All the while, Dimarco bided his time. Let the guy spend money hand over fist. Then, on the night of the grand opening, at eight o'clock sharp when the first reservations of the night were arriving, the body of the owner dropped from the third story window above the restaurant and landed right in front of the door."

"Firenze Polizia shut the place down immediately and never brought charges against anyone for the murder," Kyler finished his glass and grabbed the bottle to pour a bit more. Damn was this stuff good, he thought.

"What happened to the restaurant?" Alani asked.

"That's the kicker. It defaulted back to Dimarco."

Alani looked back at Kyler, puzzled.

"As it turns out, Dimarco had financed the whole thing to the guy."

Alani looked really confused at that, "Well then why would he kill him *after* letting him spend all *his* money on the place?"

"Maybe to prove a point?" Kyler replied. "Seems like he took the opportunity to anyone that paid attention that he would do whatever it took to own this city. Fear is powerful."

"It seems to have worked."

"Yep. That building is still owned by Dimarco and by all accounts, it's been vacant ever since. Or, at least, that's what he'd probably like everyone to believe."

Alani thought about that for a while. "Any thoughts as to what he might be using it for now?

"A few…but none that I can substantiate with any proof."

"So here we sit," she concluded.

"So here we sit…cheers."

They raised their glasses and clinked them lightly, both taking a savoring drink from their three hundred dollar bottle of vino.

Chapter 8

It was afternoon back in Langley as Dr. Ethan Goldman, as he so often did, ate his lunch at his modestly appointed desk in his office on the first floor of CIA's Headquarters. Truth be told, Goldman could probably benefit from walking on his lunches. His growing waistline from years of sitting behind the desk represented a far cry from his younger, fitter days in the field. The morning mirror now showed a reflection of a man who's formerly thick, curly hair was more than salt and pepper grey and, if he had mirror at his back, would show a growing bald spot at the top rear region. His expanding stomach was being hidden more and more by his choice of a cashmere sweater over his always-starched-white-collared shirt underneath. Goldman's closet represented about a dozen of the same white shirt that accompanied four different colors of slacks and a couple sweater options now to complete the outfit. The simplicity was a combination of Goldman's personality of minimalism and the fact that he was divorced and hence single with little to no stylistic taste.

He mused at his younger days when this white shirt and tie still represented a fit, somewhat attractive man. It was in those days that he had met Kyler Scott. Goldman had been an Agency Senior Manager then, moving up the ranks of the infamous GS pay grade after having spent close to fifteen years with the agency already. He'd moved up quickly through the seldom-used special consideration "jury" from what he'd lovingly called the "ice panel."

He remembered his first year with the CIA. He'd asked his mid-level supervisor at the time, "How long does it take to move up around here?"

The fiery, slender and sharp as nails supervisor, who Goldman considered a mentor, snorted a bit. "Kick ass, take names and work round the clock. Don't waste your time kissing my ass though. Won't help ya."

"Why's that?" the eager Goldman asked.

"I can send you to the panel but I won't be on it." By the "panel," he meant a group of senior members of the CIA that determined if an employee gets to move up. "I can only recommend sending you there."

"So, you're telling me that no matter how much you like what I do here, it doesn't really matter?" A deflated Goldman asked, his youthful naiveté showing through.

"Hell yeah it matters Goldman," snapped his supervisor. "You think I can't get you booted outta here?"

Goldman flushed red at that. He respected the man immensely and now he'd felt he'd dropped himself down a peg.

"No, sir…that's not what I meant. I just meant that…" he stammered.

The supervisor put his hand up, cutting him off, "Relax, Goldman. Jesus. You're not goin' anywhere. All I'm saying is that we've got fifteen schedules here. We also have procedure, like it or not. You just need to figure out how to work around it. Like I said, work your ass off and word will get around…mostly by me. People will see you're good…which you are. Shit, it's why a hired you. I'll throw you on the block for a bump as soon as they'll let me and then it's up to you."

"Up to me to what?" Goldman asked.

"Impress the white hairs."

"The white hairs, sir?"

"Yeah…the guys that have seen more than they'd like to admit over the years. Now they got white hair from it…assuming they have any at all." He smiled, stroking his quickly receding hair.

"The panel chooses everything. You might as well check with them before you breathe. Pay increase, schedule increase...I'd check with them before you wipe your ass!" the supervisor joked, trying to lighten the mood of the young and all-too-serious Goldman. The kid had talent, but he needed to lighten up for Christ sake. It's a long career!

Goldman smiled and eased up a bit. "I won't let you down sir," he said, nearly saluting.

"At ease soldier. I know you won't." His supervisor had been right on that.

Goldman looked back at his reflection in the window and noticed his white hair. Go figure.

Twenty years and 15 trips to the panel later, he understood what his supervisor, now dead and gone, had meant. Pace yourself. It took him a while to learn that and, as a result, worked too hard in his young years, married late, divorced quickly and still hadn't figured out how to cook. The latter being the result of the developed gut. Crazy that the body stopped figuring out how to deal with the Big Macs and Super-sized fries, he thought.

His eagerness in youth had brought him quickly to the upper half of the pay grade by the time he ran across Kyler Scott. His fervor as well as the decentralized nature of personnel management at the CIA allowed him to locate Scott, with his undeniable natural skill as a potential operative, and...get creative. Decentralization meant that Senior Managers could operate with a bit of cushion when it came to oversight.

It was that lack of oversight that allowed Kyler Scott to become an unofficial member of the clandestine organization that needed to get more and more creative in the spy game as time went on.

Goldman's wife had been good for one thing, as far as he was concerned. She introduced him to Kyler Scott. Her sister ran an agency in Hollywood and they represented the child star.

"Why do they still hang on to that punk?" Goldman had asked his wife, Joanna, after hearing one side of a conversation with her sister talking about Kyler Scott's most recent appearance in the tabloids. It was after he'd grabbed one of the production's cars over a lunch break and, spinning donuts in the parking lot after a fresh dumping of snow, ran the car into the make-up trailer, nearly taking a couple screaming make-up artists out with it.

"Money, money, money," Joanna replied curtly. Goldman would later realize she'd already decided to leave en masse exodus from the marriage at that point.

"Yeah but he just cost them…what…fifty grand, minimum, by that stunt?" Goldman retorted, sensing her tone. He couldn't blame her. Married to a ghost, as they say.

"That's nothing, Ethan. Really. He's a hit at the box office. Every movie he's been in for the last two years have been number one." She replied, her condescension of his lack of knowledge of the business showing through.

"A kid like that will self-destruct eventually, Joanna," Goldman replied in an attempt to showcase *his* worldly knowledge. His was of the nature of people…a skill he possessed very strongly.

"Then they'll just find the next hit star," she replied.

"Chew 'em up and spit em out," Goldman scoffed. "Hell of an industry."

"And yours is so much better Ethan? At least in Hollywood the only thing those supposed heartless souls kill are careers."

Joanna's dislike for Goldman's limited physical presence had quickly evolved to contempt for the CIA and everything it stood for.

"I just feel bad for the kid," Goldman replied, ignoring her scorn. "Despite my hatred for his teeny bopper flicks, he seems to have something…special. Something hidden beneath the layers of whatever he's got goin' on."

"Ah yes…there it is. The great Dr. Ethan Goldman strikes again, reading people and seeing all of their hidden qualities and potential. Maybe you should spend more time paying attention to the qualities of your wife!" At that, she had stormed off.

It would only be a couple months later that she would leave him...off to join her sister in Hollywood with hopes she'd introduce Joanna to a producer or director that would see all of *her* hidden potential.

Goldman had seen something in Kyler though. After Joanna had forced him to watch one of his recent movies, he noticed a movement in the actor. A fluidity that he rarely saw. It was in a horribly choreographed fight scene in a middle-America look-alike high school. By all counts, the scene was awful. All save Kyler. He moved with lightening speed through his fake punches and air kicks. That with what Goldman suspected was minimal training based on the performances of his co-stars. It was a short scene and undoubtedly went unnoticed by most watching it but not Ethan.

It was that scene that had given him pause when flipping through channels on a rare lazy Sunday afternoon a couple weeks later. It was a quintessentially-awkward Barbara Walters exclusive interview with none other than America's heartthrob slash bad-boy, Kyler Scott, perfectly complete with good ole Barb faltering through innocuous questions that dated her by decades. She began asking him about his family and that's where Ethan saw it. He was commenting on his father, who Goldman knew by reputation as a push-the-envelope soldier made commander. As Scott talked about his parents, he saw the love and respect he had for his mother and the sheer fury he possessed for his father.

To anyone else watching, these moments may have been just blinks...flashes. To Dr. Ethan Goldman, they were blatant personality cues. The feelings for his mother showed capacity for respect, caring and love. Those for his father showing his fire and resistance...rebellion and strength toward a man he, no doubt, also feared.

Combine that with the physical potential Goldman had seen in the movie just a few weeks prior and it painted a very interesting picture. When Scott found himself only a few miles from

Goldman at the Fishburne Military School, Ethan couldn't help but take it as a sign.

It was time to meet the young man with such hidden talent.

Chapter 9

Kyler watched Gianni Dimarco hang up the phone near the back of the restaurant. Dimarco had his back to him but he could tell that the conversation, whatever it had been about had gone well. Some nodding, a calm voice and squared shoulders that remained upright in a way that only said that he stood with confidence.

Not just a customer calling to compliment the restaurant on their dining experience, he thought to himself. No, that had been business of another flavor entirely. If he could have only been a fly on the…wire? Yeah, that'd be the term, he thought.

"Hello?…earth to Mr. Scott," Kyler finally realized that Alani had been trying to get his attention for several seconds.

"What? Oh. Yes. Sorry, what were you saying?"

"Hmm…glad to know I'm that interesting to you. You know, sometimes I just feel like you don't ever listen to me." She smiled and then added, "Actually, you were staring Kyler."

"Shit…I was, wasn't I?" he said, frustrated. He had been straining to hear the conversation Dimarco had been having that he lost his sense of awareness.

"Thanks."

"Of course. Care to share your thoughts?"

Kyler took a bite off of the plate of Gnocchi that had arrived a few minutes earlier, savoring the taste of his favorite meal. Damn, I love this country, he thought.

Mouth still slightly full, he replied slowly, "Whoever he was just talking to had good news for our friend and I don't think it was that the next shipment of cheese from the local farm would be on time."

Alani, showing a bit more elegance than Scott, finished chewing her mouthful of ravioli and then said, "Business of a different variety?"

Kyler nodded slightly but then made a quick sideways glance indicating that he was heading their way. Kyler's peripheral vision was nothing short of amazing. It was almost as if he could see backwards. It was a trait that clearly came in handy in his line of work.

Gianni seemed to magically appear alongside their table in a blink of an eye.

Clasping his hands together gently, he asked "Signore. Signora. How is everything? I trust it is to your liking? I am hoping you are enjoying our humble restaurant."

Gianni knew full well that his establishment was the finest within a hundred kilometer radius but, he thought, who likes an arrogant restaurant owner?

"Il cibo e fantastico, Signore Dimarco," Kyler replied.

He tried to throw his Italian out as often as he could. It was partially because of his love for the country but also as a sign of respect. He knew that Italians were very proud of their heritage and walked a fine line of looking down on other cultures. By speaking their language, Kyler found that he was warmed up to considerably more. He had gotten quite good at it too, including a finely refined accent.

Nothing irritated Kyler more than the Americans that pranced into this lovely place and ignorantly assumed everyone spoke English. They were the same people that complained about Mexicans or the Chinese, for example, that came to America and couldn't speak English perfectly. At least they're trying, he thought. It was no wonder the rest of the world hates us! Alas...he could only fix one problem at a time and American ignorance wasn't on the menu right now.

"Grazie, Signore.   That makes me very happy to hear," Dimarco replied.   "And for you, Signora?" he asked Alani eagerly.

"Ah...absolutamente delizioso, signore," Alani emphatically replied while making the stereotypical hand gesture of four fingers to thumb that seemed to be universal when discussing good food.

That clearly pleased Dimarco.   Much more so than Kyler enjoying his food, Kyler noticed. But, then again, he'd care more about what Alani thought too, he admitted to himself.

"Grazie! Prego. Please enjoy." Dimarco had done his duty and prepared to continue his rounds. "Please do not hesitate to find me. Whatever you need is our pleasure to give."

With that, he was off. To Kyler's delight it was finally to the table he'd been eyeing since they walked in and surveyed the restaurant from the hostess stand. Clearly Dimarco was far more familiar with this couple as he pulled up a third chair and joined them. He snapped his fingers in the air and one of the waiters brought over a glass of wine for Gianni. He leaned back, crossed his legs and said something quickly in Italian. It was a toast of sorts because all three brought their glasses together and took a healthy pull from their hearty wine glasses.

Kyler could see that this was going to be a bit of a challenge. His Italian was quite good, if he did say so himself, but with music overhead, Dimarco speaking in lowered tones and at a rate much faster than even he had become accustomed to, he was only catching two-thirds of the conversation.

With her head down, Alani quietly asked, "Can you pick up what they're saying?"

Kyler held up a hand quickly. What she didn't know was that he'd come prepared. The home office had outfitted him with a tiny, high-powered microphone that pinned to his front pocket. It was small enough that it could hide just perfectly behind his stylish, intentionally placed silk handkerchief. While tiny in size, its ability to pick up sound at incredible amplification levels was astonishing. To add to its impressive design, the contraption had built-in wireless communication capabilities allowing it to wirelessly and instantly stream the audio back to his laptop which sat back at his hotel.   The laptop was currently recording everything Gianni and his dinner guests were saying.

Unfortunately, it would pick up anything Alani said as well, hence the need to keep her quiet. Alani noted the subtle dart of Kyler's eyes toward his pocket. She was smart and they'd worked together long enough to know that his gesture meant a plan was taking place.

Got it, she thought. Time to enjoy this fine Italian cuisine…in silence.

Chapter 10

In Palo Alto, California, Jack Hawkins turned up the volume on his high-definition television that was built into his custom-designed sub-zero refrigerator. He had been preparing his favorite breakfast, an omelet with tomatoes, hot sauce and Italian goat cheese when a breaking story caught his eye. He announced to his voice recognition sound system that was wired throughout the high-tech modern house, "Increase volume to thirty-five."

The sound system responded accordingly and projected the local news anchor's voice who was saying "Now a story that has many scratching their heads." The overly tanned man said. An image of a restaurant appeared in the smaller box to the right of the newsman's head.

"A restaurant in Sausalito, California is facing some strange allegations from a local woman who ate at the establishment two nights ago."

The anchor paused for dramatic effect while waiting for the image to change to the face of the woman. She was an attractive woman with mild features who looked to be in her early thirties.

"Ellen Stratton is pressing charges against the local place, Gino's Italian Cuisine, claiming they bear responsibility in her own case of sexual assault. We'll have more on this story after this."

"What?!" Jack screamed at the TV. "Seriously? You're going to break to a commercial after that?"

As if mocking him in response, a commercial for Apple's latest computer flavor of the month came on screen. It was the juxtaposition of a cool Mac kid versus the geeky PC guy that had become synonymous with the company's marketing scheme. Jack was a PC guy, had made a very cushy living off of his own innovations on Windows computers and took significant offense to the claim that PC users couldn't be cool. Truth be told, Jack was a dork, but that had nothing to do with his computer preference and more to do with the fact that he was socially inept unless his conversationalist spoke in binary code.

It also didn't help that he didn't care to put off an appearance that countered his awkwardness, though contrary to the nerdy image on the commercial, he opted for the eclectic. He sported curly, overgrown and unkempt dark brown hair that looked as if he was constantly pulling at its locks in deep concentration and coupled that with his wire-rimmed glasses that always seemed to be slightly askew. The daily attire usually involved some variation of cargo pants, Croc sandals with socks and a t-shirt he bought online that had some saying he deemed very funny and cultish with its origins usually rooted to something from the eighties. Pac Man, Tron, The Breakfast Club. He was a walking stark contrast to his actual overwhelming wealth and intelligence.

The story came back on after a series of more ridiculous commercials that Jack was convinced were placed right now merely to piss him off.

"Ms. Stratton claims that, after dining at the restaurant, she had absolutely no recollection of the next several hours." The anchorman said and then said to a yet-unseen onsite reporter, "Jim is with Ms. Stratton and has more on the story. Jim, what can you tell us?"

"Thanks Kevin," said reporter Jim, a fortyish taut-faced reporter with salt and pepper hair. He turned to Ellen Stratton. "Can you tell us more about what happened, Ms. Stratton?"

A clearly shaken Ellen looked nervously at the camera. It looked as if good old Jimbo had caught her just as she was leaving a local hospital. Nice, Jack thought. Can't leave the poor woman alone. But yet, he was certainly curious as she began to recount the story. Hypocrisy? He overlooked the moral contradiction.

"I had dinner alone at Gino's a couple nights ago," Ellen began, clearly struggling. "I hadn't been there before but it's close to work so I figured I'd give it a try."

Jim looked at her with the practiced concern of a lifetime reporter.

She continued on, "Since I was alone, I just sat at the bar. It was busy and I didn't feel like waiting for a table. There were only a few people at the bar and there was one guy that I could see out of the corner of my eye, sitting just around the corner at the other end. I never looked at him straight on but I could...you know...feel him watching me." She started choking up, seemingly realizing what she had just been through in the last two days.

"Was that the man you think assaulted you?" Jim, Mr. Sympathetic, asked.

Ellen flinched a bit but managed to continue, "I think so but I don't know for sure. The thing is, well, I can't figure out how but I'm sure that something was in my food or my drink. I just had some pasta and some wine." She hurriedly added, "But just one glass. I never drink more than one glass...especially if I'm alone. I mean, I'm kind of a lightweight but this was different."

"Different? How so?" Jim asked. Bam...grand master inquisitor. Just how did this guy do it?

"I finished my food and my glass pretty quickly, paid my bill and then that's it. I don't remember anything after that," She answered.

"What was the first thing you remember?" Mr. Salt and Pepper prodded on.

Ellen started to tear up. She hesitated but then managed to say, "I was in the back seat of my car. I was...um..." she started to cry a little bit more now as she said, "I was naked. And I didn't remember anything. Just paying my bill at the restaurant. I don't even remember leaving." Ellen's tears were streaming in a steady flow now.

Jim, seemingly unwavering, asked what Jack had been thinking, "Did you get up at any point? To go to the bathroom, maybe?"

As if knowing he'd ask the question, Ellen shook her head fiercely, "No…that's just it! I never left my spot. I've heard too many stories about guys slipping stuff in girls' drinks at bars. And with that creepy guy sitting at the end of the bar, there was no way. That's why it had to be someone at the restaurant. I don't know…the food? It couldn't be the wine. I saw the bartender open the bottle right in front of me. He asked if I wanted the bottle and that's when I said I was just having a glass."

"So that's why you are bringing charges against Gino's then?" Jim deducted. This guy was brilliant!

"Well yeah…" Ellen sobbed. "Who else could it be?" It was then that she broke down into full cry mode. A friend or family member appeared just then, grabbed her gently by the shoulders and escorted her away while telling Jimmy boy that Ms. Stratton was done answering questions.

The consummate professional, reporter Jim, turned back to the cameras at that and said, "Well there you have it Kevin. Strange indeed. We'll continue to report more as comes in."

Back at the studio, Kevin picked it up right on cue, "Thanks Jim. Great work." Then, turning to his female anchor counterpart, "I supposed this adds a new element to restaurant ratings."

The female anchor grimaced slightly at Kevin's lack of tact, but quickly recovered to say, "We just hope that Ms. Stratton can recover from this ordeal. We will keep our ears to the ground on this story and update you all when we have more."

"In local sporting news…" the story continued on but Jack wasn't paying attention anymore. He was in shock. He knew the owner of the restaurant…his name was actually Phil but who would go to Phil's Italian Cuisine? Gino's was definitely the better choice there. Point being, though, Jack knew Phil and he was a great guy who ran one hell of a tight ship over there. He went so far as to do background checks on his entire staff, including the valet employees. Shoot, especially the valets! It helped that Phil used to be with the CIA and still had connections not to mention that he had Jack who could find out dirt on the damned head of Homeland Securities if he wanted to. Although, seeing as he didn't see jail time in his future, he wouldn't even think of it.

No, something was wrong here. There is no one on that staff that would have dreamed of pulling something like that at Phil's restaurant. And it wasn't like Ellen Stratton had gotten a bad case of food poisoning. Someone or something had been done to her and it was no mistake. Jack was sure of it.

It wasn't just his concern for Phil and the fate of his restaurant that was nagging at Jack though. It was the name Ellen Stratton. He felt like he knew that name but he couldn't place it. She'd said she worked near the restaurant. Had he met her at Gino's? Not likely. His social skills were not such that he'd strike up a conversation with a stranger, particular one of the attractive female variety. Time to call on his nerd resources.

Hawkins nearly ran back to his computer room where there was enough tech gear to make Bill Gates' head spin. He had his TV s on constant back-up mode, saving all of the live content to a server that maintained the information for two weeks, whereupon it got purged unless Jack intentionally went back and saved something separately. As an information analyst of special variety and skill, it was his job to keep record of all the news that happened. His satellite television fed into every major network in the states and most across the globe. A complex archival that pulled key words and images from the audio and video feed allowed him to search content based on a self-created algorithm at any given moment, allowing him to stay current on any topic upon request. He only kept it for two weeks because, in this information age, if someone didn't need something after two weeks, they usually didn't need it at all.

Jack pulled up the video and paused the playback at a moment in time when he had a sharp image of Ellen Stratton. He clicked a few keys, initiating a scan of the image that performed a task of facial recognition. The program indicated the scan was complete and Jack ok'd it to launch a search against his database to ID the young lady. His space station blazed through the query and Jack paled a bit at what it returned.

"Shit. I knew it," he muttered.

The profile page for Stratton listed an address in Palo Alto, picture from her LinkedIn account, status of single and, most notably, her place of employment...QTS Tek. The very same company he and the CIA worked closely with for intel gathering. The same group currently working on the case he knew Kyler and team were on.

Again to himself, he muttered, "What the fuck?"

Not able to put it together and when it really came down to it, that wasn't his job anyway, he knew just who to share the information with.

With a few keystrokes he parceled off the bit on Ms. Ellen Stratton, saved it to a compressed file and started an email with the video clip and queried profile attached.

The email was addressed to Kyler Scott, Alani Langdon and Dr. Ethan Goldman.

Chapter 11

Jacques Francois lay motionless on the dirt floor of what looked to have been a traditional wine cellar at one point in time. Unlike the wine rooms often seen in pompous and fancy restaurants, a true wine cellar is nothing more than a temperature-controlled room without windows and dirt floor. It bred the best conditions for storing wine. It was amongst that dirt and darkness that Francois slowly began to stir. His eyes strained open and his panic did not begin when he saw where he was. It started a split second before that when he realized he was struggling to open his left eye at all.

Francois's eye was nearly swollen shut. When that thought registered in his mind, he then, as if it were a mental trigger, felt the searing pains that seemed to encompass every inch of his body. With his still functioning and seemingly unscathed right eye, he took in his surroundings. Where the hell am I, he thought? But before he could even think of answering that question, he screamed out in pain.

The act of looking around moved his body, and more specifically, his left leg, which was broken. Broken was not accurate. Shattered was more like it. As if Kathy Bates herself had risen out of her infamous role from Misery and inflicted the blow onto Jacques's leg.

His scream was both blood curdling and eerily muffled. The room was completely closed off to the outside world. The pain of his leg quickly spread to panic and then, more screams. Upon doing a full scan of his body, he assessed that he seemed to have a shattered leg, broken ribs, mangled right hand, his earlier-discovered swollen left eye and, raising to feel the back of his throbbing head with his good left hand, what seemed to have been a previously bleeding skull. The bleeding had thankfully stopped but he could feel the stickiness of the freshly dried accumulation of blood in his thick and unruly black hair.

His fear was quickly rising. He was in an unbelievable amount of pain, clearly needing a doctor for his numerous injuries and had no idea if anyone would hear his cries for help. The only thought more terrifying than the possibility that he would die in this dungeon was that he had absolutely no recollection of how he got there. Not of leaving his home in Paris, none of getting to wherever…here…was and, even more amazingly, not a single, fleeting, fighting memory of the brutality that had clearly been inflicted on him.

He began to panic.

"Help!! Is anyone out there? Please! Help!!!!!" Nothing. It was absolutely silent.

Again, "Anyone!!!! Pleeeeaaaase! Can anyone hear me?!" More silence.

This time he screamed with everything his broken ribs and survival instinct would allow. "HELLO!!!!!!!" His scream carried on for what seemed like an eternity. At the end of it, his body had had enough and he passed out, head falling hard back onto the dirt floor.

On the floor directly above Francois, two men sat across from each other smoking and drinking a wine. They heard the screams but neither one moved.

Chapter 12

Kyler and Alani ceremoniously bid Gianni adieu with customary kisses on each cheek, Gianni's hand traveling a bit low on Alani's back letting her know she was welcome to come back and see him whenever she liked.

"Grazie, Signore Dimarco. We will definitely return again." Scott said, grabbing Alani in a half rescuing, half protective nature. He wasn't sure, or maybe didn't want to admit, which was more accurate. He quickly erased the thought from his mind and, with her arm easing through his, made his way through the door where the Ferrari was already waiting. First class, he thought to himself.

The valet opened the door for Alani, "Avere una buona sera, signora."

"Grazie. Buona sera," Alani returned and sleeked into the car.

A second valet was already waiting on the other side with Kyler's door open as well. The valet may have been holding the door for Kyler but his full attention was on Alani as she entered.

"Draw straws for who got stuck with me?" Kyler chided, chuckling at his own joke.

"Signore?" the valet snapped to attention, not understanding the joke but realizing he had been staring. The man was bright red.

"Per favore scusarsi," the valet fumbled his apologies.

Kyler laughed fully this time, "It's ok. It's ok," he said, patting the valet. "I do the same thing."

With that, he slid into the cockpit-style driver's seat and the valet sealed the door behind him. Scott popped it into first from neutral and hit the gas hard, enjoying the exhilarating acceleration.

"Boys will be boys," Alani said as her body seemed to suction back to her seat from the car's torque.

Kyler grinned mischievously, "Me or the googly-eyed valets?"

"Both."

"Thoughts?" Scott asked quickly, trying to avoid an awkward silence. He'd had a couple glasses of vino and knew his resistances towards her would be a bit more difficult if they didn't keep the conversation steered toward the mission.

"He's smooth," she replied, referring to Gianni. "Gracious, charming, endearing. I can see why it's been easy for him to gain such favor."

"Disarming people with his nature, making it totally plausible that he's just your typical Italian restaurateur while, if his reputation is even half-true, being purely sinister behind the scenes."

"One hell of a combination. How much of that conversation do you think you picked up?" She asked, referring to the recording of their dining neighbors earlier.

"Not sure. It's the first time I've used this little contraption. I know it's not a hundred percent…just can't be. The communication rates back to the laptop can't ever be perfect. But hopefully we caught enough and they weren't speaking too cryptically."

Alani nodded. She looked out the window as the golden amber of lights that made up the romantic and ageless city coasted by. She, too, loved Florence. Loved its pace, its people, its style and its history. In moments of, say, weakness? Sure…weakness, she thought. She could see herself here, with Kyler. Neither one of them spies. Neither playing a role in any elaborate scheme. Maybe they ran a restaurant of their own. Maybe an espresso bar where all the locals came in for their daily shot. Maybe a gelato shop? She smiled at that one. She tried to keep her figure but gelato was most definitely her guilty pleasure. Probably good, she thought, that she didn't live here. She'd live on the cold, silky treat and blow up to three hundred pounds.

"What do you think?" Scott asked her, pulling her out of her reverie.

"I'm sorry...what did you say?" She replied, embarrassed at her own thoughts.

"Can you get together tomorrow after I'm done shooting?" he asked again, eyeing her coyly. "Review what we got from the conversation? We should have the translation and its transcript back by then."

"Oh...yeah...yes. Definitely. What time?"

"I'm on set at eight in the morning" Kyler responded, suddenly feeling how early that would be. "Probably done around five or six depending on how much Jon wants to get. I may try and knock out some of the translation tonight depending on how clear it is."

"Tonight? Geez Kyler," she admired him. He was the hardest working man she'd ever known. He was seemingly tireless.

"Well, we'll see," he replied, knowing he would not only attempt to translate the entire conversation before going to bed but would also get up early for his daily workout before heading out onset. Then again, he could always play up the diva movie star shtick...bags under the eyes, late night out partying...whatever worked. Kyler Scott...blockbuster diva...or was it divo for a man? He wasn't sure. Either way, he had to maintain the alter ego regardless that played to his advantage at times like these.

"Well, sounds good to me," Alani broke into his thoughts. "You know where I'm staying. Just ring me when you get back to your hotel."

It was probably a good thing they weren't staying at the same hotel. That had been intentional on many levels, only one of them being the façade of two casually dating people in Florence.

Kyler slowly pulled up to her hotel. Two valets, seeing the car that was pulling up, nearly sprinted for his car. He waived the one heading toward his door off, letting the other that was cruising toward hers continue. She turned to him, paused briefly, and then leaned in with a kiss on the cheek.

"Good night Mr. Scott," she said so softly and sweetly that he nearly melted on the spot.

"Buona sera, signora," he responded with as much levelness as he could muster.

With that, she was up and out of his car and sauntering toward the door. All three men, him and the two valets, watched her go. The one that had let her out finally closed the door and Kyler exhaled strongly. Get it together, man! He scolded himself. With that, he punched it and raced back to his temporary home. He had work to do.

Chapter 13

Kyler pulled up to the Boscolo Astoria again and the valets that had been there when he left were there waiting for him when he pulled up. They loved Kyler. For a country that didn't have gratuities as an overwhelming part of their culture, they had unsurprisingly adapted well to Scott's propensity to tip generously whenever possible. Call it force of habit, call it playing into the image of millionaire movie star, Kyler didn't know or care which.

Truthfully, he didn't care much for the money. He had more than he'd ever be able to spend and the irony was, the more famous he became, the less he actually had to pay for. In his calmer times, he marveled at that thought. Was it envy? Was it insecurity as part of human nature...seeing someone famous and wanting to give them freebees so they could say they met Brad Pitt or Beyonce? Or was it simply good business, knowing that if Angelina Jolie wore a company's jeans and someone took a picture of it that ended up in People magazine, maybe even along with a few kudos on her style from the writer of said periodical, sales would suddenly soar?

Whatever the reason, Kyler couldn't remember the last time he paid for a suit, shirt, pair of jeans or even a DVD. With all the money he accrued from his stardom and success, he rarely had the opportunity to spend it. Maybe that was why he had four houses...one in Malibu for his passion for hanging ten, one in the Rockies of Colorado to snowboard the light and fluffy powder. He also maintained a loft in New York for the occasional upkeep of his nightlife façade and, as if to provide the starkest of contrasts, finally a place in Wilmington, North Carolina for some good old southern hospitality, not to mention food that he dared say rivaled that of his beloved Italia.

After this current visit to said country, he wondered why he didn't own a fifth and decided that he would have to remedy this tragedy when he had a break in the action. Maybe a little apartment in the more remote region of Tuscany? Cortona perhaps? He'd heard of a little town near the original home of Michelangelo, nestled high above the Tiger Valley, called Anghiari. It was said to be an old medieval castle set on a hill that had been converted to a town of apartments, restaurants, espresso bars and shops. Majestic was the word he'd heard used to describe it. That does it…he'd have to look into that as soon as this latest mission was through. Maybe he'd even stay behind….rest for a few months. The thought caused a smile to creep into his face as he entered through the beautiful glass and gold of the hotel. A lovely and lengthy Italian woman passed him and returned his smile, assuming it had been intended for her.

The now lost in thought Kyler Scott didn't even notice. His thoughts, however, had already moved past his reverie of enjoying the good life in the Italian country and onto what awaited him in his room. More specifically, on his computer.

He decided to bypass the elevator that tended to move on banal Italian pace and hit the stairs with fervor. He bounded up the five flights of stairs, exploded out of the door from the stairwell and headed toward room 512 which had been his home for a time. The recent presence of the hotel staff was evident by his turned down bed, the bottle of wine they ceremoniously sent up from the Agora Wine Bar within the hotel and, to Kyler's amusement, two glasses. Nope, he commented aloud, no guests for the famed Mr. Scott tonight. Sorry to disappoint. In truth, though he would lead them to perpetually believe otherwise, he had had not a one female visitor. Not even Alani, albeit for different reasons entirely.

To his delight, they had also continued the customary practice of opening up the absolutely stunning private terrace that overlooked the Duomo and Cathedral. Heavens, he mused, had it just been this morning that Scott Cruz had been racing around down there doing his best James Bond? The thought was both sobering and exhausting. Alas, that was the life.

With that, he made has way over to the desk where his tank of a computer was perched. Its screen told him what he was hoping to see. A single dialog box displayed two words; "transmission completed." Ah technology, he mused. Working as if it were magic. He then noticed another box blinking at him letting him know he had email. Not in and of itself a revelation or newsworthy save the sub-text indicating its sender. Jack Hawkins. This wouldn't be an innocuous email. Good old Jackie-boy was inept when it came to the socially casual. No, if Jack was emailing him, it was going to be relevant.

Putting aside the initial task at hand, he clicked on the email that carried the subject line:

"You're going to want to see this."

There was a compressed video file attached to the email. Kyler clicked on it and waited for it to extract. It was taking a while which meant, to Kyler the master of deduction, it was a reasonably large file. He wasn't sure how many mega-whatever it was, and even if he did, still wouldn't know what it meant, but it must have been a lot.

The download finally finished its duty and the media player window that would display the playback popped up and the video began. Scott watched the news story, chuckling at the newscaster much as Hawkins had, but was far more serious as the story unfolded.

When the clip finished, he leaned back in his chair trying to figure out what it meant. He then noticed that he overlooked what else Jack had added in the email.

The email simply read:

Scott,

Recognize her? Ms. Stratton is an employee of QTS Tek.
WTF?????
- JH

Kyler then realized he hadn't seen the second attachment. It was Stratton's profile that Hawkins had pulled and was pretty basic but confirmed that the victim was indeed currently under the employ of QTS Tek. Kyler didn't know her but that meant nothing. QTS employed thousands of analysts and the information that made it to the field agents was usually filtered through the same people.

Hawkins had been correct to send it. He definitely had wanted to see it but couldn't pinpoint the significance of a local sexual assault accusation halfway across the world, even if it was an employee of a highly sensitive government sub-contractor. He granted it as bizarre. He also felt there was relevancy but to what end, he didn't know.

The connection wasn't coming and Kyler knew he'd have to let that fester for a bit. He worked best when he filed information away in his brain and pulled together more details that eventually allowed the pieces to align themselves. For the present moment, he really needed to get to the audio stream from earlier.

He went through a multitude of steps his tech geeks back at HQ showed him in order to pull down the playback from earlier in the evening. Finally, another window appeared on his screen that looked a little like the recording programs he'd seen a few musicians he'd known use. Garage Band maybe? No matter. There was a bar of what resembled a sheet of music with a long string of what looked like frequency lines. As had been instructed, he clicked on play where he heard Alani's voice say, "Can you pick up what they're saying." To which he had, of course, not replied at the time.

What he could hear after that was a seemingly passable recording of the conversation he'd hoped to capture. As he'd expected, it was far from perfect and would need to be enhanced by the techs. The background noise interfered at times as did his own movements which caused the microphone to rub against his clothing.

What became clear was that he would need some help with the translation. He was good but not this good. They had simply been speaking too quickly and quietly for him to interpret accurately. He figured it was just as well. He was exhausted, after all, and had what promised to be another long day ahead of him tomorrow.

Before going to bed, he followed the other vital set of instructions he'd been given and saved the file to what he was told was a highly compressed zip file. It took several minutes during which he shed his evening's attire that he'd still had on and opened the bottle of wine for a final few pulls of the sweet nectar. He could use the help falling asleep since his mind was racing with thoughts of Dimarco, the odd video and, of course, Alani.

The file told him it was saved and ready to be sent. He went back into his email, attached the file and sent it off to the analyst team that would be able to further isolate and enhance the audio. They would then pass it along to one of many of the agency's translation experts who would translate what they could pull out and type it out with the intention of being sent back to Kyler and a few others whose eyes needed the information.

Kyler finished his glass of wine, collapsed onto the bed and despite his earlier concerns, was asleep instantly.

Chapter 14

The ringing was loud in Kyler's ears and, at first he thought he was back in school at Fishburne again. Thought it was the bell for them to get up for their five a.m. five-mile run. It was at the moment of haze between sleep, dreams, waking up and reality that it occurred to him that it was that routine that had obviously spurred his current obsession with the workout that had been his daily regimen for over a decade. He also wondered why that had never dawned on him before. Old habits die hard he guessed although that was one he was grateful for.

The second ring shook him out of his sleep entirely. What strange thoughts came in moments of that in-between. He'd heard that some of the most brilliant ideas came to great men in their sleep. Alas, all that came to him were memories of joining a dozen other angst-ridden teenage rebels just as angry as he had been at the thought of heading out, pre-dawn, for a brisk jog that was highly against their will.

Riiiiinngg! That one jolted Kyler into awareness. That moment that, for…say… a child in school or anyone that despised their job, was all-too-often accompanied by a frantic glance at the clock only to realize that the perpetually unreliable alarm had failed to do its job once again and said individual was, once again, late. That spurred a frenzy of activity that wouldn't change the fact that they would face consequences, coming from a teacher or boss. Somehow, it is a familiar feeling everyone shares having experienced it at one time or another and, at various times, gets called upon again when being awoken unexpectedly.

That familiarity of panic is what made Kyler leap out of bed, catching his shoulder on the corner of the bedside table, causing not only incredible pain but also knocking over the empty wine glass that still sat atop it from the previous night. The glass, as if in slow motion to Kyler, went airborne toward the wood floor. Before Kyler could even attempt to yell the innocuous "NOOOO!!!" accompanied by the worthless outstretched hand, neither act having any bearing on preventing the inevitable from happening, the glass shattered into a dozen pieces on the ground. Kyler groaned. Hell of a start to the morning, he thought.

The origin of the ring was finally clear to him as it rang again, coming from his computer, which he promptly cursed aloud. He strode gingerly over to the computer, holding his now throbbing shoulder as he did so, letting loose a few choice words to accompany the rude awakening.

The caller ID read Dr. Ethan Goldman. Kyler hit the accept button to initiate the incoming call and Goldman's face popped up on the video conferencing window.

"You look like hell Scott. Rough night?" Goldman began, laughing at what must have been a battered-looking Kyler.

"More like a rough morning," Scott replied, rubbing his shoulder. "Got my ass kicked by some renaissance-era furniture. The wine glass got the worst of it though, sadly. Don't think it will be able to recover from that one."

"Sorry for the early awakening," Goldman realized that while he'd been wrapping it up at eight o'clock at night at the office, it was only five in the morning in Florence.

"It's ok…I needed to get up anyway," Kyler managed. It was only true if he wanted to keep to his regimen. Truth was, he probably could have used the extra couple hours of sleep but, as he'd said in dreamland, old habits die hard.

"I won't keep you long. Seeing by the fact that I just woke you up, I'm assuming you haven't heard the latest news out of France?"

"That'd be a no on that sir."

"Ok then. Pull yourself together and check out the article I'm emailing over right...now," Goldman said as he hit send on the email with the web link included that would take Kyler to the story in reference.

"Check that sir," Kyler replied, expecting Goldman to sign off at that but he did not.

"How did things go with Ms. Langdon last night?"

The underlying curiosity of the good doctor was not lost on Kyler.

"Things went..." Kyler considered his words, "according to plan."

Goldman paused slightly, considering how much to press on the subject, "So she made it home alright then?" Ever the tactful CIA man.

"That she did sir. Safe, sound...and *alone*."

The truth was Dr. Ethan Goldman was the closest thing to a father Kyler had, without question, but he was still his boss. He was also still the director of the CIA and had big people that sat at even bigger desks, particularly ones sitting in offices of the oval variety, to answer to on these not-to-be-understated issues of national security. Simply put, Goldman knew of the complicated nature of Kyler and Alani's history, if it could even really be called that. When his supportive pseudo father hat was on, particularly over drinks and during down times between missions, Goldman listened to the struggles Kyler had with the forever-doomed, never-actually explored relationship that loomed over his prized agent's head.

The problem with being both boss and mentor is that, inevitably, the boss hat had to come back on at some point. And when it returned, so did Goldman's concerns regarding anything that could put a wrench in any mission.

Goldman knew and, more importantly, trusted Kyler though. He knew his best guy, or so he called him, wouldn't jeopardize the bigger picture. That, however, didn't prevent him from worrying. It was what CIA Directors did.

"Glad to hear it," Goldman replied, closing the book on the subject. "Did you open the article yet?" Changing the subject as quickly as it had been breached.

"It just popped up on the screen," Kyler replied and began reading the article's tagline.

Local Paris Man Doesn't Remember Beating.

The article went on to say.

Paris local, Mr. Jacques Francois, was checked into a local hospital, Hopital Robert Debre, this evening under bizarre circumstances. He was not brought in nor did he drive in of his own volition but was, rather strangely and ominously, literally dumped in front of the entrance of the emergency room. Several hospital staff members noticed Mr. Francois as they were leaving their shift whereupon they checked him into the hospital immediately to begin addressing his numerous injuries. A nurse at the hospital, Ms. Celeste Ferdinand, told reporters that Mr. Francois's injuries included a badly broken leg, hand, swollen eye and potentially broken ribs. He had also sustained a fairly significant head injury, which they are currently using as the excuse for the biggest mystery behind the story. Ms. Ferdinand let it slip that the patient was in a state of sheer panic as they brought him in by what can only be described as the most inexplicable case of amnesia the hospital has ever seen.

"He was screaming how he didn't remember, didn't remember, didn't remember." Ms. Ferdinand was quoted as saying.

Kyler continued reading as the story went on to say that Ms. Ferdinand wasn't entirely sure what the patient couldn't remember. Francois had apparently screamed words like "Broken," "Cellar" and "woke up."

The doctors have pieced together that, despite what happened to the poor man, he seemed to have absolutely no memory of it. He only remembered the pain afterwards and being stuck in what they thought to be a wine cellar. The doctors prodded on for some time trying to determine the origins of the injuries but the patient simply could not recall.

"Temporary amnesia?" Kyler asked aloud after finishing the article.

"Exactly," Goldman replied, nodding. "Strange, isn't it?"

"Certainly is considering the amount of pain that comes with even one of those injuries," Kyler winced a bit as he said it, remembering his own ribs being broken during an interrogation a couple years prior.

He'd been sloppy and got himself caught breaking into an ambassador's apartment that they had suspected of feeding secrets to the Iraqi government. Turns out, they'd been right. Small price to pay for a solved case, Kyler thought, looking back while still instinctively rubbing his right rib cage.

"Then there's the length, or lack thereof, of his amnesia. From the sounds of it, he couldn't have been out for more than a few hours."

"Too much pain to be drunk or drugged and not remember."

"Exactly."

A thought occurred to Kyler, "Not to be insensitive to the poor Frenchman Doc but…"

"Why do we give a shit?"

"Exactly." Kyler nodded.

"The part the press leaves out, either intentionally or because they don't know yet, is that Francois is former-military. His real name is Guion Baston."

"Operative?" Kyler asked, beginning to see the reason for Goldman's interest in the story.

"No, but it's no less damaging. According to the DGSE, he was an analyst who had top-level intelligence clearance." The DGSE, or Direction Generale de Securite Exterieure, being France's equivalent to the CIA.

"Was he forced out?"

"Not entirely. Apparently his wife left him, probably for the typical reasons that go with the business," Goldman said the last bit with more than a slight overtone of bitterness. "She took his two girls and moved them out to London while he was out of town on an assignment. He went nuts. Totally lost it and DGSE convinced him he should consider an alternative career...they suggested that he take some time off...maybe try and get her back."

"In other words, they got rid of the liability."

"Yep. To their credit, they helped him get a new identity, landed him alternative employment and did a commendable job of erasing any traces of who he was. He refused to leave the country though, convinced that if he could get settled into a regular life, he could get his wife and kids back. The DGSE were supposedly keeping a close watch on him."

"Not close enough it seems."

"So it would appear. The shit's hit the fan. They are in full damage control right now because, to make matters worse, rumor has it that Francois had become...*friendly*... with the reporter that broke the story. Reporter's name is Camille Blanche."

"Shit," Kyler said, more to himself. "Do we know if Blanche knew about his past?"

"They've asked us to help in that territory."

"Why?"

"Think about it. Say they send in their own personnel...if the anchor or editor doesn't already know, they'll quickly figure out that there's more to this story than just a strange case of amnesia. Not to mention DGSE has their hands full trying to figure out who snagged Francois in the first place and, more importantly, find out what he may have said."

"Want me to find an excuse to break away for a couple of days and check it out?" Kyler asked.

"I'm already sending Alani out there to check it out. She's got writing credentials and will go under the guise of an American reporter looking into the story of treatment in hospitals. She's going to do some digging. Try and talk to Ms. Blanche. Feel her out to see if they are onto the story. They need to contain the situation as much as possible and make sure the press doesn't get trigger-happy trying to break a military conspiracy story. The more we can protect Francois's identity, the more they can minimize the damage."

"Sure…makes sense," Kyler replied, trying not to show his disappointment, though he wasn't sure if it was because he wouldn't get to be in on the action or if it were due to his inability to see the lovely Ms. Langdon that night.

"Don't worry loverboy, she's gotta be back for your rendezvous to the winery this weekend," Goldman chided, reading his thoughts.

"What are you talking about? I'm not worried," he lied, badly. "Just wish it could be me, that's all." At least that was partially true.

"Uh huh…yeah…well your adoring public awaits the completion of your latest silver screen gem. You and Alani can reconvene when she gets back tomorrow. See what more she can dig up."

"Got it. By the way, did you see the video Hawkins sent over?" he asked, remembering the clip from last night.

"Yeah, that's why this concerns me so much."

"You think they're connected?"

Goldman nodded his head back and forth as if to say 'maybe.'

"We have two victims with cases of amnesia who both have government intelligence connections."

"I see your point but it seems like little more than coincidence right now," Kyler replied, not entirely believing it as he said it.

"It may be but let's call it a hunch. We'll see what Alani comes back with in France. I've got a local in California checking into the restaurant story too. We'll see if we find any more similarities."

"Sounds like a plan to me. I guess I'll handle the difficult task of bringing the females of the world one filming day closer to enjoying the prowess of Scott Cruz, defender of all things action-hero."

"You're a better man than I. Be sure to send me an autographed picture of that beautiful love interest of yours."

Kyler nodded in agreement and they both said their goodbyes, agreeing to reconvene in a couple days.

Kyler mulled the two stories over for a bit, ultimately coming up with no significance for the connection, granted a strange one, for the two stories. His workout awaited him, as did craft services on set. With that, he threw on his workout clothes, strapped on the running shoes and bounded out the door for his former-Fishburne routine.

Chapter 15

Kyler put on his best Casanova facade as he sat in the director-style chair that had his famed big screen alto ego's name elegantly embroidered onto the back...*Scott Cruz.* He sported his favorite Dolce and Gabanna aviator sunglasses while lounging under the umbrella that had been brought over specifically for him. He quickly decided if Casanova had seen him at that moment, he might just rise from the grave, slap the glasses off his face and walk away with every woman on set while looking back at him mocking victory for even trying. He'd have to work on his bravado a bit.

Instead, Kyler aimed for the amiable and slightly-hung-over schmoozing actor. A la Alec Baldwin post weight-gain era. He smiled at a few of the extras that walked by noticing that most smiled back, many lingering for a second as they past as if they were waiting to see if he would invite them over for an introduction. He did not.

It was a sort of game Scott played. He noticed that while he certainly got a few looks when out in public, which he mostly attributed to the natural tendency people have to be star-struck, those looks intensified from the budding actresses he encountered onset. Their admiration for him seemed to bypass general female-male attraction and crossed straight into the opportunistic. Sitting in the big chair, being the leading man, having the director's ear, he had something to offer them and he was guessing they weren't that focused on his anatomy. Although he suspected some would be willing to take a look if it meant it could help them. Truth be told, he could help them if he wanted but the thought of it disgusted him straight down to the core. He'd leave the sleaze to his director...he seemed to have a knack for it.

While he had never taken advantage of his status, he certainly enjoyed the ability have a little fun at others' expense from time to time. Maybe it was a bit unkind knowing he'd never help any of the "star suckers," but it kept the boredom out of the monotonous hours he spent sitting around on set doing nothing. So ensued his own personal game, feigning interest in the women only to shut them down before they approached by moving his gaze onto someone else.

If Dr. Ruth or, maybe Dr. Phil, were there, they may have psycho-analyzed him at that very moment telling him his wall for anyone seemingly interested was the reason he was still single, and, in his more honest and self-reflective moments, extremely lonely. He'd probably go with Dr. Ruth now that he thought about it. Was Dr. Phil even a real doctor? He didn't think so. He didn't like doctors, psychologists, life coaches or anyone in that realm very much. After all, didn't the widely respected author of that book Men are From Mars, Women are From Venus get divorced? How about Dr. Atkins, preacher of all things meat. Didn't he die of a heart attack? He'd heard conflicting reports on that one. He was going to run with it though since it suited his theory.

More to that end, he realized that in both the movie business and government, everyone had an agenda. The scary part was he wasn't sure which industry represented more of it. Truer still, it was evident in life. He could easily chalk it up to his cynicism from his parents' visibly unhappy marriage coupled with his own string of relationship failures resulting, in large part, from his dual personality lifestyle. Bottom line, he didn't have a great deal of faith in relationships. Careers definitely affected many marriages, friendships and relationships of any kind. The irony though, to Kyler, was that those that he encountered that had experienced those failures took the easy path of blaming it on their careers.

The athlete that was too busy traveling around to see his family but still found time to sleep with a dozen women while on an east-coast road trip. The Senator who hadn't seen his family in a month while on the campaign trail but was willing to squeeze in one more state visit to catch a rally because he might get a dozen more votes out of it. Pick a profession, find the most successful individual and plenty of others aspiring for that same level of excellence and Kyler believed he could point to most of the relationships in their lives as a failure.

That was his cynicism, at least. His walled-off, shut down mind talking. And that was what drew him to Alani. Because she, if just for a few seconds, made him believe that there was another side to that story. That maybe it was possible to have balance. Some yin to his life's yang. Maybe he only saw the relationships that failed because that's all he chose to see.

He wondered, as he did on many nights where sleep escaped him, if he truly feared that a relationship between them jeopardized their missions or if it was Kyler himself that he feared. The fact was that he was one of the best in his field equated to personal sacrifices. Ignoring the obvious demands on him personally, there was the other subject of the danger he was in on a regular basis.

He maintained what most agents in his life did. Absolutely zero relationships. They'd all been taught the same lesson. Relationships are perceived weaknesses by your enemy and if they know about them, it gave them the one thing Kyler avoided at all cost. Leverage.

Of course then, his devil's advocate reminded him that Alani was a big girl. She could take care of herself. She was an agent herself after all. She, more than any other woman in his life, past or present, knew the dangers and seemed willing to take them on. Was it he, then, that was the blockade and he alone? Was it his machismo desire to protect her even if he knew she didn't need protecting?

"YO!" Jon Christenson barked. Session over.

"Huh? Hey. Yo…hey Jon," Kyler fumbled quickly playing up his hung-over act. "Ahem. Sorry. What's up?" he cleared his throat, pushed the sunglasses a bit further up on his face and slumped back into the chair a bit.

"Yeah. Nice Kyler," Jon said, obviously buying what Kyler was selling. "One word. Sleep. Seriously. Do us all a favor ok?"

"Sure thing boss," Kyler straightened up a bit. "So what are we shooting today?"

"Cruz kickin' ass in the plaza."

"The Piazza, you mean?"

"Whatever. Plaza, Piazza, big fucking open space. Who gives a shit man?"

This was an argument that ensued almost daily. Jon was here to make his hundred million dollar film but couldn't care less about getting into the culture of Italy. He knew Kyler was a purest on the subject and enjoyed showing him how little he shared his sentiments.

"The Italian consulate that gave you the permit to shoot here, for starters," Kyler replied.

"Oh, yeah, is that the same bunch of nut-jobs that are taking me up the ass in fees to do it? Yeah, I really give a shit what they think Scott."

"You take it up the ass, Jon?" Trying to break the levity that was building.

"Fuck yourself Scott," he said but couldn't help cracking a smile.

They'd known each other for years and were, despite their many differences, great friends. Jon also needed him. He was, after all, Kyler Scott a.k.a. Scott Cruz and that name drew in half a billion dollars to the box office, DVD rental and digital download marketplace to more than cover the hundreds of millions they spent on his films.

"A lovely thought but already taken care of," Kyler retorted with a sly smile.

Jon stopped at that. He loved good juice, "Who? No fuckin' wonder you look like hell."

"A gentleman never kisses and tells Johnny boy," he said patting his shoulder as he got up from the chair to stretch his limbs. He hadn't had a chance to properly do so after his workout earlier.

"I don't wanna hear about the kissing…" Jon started but Kyler cut him off with a hand.

"Let it go man…I'm sure your imagination can take it from there." Kyler changed the subject. "So, the fight in the piazza."

Jon took the cue, "Right…yeah. We're picking up from yesterday where the chase ended. Cruz dumps the car…"

"And runs into the center of the piazza where he's surrounded. Got it."

Kyler looked forward to days like this. It was stunt work and gave him an opportunity to do what he did best. Fight. Sure, he wouldn't be hitting his opponent in this case but the movements, the actions, drove him. It kept him sharp. And it happened to look great on camera.

Knowing it was an empty offer, Jon asked, "You sure you don't want the double for some of the hairier shit?"

Jon knew the ever-present Screen Actors Guild Union would approve. Must protect the talent at all costs. Or, rather, must protect or pay a hefty cost.

"They can take the boring stuff if you want but at least leave the hairier stuff to me," Kyler said grinning.

He knew where Jon was coming from. They both also knew Kyler would handle every stunt in every scene and do it better than any of the stuntmen standing by. Their presence was also merely to appease the union as sort of a statement for Jon to say, "See, I offered and even have guys available to do the stunts but Mr. Death-wish-actor over there refuses."

All this being a charade to prevent Christenson from paying millions in penalties via the union who, for their part, where merely trying to prevent studios from taking advantage of actors. It happened enough to warrant their caution. The less prestigious and aspiring actors typically would do whatever was requested of them if it meant they would come across as amiable and, hence, more hirable for the future. Enter the union. Let them be the bad guys, or so they figured.

Nothing was perfect, Kyler knew. So they played along.

"Well, get your ass in make-up. You need it," Jon said and strode off barking orders at a dozen other people with earpieces and walkie-talkies.

Kyler smiled as he watched Jon walk away. He loved the guy with all of his abrasive qualities. Again he thought to himself, "If you only knew buddy."

Shaking his head, he made his way to the trailer marked "Hair and Make-Up."

Chapter 16

The wheels of the 747 screeched and rocked aggressively as they touched the French ground at Charles De Gaulle Airport. The action jolted Alani in her first class seat and sped her heart up a few beats as landings always did.

It was a strange phenomenon, she thought. She ran around the world looking for trouble with some of the worst kinds of people but somehow flights scared her more than anything. She supposed it was the control aspect of it, or lack thereof. Despite all the statistics people had given her in the past when she revealed her fears to them. The favorite amongst them were that infinitely more people died in car crashes.

There were several flaws she found in that argument though, the first starting with the fact that she wasn't the one with the controls in a plane leading her to her next point in that she was not your averagely-skilled driver. Alani was a pro. It was one of her finer qualities as an agent and had gotten her out of more dicey situations then she'd like to count. She'd actually tried to calm her nerves once by looking up said statistics and recalled that the chances of dying in a plane crash were something like one in eleven million versus one in five thousand in a car. By that logic, she was far more likely to die on her way to the airport than on a plane.

Still, she thought, if the plane crashes, you don't walk away from that. Unless you're the cast of Lost of course but then, in that case, you're stuck on some island that disappears, spends six seasons running from smoke monsters and time travel and then in the end nobody can even give you a good explanation of what happened for a hundred and fifty or so episodes.

Her mind stopped its rambling when the flight attendant's voice chirped through the speakers.

"Welcome to Paris where the local time is ten twenty-five. The local temperature is currently seventy-two degrees with beautiful sunny skies. If this is your final destination..." She carried on but Alani had already blocked her out.

The mention of time reminded her that she needed to kick it into gear when they got off the flight. She had an appointment with BFM TV, a French group that runs around the clock news locally. It was the station that broke the story on Jacques Francois, or Guion Baston depending on how much they knew.

She'd received the call from Goldman early in the morning right around the time that her hotel's bellhop was knocking on her door with a package that had arrived last night. The package contained a new passport to accommodate press credentials in the name of one Lucy Sykes, both fabricated of course. She was supposed to be with CNN, a cover that could be corroborated if necessary by a contact out of its Washington DC office. The fact that CNN was known to have a strong world news division made it easily plausible that there would be interest from an American journalist in a story of the local Frenchman with inexplicable amnesia. Add the element of a violent story, which the U.S. News was known to have a taste for, and it was believed to be plausible interest. For good measure, Alani had also looked into several other stories she'd could ask about to avoid the suspicion of only asking about one story. She was walking a fine line. If the station truly didn't know of Francois/Baston's true identity, she needn't give them reason to begin snooping around. On the flip side, she needed to find out if they were on to the facts so she could inform the DGSE to cut them off at the knees.

The flight attendant went through the final connections and housekeeping items as the doors were opened and the herd of passengers began their single-file departure. Alani thought she might've even heard a moo but couldn't be sure. Thankful to Goldman for booking her in first class, she was up and out of her seat and out the door before the comatose passengers could stall her with their fumbling for bags in overhead bins.

She marched dutifully up the ramp toward the gate with a journalist-style briefcase slung over her shoulder. She sported a modest pantsuit that had been off the rack at a department store back home reserved for this character she played periodically. Her hair was up in a haphazard bun. She'd kept the jewelry to an absolute minimum of a watch and a bracelet and finished the façade up with glasses that bore no prescription. She had to admit, she sort of liked this part of the job. What woman didn't spend her younger girl days playing dress-up?

She looked at her watch again and picked up the pace realizing she had an hour to hail a cab at this busy airport and make it across the city for her appointment at eleven thirty with the editor of BFM. It would be close.

She burst out of the gate entrance and made her way towards signs that pointed to ground transportation. She realized, jolted with a tinge of fear yet again that she was passing through the Terminal 2E section that had now become infamous after its collapse in a few years prior. Apparently the architects had gotten a bit overzealous with their design, focusing on wide open spaces and vaulted concrete ceilings, forgetting such things as say...stability, resilience or sound design. The result had been the death of four unfortunate passengers. Alani shuttered at the thought. They had probably just gotten off their flight with the relief they had made it safe and sound only to reach their untimely demise in an airport terminal. And people wondered why she was so paranoid about traveling?

The thought picked up her already lightening pace and she half ran toward the escalators that would lead her out of this steel trap. She saw the group of casually strolling zombies hit the escalator and stop so she decided to bypass it and opted for the stairs.

At the bottom of the stairs she looked up in relief to see what she had been praying would be the case. A driver dressed in an ill-fitting suit as seemed to always be true with transport drivers, was waiting for her with a sign that had Sykes scrawled across it. Thanks, Ethan, she thought to herself. No need to worry about hailing a cab at this mad house.

She strolled toward him, made eye contact and smiled a brilliant smile. The man flushed a bit when he realized the beautiful woman gliding his way was the aforementioned pseudonym Lucy Sykes that he was holding his placard for.

"Bonjour monsieur," she said.

Suddenly dry-mouthed, the man fumbled a bit but managed to squeak out, "Bonjour Madame. Welcome to Paris." He'd also been briefed that she was an American so he took the opportunity to impress her with his English.

"Merci beaucoup," she returned the gesture. "I'm sorry Monsieur but I'm in a bit of a hurry. How fast do you think we can get to the BFM TV studios?"

"But of course Madame. It is less than ten kilometers. We can be there in twenty minutes or less." He smiled again and extended his hand to take her briefcase.

She pulled back a bit too quickly but recovered, "Merci monsieur but I can handle it." Recovering further, she added, "I'll need to do a bit of work on the way so I'll just keep it."

She smiled hoping he didn't notice anything odd. Alani had carried all of the case files for the story she was there for, information on Gianni Dimarco as well as the story out of the states Goldman had forwarded along to her last night. It probably would have meant nothing to a random driver at the airport but she'd been in the field too long to trust anyone.

"Of course Madame," he replied apparently unphased. "Your car awaits."

With that they were off and Alani prepared for the upcoming encounter. Sitting in the car, she looked at Francois's face, an image they'd frozen from the news story. What is your story Mr. Francois? She thought to herself.

Chapter 17

Scott Cruz hit the center of Piazza della Signoria and was three steps from the David when the first bullet whizzed by his head, just inches from his face and put a hole squarely in the middle of David's fig leaf. Despite the fact that it was a statue, and a copy at that, Cruz grimaced in pain at the thought of where it landed.

"Hope that thing's gold-plated buddy," Cruz said as he cut past the statue and tried making his way for the other end of the plaza.

He hit the center of the courtyard and saw the next group of Polizia and hit the brakes. He looked left and saw another couple of men heading his way. A quick glance to his right confirmed what he already knew. Damn. Surrounded.

A quick assessment made him realize they weren't going to fire any more shots. The one that destroyed David's manhood was probably an overzealous trigger-happy guard. There were too many witnesses that were already frantically scattering. Moreover, Cruz wasn't armed. That had been intentional. Kill an unarmed man? Bad for business.

Exhausting all options of escape, he realized it was time to fight.

"Halto!" One of them yelled aiming his gun at Cruz. He raised his arms up, feigning surrender knowing he'd need them closer.

In that moment everything went into slow motion. It was where he lived in his mind's eye. As if the entire scene was preparing to play out in individual and miniscule pieces. He closed his eyes and listened to his own breathing, calm, controlled and slow. His breathing slowed his heart down to a stillness that allowed him to not be distracted by its pounding and thus putting him into a panic as most people would get in the face of battle.

Now he could hear his attackers breathing, could hear their footsteps with each individual step. He could hear that they were all measurable distances from him. It was there that his plan formulated. They had done him a huge favor without knowing it. Their approach, rather than a collective and unified one, was staggered. Not considerable but enough for Cruz to plan his attack. His movements would have to be precise and efficient. He could only afford one strike per attacker.

They'd also appeared from each angle in pairs. One hand for each.

"Wait for it," he said so quietly it was almost to himself. "Wait…." He was as still as the statues that surrounded him in the courtyard.

"Now!" And with that, his eyes sprang open just as the first two targets were practically on top of him. As if like a dance, the action began. The one on the right had a gun pointed at his face. Cruz's left hand shot up from his side, grabbed the gun, shoved it down into his waist as his right fist came up simultaneously with three quick strikes pummeling his face. His right hand, almost immediately, shot down to join the left, and swiftly swiped the gun, snapping the man's finger in half that held the trigger.

The gun was Cruz's now and the man was on the floor. Stunned, if only momentarily, the one on the left delayed his swing of the Billy club that'd originally been targeted for his head. Cruz seized the delay, sprang his body into the man's tightly so his arm, not the club, hit unassumingly into Cruz's side. In rhythm, Cruz slid his head under the attacker's arm that had been jammed onto his shoulder. As he flew underneath, he took the arm with him, yanking it tightly behind his back, separating his shoulder as the club dropped harmlessly to the ground.

The rest of the action picked up quickly as the men from the other directions realized what was happening. Their responses were merely ones of the knee-jerk variety as they started firing off rounds of their guns. Cruz used the poor bastard as a shield as a dozen or so bullets thudded into his body.

When the men saw they had taken down one of their own, one of them, probably the captain yelled "CESSARE IL FUOCO!" which Cruz knew meant for them to cease-fire.

That was the break he'd counted on. In one fluid motion a la Jackie Chan, he shot the fallen club into the air with his foot, tossed the gun from his right hand to his left and caught the club with the right all while moving forward to the next two men. His next two victims looked up in horror as Cruz swung the oak-like stick hard into one of the man's knees, shattering the knee cap into oblivion while in the same motion pointing the gun in his left hand directly at the other one's face.

Not giving him a chance to respond with the innocuous "freeze" or "drop it" yell, he opted instead to drop the stick, swing around behind the stunned soldier while wrapping his now free arm around the neck with a vice-like grip as the gun smoothly slid from the front of the man's forehead to the left temple. He pressed the gun hard against his head, cocked the jam backwards and then looked at the two other pair of men almost daring them to make a move.

The waltz of death and destruction took maybe thirty seconds in total, had amounted to no side casualties of the innocent on-lookers that had mostly scattered anyway and, most impressively, had resulted in not even a scratch on Cruz. Efficient. Highly efficient.

Now that he had full control, not to mention their attention, he calmly, almost eerily said "Farli cadere."

With that, the men dropped their guns.

"CUT! Beautiful! Great take Kyler," Jon yelled as he half-sprinted over to him with the joy a child bore as he or she bounds down the staircase on Christmas morning realizing Santa had indeed found a way into the house despite the lack of a chimney! Who knew!

"That was absolutely perfect man! What the hell?! You are a machine. What do you call that style again? Kevlar Magnum?" Jon was bursting at the seams at Kyler.

"No, that's what I wear with the ladies," Kyler chided, invigorated from the scene. His heart was pumping with the amazing sensation of adrenaline he got. A feeling he wondered if he liked just a little too much.

"No, it's actually Krav Maga." Kyler corrected.

"Sounds Jewish. Jews don't fight like that. Look at me!" Jon spread his arms out in a quasi-ta da-style.

"You're hangin out with the wrong Jews then buddy," Kyler replied while patting the healthy stomach that Jon had left exposed. "Besides, it's Israeli, not Jewish."

"Well shit, no wonder we're losing over there with shit like that. Where the hell do you learn this crap anyway? You're like an endless stream of martial art poetry, I swear!"

Again, Kyler thought, if you only knew. Jon couldn't seem to help himself from tossing softball lobs that begged Kyler to break and shock the hell out of the director.

Instead, he replied, "City of Angels my friend. We're a melting pot. You can find anything from psychics to yogis to psychos. And probably all on the same block." A truer statement, he knew, had never been spoken.

The response was at least partially true. At least the location bit. He had indeed learned the defense and striking-driven martial art in Los Angeles but not through any studios Jon or any of his fellow Angelinos would ever be in. There was a dojo of sorts located in the heart of Chinatown in a building that looked like a gigantic abandoned warehouse complete with boarded up windows, rusted steel beams on the exterior and impressive weeds growing through the cracks of the parking lot in front. The entrance for the few privileged enough to know about it was via the back alley through a door that blended so inconspicuously into the wall that if you didn't know it was there, you'd never know it was there.

Not to be fooled by the dilapidated exterior, the inside of the building was an MMA fighter's dream complete with cages, ten boxing-style rings, a gymnastics pit, dozens of punching bags of different varieties, a weight room in the back and an entire room dedicated to every weapon both imagined and some not. In the spirit of a movie sound stage, there was even a street façade that had been built to include an alley, buildings with stairs in pseudo San Francisco-style, store fronts and other obstacles that could be used to train it's fighters to deal not only with real life fighting attacks and weapons but also its physical surroundings. That had been one of Kyler's several contributions to the facility and it had proven incredibly useful.

The building also had a firing range as well as a movie theater mostly used for studying tapes of various fighting styles although there had been more than a few nights dedicated to Bruce Lee marathons. Kyler's favorite being Enter the Dragon which always made him a little sad knowing it had been the film that brought Bruce Lee to superstardom, a fame he hadn't lived to enjoy, dying of what had only been described as a mystery coma. Insert a hundred different stories of old world curses that would forever matriculate in and out of the martial arts world.

Amongst the many styles taught in the place, the one that had proven by far the most useful in the real world for Kyler had been Krav Maga. A mix of boxing, Karate, wrestling, Muay Thai and Brazilian Jiu Jitsu, its Los Angeles-like Mecca of styles adding to a deadly and highly effective combination. It centered on the premise of exploiting a person's natural reactions and movements with the primary intent being self defense against guns, knives and sticks. A person could quickly be trained on techniques that, when applied correctly, would disarm a gun in one second. In the framework of guns, one second was about all Kyler wanted to allow his attacker.

Back in the now, Kyler heard Jon say, "I must've driven by those places on my way to the strip."

The Strip, Kyler knew, meant the Sunset Strip in West Hollywood. Kyler thought it was a bit tacky and almost dated as far as locales went but he knew Jon liked it. Plenty of clubs which meant even more alcohol-induced woman that, as the night proceeded and he proceeded to sponsor their inebriation, would be likely to spend the night with the famously rich movie man.

"Just have to look closer buddy. I can take you sometime," Kyler said knowing there wasn't the snowball's chance in hell it would ever happen therefore rendering it a truly useless offer.

"I'll leave that business to you," Jon replied with a snort. "You just make sure you keep going and learning more knew stuff cuz it looks unbelievable on film."

"Thanks. You want to run it again?" Kyler asked, almost hopeful.

Jon nodded, "Once more for good measure. And just in case tweedle-dee and tweedle-dumb over there fucked up the shot." He said while gesturing a thumb over to the director of photography and his cameraman.

It was, of course, in good fun. Todd Schwartz and Chance Stevens had been with him on every movie since the first one they all did together, Detroit Destruction. Part of that was because they were some of the best in the business. The other reason was that it supported Jon's well-known beliefs in superstition. Kyler wasn't sure which pulled stronger but...no matter.

"Fuck yourself Jon," Phil shouted in the way only true long-time friends could. "We got it."

"Great, genius. Well let's do it one more time just in case, alright asshole?" The mood was light and they all moved with ease back into place for the top of the scene.

"Rolling rolling...and...action!"

Chapter 18

The car pulled up to the unassuming building on Rue d'Oradour-sur-Glane and stopped. Alani checked the time. She arrived with ten minutes to spare thanks to her driver, whose name she'd learned to be Phillipe on the way.

For his part, Phillipe managed to fly down the Parisian highways and streets with blinding speed while still managing to tell her about the one time he had been to America with his wife and two children. They'd gone to California to see Hollywood and Disneyland, commenting how rude the people in Los Angeles had been. Ironic, she thought to herself. He told her about his trip along the walk of fame with the stars and the concrete feet and hand imprints that donned the entrance to the Mann's Chinese Theater.

"I see why they call it Mann's Chinese Theater," Phillipe said while looking back at her through the rearview mirror while he whirred past cars on both sides.

"There are so many of the Chinese people there. Taking the pictures and the videos in front of the building. They are everywhere! There should be some law against that, don't you think?"

Alani didn't know where to start with that one. Would it be the blatant stereotype she chose to correct, the fact that the name had absolutely nothing to do with it or merely focus on the fact that while he focused on insulting an entire race of people, he was inches from killing them both every second.

She took the polite route and said, "I would probably do the same if I were a tourist in Hollywood. It's pretty mesmerizing."

At that, he shrugged, unaware of her discomfort with the statement and continued to carry on about the traffic, pollution and surprisingly bad food. His opinion, of course. She lived in Pasadena near the famous Rose Bowl where her Alma Mater, UCLA, played. She happened to quite like the food and the city in general. Oh well, agree to disagree she figured. So long as he'd gotten her there on time.

As they'd pulled up to the building, she said, "You'll wait here I assume?"

"My instructions are to bring you to this building and then back to the airport," Phillipe replied, nodding his head. "This is correct?"

"Correct."

With that, she raced through the entrance of the building and signed in at the front desk where a tall, thin and very attractive guard who looked to be about her age gave her the once over. She had to admit, she enjoyed the attention. Alas, another day, another time, maybe even another life. He gave her a visitor's badge and made no attempt to hide his glance for a wedding ring on her left hand as she took it. When he saw none, he gave her a wide smile.

"Où l'ascenseur est?" She asked, ready to get on with it.

He pointed directly behind her toward two rows of elevators. She thanked him, turned hard on her heels and quickly made her way for them.

The elevator doors dinged open as three men in suits made their way out, talking heatedly to each other and nearly taking her down as they passed. She slid in and hit the button for the fifth floor.

The doors were of the mirrored variety so often found in office buildings. Alani marveled at the fact that it was probably intentional since so many people, as she had been doing at that very moment, used the opportunity to give themselves one last check. Make sure hairs weren't out of place, teeth were clear of salad bits after lunch, a tie was sitting straight. She looked hard at the reflection she saw and had to say she wasn't looking half bad, particularly seeing as she was operating on four hours of sleep, had gotten dressed in twenty minutes flat and had spent the last four hours traveling in cars and a plane. Humphrey Bogart's words rang in her ears as she let loose a smile, "Here's lookin' at you kid."

The elevator dinged once more as she hit the fifth floor. The doors slid open to a cacophony of noise that was so often associated with a newsroom floor. She approached the front desk where a large house of a woman sat behind a minimalistic desk. The woman didn't bother looking up as Alani approached.

"M'excuser," Alani said as she arrived at the desk.

It wasn't until then that the portly woman lifted her rather large head up to look at her. When she saw Alani, she frowned. It was not a look that helped her cause in the effort of redeeming qualities. Thoughts of Sloth from The Goonies came to mind.

"Oui?" She asked, though seemingly very put off by the rude interruption.

Alani glanced around to see what the woman had been occupied with and found nothing save a magazine open to pictures a la US Weekly, complete with shots of what looked to be French celebrities that likely carried taglines that tore into the particular subject's choice of clothing or shoes.

Putting on her best I-just-want-to-be-your-friend smile, Alani asked, "Do you speak English?"

It didn't help. The woman half-grunted, "Oui. Appointment?"

"Oui, madame," Alani replied, still aiming for charm, no matter how futile. "I have an 11:00 meeting with Mr. Gautier.

"Name?"

"Lucy Sykes. CNN," Alani replied while pulling the faux credentials from her satchel.

If possible, the woman's expression intensified even further as she scrutinized the identification. Alani thought she heard cars slamming into each other and children screaming as they ran away in horror. She also thought to herself, you are going to straight to hell. She softened her gaze on the woman and then glanced down at the nameplate. One word. Berthe. Really, Alani thought. You're not making it easier here lady.

Finally satisfied with the identification, miss friendly picked up the phone punched a number on the dial pad.

"Madamoiselle Lucy Sykes," said the woman of seemingly few words. She hung up. "Sit," she said motioning toward the bench Alani had passed on her way to the desk.

Alani gave up on her attempt to make friends, turned without another word and sat down, crossing her legs. She nearly laughed out loud at Phillipe's comment of rude Americans. It was all a matter of perspective she figured. You could run into a coarse personality anywhere.

As if in an attempt to be a holistic contradiction to Berthe the conversationalist, Mr. Juliene Gautier bounded around the corner of a cubicle and approached Alani with a wide welcoming smile and an outstretched hand.

"Ms. Sykes? C'est un plaisir pour vous rencontrer. Oh," he stopped, "I'm sorry. It is a pleasure to meet you."

"Mr. Gautier," she replied, taking his hand and standing to meet the much shorter, much balder and very slight man that was Juliene Gautier. "Please don't apologize. I only wish my French was as good as your English."

At that, the bright man flushed, clearly pleased by the compliment.

"Won't you follow me to my office?" He said as he took her arm and guided her back past Berthe's desk. As they did so, he looked at the highly disinterested woman and said, "Café. Tout de suite!"

He looked at Alani, "I assume you would enjoy some of our fine French café after such a long trip?"

"Oui. Merci."

They walked past rows of cubicles with men and women all talking earnestly in French into the phones, probably to sources Alani could only assume. A continent away from home but yet, somehow, still the same. Symbolism of equality rang in her ears but she ignored it for the time being. Bigger fish to fry and all.

They arrived at the door of what was obviously Gautier's office. They entered and he extended his hand toward a chair that sat in front of a grey-washed Oxford-style wooden desk. It looked strange underneath the stacks of paper that were piled onto it, not to mention the very contradictory modern thirty-inch monitor that towered over it. Clearly lack of time and the aim at efficiency won out over the show of appearances in the editor's office.

The small man sat behind the large desk and looked oddly like a child sitting behind his or her parent's desk pretending to be all grown up. Alani tried to push the image out of her mind.

Gautier looked at her, his mood suddenly shifting from jovial host to grave inquisitor as he said, "Ms. Sykes. What is it that brings you all the way from America's capital of Washington DC to our humble studios here in Paris?"

He was great at the humility, Alani noted. She might have bought it had she not already known that the station was one of the largest in Paris.

"Please do not misunderstand me," Gautier continued with a sincere hand to his chest. "It is always my pleasure to do what I can to help Mr. Kranz."

Alani knew he was referring to the CNN Producer back in the states.

"After all, he has certainly assisted us on several occasions to which I owe my many thanks to. Tom just didn't tell me much of your visit. Only that it was important."

It was Alani's turn to put on the sincere eyes and warm voice. "I'm sorry for the theatrics and short notice, monsieur Gautier."

"Please, call me Julienne."

"Julienne. Yes," she continued. "Well it was important that I came here. I'm following up on a story you ran yesterday about a…" she pretended to look down at the pad of notes she'd pulled from her satchel as if she didn't know exactly who she was inquiring about, "Monsieur Jacques Francois?"

Something crossed Gautier's eyes. It was a flash, albeit brief, but Alani saw it. She tried to register what it was noting that it looked a bit like fear. She wasn't sure.

He collected himself quickly and paused, "Francois? Francois?" he muttered, clearly trying to recall the story, possibly trying too hard?

"Case of amnesia?"

"Ah! Oui oui! Mr. Francois," the smile was back and he turned his attention to his computer and hit a few keystrokes. "There it is." Julienne said while looking at a still image from the piece they ran on the man the previous day.

"He looks to have gotten quite a beating."

"Yes," Alani nodded. She treaded lightly, "I am hoping to see what more I can find out about Mr. Francois. Who he works for? If there was any reason for the attack…anything peculiar."

Gautier fumbled a bit but recovered and then looked at her more seriously, "Let us not play games Ms. Sykes. What is your interest in this story?" His stare was on her now. "We have beatings and muggings in this city every day. Why would you fly all the way here for this particular occurrence?"

Alani opted to try and keep it light, "We were interested in his strange case of his amnesia. It is sort of a psychological and physciological study piece. Scientific study on the anomalies of the mind and their connection to the physical body. That sort of thing."

"Uh huh," Julienne nodded but clearly wasn't buying it. "Where are your doctors then, Ms. Sykes?" He asked looking around at her lack of accompaniment.

"Excuse me?"

"If this is a medical study, where are your doctors?" His smile remained fixed in place. "Or are you the physician as well as the reporter?"

Alani debated how to proceed. She decided to change gears slightly, "I noticed there wasn't mention in the story of a statement from any of the local law officials. Why?"

"I'm not sure. I am only the producer. I wasn't there but I would have to guess it was because it was very late and the reporter was trying to get the story in before the deadline for the late edition." The answer seemed very quick. A little too planned, Alani thought.

"Such a strange case and no follow up? Even this morning?" She asked. She knew she was going to have to push a little harder now.

"Ms. Sykes, you yourself are a reporter so I would think you would understand," he leaned back slightly in the chair that engulfed his small frame. "A story is done the minute it airs. The next day, it is on to the next story. Am I right?"

For his part, Alani knew he was right. In the current day of short attention spans and news stories that seemed to be limited to fifteen seconds just to make sure you didn't lose the audience, follow up to previous stories seemed to be almost non-existent. But still…this was too odd of a story for such quick dismissal.

"Am I correct in quoting the reporter in saying that it was of the strangest cases of amnesia the hospital had ever seen?"

Gautier, whether for show or because he truly needed to, consulted his screen again which had a transcript of the report. "That is correct. But I don't see your point Ms. Sykes."

"A man gets dropped off in front of a hospital with massive injuries, no witnesses of the drop, no witnesses of the attack, absolutely no memory of the beating and there is no case created by the local police to find answers?" It had been her trump card and indeed the most peculiar part.

Sure, the fact that the man had no recollection of the beating that nearly brought him to the grave was beyond bizarre. But to have no activity by the police to try and find the attackers? That was the part that put it over the top.

"I can assure you, Ms. Sykes, that I certainly cannot explain the actions of the police," Gautier was shifting forward now and looked like he was getting ready to end the conversation as soon as he could. "I am sure they are indeed looking into the case. The Paris police are amongst the finest."

She looked at him squarely now. "There is no case, Julienne. That I know for certain. Mr. Krantz also has friends at the police nationale. We know it's dead."

Julienne's eyes hardened slightly but then he smiled.

"Well, it sounds like this is something you should be speaking to them about then," he said as he rose from his desk. "I surely am of very little assistance to you. I apologize but I am very busy and must get back. The news beckons."

Realizing she wasn't going to get to whatever Gautier was holding back, she opted for one last piece of information, "I understand. Well can you at least tell me which of your reporters worked the piece?"

Knowing that she could easily find this out on her own, he offered this nugget of information up to her, "Camille Blanche. But she is not here today."

"Finding the next story?"

"The stories never stop, Ms. Sykes. You understand." He nodded toward the door, "I assume you can find your way out?"

Alani confirmed with a nod of her own, "Yes. Thank you for your time. You've been extremely helpful."

The last statement was not purely sarcasm. It seemed that the station was not continuing with further investigation on the case. On the other hand, Alani thought, her 'absence' could merely be a cover to allow Blanche time to investigate deeper into the case without the police getting wind of it. In truth, the French police opened no case because they were instructed to do so by the DGSE. Alani knew that but she had to press Gautier, if nothing but to see his reactions. Any half-decent agent knew that far more was learned in what people did not say than what they did.

Alani decided that she was going to need to read someone else's body language on this. It was time for a visit to Ms. Blanche's home.

She was out Gautier's door and heading back toward the elevator, noting Camille Blanche's empty desk as she passed.

As she passed by Berthe's desk, she said, "Say hello to Mouth for me."

R.I.P. Corey Feldman, she thought and then disappeared behind the elevator doors as the woman sneered back at her having no idea what she meant but knew she didn't like it.

Yep, Alani thought, straight to hell.

Chapter 19

The satellite was moving with graceful floatation a mere three hundred and ninety miles above the earth. It is the latest and greatest model of satellite, a breakthrough in technology developed out of a Denver think tank. Its intended use being for monitoring surrounding satellites, taking images of space and making sure that there wouldn't be a repeat of the collision of the inoperable Russian satellite and working Iridium Spacecraft from a few years back. A big whoops, to say the least. NASA had taken some hits, as had space travel advances in general and stories like that not only cost a lot of money but didn't bode well for the image either.

The fact that the Air Force was monitoring it, however, allowed for some flexibility on its use. They could call it loose interpretation of its intended purpose. After all, the Air Force, once taking ownership of the craft, was quick to publicly point out how crucial the advancements could be in the "evolving need for new technology in the defense of national security." Code word for, we'll use it as we see fit so don't ask questions. That even means you, Boeing. We don't care if you helped build it because it's ours now bucko.

This was one of those special circumstances. The satellite had a very unique feature, making it unlike any other before. It had a communication feed that could be controlled from ground level coupled with a camera that could zoom with such precision, it could practically see if a card player sitting outdoors was holding a pair of aces.

Bob Buckney sat in his room of gadgetry and monitored the image that sat on one of his six flat-panel thirty-two inch high-resolution computer screens. Buckney worked for QTS Tek, a government defense contractor only slightly smaller than its rivals of Northrop Grumman, Raytheon Technologies and SAIC all of whom were mostly funded by its contracts with the various military entities. He had been commissioned to work as a go-between for the Air Force and the CIA on this particular job. Basically the Air Force had given Buckney clearance to use the newly developed satellite to gather information the CIA had expressed as matters of serious concern. Buckney was to gather the information and pass it along to the CIA. Simple as that.

Bob really didn't understand the need for the charade. Why the Air Force couldn't just pull the information down on their own and pass it along to the CIA was beyond him. Not that he was complaining. He was being generously compensated for the ruse. Call it just a passing curiosity. The Air Force had explained, not as if they really needed to in truth, that the less the public knew about this use of the technology the better. There were too many conspiracy groups crying foul over the growing concerns that technology was adding to the infringement on privacy. Big Brother was out to get them and the like.

In Bob's opinion, the public had seen one too many movies. His belief was that the people that tended to worry about Big Brother were probably giving them good reason to worry. And the constant debate ensued. Knowing the power of the technology he was, at the present time, controlling, the fear factor could certainly be warranted.

The image coming through from the satellite was crystallizing at that moment. He had locked in on the coordinates that his contact and employer at the CIA had given him. It was a location outside of Florence. More specifically, a winery and bed and breakfast.

His instructions had been clear on this. Using the ability to get sensory readings that indicated various levels of heat zones, he was supposed to look for areas that could be deemed of interest. The CIA believed that there was a lab located somewhere in the building and his directive was to locate where it might be and then plot the entire grounds out in a Geo Spatial grid to be sent off for use by a field agent of theirs.

Using what could be compared to an arcade joystick, he started panning down on the image, pushing forward on the stick to zoom closer in on the location.

"That it?" Matt Barnes asked, Bob's partner on the job, as he walked in with two giant sugar-free Red Bulls and handed one to Bob.

"According to what they gave me, looks like it is."

"Looks like that's the edge of the property," Matt said, drawing his finger in a square on the screen. His finger actually drew a line on the touch screen monitor, a feature that had been introduced to the world first in recent presidential races and now as an analysis tool on ESPN by former football coaches after Monday Night Football. It all felt very much like the culmination of Minority Report.

"Uh huh…I think I should spread it out to Big Momma so we can get in closer," Big Momma, as Bob had affectionately named it, was the seventy-inch flat screen television they used to get more detail from an image.

"It would only be fair to Big Momma to join the fun," Matt responded.

With a click here and a drag there, Bob sent the image magically flying from his monitor to the mounted display that sat on the wall. Big Momma was also touch-enabled allowing them to then manipulate the image, essentially overtaking the controls of the joystick. Somewhere in the distance Bob thought he could hear an ensuing argument between old school and new school. Atari nostalgias butting heads with new Nintendo Wii enthusiasts. Bob's take was that there wouldn't be one without the other and therefore chose to honor both.

Now that the image was about four times the size that it had been, they could easily see the winery's plot lines.

"Let's start the image here," Matt said as he started another square from the upper left hand corner just above where the field of vineyards seemed to stop. The line carried across to the right, down toward the bottom, across and then finally back up again encompassing the hotel building they knew to be Villa Santini.

"Yeah, lemme isolate that," Bob said as he hit a few keystrokes on the wireless keyboard he had carried over to the screen.

The exterior excess of image faded away and all that remained on the screen was the section Matt had carved out on the display. The image zoomed in and sharpened for a closer look.

"Save that as the base image," Matt said.

Bob hit a few more keys and a smaller screen popped up indicating that the ArcGIS image was being plotted. GIS being a Geographic Information System, was essentially an image that had data linked to it. It'd been used by the military for years and was now being incorporated by the same contractor Bob and Matt worked for to allow field agents and other military personnel to connect any GPS device to a computer and pull up the same data that corresponded to their current location. It was critical in the world of planning routes and being prepared for, say, unfriendly territory.

In this particular case, they were preparing two field agents to quickly identify what might be the point of interest on what looked to be an otherwise innocent tourist spot.

"Enable the heat zones," Matt told Bob.

Bob had already been ahead of Matt on the task and the screen illuminated with various colors. The software's purpose was to look for chemicals on the image. The stronger the chemical, the darker the color would be ranging from yellow to orange to red.

The image had all colors represented. Most of the vineyards were a deep yellow as was the hotel itself. Portions of the hotel had orange which they assumed was where there were heavy concentrations of wine bottles. Most likely those areas represented the restaurant and storage areas for wine. Nothing of interest there.

They continued to pan the image when both of their eyes drew to a building that looked to be about three hundred yards from the hotel.

"Zoom in on that," Bob said to Matt, pointing to the building.

Matt took two fingers, touched the screen around the building and spread them apart causing the image to rapidly zoom in on the target. It was deep orange in most places obviously being the actual location where the wine was being made. Near the back, however, they both saw it. Matt zoomed in to what looked to be about fifteen hundred square feet of space.

The entire area was a deep, blood red.

"That's gotta be what we're looking for." Matt said to Bob excitedly. "Send that to him now."

Bob was again a step ahead of him and was saving the colored imaged into a file. Once saved, it was sent in an encrypted email to one Dr. Ethan Goldman, CIA.

Chapter 20

Alani was revisited by her image staring back at her in the elevator. She debated what to do next. She'd hoped to get more information from Gautier but had basically struck out. The only thing she'd confirmed was that their suspicions were correct. For some reason, there was more to this story and she needed to know what. But who to question was what she wasn't sure about. She could try the Paris police but suspected she'd have about as much luck there as she'd had with Gautier. No, she needed another angle and knew where that would be. She needed to get to Camille Blanche, the woman who wrote the story on Francois. She had a feeling Camille might be her best bet on getting her some answers. She decided to use her best assets with her friend down at the security desk.

The elevator hit the ground floor and Alani stepped out with a bit more flair than she'd entered. She'd let her long hair down so it flowed past her shoulders with its natural seductive wave. She wasn't aiming for homely reporter anymore here.

She looked ahead with relief, seeing that her friend, the attractive guard that had not been shy about his interest in her, was still manning the main lobby security desk. It didn't take long for him to see her coming and the smile on his face told her he was certainly happy for her return.

"Hello again mademoiselle," he said flashing what Alani imagined was his best sultry smile.

"Bonjour Monsieur," she returned the smile while taking her visitor's badge slowly off of her jacket, which had been strategically placed very close to her chest. The action did not go unnoticed by her companion.

"You are done here?" He asked, his eyes not so subtly following her actions.

Alani handed the badge back to him and allowed her touch to linger on his hand a bit as he took it from her.

"Oui, monsieur...I'm sorry for being so rude when I arrived. I didn't even ask your name."

"Ah...it is no problem. My name is Jules. And you are Mademoiselle Lucy Sykes?" Jules said it more as a statement than a question, having obviously referred to the sign-in sheet from earlier.

"Yes, that would be me," she said, smiling and extending her hand to him.

She feared he was going to kiss her hand or maybe lean across the desk for a peck on each cheek but, thankfully, he opted for the less intrusive handshake.

"Was your visit a success?" he asked, looking for conversation to extend her time with him.

Alani gave him a smile and a slight back and forth motion with her head, "Well yes and no. I was able to see your wonderful news room but unfortunately wasn't able to locate my friend that I was really here for."

Alani nearly fluttered her eyes at the man, although she knew she had him already.

"I'm so sorry to hear that. Who is your friend?"

Yep, she thought, got him.

"Camille Blanche. Do you know her?"

"But of course! I see Ms. Blanche every day. We are good friends."

This just keeps getting better, Alani thought to herself.

"Really? That's wonderful." As she said this, she leaned across the desk in pseudo-Julia Roberts Erin Brockovich style.

"We actually met a few months ago on a story we were both covering in the States. We hit it off, promised to keep in touch but then forgot to exchange numbers. I only knew she worked here at the station. I happened to be here in Paris covering a story and thought I'd surprise her with a visit but she's not here."

Jules nodded his head slowly, "Ah yes, I believe you are right. I don't remember seeing her today. Let me see here." Jules looked down at his sign-in sheet.

"No, she hasn't been in all day."

"Hmm…that's so sad. I'm only in town for the day and have no way to reach her."

Anxious to please, Jules said, "Well I know where she lives. I could tell you where…" he smiled at her slyly, "in exchange for…maybe dinner. With me. Tonight?"

She returned the smile. "That would be lovely Jules."

She pulled a pad of paper from her satchel and slid it slowly across the counter to him.

"Why don't you write her address right there," she said, pointing to the top line of the paper while keeping her eyes coyly on him. "And then, below it, write down where you and I can carry on the process of…getting to know each other. Say…nine o'clock? That way I can have enough time to catch up with Camille beforehand." She gave him a seductive smile that would have made the most devout priest weak in the knees.

As Alani walked away she felt a pang of guilt. By nine o'clock, Alani would be on a plane back to Florence and Jules would be sitting at the restaurant alone.

"Sorry Jules. Another life maybe."

Chapter 21

The rest of the day had been quite a bit less exhilarating for Kyler. The climax had certainly been hit with the fight scenes and the rest of the day was spent getting close up shots of Scott Cruz. Reaction shots he guessed you could call it. Scott Cruz hitting the piazza and delivering his clever one-liner to the copy of the David. Cruz stopping in the center of the piazza and looking one way, then the other and then the next. All in extremely dramatic fashion. Each of which somehow requiring several takes from numerous angles. It was the part of the filming process he didn't enjoy much but knew it was all part of the big picture. He was only thankful that it wasn't the middle of the summer with the sun beating down hard on them all day.

When Jon finally announced that they were done for the day, he was gone before Christenson could even finish the words. Kyler jetted back to his trailer, changed out of his wardrobe that they'd laid out for him for the day's shooting and slipped into his own clothes. He walked through the regular routine of signing out for the day, another union policy not to be overlooked. He made his goodbyes to the assistant directors, the few crewmembers he saw and the personal assistants, often commonly known as the gofers.

After going through his rebellion and coming back to the movie industry the second time around, he had made a point of going above and beyond on his treatment of everyone on the films he worked on. Call it penance from how awfully he'd treated the same groups of people in his younger years. He recognized how hard everyone around him worked and realized how fortunate he was to be in his position. He'd even followed the lead of a story he'd heard about Keanu Reeves once who'd famously bought Harley Davidson motorcycles for all of the stuntmen that worked on his blockbuster movie, The Matrix. After a movie they'd done a couple years prior in Los Angeles, he bought all of the Los Angeles-based stuntmen season tickets to the Lakers. Not just any tickets. Floor seats. They'd gone nuts and nothing had ever made him happier.

Much like Reeves, he tried to avoid the act of generosity making it into the papers and had gifted the tickets with the condition that they made no mention of where they'd come from. He wasn't interested in the media. He hadn't done it for that. Waxing philosophical yet again, he wondered what the world would be like if we could all follow Keanu's path. Certainly not buying motorcycles or basketball tickets, but focusing on the giving more than the taking. He guessed he may not have his covert career.

And just as he was musing on world peace he realized his reality and picked up his pace towards the Enzo. By now, headquarters had probably sent over the translation of the conversation at dinner the previous night.

As he got in the car, he checked his phone and saw he had two missed calls. One from Alani and the other from a private number, which he guessed was probably Goldman calling from Langley.

He hit the voicemail button prompting the always-robotic female voice telling him he had two new messages. The first was from Alani telling him what he already knew in that she wouldn't be back in time for dinner because she was following up on the lead in Paris but was planning on meeting him at his hotel tomorrow for the trip out to the winery for the weekend. A tinge of sadness crept in him for the dinner cancellation but he was comforted by the idea of an entire weekend with her, despite the torment it would provide him with.

Miss Roboto told him that the second message from the unknown number came in an hour ago. Goldman's voice came through.

"Scott. Goldman. Need you to call me when you get to the hotel and in front of the computer. Translation's in from the linguists and also have the data you're going to need for tomorrow's trip."

Kyler reflected on the efficiency of the team of people he worked with. He knew the data Goldman was referring to was the ArcGIS information for the locale. It would have pictures, coordinates, heat zones, a blue print of all of the buildings on the premises and full descriptions of every employee that worked there. Between the recorded conversation from the previous night and the map's info, he would be extremely well equipped for the weekend, allowing him to do what he did best. Start blowing the damn thing wide open.

His anticipation for the suspense of the next few days sent a shot of adrenaline through his veins and he hit the gas hard. The quasi rocket on wheels didn't disappoint.

Chapter 22

Jack Hawkins walked out of his favorite pizza place in Palo Alto Hills. He hated chain pizza places, particularly being a Chicago native where he'd been spoiled most of his childhood life with mouth watering deep-dish style pies. He sat on the thick crust side of the on-going debate that seemed to always ensue. Which was better? New York's thin crust variety of slices the size of one's head or Chicago's hearty, cheesy, deep-dish offering that dared you to try and eat more than a slice? Call it nostalgia or just a matter of taste, but pizza only felt like pizza to him if it made him feel like he was going to burst through the increasingly growing waistline he was sporting. He tried to overlook the glaringly obvious correlation.

Having defied all odds imaginable by putting down not one, not two but three slices of coronary delight, Jack all but stumbled to his Tesla roadster that he'd parked in the spot directly in front of the entrance that had been reserved for him by the owner. Jack was one of less than a thousand people in the country that owned the innovative all-electric car. It was a bit ironic in the fact that owning the car put him into the type of community of alternative drivers that he criticized so heavily when it came to Apple computers. People who, in attempts to defy the big bad automobile giants, opted to spend two to three times the price of a normal, or even a hybrid car.

The car had cost him just over a hundred grand, which he'd only been fortunate enough to spend when his name had come up on the extensive waiting list. It was the perfect car for the somewhat leftist affluent region of the Palo Alto area. Palo Alto Hills being home to the likes of the late Steve Jobs, the founders of Hewlett Packard and Hall of Fame quarterback, Steve Young amongst others. The residents worked hard to separate themselves from the distinctly opposite make-up of East Palo Alto, which, at one point, held the title of one of the most dangerous cities in the country. The hills region, on the contrary, boasted homes in the ten million dollar plus vicinity and was not shy about its intellectual pride as the home of Stanford University.

The problem, particularly on this night where Jack felt every bit of his two hundred and twenty pounds, was that the high tech, futuristic car was about the size of a Mazda Miata. The comparison was probably a generous one, actually. Hawkins had also taken down several glasses of beer and began to question whether driving was the best idea, even if he could manage to squeeze into the car.

The cautious part of him won out and he decided he could trek the half mile home rather than risk wrecking the precious toy he'd only acquired a few months prior. Yep, he thought to himself, best to take the responsible route. Way to go Jackie boy, you're all grown up.

Jack made sure the car was locked and then poked his head back into the restaurant, Pie in the Sky. He found Craig Stevens, the owner, wiping down the bar and getting ready to close up shop.

"Craig, do you mind if I leave the car here for the night. I don't think drivin' would be a good idea."

"Sure Jack! Anything for you," Craig replied in a raspy voice commonly attributed to years of smoking which, in his case, was accurate.

"You sure you don't want me to call you a cab? We're closin' down. I could probably even have one of the guys take you home."

Jack patted his stomach, "Have you witnessed my growing waistline? I could use the exercise. Thanks anyway though. You sure she'll be ok here overnight?" Jack pointed out to the lot toward the car.

"Definitely. We installed security cameras a couple months back after some of the rich punks in the neighborhood decided to spray the place with some of their graffiti artwork." Craig pointed to a monitor behind the counter that displayed a live feed of the front of the building.

"Obviously it won't prevent anyone from taking the car but if they do, you'll have the fucker that did it on tape."

"Well, by calculating the percentages and chances of theft in this neighborhood versus the statistical likelihood of either an accident or DUI, I think I'll elect the former and roll the proverbial dice." Jack said, almost to himself, ever the easy conversationalist.

"Uh…ok. Does that mean you're gonna leave it or drive it?"

Not noticing Craig's utter confusion, Jack answered, "I'll be walking home Craig. Good night."

"Sure thing, bud. See you tomorrow then."

With that, Jack headed back out and made his way toward the path that would lead him to his house. As he did, the lights of the Pie in the Sky went out and left him with a single overhead streetlight to guide him for the next couple blocks. He wondered why the city didn't install more lights but then remembered that it had been a debate waged the year before. With the golf course in the area and the desire for privacy and seclusion, the residents had voted to keep the lights to a minimum. The common opinion had been that streetlights were reserved for areas where you wanted to keep watch on the comings and goings of potential troublemakers. That wasn't a concern in this part of town. Or so they thought.

Jack had made his way about halfway down the first block and was about a hundred yards from the streetlight when he thought he heard light footsteps behind him. He stopped, whirled around to look behind him and tried to listen to see if he'd been hearing things. He heard nothing but the occasional passing car in the distance and the night hum of insects and the outdoors. He started walking again, now wishing he'd voted for the extra lights.

He picked up his pace a bit, which was a bit of a struggle in the state he was in at the moment. He tried not to panic, telling himself that he was just being paranoid. This is a safe neighborhood. It's not New York. People don't get mugged or shot out here. It was the beer and cheese playing tricks on him.

Then came a slight crunch of leaves and he stopped again, this time with an increasing amount of panic.

"Hello? Is someone there?" But there was no response. He hadn't expected one and the lack of it only increased his fear to catastrophic levels.

"Hello!? I have a gun and I wouldn't want to shoot someone on accident!" Jack did not have a gun but wished he had. But then again, who would carry a gun to a local pizza place in this neighborhood? He knew he was moving towards paralyzing panic now and felt like his legs were frozen in place.

He circled around several times, his eyes desperately straining to make anything out in the dark but he saw nothing. He had finally gotten his legs to work again and turned to begin making a break for the direction of his house. That's when he felt the prick of the needle in his neck, a strong arm grab beneath his arms pits and another wrap around his neck firmly holding him in place. Within seconds, the already dark world around him went completely black and his body slumped unconsciously into his attacker.

"Good night, Jackie boy," a man dressed head to toe in black whispered into his ear and slung the heavy computer geek over his shoulder with surprising ease.

Chapter 23

Alani stepped out of the news building and was happy to see that Phillipe the talkative driver was still there waiting for her. He was leaning against the front of the car, one hand holding a phone that he was talking at breakneck speed into while the other held a cigarette that he waved around as he spoke with entertaining animation. Looks like the Italians aren't the only ones that say as much with their hands as they do with their mouths, Alani mused.

When Phillipe saw her approaching, he quickly snapped the phone shut, seemingly hanging up on whoever might have been on the other end of the line. He smiled brightly at her.

"Ms. Lucy, how did everything go? You had a good visit?" Phillipe asked as he opened the back door for her as she approached.

"In a matter of speaking, it was what I expected," she replied. As she approached, she felt his gaze survey her with even more interest than before. It was then that she remembered she'd pulled out her more seductive appearance for Jules and Phillipe had taken notice. He fumbled to close the door after she'd slinked into the seat, enjoying playing with him a bit as she did. He hurried around to the driver's side of the car.

"We go back to the airport, yes?" Phillipe asked, turning back to look at her.

"Actually we need to make a bit of a detour first," Alani replied, pulling out the sheet of paper that Jules the security guard had written Camille Blanche's address on.

She handed the paper to him, "I need to go here first please."

The driver took the paper and looked back up at her, "This is not a very nice part of Paris you know."

"Oh?"

"It is like...how do you say in English," Phillipe was tapping his head and his eyes looked upwards as if searching for the word lost in the recesses of his mind.

"It is...er...slums? This is the correct term?"

"The slums?   Well yes if, by that you mean run-down buildings, maybe some falling apart, dangerous streets. You know...the kind of place you wouldn't walk around at night without some protection."

"Yes, yes. That is right," he was clearly pleased that he'd found the correct slang term.

"Slums...that's it. Yes. Not a very safe part of town." His look of concern seemed to be very genuine.

It didn't surprise Alani too much. After all, if Paris was anything like the States, a beat writer, even one that wrote for a newspaper of the caliber of the Los Angeles Times or Chicago Tribune, didn't make much money. That was particularly true for the writers that were still a bit green and hadn't earned his or her proverbial stripes with a big story that would mean an editorial column or regular spot that readers looked for each day.

"You are sure that is the correct address?" As Phillipe asked, Alani wasn't sure whose safety he was more concerned with, hers or his own. He didn't strike her as the sort that could look out for himself.

Going with the idea of familiarity, she said, "Absolutely. Ms. Camille Blanche lives there. She's a friend. I'd hoped to see her here at the station but she wasn't there. I'd hate to leave without saying hello even if it's not the best neighborhood.

Still leery of going but realizing he wasn't going to convince his passenger otherwise, he agreed. "But of course. As you wish. It should only be fifteen minutes or so."

"Excellent," she said and then picked up her phone. She decided to take the bit of time to check in for any messages and then called Kyler and left him a message to let him know she wouldn't be available for dinner. She felt the pang of disappointment at that thought.

As he had before, Phillipe drove at a pace that would have impressed Mario Andretti. Alani, having finished the few phone calls she wanted to make, watched the city go by. Close to fifteen minutes had passed now and she began to laugh to herself. She looked at the buildings as they passed and, if this was supposed to be her French driver's idea of the slums than she strongly recommended he didn't visit South Central Los Angeles anytime soon.

The buildings were possibly slightly less taken care of in places but, more or less, were of the same historically beautiful and quintessentially European as all other parts of Paris she had seen.

"Are we in Gare du Norde?" She asked, wondering if she just hadn't paid much attention to the time.

"Oui mademoiselle. This is, as you say, Paris's 'slums'," as he said this, he made the traditional air quotes with the two fingers of his left hand, thankfully keeping his right hand firmly on the steering wheel. If this was unsafe territory, the last thing they needed was to get in an accident and be stranded. Still, Alani thought to herself, this is the nicest crap town she'd ever been to.

They traveled a few more blocks and the scenery didn't change much, Alani noted, silently wondering if they'd turn a corner and then, wham! Slums. Nope. Just more classic buildings that, she noted, felt like they could have also been mistaken for New Orleans.

Alani's commentary on Paris and the world's similarities disappeared quickly though as they turned down Rue de Belzunce which was the street Jules had given her as Camille's place of residence. The scene ahead of them as they turned down the street sent a quickening pulse into Alani veins. Something was seriously wrong here as she counted six Paris Police cars parked in front of what Alani feared to be Camille's flat. The lights of the vehicles were spinning and turning with an almost ominous rhythm.

"Keep going Phillipe," Alani said firmly, almost too firmly, as she sensed her driver start to slow down for the first time, clearly unsure what to do.

"Are you sure mademoiselle?"

"Yes! Go!" and then, "please."

"I don't think it is safe Ms. Lucy."

"Fine Phillipe. If you don't want to go then stop the damn car here and let me out. I'll walk the rest of the way," she said and then added, for effect, "That is my friend's flat and I need to make sure she's ok."

"Of course. Of course," Phillipe seemed to realize he was not going to win this battle and also knew his employer would kill him if he found out that he'd let his passenger out of the car to walk the streets in this neighborhood, particularly with half of the damn Paris police poking around.

Phillipe approached the scene slowly and finally came to a stop as close as the police would allow him to get.

Alani hardly waited for the car to stop and was already opening the door. "Wait here."

She ran up to a group of policemen that were standing around talking with serious expressions on their faces. One turned and saw her approaching and put up his hand to stop her.

Alani debated pulling out her government-issued credentials and then reconsidered. The less exposure the better. Instead she pulled out the press credentials and introduced herself.

"Lucy Sykes, CNN, Washington DC," she showed the ID to the policeman that had his hand held up at her, telling her not to come any further.

Thankfully he spoke English, "No press." Well, at least a little English.

She decided to take a different approach, "My friend, Camille Blanche, lives in that building." As she said this she pointed to her right where a few of the police officials were going in and out of.

The man's expression changed from one of a policeman doing his job of crowd and press control to one of concern.

"I am sorry Ms. Sykes to be the person telling you and in this way but Ms. Blanche is dead."

Though Alani had known this was coming, it still hit her like a ton of bricks.

"Dead? How? What happened?" Her concern was certainly genuine but her motives behind her questions were not exactly forthcoming.

"Ms. Blanche was shot Ms. Sykes," the police official said, concern in his eyes now.

He had separated from the other men while talking to her and began to pull her aside to talk to her one on one. Alani was grateful she had gone the route of press and friend at this point since he would clearly be more sympathetic to her.

"We believe that the killer was here to rob her house. That maybe they thought Ms. Blanche was at work and then, when they found her at home, panicked and shot her."

"What makes you think that Officer…" Alani looked for the name on his badge.

"You can call me Ferdinand, Ms. Sykes." His smile was warm and sincere.

"Thank you Ferdinand. Well what makes you think it happened that way?" She was trying to maintain her feigned grief of the loss of a friend but also needed to find out what she could while she had the chance.

"The killer made a big mess in the house. Broken lamps and mirrors, pulled the drawers out. Probably looking for jewelry or something. But, as far as we can tell, there doesn't seem to be much missing from the flat."

"When did this happen?" Alani asked, the question making it easier to show the pain in her voice, albeit put on.

"A neighbor that takes care of Ms. Blanche's dog found her and she called us about an hour ago."

One of the officers called over to Ferdinand, summoning him over.

"I am sorry for your loss Ms. Sykes but I must continue with the investigation of the crime scene. Can I have you taken home?"

Alani nodded her head, "No, thank you. I am fine. I understand."

With that, he rejoined the other officers who again engaged in grave conversation, undoubtedly over the elements of the crime scene.

As Alani made her way back to the car, her mind was swirling with what the information of the last few minutes presented. For starters, it would seem that the concern that Blanche was investigating the true identity of Francois with the intention of exposing him could be put to rest.

As for the murder itself, Alani sorted through the few details she had gathered about the murder, noting a couple things that struck her as odd. The obvious one being that nothing had been taken from the apartment. Sure, the officer's theory was a logical one. It was certainly plausible. But the second piece made it not fit as neatly as they'd probably like. The building clearly had several flats in it but the officer said the body had only been discovered when the neighbor came to look in on the dog? That didn't fit. With all of those people living in the building, nobody had heard a gunshot? *Someone* must have been home when it happened and heard *something.* She had been in the business long enough to know what that likely meant. Camille Blanche had been executed by a professional who would have used a silencer and then framed the scene to make it to look like a robbery.

If her theory was true, this then opened up a new line of questioning. Had Blanche already known Francois's true identity and paid the price for it? She thought back to Gautier's peculiar behavior and wondered what his involvement could be? It wasn't making sense and Alani wondered what she was missing. She now wished she'd pressed Gautier further when she'd been at BFM.

She needed to get back to the airport for tomorrow's trip with Kyler. It was clear that the winery was where they needed to be and she could only hope that it held the answers they needed to piece these increasingly mysterious events together. The two of them could recount this recent development and hopefully make some sense of the connection to Francois and maybe Ellen Stratton as well.

"Back to the airport please Phillipe," Alani said, seeing the worried and scared expression on his face.

Phillipe knew by her tone that now was the time to keep his mouth shut. Just as Alani had hoped. She needed time to think.

With that, Phillipe sped off towards Charles de Gaulle Airport.

Chapter 24

Kyler pulled into the valet once again at the Boscolo. The eager attendant was opening his door nearly before he could put the stick shift in neutral and pull up the parking brake.

"Buona Sera Signore," the attendant greeted him.

"Buona Sera. Grazie." Kyler replied as he hopped out of the car. "I am very rude signore and must extend my apologies. You have been tending to me each night and I have never gotten your name."

The man smiled a bit sheepishly and Kyler assumed it meant that the question didn't happen frequently.

"Napoleon, signore, is my name."

"Napoleon?" Kyler asked, unable to hide his surprise. Maybe that had been the reason for the hesitancy to offer up the name.

"Si Signore. I know it is a bit odd."

"I can't say that I have ever met anyone with that name before." Kyler staved off a hundred Napoleon-complex jokes that came to mind while also considering the irony that he was actually the one in the scenario driving the outlandishly expensive car.

"My father was a French history teacher. He gave me the name." Napoleon wore an easy smile as he explained. Kyler assumed this was one of a thousand times he'd told the story.

Eager to change the subject he said, "Well I plan on leaving again soon so would you mind keeping the car close?" He had pulled one hundred Euro from his wallet and was handing it to Napoleon.

"But of course signore. This is not necessary," Napoleon was clearly surprised by the generosity of the tip.

"It is. Let's just call it a thank you for my rudeness for having gone so long without an introduction. Everyone here takes wonderful care of me." And he wanted to make sure they continued to.

"Grazie, signore. It is our pleasure. I will make sure the car is taken care of. It will be here when you are ready."

"Once again, grazie." And with that he was passing through the already open doors to the hotel and making his way quickly toward the stairs where he would again bound up them in two by two fashion. He had a lot to take care of before heading out for what would be a brief but important task later that evening.

Chapter 25

Entering his room, Kyler was once again taken aback by the reverie it brought him to. Customarily, the bed was turned down, the doors to the terrace sat open allowing the gentle night breeze to provide a perfect room temperature and the ever-present fresh bottle of wine sat there waiting for him, again accompanied by two glasses. Despite the numerous tasks ahead of him, Kyler couldn't resist. He strode over and, after uncorking the bottle, a different offering of the local variety, poured a conservative amount.

Playing the increasingly pretentious wine snob and loving every minute of it, he inhaled the aroma of the wine with a deep sniff. He wasn't going to lie though. He had no idea what he was smelling for. He couldn't pick out the scent of raspberries, vanilla, oak, coffee and even a faint odor of tobacco. He remembered seeing a wine he had tasted in California that had those elements in its description and sheepishly admitted to himself that the best he could offer was that it smelled fruity and a little like dirt. Some friends who were connoisseurs in their own right had corrected him later on saying that it should be described as *oaky* or *earthy*. Naturally, to the owner of the winery who'd taken the famous actor on a private tour of the winery, he adamantly nodded in complete and total agreement with the description. They had, in fact, been drinking the offering directly from the barrel that housed it and he wasn't about to insult his sommelier with his own ignorance.

But he knew what he liked. His tastes were definitely evolving and he knew enough to know that what he was smelling was going to be nothing short of amazing. He took a small pull from the glass, allowing the flavor to linger in his mouth a bit before swallowing. He closed his eyes appreciatively. His winos back home would be so proud of his reverence.

He decided it was his favorite thus far. Of course, he said that with nearly every new wine but he didn't care to acknowledge that fact.

"Let's get it going Scott," Kyler said, half-scolding himself knowing he didn't have time for this right now.

Taking the glass, he sat in front of the laptop and logged on with the special key that he'd been told was called an RSA Token. It was the only way to unlock his computer, which he hadn't used the previous night because he'd unwisely neglected to lock the computer down. He'd amply cursed himself for that major oversight knowing how much data was on the piece of machinery.

The RSA Token, as the geeks had described it, was the most secure tool for logging onto an individual's company access in the world. More amazingly, the technology has been around since the eighties and has yet to be replaced with anything better.

It was the size and shape of a keyless entry box for a car. What made it so secure was that it created a two-tier password login requirement. One password being a unique pin number that the user themselves selects and remembers. The second being a six-digit pin that the little device's display shows the holder of the token. That six-digit pin was actually a simplified number driven by a highly encrypted algorithm generated by the brains of the key. The big kicker was that the pin changed every sixty seconds. That pin number matched the one that the server the user was trying to log into had, both the server and token being on a clock so as to be in synch.

Kyler looked at the device and marveled at it. Technology certainly fascinated him, even if he didn't understand it most of the time.

He entered the two pieces of information and was logged on successfully. The first item that got his attention was the email from Ethan Goldman, which he assumed was the data his boss had told him he'd sent. He decided to give the good doctor a call to go through the next steps.

He launched the videoconference and Goldman's face appeared after two rings.

"Scott…perfect timing. I was just about to call you. We've had some developments since that message I left you." The stress on Goldman's face was clear to Kyler.

"What's going on?" His thoughts instantly went to Alani and fear for her crept in.

"Do you remember the name Camille Blanche?"

Kyler's gaze went up and to the right, an action neurologists would say is instinctual when searching for facts buried in the recesses of the mind.

"I know the name but I can't place it. Does she work for the agency?"

"No, she was the one that covered the story about Jacques Francois out in France for BFM TV."

Kyler began nodding remembering seeing the name in the article from the day before.

"Right. What about her?"

"She's dead."

"Excuse me? Dead? How did you find out? When?"

"Alani just called to give me the news. She's on a plane heading back to Florence now," Goldman replied and then proceeded to relay the details of Alani's trip from her conversation with the producer at the station to her visit to Blanche's flat where she found out about the woman's demise, including the conversation with the local police on the case.

"That was a hit sir. No doubt about it." Kyler deducted coming to the same conclusion Alani had.

"Alani said the same. I concur but the question is why," it was more of a statement then a question because it was clear that neither him nor Kyler had the answers right now.

"At any rate, Alani will head back to Paris after you're trip this weekend. Have you taken a look at the data yet?" Ethan asked, obviously referring to the images he'd sent over that prompted Kyler's call in the first place.

"I just opened it up. Figured I'd call so we could review it together and you can tell me what I'm looking at."

The image file was completely downloaded according to the icon in the top of the computer screen. Kyler clicked on it and the image slowly sharpened revealing the heat zone map Goldman had received from Bob Buckney earlier. The screen that displayed Goldman's image reduced in size to about a two inch by two inch square, giving the downloaded image priority for Kyler to examine more closely.

"I'm going to take over your computer." Ethan told Kyler.

"You're going to what, Doc?"

"Take over your computer. You know, remote shadowing? You really need to read the damn technology memos the agency puts out. I'm an old man and I know more about this shit than you do."

"Do I need to do anything?" Kyler asked, showing his benevolence to the technology.

"Christ. No…look. Is the cursor on your screen moving right now?"

Kyler looked in amazement at the screen and realized that the arrow on his screen was dancing all over and he didn't have his hand anywhere near the laptop's track pad.

"Sure is."

"That's me. I have the ability to take control of your computer from here. We're tied together essentially. It's pretty basic management software. Haven't you ever had to call into tech support before?"

"Nope. Just lucky I guess. Sorry sir, I'll dive into the trainings after this mission's up. The guys did walk me through how to use the latest bag of tricks they sent me here with."

Kyler had been referring to a bag full of various gadgets he'd been sent with, one of which would come in handy that evening.

"I'd hope to hell they would. You're going to need that this weekend. Can we carry on now that you've done your best to terrify me with your ignorance?"

"Absolutely sir. Please continue."

"The guys isolated this image to only include the grounds of the winery. So what you are looking at right now is the property lines." Goldman had switched the arrow to an object that looked like a virtual pen to make his point.

"What we are interested in, as I'm sure you've already figured out, is this area right here," Goldman used the tool to draw a circle around the area in the warehouse that Matt Barnes and Bob Buckney discovered.

"I see that. Looks like there's heavy chemical concentration there." Kyler was scrutinizing the screen and, at the same time, committing the layout of the grounds to memory. He may not have the benefit of this image when he needed it.

"Right. Obviously, priority number one is to get in that room, determine what's causing this hot zone and gather as much intel on whatever it is as you can. Some of those toys in that bag of gadgets should help with that."

"Number two, I need you to find out as much about Vitale Baldacci as you can. He's running Villa Santini for Dimarco so I'm sure he's tied into what's going on over there."

"I assume you have images of Baldacci so I'll know who to look for?" Kyler asked.

Goldman was nodding his head, "Image and bio are on the second page of this attachment. You can scroll to it when I'm done, read up on him, get to know our friend."

"If you can find a way to track Baldacci, keep tabs on him, that'd be a plus," Ethan moved on to the third and final point.

"Last thing is that the video shows trucks going in and out of that warehouse on a pretty regular basis but we don't have the feeds to track it beyond a radius of a few kilometers. Too many trees and hills around there so we lose it."

Knowing where that was headed, Kyler said, "And you need me to get a tracker onto it?"

"There are those superior brains I recruited you for."

"You should see me at Trivial Pursuit. It's truly a wonder that I'm able to mingle with commoners with the mass of brilliance perched right up here," Kyler retorted, pointing to his head.

Goldman ignored him, "We need to know what's in that room Scott. I have a feeling that it ties this all together. Not sure how yet but I am certain it does."

"What about the transmission from the restaurant conversation? Anything eye-opening there?"

"You have a separate email with that. Confirm that you received it." Goldman instructed.

Kyler moved the mouse, having gained control of his machine back again. He minimized the image of the grounds so he could pull it up again later to study it further. Looking at his inbox, he saw the other email from Goldman with the audio file attached.

"Confirmed sir."

"Ok. You can listen to it on your own, maybe review it with Alani tomorrow on the way to the winery. They're mostly talking in code. No names, no real details but maybe you two can find something there. It'll probably be relevant later but I can't discern anything in there that means much right now."

"Copy that sir. Anything else?" Kyler was anxious to get moving. He was starting to sense they were going to start seeing a lot of movement on the case soon and he needed to get ahead of the curve.

"That's all I've got for now. By the way, how's my favorite co-star of yours doing?"

The ease of changing gears to lighter topics, even amidst the tasks at hand, was always amazing to Kyler. It was a great balance and likely had a great deal to do with how they were able to keep their sanity in a very unsettling business.

"Got a picture coming your way. Snail mail of course. She signed it for you." Kyler gave Goldman a cheesy wink.

"You're a gentleman and a scholar agent."

"Thank you sir. I try. I'll check in with you tomorrow once we get settled."

"Be safe agent. This case is starting to get interesting."

"Will do sir."

Kyler hit the end key and Goldman's image was gone. He was up and out of his chair immediately and making his way back to the closet for a change of clothes. He felt the surge of urgency on the case and it had him moving at breakneck speed. He couldn't get out of the room fast enough.

Chapter 26

Back on the plane again, Alani silently thanked Air France for having instituted Wi-Fi internet access on their planes, which was the case with the one she was flying back to Florence. Diving into her work gave her the ability to ignore her overwhelming fears and, more importantly, allowed her to try and connect some of the dots on the case during the two-hour trek back.

Ever since she'd gotten into the car at Camille Blanche's flat, now an active crime scene, she'd been trying to put the pieces together. It was obvious to her that there had to be a connection between Camille and Jacques Francois. The coincidences were too glaringly obvious to assume anything else.

She reviewed the connections in her mind. Jacques Francois is dumped at a hospital not far from where Camille Blanche lived. However, it was also close to where Francois lived as well so that didn't prove much in the way of a connection. Plunging ahead though, then she added the fact that Camille was the reporter who'd covered the story on Francois's mysterious beating and amnesia case. Then there was the curious avoidance of offering much information on the story by Gautier, the station's own producer. Was there something to his seeming secrecy? She couldn't be sure but her gut was telling her that he wasn't giving her everything.

Then there was the fact that she wasn't at work. Again, that in and of itself would prove little until she found out the time of death. Her question being whether she didn't make it in to work because she just so happened to be dead already or whether she had not gone to work and then wound up dead. The latter scenario clearly proving the possibility that the Paris Police's theory would be more plausible, though not certain either.

The glaring question to Alani was the obvious one. Why kill Camille Blanche. She simply didn't buy the idea that it was a robbery and knew Kyler and Goldman would come to the same conclusion hence a respectable consensus to what she already knew.

So what then? Had Camille seen who took Francois and then they killed her to keep her quiet? That was one possibility. She let that thought mull over her a bit. It was a decent, theory but she still saw a potential problem in that brought her back to the time of death. If Blanche was killed after the time when she was supposed to have been at work and if Alani disagreed with the robbery theory, then that meant that she needed to find out why Camille had not gone into work that day. She had clearly not, as Gautier had tried to lead her to believe, been out pursuing the next story.

The other possible theory felt like it had more legs. Camille Blanche knew Francois and, more importantly, knew who he really was. She was killed for the same reasons that Francois was nabbed and beaten within an inch of his life, though those were still under a black cloud of mystery. This line of connections in essence tied all three stories of Stratton, Francois and Blanche together by a common thread…their employers…albeit Blanche's connection was somewhat indirectly associated.

As logical as it was to make the connection, there were still too many questions with too few answers, she thought to herself. The flight attendant came over to her seat at that moment.

"Can I bring you anything to drink, mademoiselle?"

Alani was shaking her head, preparing to decline the offer, determined to focus on the task at hand when the plane hit a rather sizeable pocket of air and lurched downward making her stomach and nerves do a triple back flip.

"On second thought, I think I'll take a vodka and ginger ale if you have it." She was thankful for being in the first class seat at that point. If this trend continued, she may need more than one of the libations.

"Oui mademoiselle. I'll be right back with that."

Alani turned her attention back to the computer, pulling out her own RSA Token to log into her system. She, unlike Kyler, had taken the agency-offered courses and was far more familiar with the tools of their trade. She supposed it was a trade-off. He was by far the best covert agent and, more specifically, the most lethal in hand to hand combat that she'd ever seen. His instincts were also off the charts. She supposed it all made them a good team.

The flight attendant came back as quickly as she promised. She had two cans of ginger ale and four individual sample-style bottles of vodka. She must have seen the color disappear from Alani's face with the turbulence. Either that, Alani mused, or Alani came across as an alcoholic to the attendant. She doubted the latter to be true but it was humorous to consider nonetheless.

"Merci boucoup mademoiselle," Alani said as she unscrewed the cap of the vodka and poured it over the ice. She was generous on the amount and then finished off the top with a bit of the ginger ale.

"I'm sorry to trouble you with this but you wouldn't happen to have a straw, would you?" Alani had a thing with drinking directly from cups, particularly those that had been in public places.

"Oui, of course," the flight attendant handed her the short black straw and then was gone as fast as she'd appeared.

Alani took a long, hard drink from the concoction suddenly feeling quite a bit more at ease. Without realizing it, she had taken the entire drink down in thirty seconds flat which was pretty uncommon for her. She usually tended to nurse her drinks, being the petite woman and, hence, lightweight, that she was. She felt the effects significantly and immediately.

The computer, meanwhile, had gone through its series of logging in and launching her various programs. She glanced back at the screen and saw a smaller window had popped up. It was the agency's private, secure messaging program. It was like Yahoo Instant Messenger without all of the advertisements, news articles, emoticons and security vulnerabilities.

The message was from Goldman.

"Are you there Alani?" the instant message inquired.

"Yes sir. On the plane but it has Wi-Fi connectivity."

"Thank goodness. Been tryin to reach Scott. Not answering."

That made Alani draw in a sharp breath of fear.

"He ok? What's wrong?" Alani tapped her fingers wishing for the first time that instant messenging could somehow be just a bit more instant. The anticipation was killing her.

"He's fine. At least I think he is. Not about him but was trying to reach him. Got a problem."

Alani let out a sigh of relief and then responded, *"What is it?"*

"It's Jack Hawkins. He's missing."

At that moment, Alani wasn't sure if it was the vodka or not, but her head began spinning.

"Missing? How do you know? What happened?" Alani was baffled. She liked Jack and, equally important, needed him. They all did.

"Call me when you get in. Fill you in on the details."

"Should I get on a plane to come back to the states? Start searching?" She also knew what the answer to that would be but her mind felt like it was going a million miles a minute.

"Need you to go with Scott. A little weird...guy showing up at a romantic bed and breakfast solo. You guys will need to split up your resources anyway."

The mention of a romantic bed and breakfast added to her already swirling brain and Alani made another concoction.

"True sir."

"Try and reach Scott when you land. Not sure where he is but you know him."

Alani knew what Goldman meant about knowing Scott. He tended to execute side-plans at times but neglected to share them with others. She thought it was his way of surprising Goldman since it usually produced extremely valuable information. Sort of a game to prove how good he really was.

"Will do sir. Call you when we touch down."

"Fly safe agent. If the pilot fucks up just shoot him and take over."

Had the program had emoticons, that probably would have been the place for a traditional smiley face but she got the humor and appreciated it greatly anyway. Goldman was a good man and a heck of a boss, she thought thankfully to herself.

"Consider it done sir."

"Signing off."

"Goodbye Doc."

Significantly wavering from the vodka now, Alani tried to process the news logically without the attachment of her personal relationship to Jack Hawkins drawing her emotions out. What would someone want to snag him for? This merely added more fabric to the thread of similarities between the growing number of cases that they all couldn't stay in front of...this one much closer to home.

Then there was the other question Alani didn't quite want say out loud but her mind couldn't help asking. Was Hawkins alive or dead?

She gulped down the rest of the second drink, shut the lid of the laptop and decided to close her eyes, feeling her exhaustion settle in. To her surprise, she was asleep almost instantly.

Chapter 27

Kyler, after a shower and fresh change of clothes, was bounding down the stairs toward the lobby. He'd donned another Luigi Borelli suit, opting to stay in the theme of the country. He then slipped into a pair of thousand-dollar Salvatore Ferragamo shoes. What was it they said, whoever they were? Shoes make the man? He had to admit that the price tag certainly provided for a comfortable dress shoe. He was only hoping he didn't have to test their ability to run.

The task should be an easy one, at least this time. He was heading back to Via di Santo Spirito to take Gianni Dimarco up on the offer to come again anytime. He couldn't think of any time better than the present.

He'd called down to Napoleon at the valet station before leaving the room and, pleasantly, the car was waiting for him when he exited the building. Napoleon stood waiting by the open door as he approached. Kyler slipped him another hundred Euro for which Napoleon began to argue but Kyler just smiled, closed his hand around the man's fist forcing the bill into his, released it and closed the door to the Enzo. With that, he was off to the races.

Before leaving his room, Kyler had also sifted through his bag of tricks Goldman had referred to, finally finding what he'd been looking for. It was what appeared to be an elegant Mont Blanc fountain pen in the Greta Garbo edition. It was the type that was, in its own right, an attractive accessory that could be positioned conveniently inside a suit jacket pocket only to impress all those around when it was pulled out.

The pen was a limited edition but not in the way of the three thousand dollar 1905 Commemoration Edition was. It was indeed a genuine Mont Blanc but it had been modified. While the end of it still housed the ink cartridge, its upper region contained a high resolution digital camera that fed into a completely undetectable pin hole that blended masterfully into the etchings of the pen. It was the etching that made the pen's style the best choice since it had made it easy to hide the opening. It also didn't hurt that it didn't go unnoticed.

Kyler felt for the pen once more inside his jacket, making sure it hadn't fallen out while he'd ran down the stairs. It sat firmly in place waiting for showtime.

Kyler had also again packed his thirty-eight special into his ankle holster. While it was not the most efficient of guns, having far fewer rounds that of the Colt 45 and Glock varieties more commonly chosen as well as the double action that made firing rounds a bit more deliberate, he loved how it felt. It was as if it were an extension of his hand and he was a deadly shot with it. Besides, he had justified to himself, it was far less conspicuous than some of his other choices. After all, he wasn't about to go Secret Service style, packing a Mack 10 under his jacket circa 1981 when Ronald Reagan was shot and the Service all pulled them out of seemingly nowhere. It was an image most Americans of that time probably had forever engrained into their minds.

Kyler enjoyed just about any kind of gun. He could shoot just about anything he put in his hands and was frighteningly accurate. It was another region of his mind that wondered if it were something he enjoyed, like fighting, a little too much. No time for reflection now though.

Before long, Kyler pulled up to the elegant restaurant again and was greeted by an eager attendant. He noticed that it had been the same attendant from the prior evening and thought he caught the man scanning the passenger seat for Alani. He let out another laugh and a shake of the head, understanding the effect she had not only on him but all men.

"Welcome back signore," the attendant said while opening the door for Scott.

"Grazie. I enjoyed it so much that I couldn't resist coming back for more." Kyler handed the man a twenty and strode toward the door. As he did so, he scanned his surroundings and then assessed the restaurant, quickly spotting Dimarco. He had sort of wished the man, however unlikely, wouldn't have been there. This wouldn't be the tough night though so it didn't bring him too much concern.

Dimarco took notice of Kyler immediately and made his way to greet him.

"Signore Scott. Buona sera. I did not realize you were coming back in tonight," as Dimarco said this, he shot his hostess a look as if to ask *why wasn't I notified that he was coming in tonight?!*

Sensing Dimarco's question, Kyler offered his explanation, "My apologies Signore Dimarco for not having called ahead to make a reservation. We just finished filming and all I could think about all day was the wonderful meal from last night. I simply had to come back again. I'd love to sit at the bar if that would be ok?"

"But of course! Prego, prego," Dimarco said turning and signaling toward one of several open chairs at the small bar.

"Grazie," Kyler replied and followed Dimarco. As he did so, he surveyed the place with a quick scan, particularly looking for the couple that had been there the previous night but did not see them.

"Where is the bella donna this evening?" Dimarco asked looking around to see if Alani was coming in behind him, his disappointment at her absence being more than noticeable.

"She had to meet with a record producer that was here in Florence for the evening so she won't be able to join me." He'd prepared the response ahead of time for fear of forgetting which cover Alani had used on their last visit. It had, after all, felt like a long time ago despite being only roughly twenty-four hours prior.

"Please send her our best and let her know she will have to visit us next time. You both are welcome anytime."

We'll actually be taking you up on that sooner than you think, Kyler thought to himself but instead replied simply with, "Grazie, signore. We will keep that in mind. Please, don't let me keep you from your other guests."

"It is no trouble at all. I will have a bottle of wine brought to you right away," with that, thankfully, Gianni was off to make his rounds again.

Kyler scanned the menu, debating on trying something different this time around but ultimately settled on sticking with his favorite plate, the gnocchi. He ordered when the waiter came back with the bottle of fantastic house wine and settled back comfortably surveying his surroundings. He was scanning the area to see if there was anything of interest. Possibly a hidden door to a back secret room? He monitored Gianni's movements through the mirror that was in front of him as was the case so often with bars. He wasn't sure why there always seemed to be a mirror there but he was grateful for it at that moment. He'd taken stock of it the prior evening, which was, in part, why he'd opted to sit there.

Unfortunately, Dimarco's actions were relatively innocuous this time around. He mostly spent his time walking around, talking to his clearly wealthy patrons and occasionally chatting with the hostess to check the reservation list. Probably making sure there were no more surprises this evening. He didn't strike Kyler as the type to enjoy surprises much.

The meal had been what he'd expected, being fairly uneventful. Dimarco came over to check on him a few more times while he sat but had the presence of mind never to linger too long.

When the check finally came, Kyler gave the waiter his credit card and then finally pulled the pen out as he appeared to be prepared to innocently sign for his meal. His bigger reason for having positioned himself not only at the bar, but near the end, had been because it provided him with a clear view of the telephone that Gianni Dimarco had used the night before.

As Kyler continued to wait for the waiter to return, he pretended to observe and scrutinize the elegant writing instrument, turning it this way and that, running his hand along its edges and feeling the weight of it in the palm of his hand. He was certain he looked a bit pretentious and probably even a bit obsessed with the object but he didn't care. While he made a bit of a charade of the admiration of the instrument he was, all the while, clicking the clip of the pen's cap that fired off a serious of pictures of the phone that sat no more than three feet away.

Kyler's goals were two-fold. He wanted to make sure that he got a great shot of the phone that hung on the wall. It was the same phone that Dimarco had been talking on the other night and, as far as Scott could tell, it was the only phone in the restaurant. That was, at least, in plain sight.

More importantly, though, Kyler wanted some images of the entire restaurant that he could go back to his hotel and commit to memory. There was a door to his right that could only be accessed from behind the bar counter. It was one of two doors in the restaurant and Kyler would bet the house on it being Dimarco's office. The other was of the free swinging variety that led to the kitchen. Not exactly Ft. Knox. Kyler wasn't a genius but he felt good about his assumption that Dimarco wasn't conducting business with his Sous Chef within earshot. Just a hunch.

A few minutes later, and after Scott had successfully clicked off several dozen high resolution snapshots, the waiter returned with the bill and took note of the pen.

"That is a very special pen, signore."

You have no idea, Kyler thought to himself. "Grazie. It is very special to me. My father gave it to me before he died. I think of him every time I look at it. It means a great deal to me."

"I am very sorry for your loss signore. Have a good night."

Kyler thanked him, signed the bill and was grateful that the waiter didn't ask to look at the pen. He rose to leave and Dimarco met him again near the door.

"Please remember to tell the lovely lady we missed her. We hope to see you both very soon." Dimarco said, shaking Kyler's hand firmly.

"Si Signore. I will be sure to tell her and you can certainly expect to see us both again." *Much sooner than you think, as a matter of fact, Kyler mused.*

He then flashed his best winning movie star smile to Dimarco and added, "Have a wonderful evening. Buona Sera." *I can't wait to see what you're cooking up in the oven, he thought, and then turned to leave.*

"Buona Sera, Signore Scott."

Back in the car again and feeling exhilarated from the mini-success, Kyler sped home. He wanted to be sure to get back to the hotel and in front of the computer so he could send the pictures off to the geek squad back at Langley and begin committing the pictures to memory. He was going to be short on time and would need to make quick work of gearing up to return. He'd glanced at the reservation book as he'd left and noted that the last reservation of the night was at Ten O' Clock. Given the typical three-hour dinner that was Italy's style, he figured a return to the restaurant at three should ensure he'd have the place to himself.

Steeling a look at his watch, he noted that left him approximately three hours. With that, he popped the machine into sixth gear and stomped on the gas, the amber evening lights of Florence flying by as if it were a watercolor painting.

Chapter 28

Hopital Robert Debre was quiet and relatively abandoned. The constant but faint beeps of the equipment came from each of the rooms in the Intensive Care Unit as if in a somber orchestra of machinery. Somehow it possessed the rare ability to both sooth and panic, reminding the patients and visitors that, in many cases, the equipment was keeping them alive, healthy and prodding on but also represented the reason they were there in the first place. The rest of the sounds, as in all hospitals, were of the hushed varieties. Doctors talking to nurses, family members talking to patients, visitors talking to other strangers bound together through the wonderfully human in-it-together attitude. In many ways, a hospital could be compared to church. All feelings of hope, happiness, sadness and despair were represented. On one floor, lives were being born into the world and on other floors and wings, souls were moving onto the afterlife.

The quiet carried even to the shoes the doctors and nurses wore, usually being running shoes of some variety. Naturally the purpose being to accommodate the hours said individuals spent grueling out twelve, twenty-four maybe even forty-eight hour shifts. No place for Steve Madden's of the male or female variety with that kind of stress. But yet, though the intent was certainly for comfort, the rubber soles also fit perfectly with the quiet ambience of the building.

It was those same shoes that calmly made their way from the elevator of the fifth floor supporting a tall and lean male nurse who looked to be around thirty-five years old with the beginnings of graying hair around his temples, two days of stubble on his worn face and wearing the prototypical green scrubs that always seemed as if they could double for pajamas.

The man was pushing a cart with what was presumably the evening's medications for the ICU floor's patients, most of which likely being of the pain suppressant variety judging by the state of many of the floor's inhabitants. With one hand he pushed the cart whose wheels also seemed to have gotten the memo on tranquility, seemingly gliding across the freshly polished tile floor. The other hand held a chart that he stopped to consult, then looking up to survey his surroundings of patient rooms.

The nurse crossed over to the nurse's station and found it to be empty. He momentarily left the cart at the desk and walked back to the room that was closed off and was positioned behind the desk. It housed cups, fresh linens, a microwave-looking appliance that provided patients with warm blankets upon request and other miscellaneous items. The man opened the door to the room and found it empty as well.

Walking back to the station, he glanced at the clock that sat on the wall and noted the hour to be exactly midnight. The hospital was either running lean due to the hour or was in the middle of a shift change. Either way, it was a ghost town. The man's face crept up into a crooked smile.

Grabbing his clipboard again, he consulted the patient registry and found the name he was looking for along with the bed his person of interest was currently resting in, probably waiting somewhat impatiently for something to dull the extreme pain. Soon enough, the man thought to himself, and his smile grew just a bit wider.

Looking around the floor for bed 514, he finally located it after turning a hundred and eighty degrees from the vacated desk. He turned the cart toward the room and began calmly strolling toward it, whistling softly to himself as if he were out for an evening walk.

In a few more seconds he arrived at the door, opened it slowly and saw Jacques Francois laying there staring blankly at a TV.

Francois turned to look at the nurse and said in French, "Thank God you are here. I'm in so much pain. I'm exhausted but can't fall asleep. Please tell me you have something for me."

The nurse replied in French, "Absolutely sir. I promise you will be out in no time."

"Thank you! You are an angel!"

The nurse suppressed his laughter and made his way to Francois's bedside. He pulled out a fresh bag of liquid from the tray and grabbed the bag that hung beside the bed. It was empty, having been feeding a controlled drip of what the nurse presumed to be morphine through the tube into Francois's vein.

"Well of course you are in pain. You are completely empty here. Why don't we take care of that?"

Before the nurse replaced the bag with the full one, he consulted his clipboard again, though looking at nothing in particular. He had a pen out ready to make notes.

"What happened to you, Mr. Francois?" The nurse asked, scanning the man's injury-ridden body.

"I guess I had the shit kicked out of me. I'm just happy to be alive to be honest." Francois replied in a pained and anxious voice. Why wasn't the guy giving him his damn morphine, he thought?

"You guess, sir?" the man asked.

"Yeah. I mean obviously I did get the shit kicked out of me. I have more broken bones that not."

"Why did you say you guess then?" the nurse prodded while pretending to keep busy, adjusting the bag, checking the tube from Francois's arm and then referring back to the clipboard again.

"Because I don't remember a damn thing. Hell of a thing, huh? To end up looking like this and literally not remember one thing? All I remember is waking up for a second in this dark room with a dirt floor and being in more pain than I could have ever imagined."

"Really?" The nurse asked. "You don't remember *anything*,"

"Nothing at all. Then, I must have been in so much pain that I passed out again and the next thing I know, I'm sitting in this bed with tubes in my arm, machines beeping around me and doctors standing over me as if they're waiting to see if I'd wake up."

"I see," the nurse replied, making a few more notes.

"To tell you the truth, I'm glad that I don't remember. I don't know how it's possible but that's not the kind of thing you want to feel, you know?"

"I do. Well thank you for sharing that, Mr. Francois, that is very helpful to me."

A bit puzzled, Francois looked at the man and said, "Sure. So…can you help me out here please?" He cast his eyes over to where the bag should be. "I'm dying here."

You couldn't be more correct the nurse thought as he nodded and looped the bag onto the hook and connected the tube.

The liquid quickly made its way into the man's veins and his eyes relaxed almost instantly. His pupils dilated and, in a matter of what seemed to be just a few seconds, his jaw fell slack and his head fell loosely to one side. The machine that was monitoring his pulse stopped its rhythmic beeping song and confirmed what the nurse already knew. Jacques Francois was dead.

Chapter 29

Kyler circled the block of Via di Santo Spirito three times before he felt reasonably certain that it's last employee was nowhere to be found. He settled on parking in the darkest alley he could find about four blocks from the restaurant. As helpful as the Enzo could be for a quick get-away, it didn't fair well when it came to blending in amongst a row of Fiats and scooters. Not to mention the fact that his visits to the restaurant had created an association back to the famed Kyler Scott. He'd now wished he'd asked for a second car in his contract for Fire in Firenze but there was no time for worrying about that now.

In truth, his mission for this evening should be an easy one. He wanted to get a bug on the phone he'd seen Dimarco use during his and Alani's first visit. The geeks at Langley had of course taken the liberty of sending him with the tools he would need for such an occasion. With the picture he'd snapped during his solo visit, they had been able to direct him to the appropriate version of the phone tap that would prove most inconspicuous based on the make-up of the phone in the restaurant. Kyler could handle the rest as he'd done probably hundreds of times by now.

Kyler was dressed in black from head to toe and carried a ski mask he'd don as he got closer to the restaurant. Included in his arsenal was the tap that consisted of a small semi-conductor with red, green and yellow wires connected to it, a small flat-head screw-driver to disassemble the receiver of the phone and a shoulder holster that housed his Glock 21 complete with the latest military-grade LaserMax sight. Instead of a spare mag in the other pouch of the holster, he'd fitted it with his lock-pick kit even though he'd hoped his earlier actions from his visit would prevent him from having to use it.

Shortly before leaving the restaurant, he'd made a trip to the bathroom and scored a minor victory. The bathroom had a window that faced an alley behind the restaurant. Scott made sure to unfasten the latch before leaving the room and hoped that those that locked up for the night wouldn't notice the small detail. He'd actually picked up the trick when his random curiosity found him reading a website that gave away the "top secret tricks" of home burglars. Kyler had been amazed by the number of unsuspecting home owners that took great care of locking their homes and setting their alarm systems only to leave a window unlatched or, worse even, slightly cracked to let in some fresh air. The seemingly innocent oversight was all but an open invitation to a burglar casing houses. It was as if the house screamed, "Come on in and take whatever you like!"

Kyler was more than averagely skilled at picking a lock, including some of the most complex varieties, but he knew the path of least resistance was more likely to minimize unforeseen complications. He liked to refer to it as *risk management*.

As Scott traversed the few blocks toward his destination, he reviewed the layout of the restaurant from the mental snapshots he'd taken earlier. He knew there was an alarm system that was monitoring the front entrance via a run-of-the-mill sensor method. Yet another advantage of the window entry option which, he noted, did *not* have a sensor visible anywhere. Scott had scanned the restaurant for motion detectors and came up empty in his search. All in all, it was surprisingly light security for a man seemingly involved in a great deal of questionable activity. The lack of security actually told Kyler much about the restaurant. Namely, aside from his phone conversations, Dimarco's *business* didn't take place in there. Kyler's final assessment was that the phone was likely the only object of interest in this particular establishment hence his plans for a very brief visit this evening.

As Kyler rounded the corner to head down the alley that led behind Via di Santo Spirito, he slipped the ski mask over his face. He hadn't noticed any surveillance cameras but he wasn't about to potentially blow his vitally important movie star cover because of an amateur oversight.

Kyler noted the time. Three o'clock. The alley and surrounding streets were deathly quiet. Another benefit of Florence, he mused. For the most part, it turned into a ghost town after midnight. A far cry from the hustle and bustle of Times Square or Hollywood. Despite the barren surroundings, Kyler's instincts remained on high alert. Call it force of habit.

He approached the window that led to the bathroom of the restaurant. Whispering a silent plead to the Gods of Simplicity, he angled his view through the window so as to eye the position of the latch at its base. *BAM!,* as the famed Chef Emeril would say. The latch remained in the same unlocked position as he'd left it just hours earlier. Kyler reached into his shoulder holster pouch and extracted the flat-head screwdriver. He carefully slid the flat end at the base of the window and wiggled the tool until it had sufficiently wedged itself to a point of leverage. Kyler let go of the tool as it freely protruded from the window so he could reposition his right hand underneath it while his left hand pressed flat against the glass. With a simultaneous motion, he moved both hands upward. After overcoming a little resistance initially of a window that hadn't budged in a while, the glass eventually eased upward. Once it was at its maximum height, Kyler slowly let go of the window, ensuring it wouldn't come crashing down on its own. It did not. Time to climb aboard.

Kyler put the screwdriver back in his pouch and reached into another compartment of his holster, extracting a pair of lightweight night vision glasses. He slipped them on over his head and flipped the switch to activate the green glow of vision to guide his way through the darkness. To complete the ensemble, he reached into the pockets of his cargo-style pants, pulled out a pair of black gloves and slipped them on.

Checking his surroundings one last time and deciding he was seemingly alone, he hoisted himself up and through the small opening of the window, grateful for his lean frame that easily allowed him to slide through without much difficulty. After slowly lowering himself to the ground of the bathroom, he closed the window behind him, deciding it was best not to draw any suspicion from a casual passerby in the night.

Kyler did a quick check of his holster and, once confirming all items were in tact, he exited the bathroom. It took his eyes a second to adjust to the green hue of the goggles and he took a moment to take in his surroundings. He located the bar and then shifted his eyes to the right where he found the phone nestled into the corner of the room on a small desk.

Navigating through the staggered placement of tables that were already finely appointed for tomorrow's lunch patrons, he arrived at the desk and stopped just short of it. Before he began, he pulled out his iPhone, launched the camera application and snapped a quick picture of the desk and phone. He glanced at the digital image and confirmed he had a clear shot and then began extracting the items he'd need for his task.

The screwdriver and bug were all he needed. The phone was not a newer wireless model, probably out of concern for its susceptibility to being intercepted via its relatively open frequencies for even the most amateur hacker. Dimarco was likely using the corded landline because of a common misconception that it was more secure than a mobile. While Kyler may not be a tech head, he knew plenty about spying and would be the first to point out that, in the wave of modern digital cellular technology, mobile phones were now far more secure than any landline phone. Most people still shared Dimarco's belief that anything wireless couldn't be secure. Kyler thanked him for his ignorance.

He picked up the screwdriver, a smaller version than that used to pry open the window, having a thinner blade at its end designed to fit a narrower crevice like the one that divided the phone in two parts. He gently eased the tip into the crease. Kyler was careful not to scratch the surface of the phone as that would certainly draw attention to the tampering. After some jimmying side to side, the two parts gave way and he popped off the top half of the handset that housed the earpiece. Kyler set the piece down on the table and picked up the tap, making sure he could distinguish the colors of the wires so as to attach them to the proper corresponding lines in the handset. He attached the semiconductor to the top portion of the phone, fastening it into place, and then used the tiny clamps at the end of the wires of the tap to attach to the appropriate colors of wires near the bottom of the device. He held the hand piece close to his face to carefully examine that all components were where they belonged and determined he was satisfied with his handy work.

Kyler then made quick work of putting the two halves back together, firmly sealing it in place throughout. He closely examined it once more to ensure that it looked as it had previously and then rested it back onto its base. He put the screwdriver back in his holster and pulled the iPhone out once more, pulling up the picture he'd taken just minutes earlier. He held the phone up in front of him, its juxtaposition allowing him to compare the image to what he now saw before him on the desk. Kyler made a few small adjustments to the positioning of the phone and was satisfied once again that the desk looked identical to its prior arrangement. It was possibly a bit on the obsessive-compulsive side but he'd learned that paying too much attention to details never hurt but the flipside certainly could and, on more than one occasion early in his career, had.

Just as Kyler had scanned his surroundings to make sure he wasn't leaving anything behind and began to prepare to leave, he heard two voices. Definitely male and definitely not coming from the street. They were speaking in Italian and the voices were getting louder as they approached in the alley. Kyler hoped the men were just passing through and that their voices would began fading as they carried further away but they did not. The next sound he heard was of keys being inserted into a door. The door, he was certain, was the one in the back that led to the room to his right. It was, he had assumed, what led to the kitchen and possibly a back office if it were like the layouts of most restaurants.

What would prompt a late night visit from these two? Kyler questioned. They weren't approaching urgently which would have indicated they were tipped off to his intrusion via some silent alarm he'd overlooked. No, they were casually talking and in no rush to get inside. He listened closely, curious if either voice was that of Gianni Dimarco. After a moment, he concluded neither belonged to the restaurateur.

Kyler quickly assessed his best course of action and decided that exiting the window without being heard wouldn't be possible. It was closed and, judging from its previous prying, would not reopen without drawing some attention. More importantly, Kyler's curiosity for the purpose of their late night rendezvous outweighed his concern for his own personal safety.

His mind made up, he glided to the door and gently pressed his ear to it. The two men were inside now and continued their dialogue. Kyler cursed himself for not being more fluent and was struggling to make out any details until he heard the one with the deeper voice say "Che e quello" which Kyler thought meant *that one.*

The two walked to another part of the room not far from where they'd been and stopped. The other man, a squeaky-voiced fellow, said "Aprirlo," or *open it.*

There was a pause and then a burst of what sounded like cracking wood filled the air. Kyler imagined the gruff-voiced man was prying something open and after a few more moments, a crash on the floor ended the cacophony.

In a brief moment of silence, a ding rang out and Kyler realized it had been his iPhone getting a message and he froze in disbelief. How had he forgotten to silence the device? Any hopes Kyler had of the mistake going unnoticed were dashed when he heard the two men pause momentarily and then began quickly approaching where he stood.

Shit, Kyler hissed. Change of plans. Kyler was going to have to take care of the two. *And you thought this was going to be an easy night,* he thought to himself. Never a dull moment.

Kyler quickly planned his attack in the few brief seconds he had. The door would open outwards. That was good, Kyler thought. In a quick movement, he stepped back and pulled out the Glock. Instead of aiming the weapon, he gripped it with his right hand almost like a knife, with the butt of the gun facing out.

Kyler held his position and waited for the perfect moment.

He eyed the knob as it slowly turned and then the door began to open slowly. Cautiously. He envisioned the two men, one in front of the other, both likely with a gun trained ahead of them for whatever was on the other side.

The door continued to glide open. It hit the 45-degree angle and, in the blink of an eye, Kyler wound up and delivered a crushing kick that rocketed the door backwards. It drove the outstretched hands of the leader, gun included, into his own skull, crushing his nose which exploded with blood that blinded him. The man cried out in agony as the door slammed shut.

Kyler seized the moment of surprise and confusion, pulled the door open and spotted the second man who was struggling to keep his balance as the first fell back into him from the blow. The man looked up just in time to see the rear end of a Glock come in a blur toward his face. With every ounce of strength and speed he had, Kyler drove the weapon hard onto the man's nose. The surprised look quickly changed to one of excruciating pain as the man's hands flew up to his face to catch the rush of blood that began to spurt out. He now matched his partner who lay writhing on the floor beneath him.

The second man, though still on his feet, was hunched over and Kyler quickly drove his knee upward into the man's face, catching under his jaw with brutal force. Kyler heard the sound of bones breaking as he crushed the man's jaw and watched as he dropped to the ground, unable to scream aloud since he could no longer open his mouth.

Without missing a beat, he swung a kick to the first man's temple. Kyler knew it would not kill the poor soul but, rather, knock him unconscious which was precisely what he wanted. He had no desire to kill either man. Kyler returned the second goon, who was kneeling on the ground and likely close to passing out from shock. Scott couldn't take any chances though and swung the gun downwards and connected with the temple in similar fashion as the first. He watched the body go limp and crumble down into an almost fetal position.

Stepping back, Kyler was convinced that both were down for the count. He now needed to stage the scene. He didn't want any suspicions being drawn and decided that he needed to make it look like a robbery that the men had interrupted.

Going back to the front of the restaurant, he located the cash register. He pulled out the larger screwdriver and quickly forced open the cash drawer. Kyler wasn't surprised to find it empty. Most restaurants collected the night's earnings and, after accounting for the bills from the evening's patrons, settled the books and deposited the cash and credit card slips into a safe deposit box. The money would be gathered the following morning and taken to the bank for the daily deposit into the business's account.

Kyler knew this was how the business operated when he pried open the draw but had done so anyway so as to give the impression, to those that would find the scene tomorrow, that the robber was a run-of-the-mill thug thief too dumb to check into such details.

Kyler then returned to the back and found a desk pushed up against the wall to his left. He quickly rifled through it, making a certifiable mess both for looks as well as hoping that, on an off chance, he'd something of interest that Dimarco may have been careless enough to leave behind. Finding nothing that caught his eye, he removed the drawers entirely and scattered them in chaos across the floor. Satisfied that the scene would adequately pass as an attempted cash and dash gone wrong, Kyler took a moment to investigate what the two thugs had been doing before his phone had drawn him into action.

With a quick scan of the room, he spotted a box on the floor about ten yards away that had been opened. He walked over to it, looked inside and, to his disappointment, found it packed tightly with about a dozen bottles of red wine. He extracted one of the bottles and held it close to his face. The label read "Villa Santini" and indicated it was a 2009 bottle of Sangiovese.

Damn. Kyler said aloud. The men were probably just coming in for night inventory. He wasn't sure why they'd be carrying weapons but surmised that most of the men in Dimarco's employ probably did. None of them were likely to be amongst Florence's most up-standing citizens.

Deciding there was little else in the place to explore, Kyler made his way to the back door that the two unconscious unfortunates had entered through. Before leaving, he sufficiently tampered with the lock on the side of the door that faced the alley, giving the impression of a clumsy break-in by an amateur.

Kyler closed the door behind him, scanned the alley, confirmed he was alone and began calmly making his way back towards where he'd left his vehicle. Once nearing the corner, he removed his gloves and ski mask and slipped them into the deep pockets of his cargo pants.

He quickly covered the few blocks with, thankfully, not a soul in sight. Firenze was peacefully asleep and, as Kyler finally settled into the comfort of the Enzo, he laughed at the stark contrast of his experience of the last twenty minutes. It hadn't been clean, he mused, but… mission accomplished.

Back to the hotel for some painfully few hours of sleep before tomorrow would slap him in the face. He wished the glowing city a good night as it whizzed by in a blur.

Chapter 30

Dramatic music played as a video montage played clips from all over the globe; Military tanks in Baghdad, factory workers slaving away in Anywhere, USA, Aerial images of a tropical location post-hurricane and children actively learning in a classroom that looked to be somewhere in Africa. Then a women's voice broke in over the imagery.

"This is BBC World. Putting news first."

The footage then shifted to what looked to be the inside of a medical emergency clinic that was, judging by its patients, somewhere in Asia. A male's voice began by saying:

"Tonight's top story comes to us from SaPa, a tiny Vietnamese village tucked high into the mountains near the Chinese border. While it is mostly unknown and populated only by its lifelong natives, it's a wonder the village isn't a tourist destination purely for its spectacular views and rich cultural history. That beauty is likely the only reason this story has come across our desk. An Australian photojournalist named Paige Walker was passing through the village to document illustrations of this relatively untouched area only to come upon an even bigger and wildly enigmatic story."

The footage cut back to the inside of the BBC newsroom where the voice found a face in a handsome dark-haired anchor in his mid-forties. He'd put on his best look of gravity and concern as he then introduced himself.

"Welcome to BBC World News. I'm John Mackenzie reporting on this shocking story of what is one of the most fast-acting and inexplicable disease infiltrations we have ever seen."

A small image popped up to Mackenzie's right as the newscast brought it's viewers back into the scene of a tiny make-shift medical clinic.

"SaPa, Vietnam has been struck with a bizarre illness that seems to have spread to nearly all of its inhabitants in less than 24 hours' time. The local medical staff, seemingly ill equipped to determine the source of the disease, is mystified by the sudden epidemic and is scrambling to find space in its modest and already-cramped medical clinic, if you can really call it that. As you can see from the images, the clinic is not much more than a one-story office building with beds and rudimentary medical equipment jammed into a tiny space. We spoke to one of the leading doctors of this small clinic who told our reporters that patients began checking in late last night with complaints of extreme abdominal pain and dangerously high fevers which were quickly followed by violent vomiting and bouts of debilitating chills. Shortly after checking in, several of the patients fell into comas which the doctors described as the body's defense mechanism against a violent attack on its immune system."

The footage shifted first to sweeping aerial images of the beautiful mountain town followed by coverage of the villagers as they go about their daily activities.

"It is worth noting that this footage of the people of SaPa is not current. That is relevant because, according to our most current count, nearly 85% of its residents have checked into the medical clinic. All with identical symptoms. Current images of this village would reflect one reminiscent of a ghost town."

Mackenzie paused after the last statement for effect. Mission accomplished. The statement hit home in astonishing fashion.

"Thankfully there has only been one death reported amongst the nearly five hundred cases currently being treated and it is unclear if that death was in fact directly related to the disease in question. The only conclusion local doctors have been able to

ascertain is that the illness was airborne but, thus far, none have any clue as to its source."

The virtual image box disappeared and John Mackenzie shifted to face the centered camera angle. Looking deeply into the eyes of his transfixed viewers, he concluded the story.

"Those are all the details we have been able to gather thus far. BBC thanks Paige Walker for her contributions to this story. Ms. Walker quickly made her way out of SaPa after contacting us to make sure she did not contract the mystery virus.

We will continue to update you as more information becomes available to us on this bizarre and horrific medical phenomenon. We'll be back after this brief commercial break. Next up...we'll bring you the latest news on Princess Kate's pregnancy progress as possible suggestions for baby names circulate about."

With that, BBC World's coverage ceased momentarily, replaced by an ad for Manchester United that told its viewers that they absolutely couldn't miss the most important event of the season. The irony was likely overlooked by its viewers.

Chapter 31

To most, Saturday was a day off in many ways. A day when the alarm lay dormant with no need to rush up to go to work presenting a rare opportunity to sleep in, unless of course there were young kids in the house. It was a day when the workout clothes may stay in the drawer save the overtly ambitious and disciplined few. Maybe it was a day when Dad cooked up his famous chocolate chip waffles while leaving a mess in the kitchen for Mom who, knowing he probably wouldn't get around to cleaning it up, silently wondered if it were better if he didn't do it at all. For some it was a day of taking care of the many errands or projects that couldn't fit into the frantic week-day pace while for others it could merely be a day of going to the movies, possibly a long dinner with some wine with a husband, wife, girlfriend, boyfriend, friend or loved one.

For Kyler Scott, Saturday was just another day. People didn't stop trying to terrorize the world on the weekend, though it would be an interesting gentlemen's agreement of sorts, he mused. It could be a throwback to the general acceptance in the old wartime era in which certain days were respected. Scott recalled stories he'd heard of soldiers holstering their guns on Christmas, even just for a brief moment.

An interesting thought indeed, he concluded. He'd have to pitch that one next time he was in mid fight for his life with a member of the opposite side. He could imagine how that might go. Maybe as they were both positioned behind their respective shield of a wall or car, both maybe loading fresh clips into their piece of choice, he could throw it out there.

"Hey, guy. Yeah you. The one that's trying to put one in my brain. Any thoughts on pushin' for a five-day workweek? Pass it along to your terrorist buddies. See what they think. I'm in if you are."

Somehow, Kyler didn't see it playing out well, particularly since in those scenarios, one of the two negotiating parties typically ended up dead. Nothing like fruitless negotiation, Kyler thought. Guess he'd have to carry on with the seven day, twenty-four hour method he'd been running with. At least he got to play with cool toys. Alani's words of boys will be boys rang in his head. Of course, she didn't seem to mind the toys either. He'd have to remember the counter argument for next time.

Settling his mental tangent, Kyler rose from the bed and consulted the clock which confirmed what he'd already known. Just then, the alarm sounded letting him know it was both five in the morning and time to rise and shine. His brain had been waking him up at the same hour for so long he wondered why he even bothered with the alarm at all. It was irrelevant that he'd only finally drifted into sleep roughly two hours ago. It had taken a little while to come down from the adrenaline surge from the previous night's excitement. He longed to stay in the comfort of the hotel bed but his discipline and routine overrode that desire. He peeled himself out of the bed and shuffled over to the beautiful view he certainly had not grown tired of.

As he looked out through the French doors and through the terrace to the city he loved so much, he couldn't help but think how much he loved mornings, particularly right at this moment. Who couldn't be a morning person with that view to look at, he wondered?

Kyler knew it was going to be an interesting and potentially dangerous weekend and decided he needed his run more than ever this morning to help clear his head.

After throwing on his running attire and bounding down the steps, Kyler hit the streets of Florence. The city must not have shared his enthusiasm for the morning and he seemed to be the only one awake, no less going out for a five-mile jog. That would be perfect for the moment, he thought.

He'd gotten several frantic messages from Goldman last night where he, after nearly reaching through the phone to rip his head off for not answering his calls, gave him the news about Jack Hawkins.

What the hell was going on, Kyler wondered? Sure, Jack definitely had plenty of connections to various divisions of the government but, when it came down to it, wasn't he just a highly glorified computer geek? It hardly seemed worthy of kidnapping. Had Hawkins seen something in the stories he was regularly monitoring and sent it off to someone within the agency with some incriminating hypotheses which then got intercepted by a third party that was in turn monitoring his communications?

He just didn't see that theory playing out. First of all, he knew the lengths not only the agency but Jack himself went to keep all communications secure. It would take nothing short of a genius the level of Dr. Spock himself to crack it. Scott questioned if even his pointy-eared Vulcan doctor could do it. No, Kyler concluded, that couldn't be it.

Then there was always the off chance that it was completely unrelated to anything having to do with the government. People were kidnapped across the country every day. Jack could have been out and an eager criminal spotted his fancy car and decided they could grab him and hold him for ransom. There were again, of course, too many problems with that theory as well. Wouldn't it just be easier to jack his car, no pun intended? Beyond that obvious quandary there also existed the fact that there had been no calls for ransom. And, even if there had been, where would those calls have gone to anyway? After all, Jack was a single man with, from what Kyler understood, no family to speak of. Kyler had heard that Jack's parents had died when Hawkins was in school in a car accident. Jack had been an only child so, save maybe some aunts or uncles, he was left by himself.

But still, Kyler thought, he just didn't see Hawkins being a target of a capture and ransom scenario.

He was moving at a good pace as he wove toward the cathedral, the historical and timeless cobblestone guiding his New Balance running shoes along the quiet streets. He'd driven his morning run in the car the first day he arrived so as to gauge his pace, picking landmarks to note at each mile marker so he could cross-reference it with his watch. He passed the first mile marker, a small café that hadn't even dreamed of opening yet, on his right. He checked the watch and smiled. Six minutes flat. Not bad for the warm-up mile. He'd push to bring it closer to five for the last four miles.

The questions of Jack Hawkin's disappearance continued to swirl around in his head. He was going to need to talk it out loud and knew he'd have the opportunity in couple short hours when he made the drive with Alani to their weekend destination. His feelings for her aside, she was an excellent partner and great agent. Bouncing theories would go much further with her on the receiving end.

They would also have to take the time to sift through the translation that the linguists sent over. While he wasn't sure that much would come from it, there could be a hidden gem somewhere that could benefit them going into the weekend.

Kyler passed the second mile marker which was, conveniently, the bell tower that rose high above the city next to the cathedral. He saw a few ambitious street vendors slowly rolling carts out to the piazza around the cathedral. He checked his watch again and was happy to see mile two had indeed improved to five minutes and fifteen seconds.

As his thoughts began carelessly drifting towards his up-coming alone time with Alani, he decided to kick it into high gear to push them out of his mind altogether. His legs were pumping at a solid pace and the city began moving by very quickly. He noted the restaurants, shops and espresso bars that he'd come to find solace in as he made the turn down Via de Conti.

Miles three and four came in at a solid five minutes flat as he glided down Via Dei Banchi when a car came flying out of the side street a mere fifty meters in front of him. The car screeched to a sliding stop a la car-chase-pull-the-parking-brake-style so close to him that he almost didn't have time to cut off his sprint before slamming into the hood of the black sedan.

Kyler's initial shock settled almost immediately as he registered who was in the driver's seat. Alani stared back at him through the windshield, unsmiling. Of course, he thought, who else drives like that.

Kyler started easing the twenty-two he'd pulled in insanely fast fashion back into its ankle holster. It had been so quick that he hadn't even registered he'd done it until he saw Alani give him a slight eye brow raise at the piece he'd had trained on her forehead.

"Is that a gun in your hand agent or are you just happy to see me?" Alani asked as he walked to her window.

Kyler was considerably out of breath although he wasn't sure if it was more due to the run or the fact that he'd momentarily thought he was going to get mowed down by an Audi A6.

"Yes and yes." Kyler replied. He started catching his breath and said, "Jesus, you scared the shit out of me."

"Sorry about that but you haven't been a good little agent boy," she said as she held up her phone to him. "Goldman and I have been calling you non-stop this morning."

"I know, I got Goldman's message last night about Jack. I was just running through the possible scenarios in my head." Kyler opted not to share the details of the previous night's self-assigned mission with Alani. At least for now.

"Glad to hear it Kyler but you're gonna have to add one to the mix."

"What are you talking about?" Kyler asked, his breathing almost back to normal again.

"Jacques Francois was found dead in his hospital early this morning. Apparently he'd be given a lethal dosage of morphine in the nurses' rounds last night. There was a shift change and nobody else was on the floor. One of the nurses came in shortly after midnight to check on the patients and found Francois flat-lined."

"Oh shit," Kyler replied, letting the news sift through what he already felt were a few too many oddities.

"So what about the nurses? Who was on staff? Have they interviewed all of them already to see if one of them screwed up on his dosage?" Kyler asked.

"Already done. There were only a handful of nurses on staff before and after the shift change and all of them claim that nobody had been in to check on Francois since a dosage given at nine last night."

"Meaning either they're lying or..." Kyler continued, "more likely, that someone came in and killed him.

"Yep. My bet's on the latter."

"I'll second that one," Kyler agreed. Then, "Well I gotta get showered and changed. I also need to grab a few things before we go. There's a café called La Madia across from the hotel. It's the only one around here that opens early. If you want, you can wait for me there. Ask for Vincenzo and tell him that you know me. He'll make you the most spectacular cappuccino you have ever had in your life."

"The perks of Scott Cruz I presume?" She teased.

"I'd like to think that it's my stellar personality that won him over, not just my movie-star good looks."

"Hmm...I think it actually must have been your modesty." She chided while putting the car into first gear in preparation to take off.

"I shouldn't be more than twenty minutes and we can get going."

"I'll time you Mr. Scott," and with that, Alani sped ahead and around the corner. Kyler jogged the last half-mile back to the hotel, suddenly far less interested in his time.

Chapter 32

Kyler raced back up to his room and made quick work of getting ready. He jumped in the shower just long enough to rinse the sweat off his body and brush his teeth. Nobody likes morning breath, he thought. He threw on some designer jeans and a button down that aimed for the stylish without trying too hard look. He was, after all, Scott Cruz whom the bed and breakfast had made room for during what he knew to be their very high season. Best play the part. Always play the part.

He'd thrown the rest of what he'd need for the weekend together the night before so he'd be ready to go without much preamble. As promised, he was back down in twenty minutes where the Enzo was waiting for him.

"We won't be saddling the horse this time my friend," Kyler said, patting the valet on the shoulder. The man clearly missed the metaphor.

"Signore? I'm sorry, but I'm not sure I understand. You would like to make arrangements to go horseback riding with the lady?" He asked, trying to recover while nodding at Alani who'd approached when she saw Kyler exit the hotel from across the street.

Kyler laughed at the confusion he'd created for the poor man, "No, signore. I am sorry. Stupid American sayings. What I meant to say is that we won't be taking this car this weekend." At that, Kyler nodded down at the two bags he'd brought down with him.

Understanding now, "Ah si, signore. That *would* be very difficult." They both eyed the sports car, which, for all its glory as a fine driving machine, had no storage to speak of.

"We'll be taking the fine lady's vehicle this time."

Alani, having just crossed the street towards them, smiled while dangling the keys to the Audi for the valet to see and then thumbed over her shoulder at the sedan that was seemingly illegally parked across the street.

"Livin' on the edge I see," he smiled as he said it.

He knew it was symbolic for her in that the car was parked in a place that was poignantly ready to make a quick exit, mirroring her love and her approach to driving. He also pondered the idea that it emulated both of their feelings on relationships. Symbolic indeed, he decided.

As for driving, Kyler was certainly amongst one of the most skilled drivers in the agency but Alani hovered in another stratosphere in that department. She could pull off maneuvers that he hadn't seen duplicated by any agent or film stunt driver he'd ever been around.

"You know me," she smiled and turned on her flats back toward the car. Flats, he thought. Even her choice of shoe was associated with her driving. Who knew when she'd have to turn on the James Bond tactics and high heels of any kind were definitely not going to cut it. Despite the unassuming shoes however, Kyler and the valet wound up being entranced as she walked away from them. The long legs and hip sway were enough to make cabbies in New York during rush hour stop and appreciate the view.

The valet looked over at Kyler with a look of envy.

"I know," Kyler replied, reading the man's thoughts. "Lucky as hell."

With that, Kyler followed Alani, two small roller bags in tow as he made his way toward the now open trunk. He looked inside seeing only one bag for her and laughed at the clear paradox at play. He knew, though, that looks were deceiving since only one of the bags had any clothes in it.

"Went with the Audi this time huh?" Kyler was always impressed with Alani's knowledge of vehicles, which made sense considering her love and necessity for driving.

"Well, according to Car and Driver, it performs better than BMW and Infiniti," Alani replied sounding like the very car company's commercial itself.

"I had no idea. I always assumed by the hideous interior that it drove like my Dad's old Buick."

When Kyler got in the car, he realized this was no off-the-line Audi. The most obvious indicator was the significant modification that had been made to the dashboard. Where the radio used to sit, a mounting mechanism had replaced it. It consisted of a flat plastic panel with audio and USB inputs along the bottom. Above that, a round-ended mounting stick protruded out about two inches. That allowed for another mounting bracket that would hold an iPAD-like device into it while still giving it the ability to tilt in all directions. The finishing touch being a cable that plugged into the audio and USB inputs on the panel, feeding through the car's audio and charging system and out to the mounted device.

Essentially, the device gave Alani and Kyler a mobile moving office on a panel that both could look at simultaneously. They, of course, had a device a bit more suited for their purposes than a traditional iPAD. They had plans to do more than listen to a playlist or surf the web. Kyler couldn't help but muse over the thought of how many laws would be put in place if something like that started ending up in cars in the states. Texting was one thing but hitting Facebook, YouTube and Twitter while trying to keep your eyes on the road? Not a chance.

Kyler pulled out what looked to be a slate of a device from his messenger bag and mounted it onto the bracket, plugging in the cable and powering up the device. It was, in fact, a touch screen device but the shell was completely ruggedized much like his laptop.

Being equipped with internet access through the local cell phone provider, they would be able to access the internal CIA intranet portal to review the items that they needed to mull over on the drive. It would probably be one of the few times they'd be able to do so without worrying who might overhear their discussions. It'd also give them an opportunity to plan their approach to the task.

"Will this feed into the Bluetooth in the car as well? My video phone account is set up on this too and we should probably give Goldman a call on the way."

Alani shook her head. "Yep. It will even silence any audio playing from the computer if a call comes in."

"So you're telling me that if we're groovin' to a little Let's Get it On, Marvin Gaye style, Goldman could literally call in and ruin my mojo?"

"I don't think Goldman will be the one affecting your mojo but…yes."

The dig, albeit good-natured, hit him a little more than expected. He shoved it off though.

"So what did they do to the engine on this puppy?" Kyler said, patting the top of the dashboard in front of him affectionately.

"Well they took the six cylinders it usually has and bumped it up to eight for one thing which says a lot for an already supercharged engine."

"Nice. And I see by your arrival that the brakes and tires are all in perfect working order."

"Yep. There's also a nitro boost installed just in case we need a little extra help getting outta somewhere."

"So what you're saying is that I am in very capable hands."

"That'd definitely be what I'm saying."

With that, reminiscent of Kyler's actions at dinner the other night, Alani slammed the car into first and rocketed down the street back in the direction of the Arno River. Kyler's head slammed back against the headrest and he felt the seat belt lock up against his chest hard.

"Girls and their toys," he chided back.

"Girls will be girls. Well actually, this girl will be one bad-ass chick."

"Dutifully noted."

Kyler turned his attention to the computer and started thinking about the list of items they'd need to cover in a relatively short period of time. Time to get to work, he thought. There were already two dead bodies that they hadn't been able to keep alive so it was time to kick it into…high gear?

Chapter 33

Jack Hawkins' eyelids felt as if they weighed about a thousand pounds. It was the most bizarre feeling he'd ever experienced. He couldn't actually open them and he was staring into the back of his lids into an abyss of darkness. He wasn't sure where he was or what he'd been doing. Was he asleep in his bed? That was ruled out immediately as he realized that he could feel his body was sitting upright although tightly bound to a chair. He couldn't remember anything that seemed to make sense. His mind was still too groggy, as if he'd been recovering from the most intense night of drinking and drugs and was just sobering up. He felt like what he'd imagined Ozzy Osbourne must feel every day.

Jack was starting to panic then. Even if he hadn't been tied down, he wasn't sure that he could control any of his extremities anyway. They felt much like his eyes in that they were foreign dead weight that was merely attached to his body and the physiology from brain to muscle movements to actual movement was completely severed.

Calm down, he thought to himself but it wasn't working. He frantically tried to trace his memory back in time to how he got here. Wherever *here* was that is. Some of it started coming back to him. He remembered going to the pizza place, remembered eating and having a few beers, but just a few, right? He remembered leaving and starting to walk home and then it came to him. The horrible sound of footsteps and the stab of something sharp, probably a needle he guessed, in his neck.

Things were starting to come together for him then, though what he knew did little to calm his nerves. He'd obviously been given a sedative of some sort but then where the hell was he? He tried his best to relax and do what he could to harness control of his mind and his body. He cursed himself slightly for not taking his friend Mary's advice to join her in Yoga. Her words were ringing in his ears about become centered in order to gain full control of your thoughts and being one with your body. He wasn't all that certain Mary would be doing much better right now though. Whatever he'd been given had done a number on him.

After a few more breaths and a great amount of effort, he was able to open his eyes, feeling nothing short of great victory at the achievement. His glory was short lived though when he realized wherever he was at the moment seemed as if it was going to remain a secret. It was pitch black.

It was then that he felt it. The familiar drop in his stomach and elevation change could only be attributed to one thing, save a roller coaster ride at Disneyland. No, he thought, he was most definitely on an airplane and that had most definitely been the aircraft hitting an air pocket.

What the hell was he doing on an airplane, he thought, his panic returning in full effect. And, even more puzzling, where on the plane was he that could be so dark.

Jack's eyes finally started adjusting to the dark and he was beginning to regain his focus. He started looking around, seeing nothing but four walls surrounding him. His eyes darted in each direction and finally concluded that he seemed to be in a closet of some kind.

Closet? On an airplane? Since when did planes have closets? It was then that he had remembered the trip he'd taken his one and only ex-girlfriend from college on a couple years earlier. Susan Winters had been her name and she'd been the love of his life, which seemed to always happen when a girl was the only one in a man's life. Ever.

She had broken off their extremely short-lived relationship of three weeks by telling him that she felt they were too good of friends and she hadn't wanted to potentially lose his companionship if things didn't work out. He'd bought the story hook, line and sinker until he saw her making out with the Stanford quarterback less than a week later.

He'd reunited with Susan through Facebook, the seemingly quintessential arena to find anyone you'd ever known and most who you didn't actually remember. Even if you did remember the classmate from first grade who you'd be nice to once when he peed his pants in class and you'd stuck up for him, it became painfully obvious that you in fact had zero in common with the guy. It would be at that point that you'd end up pulling the ultimate social networking snub of un-friending the person, having grown tired of five posts per day on what he or she was doing at that very instant. The posts usually involving something along the lines of *Timmy is...hungry. Should I eat an apple or an orange?* Sadly, usually being followed by twenty comments on the subject when in most sane scenarios, outside the realm of this bizarre twilight zone of social commentary, people would respond with...uh, who cares?

In this case, Jack had been ecstatic to reconnect with Susan and it quickly led to him offering to fly a chartered jet from Palo Alto airport to pick her up in Phoenix where she had been living with her now ex, and has-been quarterback of a husband that had been drafted by an Arena football team only to be out of a job when the league shut down. Mr. Stud was presently a raging, physically abusive alcoholic who Susan had wisely decided to get far away from.

Looking to show the woman who'd broken his heart all those years ago what she'd been missing out on, Jack had flown the chartered luxurious Cessna from the very same airport that the likes of Steve Jobs and Steve Young regularly departed from, albeit in their own personal jets. The jet was first class on crack complete with plush brown leather seats, mahogany polished paneling throughout and a sixty-inch flat screen television. He picked her up and, together, they flew to a romantic bed and breakfast in Vermont.

It was on that flight that he became an unlikely inductee of the mile-high club. Attribute it to rebounding from a bad marriage, being entranced with the lap of luxury on the jet, not to mention Jack's newfound wealth and success, or a combination of all of the above. Whatever the reason, Susan jumped Jack as soon as the captain had turned off the seat belt sign and they found themselves in a closet just like the one he was now locked into. It officially made it the spot of his best and worst memory.

Alas, Susan ended up being a mental train wreck with more baggage than Paris Hilton on a transcontinental flight and Jack wound up taking her home a day early with promises to keep in touch. He would later un-friend her as well.

Not sure if the drugs he'd been given had placed his brain in such a reverie or if it was simply the strength of the memory, Jack shook his head fiercely to try and focus so he could assess the situation. Not as if he'd know what to do when he did that but it seemed the best option.

He heard some muffled voices behind the door. It sounded like two, maybe three male voices but, as much as he strained to hear, he couldn't make anything out.

He then realized that, having been the paranoid geek he was, he had his beacon bracelet on. It was what looked to be a basic run of the mill stainless steel fashion piece. In actuality it was a tracking device of sorts, which, provided it was within view of a satellite signal, could communicate a rudimentary SOS back to the computers at his office. It would broadcast his location to the computer and track his movements as long as the bracelet was activated. Being on a battery, it wasn't on at the moment. Even more frustrating to him was the fact that he had not set up his computer to forward the communication anywhere meaning that, even if he did turn the device on, he'd still have to count on a bit of luck that someone back home would think to search his house when they found out he was missing and notice the computer notification identifying his location. One thing was sure though. He had to try.

Jack looked down at his hands that were bound to the arms of the chair through a painful zip tie that was pulled tight. He was definitely not going to free himself of the restraints but needed to find a way to move the slider on the underside of the bracelet from the off to the on position.

He began to rock forward and back on the chair, trying to use the end of the arm of the chair to slide the button, counting on the movements of his body to create just enough leeway to do so. He pulled up and back hard and thrust his wrist forward several times with no luck. He could just see underneath the bracelet where the button was positioned and would be able to see if he was successful. After trying a few more times, he grew frustrated and desperate and he made an aggressive attempt at it. As he lunged forward, though, he and the chair went tumbling to the ground, making a crashing sound as he landed.

The voices on the other side of the door instantly went silent and he could hear quick footsteps coming his way. He looked down at the bracelet and was relieved to see that the last attempt, although potentially detrimental for his cause, was at the very least successful. The button was resting comfortably in the on position.

Just then, the door opened and light from the cabin of the jet came rushing in, blinding Jack who'd finally fully adjusted to the darkness. All Jack saw was a hand coming toward his face and in it held a needle. The hand continued forward and thrust a shot into his neck again and the possessor thrust the depressor down to inject the liquid into Jack's neck.

Within seconds, Jack Hawkins' world went black for the second time.

Back in his home in Palo Alto, California, inside the labyrinth that was Jack's computer lair, a black box that was attached to one of the several computers started blinking an active red light as it picked up the signal from thirty thousand feet in the air.

Chapter 34

"Not to burst your bubble there bad-ass chick but do you know where you're going?" Kyler asked as he saw them fly narrowly close to scooters, cars and pedestrians on the Florentine streets.

"I know how to get us out of the city but you'll have to point me from there. We have to pull up the GeoSpatial image Goldman sent over anyway, right?" Alani nodded to the tablet that Kyler had affixed to the dash in between them.

"I already logged in and am pulling it up. You just focus on not driving us into the river."

Alani had made the turn down Lungarno Torrigiani which had been the very same street Scott Cruz had flown down merely days before with his Hollywood-style Polizia in hot pursuit. The shoot felt like an eternity ago to Kyler.

Scott had opened the image Goldman had sent him with a few touches on the panel of the computer. He'd enjoyed learning how to use this device back home the most. The ability to take two fingers on an image and spread them apart to zoom in closer, all in blazing fast speed, absolutely fascinated him.

"What sort of people have the brain capacity to think up this kind of stuff?" Kyler asked aloud while he pinpointed the destination they were headed to, selected an icon at the top of the screen giving him the option for directions and then clicked on *current location* when the program asked for their starting point. In seconds, the program rendered a three-dimensional street-level image of where they were that second, including the buildings they passed and the Ponte Vecchio that they were rapidly approaching.

"People like Jack Hawkins," Alani replied poignantly.

At that, Kyler nodded his head understanding the cue.

"I'm not in the Northern California office much and don't have the need to talk to Jack nearly as often as you do so what do you know about him?" Alani said. She made a series of left and right turns and was now heading over another bridge, the Ponte alla Grazie, meaning the bridge of thanks or bridge to thanks depending on one's interpretation.

"There's the obvious," Kyler said, considering the question.

"Computer geek, introverted, genius, socially inept. Yeah…got that much," Alani filled in where he was heading.

"And relevant because someone who has that make-up doesn't usually meet many people, make tons of friends and, more importantly too many enemies."

"Is he the type that might take advantage of his…unique skills?" Alani asked. She'd made the turn down Lungarno delle Grazie and was now cruising along the other side of the Arno River.

"Meaning what?" Kyler replied.

"Come on. A guy that has those skills and that knowledge of computers? I'm sure he couldn't help but think of how he could take advantage of what he knows. Maybe break into a few bank accounts, pad his savings a bit?"

"No, you're way off the mark on that one," Kyler replied shaking his head and, in the meantime was keying a couple locations on the computer clearly searching for something specific.

"I know he's your friend Kyler but we can't rule anything out there," Alani replied gently.

"It's not that. I'm objective. And trust me we're not that close. Jack isn't close with anyone."

Kyler, seemingly finding what he'd been looking for, tilted the screen of the computer toward her.

Staring back at her was the face of Jack Hawkins on an article in Forbes Magazine from several years back. He looked like the prototypical computer guy, though about forty pounds lighter than the current version.

The headline read *A New King in Town?* Underneath it said, *Palo Alto-based software developer, Jack Hawkins, stands to compete with his local companions for the next big player in the Silicon Valley.*

"Have you seen his house?" Kyler asked.

"No, like I said, I don't get up to that office much."

"Well let's just say it makes the Playboy Mansion look like a dollhouse. Not to mention it's wired with more gadgetry than a James Bond movie. Seriously, the last thing he needs is more money. That's all I'm saying."

"Do we know how he made it all?" Alani asked, still considering it a possibility.

"Not entirely. If you read the article, it's pretty vague. It was something he sold to QTS Tek who then took it and sold it in mass quantities to our own government branches. Part of the deal was that they didn't disclose what the patent or technology was."

QTS Tek being the same government contractor that Bob Buckney and Matt Barnes also worked for. Alani knew this and wondered what that might mean. All victims were government-connected in some way or another.

"Why would they want to do that? That sounds suspicious in and of itself."

"I asked Jack the same question once. He'd had a few beers and told me it was during a time when QTS was on the ropes. They'd lost a few major contracts to the big boys and were going down in a blaze of glory."

As Kyler spoke, Alani had made the final turn and pointed the car down SS67, the stretch of semi highway that would eventually lead them to Rufina.

"Anyway, they apparently needed something to resurrect the company. One of their engineers had been a roommate of Jack's in college and they got to talking during one of those catch-up-on-old times sessions at a bar one night. One topic led to another and Jack had given the guy a run-down of something he'd been working on."

"What was it?"

"He wouldn't tell me. Part of the privacy clause."

Kyler looked beyond Alani to what had quickly become the beautiful countryside that was, courtesy of her lead foot, rapidly flying by.

"Anyway, they created the clause so that QTS could take credit for developing it. Sort of a major about face."

"Or save face," Alani retorted.

"True. The result for Jack was a gigantic sum of money up-front and a piece of the action for everything sold in the future. Basically, he never has to work again." Kyler concluded.

"So then why does he?" Alani asked. "Why still work with the CIA and whoever else he helps provide intel for?"

"The guy's in his mid-thirties and is full-fledged geek. What else is he gonna to do for the rest of his life? Once a computer genius always a computer genius. Not exactly something he can just turn off. Seems to thrive off of it all."

"I suppose that makes sense," Alani nodded her head. "So this technology he sold…do you think it's something worth kidnapping and killing over?"

Kyler again shook his head, but not as confidently this time. "I can't be sure but Jack had been pretty convincing about the fact that whatever he developed, though certainly innovative, didn't seem to be a threat to national security if in the wrong hands."

Alani gave him a look that told him she wasn't buying that for a second.

"Then again…that amount of money can make for a pretty good actor if he needed to be." Kyler self-countered, considering the possibilities.

"We've seen it before, Kyler. Money can make people do a lot of inexplicable things. In fact, I'm not sure which is the bigger threat to peace and calm. Money or religion?" Alani said this knowing they'd both seen each origin cause destruction and death in staggering quantities.

"Ironic isn't it? Money is supposed to be the root of all evil but we've seen more bloodshed because of religion then I could have ever dreamed…not even in my worst nightmares."

"My point being," Alani said, trying to keep the focus off the philosophical and onto the tactical.

"It doesn't really make a difference what he told you. We have to consider that what he created could have been what put him in his current predicament."

"Agreed. I think we may have to find out exactly what that is."

After a brief pause, Alani asked the question that Kyler was thinking, "Do we think Hawkins is at Villa Santini?"

Kyler shrugged, "We'll see. It's in the middle of nowhere. I guess it depends on what their plans are for him. But that's assuming that this group of Dimarco's are even the ones who grabbed him in the first place. In truth, we have absolutely no substantial evidence to support that Dimarco has any connection to any of this."

"Come on Scott, of course we do."

"Really? What?"

Alani opened her mouth to answer and then closed it realizing there was little to nothing. He was right.

"All we really have is a message on a wine bottle, cryptic as it may be, that just so happened to come up before a random string of events occurred. The question we have to ask ourselves is do we think Dimarco is involved because he *is* or because we *want* him to be? Are we just trying to make it fit to accommodate our theory because that's easier? We can't get blinded."

Despite Alani's frustration, she knew Kyler was right.

"I guess we can only hope to find something…anything…this weekend," Alani concluded.

With that, Kyler turned his attention back to the computer and prepared to dial Goldman.

"Wait, before you call Ethan, we should probably take a look at the transcript from the restaurant. Our drive is only about forty-five minutes and we have plenty to go over while we have the freedom to talk openly."

Kyler nodded his head in agreement. They also hadn't even gotten to the murder of Camille Blanche or Jacques Francois yet, though there wasn't much they could figure out at the present moment.

Using a flick of the finger on the screen of the computer, Kyler did the virtual equivalent of tossing the Forbes article away as the electronic paper flew off and disappeared from the screen. His email inbox was left in a small icon and the running navigational map was in the upper left-hand corner so that Alani could consult it periodically to ensure they stayed on course.

Locating the email that Goldman had sent him with the transcript, Kyler double-tapped it with his finger and then did the same with the document attachment that had joined the file. The document opened up and he realized that he'd underestimated how large it was.

"There's a lot here. Can you give me a few while I scan through it?"

Kyler had an extraordinary gift for speed-reading, a skill he'd also had his public profession to thank for. He couldn't count how many scripts he'd read over the years and had gotten quite good at flying through them over time. It'd been particulary useful for the awful ones.

"Sure," Alani replied, turning her attention to her beautiful surroundings.

She had done her homework on both the region they were in as well as the area, the Rufina Commune as it was termed, that they were headed for. In the interest of fitting in as the wine aficionados they were playing, she'd focused on the history of the region as it pertained to the wine.

Alani had been a cursory appreciator of wine without a doubt but did not claim to be an expert. Proving that fact, she'd been surprised to learn that the famous Chianti wine she'd forever associated with Italy actually referred to a region of Tuscany and sported both an elaborate history of its own as well as some specific rules about its definition as a wine.

Always amazed with how much information she could find by a simple search on Google, she'd learned a little-known fact in that the first Chianti dated all the way back to the fourteenth century and had originally been a white wine. In some circles of Italy it was disregarded as being unproven, claiming it wasn't the same wine that was developed in the late eighteenth century and associated to areas in and around what was currently Sienna.

Like most things, the originator had kept the region to a small, exclusive area until treacherous weather all but destroyed the country's famed export. Italy then made the entrepreneurial decision to extend the name of Chianti to surrounding regions, Florence being one of them, to take advantage of additional acreage and growers.

The result was the present scenario. Now, nearly the entire Tuscan region, which was roughly ten times the size of the original, was allowed to label their wines with the name synonymous with Italian fine wine. That was as long as the mix met the minimum criteria of types of grapes, namely the Sangiovese variety that had to make up at least seventy percent of the overall mix.

The expansion also brought a wonderful variety of wines as the climate changed significantly throughout the various Tuscan regions.

Alani noticed this now as the temperature had begun to drop outside. She knew Rufina was cooler than Florence, sitting at almost three thousand feet above sea level and amidst lush rolling hills. As she looked out her window again, the scenery had continued to follow suit with her research, each bend in the windy two-lane highway producing more stunning views then the last.

Despite the dangerous nature of their visit, Alani silently looked forward to tasting what was supposed to be considered the most multi-layered, complex and elegant wine that the Chianti region had to offer. Again she pondered the fantasy of a different life where she could merely visit and enjoy exploring. Almost in the same breath, she admitted that her desire for action would quickly overtake her.

While Kyler continued to hurriedly read through the transcript, she continued to allow her mind to do battle through the prompting of her stunning surroundings. Her true spirit eventually winning out, however, as her thoughts returned once again to the many mysteries that had unfolded in the past forty-eight hours, how it all tied together and what this weekend may do to help shine some light on what it meant.

With that, Alani eased her foot onto the pedal just a bit harder and the car responded gleefully.

Chapter 35

The French officer, Ferdinand Martin, who'd been on the scene of Camille Blanche's murder and had spoken to Alani the previous day sat at his desk in the Prefecture building in Paris. The Prefect of Police was responsible for policing Paris and three of its surrounding regions, none of which included Gare du Nord where Blanche had been found dead. That area had actually been under the jurisdiction of the police nationale leading him to wonder why he had been assigned to work on the case to begin with.

The order to head onto the scene, however, had been given to him directly by the Prefect, the American equivalent to the Chief of Police. It wasn't to be questioned. He was to go onsite and gather everything he knew while still working alongside the police nationale while making it clear to their team that he would be taking the lead on the case. They were instructed to report all findings, pictures, interrogation results and other relevant material directly to Martin. He then, in turn was supposed to do the same for the Prefect on a daily basis.

It all felt very odd to Martin. He had, in fact not seen anything like it in the twenty years he'd worked for the Prefect of Police but decided not to question such orders. It didn't typically end well for those who did.

Still the case, and how it'd come to him, had him intrigued to say the least. He could also justify his participation by the fact the Camille Blanche had worked here in Paris for BFM. He'd seen a few of her pieces in the past and had been impressed by her skill, insight and professionalism despite being what the journalist community considered as relatively green.

The face of the twenty-eight year old woman looked back at him. He'd pulled the picture off of the station's website, printed out and added to her file. He liked physical connection with victims even if was merely the paper of a photograph.

Her picture was both unimpressive and pleasant at the same time. He noted her light blue eyes that seemed could border green on occasion. She had a light complexion with what looked to be a good amount of freckles, only adding to her youthful appearance. The auburn wavy hair had been pulled haphazardly back into a semi-ponytail with strands of hair tangling errantly in places. She didn't appear to wear much make-up, if any at all, for the photo. Martin imagined she'd probably come in one day and was told that it was the day for column photos whereupon she cursed herself profusely for not having been prepared.

Looking more closely at her soft features, Martin noted she was actually quite pretty. He wondered if, like with most professions and particularly those that required people to like you personally, the lack of attention to her appearance had held her back. It all probably wasn't that relevant but he'd learned over the years to do the best he could to create a profile of his victims. Details always proved to be a pay-off down the road.

Martin set the profile photo aside and moved on to the much more disturbing images. These being the crime scene photos that the forensics team had taken and printed copies out for all the pertinent parties.

The once kind, young and innocent eyes now stared back at him lifelessly. More gruesome being the hole that had penetrated her brain just above the eyes, which had proven to be lethal. It was, in fact, the only wound on her entire body. A single head shot with what, by the size of the hole and type of damage it had done, appeared to be a forty-five caliber bullet. They couldn't be sure though because, although it had entered through the front of the woman's head and exited cleanly out the back, they found no trace of a bullet or casing from the gun. The medical examiner and forensics team would soon be able to confirm the bullet through the autopsy, but it wouldn't present much assistance. The bullet was so commonplace that, without it, or at least the casing, there would be nothing to trace. It's not like a bullet left a trademark etching as it passed through a person's body, screaming, "I'm Phillip's gun!"

One thing was obvious to Martin, though. The murder and, hence, the murderer, had been efficient. None of the neighbors had seen or heard anything. Sure, it'd been in the morning, though the exact time of death hadn't been determined yet. Most of the people would have been off to work, school or other morning duties but the place couldn't have been empty.

Ferdinand, looking at the notes he'd made as well as the pictures of the scene, remarked that there'd been no sign of forced entry either. That, as anyone who'd ever seen a TV cop drama would point out, would normally indicate that the victim knew the killer. Maybe she lets him in or maybe the killer even has a key. That would be consistent with the unlocked door they discovered.

Then that same murderer shoots her, execution style with a single shot to the head? There'd been no struggle suggesting that if she did know the killer, it wasn't a lover's spat that ended violently. In that case, there probably would have been other injuries to point to. Maybe a bruise to the face or body indicating she'd been shoved. Not likely that Johnny sharp shooter walked in on Ms. Freckles when she was doing the humpty dance with some other guy.

Just then, Martin's partner, Noelle Broussard came in with a baguette sandwich in hand for both of them as well what looked to be espresso in two shot-sized paper cups.

Handing them to Martin, Broussard said, "Anything on who could have killed Ms. Blanche?"

Shaking his head, Martin replied, "Theories, pieces, details but no. Nothing makes sense here."

And, after looking around him, he added, "Including why *we* are investigating out in Gare du Nord in the first place."

The two had been partners for a long time and didn't pull any punches when it came to certain *bureaucratic anomalies,* as they liked to refer to them.

"Making friends with the press maybe?" Broussard suggested while taking a sizeable bite into his sandwich.

Broussard tipped the scale at about two and a half bills on a short five foot seven frame. He didn't often see a piece of food he didn't like. He also didn't see the inside of a gym too frequently either. Ferdinand was giving him the look that said he didn't see where he was going with the comment.

Broussard continued, "You know. Relatively pretty young girl that works for one of the largest news stations in Paris. It makes a big story. We are the ones who find her killer and avenge her death and maybe they don't go so hard on us the next time a riot breaks out or a drug bust goes wrong."

"It's possible but why would BFM give a shit?" Ferdinand picked at his sandwich, his mind keeping his appetite at bay for the moment.

"No disrespect to the lovely lady but she wasn't the damn producer or even an anchor. She's a nobody." Ferdinand opted for his espresso, which he sipped on.

Martin put his attention back to his notes.

"The more I look at this the more it feels like a pro."

"A hit?" Noelle replied, slightly puzzled. "Who'd want to take a hit out onto a low-level journalist-type?

"I don't know but the theory of it being someone she knows and possibly fought with or something doesn't fit in with the MO of the murder. The whole thing contradicts itself and screams to me that it isn't what we're supposed to think it is."

Martin continued looking through the files and started searching the pictures for anything that looked out of the ordinary.

"Here's the three biggest things we know," Martin said, ticking them off on his hand.

"First, no forced entry so the killer is obviously either very good at breaking and entering or little Ms. Blanche forgot to lock the door."

"Which is unlikely for a single woman in that area," Broussard added, following his train of thought.

"Second, only a single shot, perfectly placed in the head but no traces left behind."

"The guy had done this before," Broussard said this again with an unimaginable amount of food in his mouth.

"But then the last point throws the first two off. The place is trashed making us assume it was a general B and A robbery gone wrong but the guy decides to ransack the place anyway."

"But nothing seems to be missing," Broussard added.

"At least nothing we know of." Martin let that rattle in his brain a bit. "We need to look at the stories she'd been working on recently. See if there was anything controversial. Controversial enough for someone to want her dead."

Martin had been saying that while also continuing to look through the scene's photos. It was then that something caught his eye. It was a photo taken from the window side of the apartment. It'd been a wide angle shot with the intention to get as much of the room as possible while facing the front door. Near the front coat rack of the entrance, on the floor, Ferdinand thought he saw something shining back from the light coming in through the window behind the camera.

"Do you have a loop over there?" Martin asked excitedly, referring to the magnifying glass device usually used by photographers to look at thumbnail versions of stills.

"What you got over there?" Noelle said while tossing the device over to him.

Martin didn't answer right away but, instead put the device up to the picture focusing on what he'd seen.

"No fucking way," Martin said slowly.

"Jesus Martin, what?!" Noelle was up out of his chair now and walking towards him.

"Listen, I need you to look into every story Blanche ever wrote so we can see if there is a connection there," as he said this he was grabbing his holster and keys.

"Where are you going? What did you see?"

"I'm going to back to Blanche's apartment. I can't be absolutely sure but I think the killer may have left his casing. I need to go see if I'm right."

With that, Ferdinand snatched the picture for reference and was out the door leaving a surprised Noelle, still a mammoth-sized portion of food in his mouth, staring after him.

Chapter 36

"Are you going to share what you have over there Agent Scott?" Alani asked, getting anxious to hear if there was anything worthwhile from the translation.

"Or am I going to have to beg?"

"I vote for the begging," Kyler replied, giving her a wink.

As he said that, he looked up at their passing surroundings and couldn't help but take a sharp breath in admiration. He'd had his head buried in the computer for the past several minutes and somehow they'd been embedded into a land of rolling hills and countryside.

"They're still pretty vague," Kyler said, answering her question.

"We kind of expected that."

"They start with typical conversation. Talking about the wine the waiter just brought over, Armand Amici asks Dimarco what the specials are, they talk a bit of futbol and the chances the Italians have in the world cup. It's like that for a while."

"What about the woman they were with? Seem like she's involved? Does she say much?"

"A little here and there. Nothing much."

"She may just be playing the part," Alani said.

"The wife just out with her husband for a nice dinner with their friend, the owner?" Kyler said, nodding.

"Just like you were. Looks a little more suspicious for the guy to go to a fancy restaurant all by himself."

"Good point." Kyler said in agreement.

"What else?" Alani said, prodding forward.

She noticed that they were making good time. Great time, actually. At that, she eased off the gas a bit. They could use a little extra time.

"The first thing that stood out was that, after they order and the food comes, they go back to talking about the wine pretty extensively."

"What do you mean? Isn't that what Italians do? Talk about their great wine?"

"Yeah but Amici was almost a little too interested. Asking questions about how long it took, how production was going with the wine, what the sealing process was, how the current batch was looking, that sort of stuff."

"Could be just very curious about the process. Maybe Amici is thinking of opening up a winery of his own." Alani suggested.

Kyler was slowly shaking his head, "I guess that's possible but it doesn't feel like that. The two seem to know each other pretty well and if he was so interested, it seems a bit strange that this would be the first time they talk about it."

Kyler pondered that a bit while feeling the car continue to climb higher in the elevation toward the Rufina region. He, like Alani, had researched the area and knew the region provided cooler climates, different grapes for wine and what most would find as a memorable experience of learning the history of the area's vino.

"Do you know what Mr. Amici does?" Kyler asked.

It was Alani's turn to fill Kyler in, having had time on the plane to dig into the file a bit. She began recalling what she could remember.

"To an extent. At least as much as we know about any of these guys. Click on his bio."

Kyler clicked on the file associated with Armand Amici's biography.

"He's Founder and CEO of *Amici Corporation*," She explained, highlighting the contents.

"Self indulgent," Kyler said.

"Shocker…businessman with an ego. Well the corporation is, as you can imagine, privately held and spawns several tentacles."

"The public website says they have several divisions of shipping, both domestic and international, complete with a fleet of vehicles." Kyler noted having clicked the URL for Amici Corporations website.

"That caught my eye as well. It certainly offers up a broad spectrum of potentially questionable activities," Alani responded.

"Right. They also talk a lot about how they utilize top of the line technology for efficient shipping and even have an internal division dedicated to their technology development."

"An Italian group that claims to be efficient?" Alani laughed. "Didn't know such a concept existed. I wish the airports would take a hint."

She had lost her bag to the hands of the Italian airlines more than once and getting them back had been even more interesting.

"What kind of technology are they using?" Kyler asked.

"What you'd expect from a transportation company. GPS location monitoring on the trucks so customers can track where their shipments are at all times."

"Not to mention it allows the company to make sure drivers aren't stopping off at a local bar for a long lunch and bottle of wine," Kyler added.

"Yeah…I'm sure that never happens," Alani said.

"The site also talks about some high-tech wireless bar code scanners that can capture pictures and videos of deliveries. Those can be instantly added to the shipping confirmation so when the customer tracks a package online, they can see its live progress."

"Why would you want to do that?" Alani asked.

"Hell if I know," Kyler said.

"Does the website have a list of their customers by chance?" Alani asked, looking for anything that would give them a lead on what Amici's company may or may not be involved in.

"No but they do list one heck of a diverse shipping location map. They ship mostly by air but some of it's by sea. They use the Livorno Port off the coast of Western Italy."

"Where do they deliver?" Alani asked.

"The states for one thing. Specifically California, Florida and New York."

"Logical. Covering all of the hot spots. Where else do they ship?"

"Everywhere," he answered.

"That includes places like China, North Korea, Iraq, Afganistan…"

"Places that aren't exactly on our top ten peace-keeping lists," Alani said.

It didn't mean much when she thought about it. Sure, they could start dramatizing the fact that they could be shipping weapons, artillery, maybe throw in some of the famous weapons of mass destruction for good measure. In reality though, with restrictions as tight as they were these days, if a company was smuggling that sort of thing into countries, they certainly wouldn't be advertising it on their website.

Kyler seemed to be reading her mind, "I just don't see the threat being there since they are being so public about it."

"Unless that's their plan. Get people thinking the way you and I are right now, making it that much easier to slip things in and out." Alani was just speculating because in reality, she couldn't see the relevance.

"Well I guess that we should just file that under good to know for now. What else did they talk about?" Alani prodded on seeing that they were getting very close to the winery now.

Kyler closed the internet page that talked about Amici's company and went back to the transcript.

"Well this part makes a bit more sense now that we know all of that. Dimarco asks if the shipment from the states came in successfully. Amici confirms that it did and goes on to say that the process was smooth and problem free."

"Sounds like he is checking on an *arrival*. That's a bit strange for someone who specializes in shipping *out*," Alani commented.

"Agreed but what would someone like Dimarco need from the states? Nothing against our fine country, mind you, but we don't have much to offer a guy like Dimarco. The guy's a goddamn elitist and people like that don't see American-made as quality-made."

"Well then the guy clearly hasn't seen American Chopper," Alani joked knowing Kyler was right.

"Dimarco does ask Amici if he's handling the delivery personally and Amici confirms that he is. That strikes me as interesting." Kyler continued reading.

"Why do I believe that we need to find out what that shipment was?" Alani concluded.

"Probably because you're right. We need to see if Goldman can find out about that it. Amici says it was leaving California for Pisa. If we can pull the bill of lading under his company maybe we can see what was in that cargo."

Kyler looked to see if there was anything of relevance on the transcript but the rest seemed to be more table conversation. "That seems to be about all we have."

"So all we've got is this guy Amici who's really interested in how his friend, who's also his business associate, makes wine. That and a shipment that we know next to nothing about which just so happened to be coming out of California." Alani summed up, slightly disappointed.

"That's about right," Kyler confirmed, feeling some of the same frustration.

"There *was* one more strange comment that didn't make sense at all," Kyler added.

"Which was…?"

"Armani asks Dimarco," Kyler paused as he found the quote in the transcript to make sure he repeated it verbatim.

"*Did the lilies wilt*? To which Dimarco responded with *Indeed they did. Almost the entire patch in one day.*"

Alani was lost, "What the hell is that supposed to mean?"

"I don't know but I'm pretty sure Amici isn't taking an interest in Dimarco's garden. This means something to them. I'd be willing to bet on that."

"We just don't know what," Alani finished.

"Well let's hope this weekend shines a bit more light on this. We have too many questions and not enough answers."

Kyler noted their progress on the map and realized they had maybe ten minutes before they arrived and they hadn't called Goldman yet.

"Why don't you pull off up there so we can call Ethan before we get too far," Kyler said pointing to a sign that read *Veduta Scenica,* or scenic view. Kyler could only imagine what this region's scenic view was going to look like.

Living up to its expectations, they pulled off the road and looked to their left only to find a scene that looked as if it could have been straight out of the footage from Under the Tuscan Sun. It looked surreal to Kyler, with what seemed to be perpetual mountain lines that were covered with the greenery of forest. Acting as the scenic tip of the iceberg, there was a small village tucked in the valley so picturesque that it looked like DaVinci himself had painted it into their glorious scene.

"Isn't it beautiful?" Alani asked him, wholly reading his thoughts.

Kyler was taken aback by the double meaning of the comment as he stared back at her. Turning his attention back toward the scenery, conveniently avoiding the obvious tension that could have been tantamount, he said, "More beautiful than anything I've seen."

Shaking himself out of it, Kyler then turned his attention back to the slate computer that had been loaded with the same video conferencing software that was on his laptop. He pulled up the virtual console that listed Dr. Ethan Goldman as a contact, tapped the screen and it was dialing out, the call ringing through the car's audio system as a speakerphone of sorts.

The image of Goldman seemingly sitting at the desk of his home office came into view as he accepted the incoming call. It was just before midnight. He didn't look pleased when he saw Kyler.

"Where the hell have you been Scott? Don't you know I've been trying to reach you for the last six goddamn hours?"

"Would you believe me if I told you I had a good excuse?" Kyler replied.

"Not unless that excuse was that you were literally having your balls ripped off and you had to go to the emergency room for immediate surgery to have them reattached otherwise you would never be able to have sex again. Do you think I call because I wanna chat Scott? See how craft services was on set?"

"It was actually amazing. They brought in a Sushi chef...guess the crew was getting tired of Italian every day or something," Kyler, the perpetual smart ass.

"Do you know what time it is here Agent?" Not letting Kyler respond he said, "Too late to deal with your smart ass. Just answer the phone next time...got it?"

Despite the lecture, Goldman knew that Kyler neither got it nor would it be the last time he'd have the conversation. He knew that this independence, which he'd actually recruited Kyler for in part, had helped close cases almost every time. There'd been times he went off the grid for days to follow the trail of a mark. At the same token, he also knew that an agent with too much free reign was not something the agency could afford, no matter how loyal he or she was.

"Affirmative sir. Moving on?"

"I assume Langdon is there with you?" At that question, Kyler panned the screen enough to allow the video feed to catch both of them.

"Hey Doc," Alani said lightly.

"Smack him for me, would you agent?" Goldman said and then finally let a small smile loose. Alani had that effect on men. Even the director of America's most critical agency.

"Already done sir. Almost ran him over with my car."

"Good. Ok. You have plenty to do but as you now both know, our problems are growing by the damn fucking minute here. The murders and now Hawkins' disappearance."

"Do we have any leads on any of it?" Kyler asked.

"It's coming in slowly. I have connections with the Prefect of Police out in Paris so they'll feed me what they have out there on the Camille Blanche case as well as Francois's murder. I told them it may have some tie into these other cases so they have the locals reporting every single detail and findings back to the French military."

"I'm sure that sits well with the locals," Kyler commented.

"Who gives a shit," Dr. Ethan Goldman, king of compassion. "If Blanche in fact knew and let it slip that Francois was not, in fact, Francois at all but instead a goddamned former French black ops agent, they'd have every media personnel digging around trying to get every angle on the story. That'd be a fucking nightmare."

Alani added, "Sure…it opens up the questions of what Francois's role in the military was and, once that's out, panic over what someone would want to beat and eventually kill him for."

Kyler chimed in, "Not a dream scenario."

Goldman nodded, "Like I said…a fucking nightmare. The local police may not like reporting to the military but they won't question it…at least not out loud to anyone that matters."

Goldman had dealt with the overzealous local police on too many occasions and was more than familiar with their tendency to get possessive over their cases. It probably didn't help that they, being the all-powerful government agencies like the CIA or FBI, famously trounced around their local neighborhood while sharing little with the same police that were supposed to be communicating with the community on progress. It was the nature of the beast. Cases that the agencies got involved in were typically sensitive and containment of information within groups that were accustomed to being careful with those details was critical. And thus, the battle raged on each time.

Continuing on, Goldman said, "We're also trying to track down the video from the restaurant Hawkins went to. Apparently the owner had some vandalism a while back and installed a camera. I should have the footage by the morning. I'll shoot it over when I do. Not sure what you can do from your end but more eyes on it can't hurt."

"What about Ellen Stratton...the rape case?" Alani recalled the story from the case files she'd reviewed on her way to Paris.

"We actually have her under surveillance," Goldman replied.

"Surveillance?" Kyler asked. "What for?"

"We want to make sure she doesn't find a way to disappear too. Either temporarily or permanently. We put a tail on her after Hawkins disappeared. We are hoping to get a little lucky there." Goldman explained.

"So you're using her as bait?" Alani asked, scared for the woman who'd already been through enough in her opinion.

"Bigger picture agent."

Goldman didn't want to get into an ethical debate on whether it was acceptable to follow a seemingly innocent citizen.

"If she can lead us to who grabbed Hawkins, maybe it leads to the murders and, more importantly, to the link between them all."

"We understand sir," Kyler said, trying to prevent the debate that seemed close to developing. He put a soft hand to Alani's as if to say it wasn't worth the fight, which she also knew.

Goldman hesitated for a moment, calculating how to phrase what he was about to say.

"Due to the recent incident, there is something you need to know about Hawkins. More specifically, what could have gotten him kidnapped."

Alani and Kyler exchanged a glance.

"As I'm sure you both know, Hawkins's invention that made him his millions is highly classified. So much so that neither of you, despite your near top-level security clearance, are privy to this information."

Alani and Kyler said nothing, encouraging Goldman to continue.

"This information would have remained a secret to you both if not for its possible relevance to his disappearance. You are now on a need-to-know basis."

The two again said nothing, only slightly nodding their understanding.

"I'm sure you know the general nature of Hawkins's relationship to QTS Tek. What I'm certain you don't know is what he created that was worth keeping secret."

Feeling the need to say something, Kyler said, "Confirmed sir. We only know that whatever it was made him rich as hell."

Goldman nodded and continued, "Without going into extensive detail, Hawkins invented an Iris Scanner unlike anything created before or since. The scanner itself wasn't ground breaking…you've seen them on military bases all over…but it's ability to cross-reference and confirm identities across an unprecedented number of multi-national databases and watchlists is unparalleled."

Goldman paused to allow the information a moment to sink in with his two agents.

He then continued, "Don't ask for details of why or how because I won't tell you but you needed to know because I'm assuming Hawkins was taken because of it."

Kyler chimed in again, "To show them how to re-create it?"

"That or force him to re-create it himself. Either way, you both are bright and were likely wondering what I have been wondering since I heard the news…if Dimarco is in fact involved in all of this as we suspect, what is the possibility that Hawkins may be at Villa Santini?"

More nodding from Alani and Kyler.

"While it wasn't the initial purpose of your trip, it should now be considered not just a possibility but one of your top priorities."

"Absolutely sir," Alani replied.

"Great. Well you both know what you need to do so get to it. I'll get you more intel as it comes through including any leads we may get on tracking Hawkins to a location. Be sure to check in regularly in case something pops."

"Yes sir. Righty-O!" Kyler said, throwing in the thumbs up for good measure.

"Righty-O? You're an idiot agent. Good but an idiot."

"I'll take it as a compliment. By the way, we'll be off the grid for a while, you know. Can't exactly be talking to you while we're there. Just making sure you weren't going to freak out on me sir."

Kyler was pushing Goldman now and he knew it but he couldn't help taking the opportunity to get under his skin.

"Always a wise ass. Get your game face on agent. This is growing in complexity by the minute and we still have no clue what the fuck we are looking at."

They said their goodbyes and Goldman was gone. With that, Alani sped off, leaving the picturesque scene behind. Poetic, Kyler thought. It was about to be a very long weekend.

Chapter 37

Ethan Goldman had just pulled into the two-car garage of his classic white colonial home in McLean, Virginia when his cell phone rang, startling him. He glanced at the classic style clock of his Cadillac CTS and noted it was nearly midnight. Granted, he was in fact just getting back from the office, having stayed late after talking to Kyler to work with who he could in Paris and Italy to gather up as much information as possible, but the number calling him was in the states. A bit late, he thought, but that came with the territory for the man in charge of the most relied-upon intelligence agency in the country, if not the world. He arguably worked harder than the president. After all, the commander in chief was not trying to keep Ethan Goldman safe along with the rest of the country. Unfortunately, Goldman also didn't even earn half of the four hundred thousand dollar plus salary of the country's fearless leader. In his more masochistic moments, he calculated what his earnings broke down to per hour, occasionally making him wonder aloud why he didn't take one of the hundreds of offers in the private sector that he'd had over the years. With his knowledge, experience and general value to nearly any company, he would easily triple his current income.

Ultimately, in those same honest moments, he realized he liked…no, loved…the power and excitement of the job. He relished in the idea that he would have the final say in so many critical decisions, many of which could lead to deaths of a few, maybe thousands of people or the right decision preventing minimal or even zero losses. He loved the artistry of orchestrating the many tentacles that made up the agency, relying on his ability to find exceptional agents, analysts and other key roll-players to assemble all the necessary pieces to keep his fine country safe.

Ethan practiced as much humility as possible but, just like any other leader in a position of extreme power, one that had risen to the absolute echelon of their field, Ethan wanted to firmly cement his own legacy. He had kept four presidents safe, some he felt he was keeping safe from themselves. More importantly, he had limited the agency's mistakes, since those also unfortunately came with the territory. The errors had been minimal in their damage to the people of the country as well as its secrets.

His pride and his legacy were why he took calls at midnight when he'd sometimes rather park his car, settle into his mahogany-rich library with a glass of cognac and read a good fiction book for once. His life was non-fiction, which, with its insanity at times, he wondered wasn't a work of farce.

"Ethan Goldman."

Ethan clicked the button of his Bluetooth headset to answer his Blackberry so he could still have his hands free to lug his briefcase and files back into the house. There were certain files he simply didn't leave at the office.

"Can you tell me why you have two CIA Agents tailing one of my best cryptologists, Dr.?" the curt voice on the other line started, not introducing himself.

Not recognizing the voice, Ethan said, "Why don't we start with who the hell you are and why you are calling me in the middle of the night?"

"This is Ian Collins, head of security at QTS and I'm calling you at this hour because I got an emergency call from my local security supervisor in Maryland who tells me that Ellen Stratton called *him* in a panic because two guys in a black clearly government-issue sedan had been following her all night."

Feigning surprise, Ethan said, "Wait a minute. Ellen Stratton works for you? She's a QTS employee?"

Ethan was pulling out his files now to review his notes on the woman. He'd been waiting for this call. In fact, it was why he'd put a tail on Stratton in the first place. Nowhere in the file was it noted that Stratton worked for QTS Tek, which was strange to keep from him, considering that they worked almost exclusively for the CIA. That would have certainly registered.

"Technically, no. Not on paper she isn't but she does work for us."

"You're going to have to do a little better than that Ian. And it's too damn late to be playing word games. Does she work for you or doesn't she?" Goldman had settled into his library. It was his office away from the office. There would definitely be no reading or cognac tonight. Maybe the cognac.

"It's just not exactly what we want to be disclosing to the director of the CIA Doctor Goldman."

Irritated now, Goldman snapped, "Listen to me. Clearly we have an interest in the woman. That much is obvious and we weren't working very hard to hide that. Do you seriously believe, knowing that we're interested, that I don't have the resources to figure out her whole goddamned life story Mr. Collins? So again, you might as well tell me now or else I'll make it my point to figure out what I can about you as well."

Ian sighed on the other end, apparently resigned although not nervous at the threat.

"First sir, if you did, you would find nothing both because there is nothing to find and because our privacy capabilities are why your government agency spends over three billion dollars a year with us. With all due respect, sir, I don't appreciate being threatened any more than I appreciate one of our employees being harassed without a heads up."

Goldman considered informing the prick on the other end that his arrogance could easily land him in a federal prison for forty-eight hours merely because Ethan felt like it. That and a convincing story that the CIA considered Mr. Ian Collins a threat to national security. Pretty much carte blanch particularly when the order came from his desk. The Patriot Act gave people in Goldman's position a lot of leeway to bend the rules of the constitution.

His interest in where this was all going though kept him from his regular reaction of tearing the guy a new one and, instead, resigned to give in a bit.

"Fine Mr. Collins. Threats aside, why don't we just agree to have a little friendly openness and we can figure out what the hell is going on. How does that sound?"

Though in the recesses of his mind, Goldman practically dared him to say no, give him a reason to drive a little fear into to the heart of the private sector James Bond wannabe.

To Ethan's partial dismay, Ian decided to bend as well.

"Frankly, it is not an issue of any national security. Ms. Stratton is a paid contractor and not an official employee of QTS because of some…difficulties…with her citizenship status." Ian had paused to choose his words carefully.

"As in she is not one, Mr. Collins? You have an illegal immigrant working for your company who, as you say, deals with some of the most sensitive material and you don't consider that an issue of national security? Particularly one that I might be interested in knowing just a little more about? How the hell do I know she isn't a spy that you've given a golden key to?!"

Ian seemed to weigh his response.

"I don't mean to stereotype here or come across as insensitive but Ms. Stratton is from Canada, sir. It's not like she's from the Middle-East or China and we're giving a possible terrorist the keys to the castle."

"How can you be so sure, Mr. Collins? If she was interested in becoming an employee of a company that I would hope takes its vetting process seriously, why not become a citizen?" Goldman had decided for the cognac to help him settle his frustration with the man on the other end of the line.

"Not for lack of trying doctor. She's failed the citizenship exam three times. As I understand it, she is taking it again in a few weeks."

As much as Goldman wanted to fling judgment on the failures of Ellen Stratton, he couldn't bring himself to honestly do so. It was relatively common knowledge that the test to become an

American citizen would be failed by most natives if given the test without a fair amount of preparation. Knowing the dates of pertinent historical events, rules of the presidency and other particulars was about as akin to common knowledge as the details on a state's driver's written exam. Most people, without looking it up first, could not list the original thirteen states that made up the first landscape of the country. Sad but true.

Ian continued, "She's been here for a year now and QTS made a special employment arrangement for her because, frankly, she's the best damn cryptologist we know. Maybe the best in the world. At least the best that hasn't chosen to make her fortune working for the other side."

"Or so you believe," Ethan countered.

"I can assure you doctor that our vetting process rivals that of the CIA and FBI combined. You have to deal with your spies but that doesn't hold a candle to the lengths people will go for corporate espionage. It factors in a very powerful driving force. Money."

Ethan took a small sip from his snifter glass and let the warming liquid pass over his gums and into his throat. The simple act calmed and even focused him. He was trying to decide if he should continue his tail on Ellen Stratton with the previous pretense of her protection or the possible alternate. That of a threat. The fact remained that he still needed to find out whether her amnesia case could have anything to do with her ties to QTS. He decided for a blend of the two but wasn't about to let Ian Collins in on his plans at the moment.

"I'll hold up my end of the bargain then, Mr. Collins. Our purpose in tracking Ms. Stratton is for her own protection resulting from her recent unfortunate incident and affiliation to QTS. Despite what you may think about your secrecy, I was well aware of Ms. Collins employment long before your call and, frankly, that employment scares the shit out of me. But the fact that someone grabbed her should scare the shit out of you too," Goldman said.

Collins paused and Goldman knew he'd taken the security chief off-guard. Collins was certain he'd kept Stratton's employment a secret and would have to do some research of his own to find out how Goldman had found out. In truth, it was no crime but he preferred to be the one who held all the cards.

"I'll admit, we are concerned, maybe even a little on edge," Collins replied.

Goldman listened closely as Ian said the words. They seemed to register as genuine leading him to believe that QTS was not involved in any duplicitous activity. He would, of course, remain cautious though.

"Well then why don't we all agree that we have the best interest for Ms. Stratton's safety in mind and leave it at that?"

"So what am I supposed to tell Ms. Stratton then? Don't worry, you aren't safe but because of that, the CIA will be keeping an eye on you although they can't tell you what they are watching for."

Ian could see the explanation wasn't going to be an easy one but could also tell from Goldman's voice that he wasn't going to have a choice.

"Sorry to say it but, yes, that's precisely what you'll have to tell her although you may want to word it a little differently. I'm not certain that will instill much peace of mind in the poor woman," Goldman said.

Ian scoffed at the comment, "Can you at least give me assurances to pass along that her status as a citizen, or lack thereof, won't be of interest to the CIA?" Ian was hoping to give Ellen Stratton at least a sliver of good news while informing her that she was under the watchful eyes of the United States Government.

"Currently, you may tell her we are not interested in that detail but Ian," Goldman said, leading.

"Uh huh."

"Encourage her to pass the test. Let's just make life easy on us all."

"I'll be sure to pass that along with minimal pressure I'm sure. Sorry to disturb you at such a late hour." Ian concluded, completely resigned to a conversation he'd basically deemed a failure.

"It seems we were both disturbed. Good night Mr. Collins."

"Good night doctor."

Ethan clicked the button off on his headset and tossed the uncomfortable piece of equipment down onto the desk. He took another sip of the Remy Martin, his middle of the road option when it came to cognacs.

As he looked around the old English style library, complete with a sliding ladder attached to the finely appointed built-in bookshelves, he wondered if it were possible that Ellen Stratton may not have his best interests in mind. He knew Ian claimed to check the woman out and believed they had done so thoroughly but he had also pointed out that she was possibly one of the best cryptologists in the world so manipulating what they found out about her wouldn't be a stretch.

He'd have to take the more aggressive approach, he decided. He picked up the phone, minus the headpiece this time, his ear still feeling the annoying discomfort of having had it on all day.

"Good evening sir," the agent's voice said, answering on the second ring.

"Agent. Sorry to call so late but I need you to change the tactic on your point of interest to one far less clean."

Clean was a term within the agency to indicate that an area or situation was clean or void of any surveillance materials or other tracking mechanisms. The agent on the other end understood this to mean that the agency needed to know a bit more about their target than originally thought.

"Copy that sir. We will commence immediately."

"Commandment 11 agent," Ethan said.

It was the number one agent rule. Don't get caught. He wasn't even sure if there was anything there, and after having partially committed to Collins that their surveillance would be innocent for the time being, he didn't need the headache of showing he'd been less than completely honest on the topic. At least not until he had good reason to discuss any findings.

"Thank you agent. That's all."

"Good night sir."

Goldman hit the end button on the phone, finished off the remainder of the drink and decided to get at least a few hours of sleep. The weekend may be coming but he knew gardening or ball games weren't on the docket.

Chapter 38

The microwave rang loudly in the barren kitchen and shook the man out of his daze. The place was so damn depressing that it was a wonder he hadn't offed himself by now. How long had they been here? Two months? Three months? He'd lost count by now and was beginning to question whether he would ever leave. It was supposed to have been just a month initially. One extended to two, two carried in to three…for all he knew now, it could be five months.

No sense in dwelling on it but boredom left him with little else to think about. He walked across the kitchen, opened the door of the microwave and pulled out the macaroni and cheese. Taking a fork, he poured in the cheese, stirred up the noodles and, once satisfied that it was ready, grabbed the first bowl he'd made just minutes ago and made his way to the back of the house.

It was a one-story, two-bedroom, one bathroom dump. Furniture amounted to a couch that had seen far better days, a card table serving as a dining/kitchen table and a tube TV that picked up two channels on a good day perched atop a milk crate. A five-star hotel it was not.

A bowl in each hand, the man found the door to the bedroom at the back of the house. He stopped and set the bowls down on the ground and reached into his pockets for the keys to the room. He unlocked the handle and two dead bolts that had been installed prior to their arrival months ago, returned the keys to his pocket, opened the door and picked up the two bowls of food.

As he made his way through the entrance into the dimly lit room, he found the woman and her baby girl as he always did. Huddled up together on the barren bed as they numbly stared at the television that, at the moment, was playing I Love Lucy reruns. He doubted they had even been watching though their eyes had shifted in fear to him as they always did when he entered. He had never physically hurt the two but had been forced to lay the threats on pretty thick in the first few days and weeks to make sure they didn't make any attempts to escape, fight back or anything else that might make the situation worse than it already was.

He knew they wouldn't take the food from him and neither moved an inch while he crossed the room and set two bowls on the cardboard box that sat next to the bed and served as a bedside table. He didn't look at the two but could see them both tremble in fear as he approached out of the corner of his eye and he couldn't help but feel a little sorry for them.

As he left the room, he felt guilty as he had every time he walked into the room since day one. *I can't believe I can't even remember how long I've been here,* he thought to himself. As he closed the door, relocking the bolts and handle behind him, he cursed himself out of guilt for the two innocents on the other side of the door.

What could he do though, he thought to himself? *Nobody said no to Gianni Dimarco.*

Chapter 39

Alani dropped the Audi down into third gear as they hit what the computer display told them to be the heart of the town of Rufina. It was as historic and picturesque as any of the smaller villages in Italy both Alani and Kyler had seen. They noted a building called the Villa di Poggio Reale, which effaced the street with its three large open archways, inviting all those that passed by to come inside. They both noted a sign etched out front that read museo di vino.

"What do you figure they would have inside a wine museum?" Alani asked Kyler as she read the sign.

"I'm guessing it's not just some really old wine," Kyler joked though he'd pondered the same question in his head as well.

They passed another building that looked to be even older, possibly twelfth or thirteenth century. It was a Romanesque church that read as the Chiesa di Santo Stefano a Castiglioni. Alani looked at the building thinking it undoubtedly had no shortage of historical pieces inside seeing as it seemed to have been untouched for as many centuries as it had been standing but still beautiful and stoic in its solidarity.

"The Italians most certainly love their churches," she commented.

Nodding, Kyler said, "Not much different than the rest of the world, I'd argue. They just know how to build them right. Almost makes me want to be Catholic."

Alani smiled knowing their lack of ties to a specific religion or even a certainty of where they stood on the subject was a common ground between them both. It had been one of the few personal topics they'd discussed on their infamous evening, both commenting on how they felt faith in something but, after all the horrors they'd seen, they weren't sure how it all fit together.

"According to the map here, the winery is just outside the edge of town," Kyler said pointing to the screen as he zoomed out of the image a bit to include their final destination for Alani to see.

Alani glanced over and noted the destination that was listed as a little over three kilometers away. She said, "Same story as the restaurant?"

"Same story. You are the famous musician and I am, of course, who I am. Sort of."

"You mean the arrogant, self-absorbed mega-star that is invading the fine city of Florence?" Alani joked coyly.

"I prefer the description of wealthy and refined artist of major motion films thank you very much. One with rugged good looks and an appreciation for the finer things in life."

"You forgot humble," she said smiling.

"Well you can't have it all."

Alani, seeing that they hit the edge of town, popped the car into fourth gear and the Audi lurched forward and toward the winding stretch of road that, according to the map, would lead them to Villa Santini.

That car made the final turn around the bend and dipped its nose downward and the scene that unfolded before them caused them both to take in a sharp breath. Neither said anything but their sentiment was shared. Down below where the road was summoning to them sat a castle that was tightly nestled in between tree-ridden hills on both sides. There were mammoth pine trees rising all around it that seemed to hug the structure, keeping it in place and making sure it stayed put. The last hundred yards before the entrance, the road turned to dirt with a horse path fence guiding toward the massive entrance that looked like it would only be complete were there a moat in front of it.

The castle's rustic stone looked to be dated back at least eight centuries and was complete with inset windows near the top of structure that loomed at least five stories and seventy-five feet high. As Kyler stared in amazement at the live snapshot of age-old history, he envisioned what the castle could have been used for in its original form. It looked to be a structure built with the intent of keeping up some level of defenses. He noted the walkway that spanned the top of the building that he imagined would have been used by guards to walk the perimeter and watch for a potential approaching enemy. Noting by their descent down to the largely intimidating yet awe-inspiringly beautiful edifice, it would not be difficult to spot an approach from a considerable distance.

At several points of its top line, towers rose above the rest of the structure as additional points of positioning. Kyler imagined setting himself up in the building in modern day battles with an SR-16 Sniper rifle and answered the question that so many often posed. Why don't they make buildings like that anymore? Kyler mused to himself at that knowing that he, like many other of the top trained sharp shooters with the right equipment and the acceptable conditions, could pick off a target at a distance as far as twenty-three hundred meters. That being nearly a mile and a half of range was just a little bit more than the medieval weaponry of a bow and arrow that was lucky to peg off man on horseback at five hundred feet. Combining today's capabilities with a vantage point to see attackers from a great distance, the building's strategy would be excellent except for one small detail. That element was the modern-day airstrike, which could blow the beautiful building into oblivion with one pass over.

And that, ladies and gentlemen, Kyler thought to himself as if giving the closing argument of a speech is why the military of today does not fight on the ground. We fight in the sky, in shadows and, in his case, incognito.

"This is the Villa Santini?" Alani asked Kyler who'd been so consumed in thought and theory that he started a bit, immediately flushing red. Alani noticed his startled jump.

"Imagining history are we?"

She knew of his propensity to get lost in his own imaginative thoughts, which were so vivid, it was as if he was there. She hated to admit it, but it was a quality that probably made him a great actor, which she regrettably acknowledged that he was.

Covering a bit, he replied, "Actually I'm considering the strong possibility that Dimarco chose this location specifically and that fact tells me a good deal. Or, at least it confirms for us that something is definitely going on here."

Letting his lie, or at least his semi-truth, go she asked, "What makes you so sure?"

"This is the only way in to the property, right?"

He was sort of asking himself as he keened back in on the map, expanding its view out to see if there were any other visible roads accessing the property.

His suspicions were correct, "Yep, see that," he said pointing to the screen. "There is no road to the backside of this property for miles. If the plot lines that the boys back home marked out are accurate, then the property looks like it is well over five hundred acres putting the edge of the plot right here."

As Kyler pointed to the spot he was referring to, he manipulated the view of the map to the equivalent of a street-level view that resembled a Google Earth image. The surroundings were three dimensional at which Alani said, "And that back edge as well as the sides are kept in by the mountains which don't appear to be inhabited with any sort of access road."

"Right. So we can assume that between their medieval-style defenses of castle towers on the front edge and its aids from the geographic surroundings, Dimarco's people, whoever is running things here, knows exactly who is coming and going around here."

Alani nodded her head and said, "Well it's a good thing we have a way in Mr. Hollywood."

"And it's good I came prepared," Kyler thumbed back toward the trunk that housed the bag full of toys which they were definitely going to need all of.

"So who is running Villa Santini if Dimarco isn't?" She asked.

Though he knew the answer, he clicked on a thumbnail-sized image of a document that was embedded into the picture of the castle. It expanded out and revealed a picture of Vitale Baldacci. It seemed to have been taken at an event as he was done up in traditional black tie garb of a tuxedo that no doubt cost in the thousands and his jet black hair was combed back a la Cary Grant.

Kyler turned the screen back to her, "That's him. Vitale Baldacci. Forty-four years of age. Been in the employment of Dimarco for what looks to be twenty years. Grew up in a small village in Sienna as did Dimarco so we can assume they were probably childhood friends that have stuck together. Baldacci spent time in the military though. Looks like he enrolled into the Italian Armed Forces at eighteen and was honorably discharged at twenty four when he was injured."

"In battle?" Alani asked. "That would have made it twenty years ago."

"It doesn't say he was in battle. Doesn't even list what his injuries were or what his role or title in the military was."

"Agent maybe? Spy?" Alani considered.

"Quite possibly by the looks of things. What was going on in the nineties politically?" Kyler pondered aloud.

He closed his eyes, casting his memory banks backward. Though he would have only been a teenager trolling around Hollywood at the time finding trouble wherever he could, he'd since become a history magnet and soaked in all he could for the job, not to mention his own keen interest.

"Olive Tree?" Alani asked, referring to the coalition that was put into power made up of leftists that included, strangely, an economics professor named Romano Prodi as its Prime Minister. It'd been a huge turning point in Italy who, up until the mid-eighties still had Catholicism as its state religion.

Kyler shook his head, "No...that wasn't until ninety-six and Baldacci was out for nearly six years by then."

Still racking his brain, he snapped his fingers, "Ah...I remember now. I think there was a big political scandal around that time. Probably one of the biggest, actually. It brought down the Christian Democratic Party that dominated for decades. Huge corruption, scandal, the works."

"Maybe he played a part in bringing them down?"

"Could be. Then he is asked to leave to minimize the damage or possibly prevent them from finding out even more. Either way, we can assume he's good at sniffing out deception and maybe even agents so we'll need to be careful."

Just then, the wheels of the car hit the dirt that led them to last stretch of hundred meters or so to the entrance. Neither of them could have known at the time that they would not be leaving nearly as quietly before the weekend was up.

Chapter 40

Ferdinand Martin pulled up to Camille Blanche's apartment building in the Subaru Impreza WRX. It was the new standard-issue vehicle for the French police. It started just a few years ago when the car manufacturer beat out the old traditional Peugots and Renaults, resting primarily on the fact that the Subaru could top the others by fifty kilometers per hour faster. Size, handling and speed made it ideal for use, which Martin had fully tested on his way out from Paris. He'd arrived in half the time it took him on the first call and his blood was pumping, hoping he would find the bullet casing he thought he saw in the crime scene photograph.

Martin jumped out of the car in a frenzy, leaving the flashing lights atop the vehicle running which drew no shortage of attention from the neighbors who'd heard the car's wheels screech as he'd slammed to a stop seconds earlier. They probably thought this was their very own American-style inner city drug bust. The lone police car and lack of S.W.A.T. truck should have tipped them off otherwise though.

Martin put his hand on the holster of his Sig Sauer nine-millimeter standard issue. He didn't anticipate running into problems in the building but his training had permanently engrained the idea of preparedness in his mind.

Taking the steps to the building in bounding twos, he hit the front door and swiped the card issued to law enforcement for access to public buildings. The door responded accordingly as he heard it buzz encouraging him to enter, which he did quickly.

He'd already been in the building so he knew he needed to get to the third floor. He panned the elevators that were in the small lobby that was apparently equipped merely to house the mailboxes for the building, a couple of chairs and the elevators for access to the six-story apartment complex. Martin decided to bypass waiting and fixed his eyes on the sign pointing to the stairwell.

Crashing through the steel door to the concrete stairwell, he began the short climb to the third floor, noting each door of the levels he passed to make sure he knew when he'd arrived. Despite the short, three-flight sprint, Martin was breathing heavily. Dare say, he may have been gasping a bit and he told himself that he'd need to get into the gym starting tomorrow. Having been a marathon runner in his thirties, he was surprised by his clear ineptness at running up a few flights that would have made him yawn in his younger days.

He exited the stairwell, albeit with a little less intensity than he'd just entered into it with, as he tried to calm his breathing. He made the corner around the hallway that led to Blanche's apartment and saw the police tape across the front door no more than twenty feet ahead. He hit the door and checked the knob. It was unlocked which was odd. He instinctively drew his weapon before ducking under the cautionary tape to enter. The door was supposed to have been locked by the crime scene team. The last thing the police wanted on an investigation was a curious, overzealous soul wandering into the room and contaminating the scene into obscurity.

Either the crime scene team neglected to practice due diligence, for which he'd have to rip them a new one for, or someone else had been inside and still could be. With his Sig at the ready, he slowly opened the door and entered, clearing each direction quickly. He debated announcing his police presence but then thought better of it. Instead he elected to go the quiet route in hopes to catch the intruder if there was indeed someone in the place.

Seeing no movement in the living room, he silently made his way toward the bedroom. The door was closed. Of course, he cursed to himself. As if he wasn't on edge already, now he had to open a door blind and hope that if there was anyone on the other side, his reflexes would be better than theirs. Despite what some may think, this was something no police officer ever got accustomed to. Adrenaline in situations like these was like breathing. It happened no matter what a person did.

Martin took a deep breath and decided to approach it like tearing off a band-aid. Quick and painful. He turned the knob with his left hand keeping the gun leveled in his right, and jammed the door open with his whole body.

He'd expected to see someone on the other side, had even cursed himself for leaving his Kevlar bulletproof vest in the car in his haste. To his surprise, the bedroom was completely empty. He walked gingerly over to the bathroom. The door sat wide open, inviting him to enter into his potential doom. He crossed through the entrance of the stark white room and rocketed looks each way, only to find it desolate as well.

Back in the bedroom again, he found the door to the closet slightly ajar. Martin crossed the room and swung the door open only to find a tightly packed space of coats, jeans, dresses and shoes on the shelving of the small closet.

Martin returned to the living room and made the short trek to the narrow galley kitchen. He turned to his left as he entered and, as he now suspected, saw nothing. At that last check, he finally relaxed a bit as he told himself it was all clear. He re-holstered his weapon and took a deep breath as he entered back into the living room.

As he came back in, trying to slow his heart down that was practically exploding from his chest, he noticed something he hadn't seen when he first entered, primarily since his focus had been on not getting shot at the time. The apartment was clean. No, it was spotless.

"What the hell," he said aloud as he panned his view around the room. There was no doubt about it. Someone had been in here and cleaned up the wreckage that it had been put into and he was absolutely certain it hadn't been anyone from the police or crime scene division. No, he thought, someone came in here to clean up the job. The furniture was back in place, papers were no longer strewn all over the place, trash no longer littered the floor and the broken television that had fallen from the stand in the corner was gone.

It was then that the thought occurred to him. "Shit," he said to no one. That meant the casing was probably gone too.

He quickly got his bearings and positioned himself as he had seen in the picture. He imagined where the picture had been taken from near the window and noted where the light would have been coming from to shine down onto the casing. Knowing the sun had changed positions, once he got to what he believed to be the spot, he began shifting to the side slowly to see if he could catch a glimmer of hope, though his confidence had been significantly reduced by the cleaned surroundings.

As if accompanied by a choir of angels singing hallelujah, just then he saw a flash. He shifted slightly back to where he was a second prior and saw it then as clear as day. It was behind the leg of the coat rack and slightly hidden by a raincoat that extended nearly to the ground.

He nearly sprinted over to the spot and bent down. When he did, though, he was struck with a strong pang of confusion and disappointment. What he saw was not a bullet casing. It was half of a set of cuff links. He picked up the single piece and noted that it was no regular article. By the look of the gold of the piece and the lettering, which was in a ruby stone, these were custom-made and undoubtedly extremely expensive.

He examined it more closely and noted the letters to be two A's which were the same size but intertwined in a fashion where one of the letters sat slightly over the other as if the second were a shadow of the first. The letters themselves were in a sort of old-english calligraphy style giving the already impressive piece an extremely elegant look.

Martin was absolutely puzzled but knew there had to be something to it. He pulled out his cell phone that was equipped, as almost any phone was these days, with a high-resolution digital camera. He snapped a picture of the cufflink and sent it off in a message to Broussard who he hoped was back at the office and could hop on the computer to see if he could find anything out about the piece.

He hit speed dial on the phone once he confirmed that the picture was sent successfully and Broussard answered the office line on the second ring, "Officer Broussard."

"Shit, great, Noelle. You're still there."

Recognizing Martin's voice, his partner replied, "Where the hell are you Martin? The big wigs are out here asking what you're doin?"

"I'm at Blanche's apartment and the damn place has been wiped clean. It's spotless."

"I know…that's what I'm trying to tell you. The officer that was watching the place is MIA. He disappeared right after he checked in for his shift and told dispatch the same fuckin' thing. I've been trying to call you for the last fifteen minutes."

Martin looked down on his phone, which he'd put on silent earlier and saw the dozen or so missed calls in the log. But instead of answering Noelle, he asked, "Did you get the picture I just sent to your cell phone?"

There was a pause on the other end and then Noelle said, "Is that a cufflink? So what?"

"The object I thought I saw in the picture wasn't a bullet casing, it was that. The place is clean but it was pretty well hidden. They must have just missed it somehow."

"That could be anyone's Martin. Boyfriend, friend…you name it. It doesn't tell us anything."

"Look closely at that thing Noelle. If Blanche had people visiting her that could pay for something like that…well…let's just say she wouldn't be living in this place. It's gotta be worth over a grand. For goddamned cufflinks! If we can figure out who's they are, we may have an idea of who killed Blanche."

Before he could hear Broussard's response, the phone was ripped out of his hand and he felt the cold of steel that was unmistakably a gun pressed against his right temple. Ice ran through Martin's veins as he realized that the circumference of the pistol was flat and rounded not in the way the end of a gun typically was. He would have bet money on the fact that the gun had a silencer attached to the end of it and anyone taking the time to add that to their gun did so because they planned to use it.

A rough voice said into the phone, "Say goodbye to your partner Mr. Broussard. I suggest you ignore what he sent you unless you would like to join him." What that, he snapped the phone shut not waiting for a response from Noelle.

The man slipped the phone into his jacket pocket and then used the now free hand to take Martin's sidearm as well.

"Wouldn't want you getting any crazy ideas," the voice growled into his ear and Martin felt a jolt of fear rocket through his body. His mind searched for any way out and, in its panic, also scanned furiously to figure out where the man had come from. He then realized his fatal error. He hadn't checked the fire escape out of the window. He couldn't remember if the window had been open but then rocked his mind back because he realized it didn't matter. He had to figure a way out of what was quickly seeming to be a situation with little window of hope.

"Who are you?" Martin asked, wishing he could think of something better.

"You can just consider me the janitor who's cleaning up a little mess. You shouldn't have come here Officer." His tone was calm and steely, as if he were responding to a simple inquiry about the weather. It petrified Martin even more.

He tried a different approach, "Do you realize what kind of hunt will be out for you if you kill an officer of the Prefect of Police? Do you really want that kind of attention?"

"I do not but you and your clever discovery...clearly an oversight on my part which I'll have to rectify in the future...have given me no choice. I can't have you running around town trying to figure out what you found. Furthermore, how can I make sure your fat partner who, let's be honest, isn't difficult to scare, doesn't attempt to seek revenge for his long-time friend and partner? Now what message would I be sending him if I merely let you walk away?"

Martin was desperate now, "I'll drop it. It's not worth it to me. Listen. Whoever it is you're working for, whatever it is your doing, it's not worth losing my life. I can walk away just as much as Noelle will. As a matter of fact, not killing me would give you someone out there making sure that he doesn't go rogue and try to do it anyway. Please."

"I'm not worried about your lazy partner, Mr. Martin. Your attempt at sincerity, while touching and nearly moving to me, rings false. I know your professional track record and, sadly for you, it is commendable. No, Ferdinand, you would not drop this and that is something I simply cannot afford."

Before Martin could respond, the sound came.

Pfft.

It was soft and deadly and, in an instant, Ferdinand Martin was gone.

Chapter 41

Alani pulled the car up to the front of the building and two attendants dressed in suits with shirts but no ties, the epitome of the Italian style of classy yet not overdone, emerged seemingly out of thin air. Each was at Alani's and Kyler's doors respectively before the car even settled into its complete stop. The finely appointed man that came to Kyler's door's rescue, heaven forbid he open it himself for once, he thought, was well-built. He wasn't stocky in a body builder sort of way but, rather in a, save for a better term Kyler concluded, a militaristic way. Muscles built for use rather than appeal. At roughly six foot even, he was of notable physique, which Scott didn't fail to take in.

"Bonjorno signore," military man greeted him in eloquent, refined Italian. "Dare il benvenuto al Santini di Villa."

We'll see just how long we are welcome, Kyler thought but instead responded by saying, "Grazie. Siamo grati per essere qui."

He then looked across the car at the interaction taking place. More specifically, he took note of the other attendant's make up as well, and he didn't mean the Cover Girl variety. He was, like his own greeter, of an athletic build and carried a striking resemblance to Jason Statham, the actor not to mention friend of Kyler's. Jason was not a guy that ought be categorized as purely a Hollywood movie fighter. He, in his own right, was the real deal but from the looks of Alani's new friend, he wouldn't last ten seconds in the ring with this guy. Beneath the smooth exterior of Mr. Hospitality extraordinaire, Kyler was certain there was a trained killer.

If this is what all of the staff looked like, they were going to certainly have their hands full.

Then, the Statham look-alike asked in strikingly perfect English, "May we assist you with your bags Ms. Gannon? Mr. Scott?" he asked looking from Alani and then over to Kyler. Kyler realized that the root of the question likely came from the fact that Alani had not popped open the trunk for their access. That, of course, had been intentional.

Alani chimed in, opting for her charm to offset the suspicion of the response. They were, after all, at what could only be classified as a five-star establishment and were celebrities to boot, one real and one fictitious.

To ease any concern, Alani gently touched the man's arm and said, "Oh thank you very much but Mr. Scott over there enjoys his own bit of chivalry." She had made the gesture complete with a smile and a slight nod over in his direction though never taking her penetrating eyes off of good old Statham.

"He prefers to carry our things. He says it keeps him 'grounded.'"

At that, she made the familiar air quotes with her long fingers, letting her hands careen down onto the man's shoulders. She then leaned in slightly and semi-whispered as if confiding in the man that had her full and undivided attention.

"You know…big Hollywood actor and all."

It was a passable excuse at best, but the attendant was mesmerized enough by Alani's little act and her engaging touch that he didn't much care what the reason was. As a matter of fact, he probably hadn't even heard it.

As if on cue and not giving the customer-first trained men an opportunity to overrule his decision, Kyler made a beeline for the trunk while Alani reached down and hit the button for him, taking her time in doing so to keep up the distraction of Statham.

Kyler first slung the bag over his shoulder that housed all of the items that he wanted to make sure the two-man wrecking crew didn't pick up a scent on. Once that was in his possession, he breathed a little easier and pulled out the other two rolling suitcases that housed their personal effects for the weekend. He was able to easily handle the carry-along as well as the two suitcases, one rolling behind him from each arm.

His own attendant, who'd been observing his cohort with envy wishing that he'd strode to Alani's door rather than Kyler's, snapped back into form when he noticed that his guest had his hands full. He rushed to the back of the car and had his hand on the trunk in seconds, closing it while he quickly added an apology, clearly embarrassed by his own distraction and thus lack of attention to his duties. Kyler again thought the man had to be from a military background since the intentionally coifed man appeared ready to chastise himself for his lapse.

Kyler smiled sincerely and added, "No need to apologize. Usually people seem to be one step away from wiping my ass for me. It's nice to do something for myself from time to time."

The man flinched a bit at the comment but it seemed to ease his mind a bit. He then extended his hand toward the arched dual oak doors that represented the entrance to the grand building.

"Please sir, follow me. Mr. Vitale Baldacci awaits your arrival. He is our…direttore di un hotel and would like very much to welcome you to Villa Santini."

"Grazie, signore. Your hospitality precedes itself."

Kyler once again remarked how impressive the man's English was. There was the ever-present Italian accent that could never be avoided as a native, but the command of the language and pronunciation was perfect. He wondered what would cause him to need such a skill.

At the sound of his partner's voice, the Statham look-a-like snapped back into reality to the task at hand, flushing slightly with embarrassment at the wonderment he'd been lost in momentarily. He extended his hand toward the door as well.

"Please follow Mr. Scott. It is my pleasure to take care of your car. Should you need, please do not hesitate to contact the main desk and we will bring the car up for you whenever necessary. Please enjoy your stay at Villa Santini."

With that, Alani gave the man a small kiss on the cheek, freezing him in place once again.

"Grazie, signore. I have no doubt that we will have an enlightening weekend."

At that, she turned fluidly toward the door and followed Kyler to the entrance, giving him a little wink as she joined his side and then a raise of an eyebrow. He knew she was thinking what he had been. That their tag-team effort had certainly worked but they were going to need to be at the top of their game this weekend to make sure it continued to.

Chapter 42

As the massive dark oak doors opened up by the hand of the Statham attendant, Kyler thought that he could hear classical music playing from the famous Italian composer, Giovanni Gabriel, best known for his sacred compositions for the church of San Marco in Venice. The grandiose doors opened, cueing the strike of the elaborate and ominous organ. That was followed by beautiful voices of a choir singing O Magnum Mysterium as the entrance to the interior came into view for Alani and Kyler. At that, Kyler was reminded how much his life was intertwined with movies. Even this part of his life would be accompanied by a soundtrack.

As they stepped across the threshold of the castle's entrance, and sticking with the musical interlude, Kyler heard a choir erupting into a rich melody of hallelujahs that was supported with the quick notes of light organ and beautiful pulls of a full ensemble of strings. The music of his mind continued as he took in his surroundings. To his left and right sides were smatterings of strategically placed large Renaissance-style wingback chairs that sat atop beautiful tapestries of large rugs to warm up the cold of the castle's stone floor. Within the spread of the chairs were ornate oak coffee tables as well as end tables on which tall brass lamps sat that were topped with elaborate shades that hung pearls around its bottom edges. There were a few guests of the Villa Santini seated quietly around the area, all of whom held large glasses of red wine that they occasionally drew from appreciatively while stopping to comment to one another on, no doubt, the fine nature of the libation.

On each side of the lobby, the seating areas presented a backdrop of 15th century stone walls which also held an occasional tapestry and appropriately spaced sconces that floated candles, all of which were lit providing the most intimate of illumination. The picture of the quintessential retreat into centuries gone by was completed on each side with an elaborate stone fireplace that was seemingly large enough for Kyler to walk into. It held a tall stand for the wood that burned within, kicking up a sizeable fire, which was protected from the surroundings by an almost equally tall wrought-iron cover.

The music in his mind kicked up into a joyful musical interlude of violins as he observed more of the visitors sitting beside the fire, again, glass in hand, talking lightly and laughing pleasantly as if they didn't have a care in the world. The scene pulled Kyler into a trance of longing, wishing to share in their blithe enjoyment.

Forcing his eyes away, he looked upward which carried his view to what seemed to be two, maybe three stories of the overall castle height. The ceiling reached its peaks from the left and the right sides via oak beams that appeared to be at least two feet in width. Large chandeliers hung at spaced out points in the beams that were clearly newer than much of the surroundings, possibly only a century old, with the advent of electricity. They cast a moderate level of illumination, serving more as an aide to the light provided on the ground level of the room.

Kyler's mind's song built perfectly with the quickening pace of the strings playing frantically. The organ climbed its steady crescendo to one final note while the choir hit a harmonious closing chord as the entrance door closed behind them in perfect timing. Kyler's gaze settled in front of him on the man he knew to be Vitale Baldacci who'd just hit the bottom of the elaborate staircase in front of them. The music ended in perfect time and Kyler thought how the revered composer, Hans Zimmerman, who seemed to be all things film, would have been proud to score the entrance.

"Signore Kyler Scott and Signora Grace Gannon, si?"

Baldacci strode powerfully over to them with an outstretched hand. Vitale wore a perfectly appointed suit that, like Dimarco, had no doubt been handmade specifically for the wealthy Italian. Similar to the picture they had reviewed during their drive, his hair was thick, straight and combed back neatly though now showing just the beginning touches of grey at its edges.

The handshake was deceptively powerful. It was a stark contrast to his seemingly soft, meager, well-manicured hands. Kyler returned the strength of the grip.

"Grazie. And you, I presume, are Mr. Vitale Baldacci and owner of this beautiful establishment?" Kyler knew he was only its caretaker and not its owner but flattery and exaggeration never hurt a situation in his experience.

"Sadly, I am not the owner of Villa Santini. I have merely been given the dubious honor of being its manager. It's senior concierge if you will. It is my duty and my pleasure to look after the surroundings, keep our fine winery up to our highest of quality standards and to ensure our lovely guests are treated with the utmost luxury."

Kyler was mesmerized with how Dimarco had rounded up such an abundant cast of characters that had an absolute refinement of eloquence, hospitality and intelligence to accompany impressive physical and mental strength. It made for a frightening combination. There was little mystery why so many of Italy's people feared his power. It appeared to be unmatched and extremely well thought out.

"Well we have to thank you for making space for us on such short notice. My agent informed me that you are the most sought-after hotel within two hundred kilometers and most of your guests' visits are planned months in advance. So I understand that you must have made arrangements with other guests to open up space for our trip. We greatly appreciate it and can't wait to enjoy everything the Villa Santini has to offer." So there, Kyler thought. Two can play the eloquence game.

Vitale smiled warmly at that, "We are happy to accommodate and are particularly honored to have someone so famous stay with us. We've all seen your movies Mr. Scott. There is much excitement among the staff to have you here. But do not fear...I have instructed the staff to allow you your privacy during your stay here. Discretion is of the utmost importance at Villa Santini." As he said this he glanced at Alani, clearly not having been briefed on who she was supposed to be.

Kyler wondered how much of what he said was true. He suspected that a man like Baldacci had minimal interest in Hollywood, movies or actors. Would he even know who Kyler Scott or Scott Cruz was, much less have taken to time to see his movies? Kyler guessed he hadn't but pegged Baldacci as a smart businessman. The hotel manager, or possibly one of his staff members, would have spent a few minutes on the Internet and quickly discovered Kyler's impressive standing in the film industry. He would have to be an imbecile to not recognize the advertising potential in having Scott stay at the bed and breakfast. And Vitale Baldacci was definitely *not* an imbecile.

"I appreciate the gesture Mr. Baldacci."

"Please, call me Vitale. Only my staff calls me Mr. Baldacci," with that, he smiled and gave a little wink in Alani's direction.

Ugh, Kyler thought. Him too?

Carrying on, "Agreed but only if you call me Kyler. Only my agent, my staff, my butler, my personal assistant, my driver and my barista call me Mr. Scott."

With that he gave Baldacci a laugh and a good-ole-boy pat on the shoulder to which Baldacci responded with a hearty laugh in return. Friends already, Kyler thought.

Alani chimed in, "And everyone else calls him diva, over-actor, jack-ass and no-talent-hack."

"But my friends...my friends call me Kyler." Scott finished, taking the dig in stride.

More laughing ensued at that.

"Anyway, Vitale, I'd like to return the favor of your hospitality and would be happy to take any pictures with you or your staff, sign anything you'd like…whatever may help you in the future. Not sure if it'll do you harm or good though." Ever the self-deprecator: Mr. Kyler Scott.

"And I presume you are familiar with Ms. Grace Gannon, musician extraordinaire back in the states."

Mirroring Dimarco's response from a few nights ago, Vitale nodded furiously. There seemed to be a bit of hidden anger likely targeted toward his staff that'd failed to add this information during his preparation for his guests' arrival.

"But of course! We are deeply honored as well. I'm told that your music is incredibly popular in America. Sadly, we are out here in the middle of the mountains and don't get much of the music that's out there."

Man these guys were good, Kyler thought. He covered the lie and didn't even miss a beat.

Alani reached graciously for Baldacci's hand and said, "You are too kind and Mr. Scott here exaggerates my success." She leaned in and gave Vitale the customary two-cheek kiss greeting.

"I'm sure much of it is true but clearly Mr. Scott…I mean, Kyler, is quite the gentleman. You, may I say Ms. Gannon are a…bellezza di sbalordire. So beautiful. Bella Bella."

"Grazie, signore. It's kind of you to say."

Breaking up the love fest that had gone on long enough, Kyler said, "I don't mean to be rude, but could you please direct us toward our room? We would love to settle in, unpack our things and change clothes."

"Of course, of course," at that Vitale snapped his fingers at a bellhop and said, "Portare questi alla loro stanza," pointing to the bags behind Kyler and Alani.

The dutiful bellhop first reached for the bag slung over Kyler's shoulder, which he suddenly clutched tightly and said, somewhat hurriedly, "Please, I can handle this," then adding toward Vitale while flicking his eyes toward Alani, one guy to another, "I just have some…private items in here that I'd like to keep to myself."

Kyler knew it was an awful and somewhat roguish offering of an excuse but Vitale seemed to enjoy the thought of what it might be and, in particular, how his newfound attraction of Alani might be involved. Kyler felt embarrassed for the ruse, particularly on Alani's behalf but it was the best he could come up with on the fly.

"Solo portare quei due," Vitale said to the man, pointing toward the two rolling suitcases. And then to Kyler and Alani, "Please follow Alonzo. He will show you to your room. Feel free to join us here in the lobby for wine tasting anytime. Day or night. We will always be here to serve you. You may call down to the concierge to make arrangements with our ristorante for dinner. You may also find my lead concierge, Carmen, who can make any arrangements you wish for the weekend. We usually have group tours of the grounds but it would be our honor to set up a much more private tour for you whenever you like."

Perfect, Kyler thought. Just as he'd hoped.

"That would be marvelous Vitale." Extending his hand to end the conversation he said, "I won't keep you any longer. I'm sure you're a busy man. Buona sera, Vitale."

"Buona sera signore, signora," Vitale repeated the double kiss, this time for both, stepped aside and extended his hand toward the stairs that led undoubtedly to their room.

Kyler smiled as he passed thinking how things were aligning just according to plan.

Chapter 43

Jack Hawkins heard it first and then felt the throbbing in his head that seemed to beat twice with each pound of his heart. At first he couldn't even think of opening his eyes but then his survival instincts and desire to figure out where the hell he was took over. His senses were on overload and it smelled like a combination of sweat, machinery and stale air. His hands were bound behind him to the chair he was sitting in, a thought that had interestingly not registered in his brain until just then. He attributed the oversight to the overbearing thumping in his skull that left his mind in a dizzying haze.

As he fluttered his eyes open, his brain started remembering flashes again. The difficult act of getting his eyes to open combined with the darkness that settled in reminded him of waking up on the plane, though he had no idea how long ago that could have been. He had a brief moment of panic as he realized that despite any initial hopes that he was in the middle of a bad dream and would soon wake up in his California King bed back home in Palo Alto, this was indeed real. He didn't know where this was but it was most certainly not home.

More flashes came back to him again, remembering when he must have been abducted and then, more importantly, remembering how he'd managed to trigger his beacon bracelet on the plane just before getting knocked out again.

The thought brought him a glimmer of hope as he prayed aloud that his government connections would pay off. Yes, he thought, they would notice that he was missing, someone would decide to search his house and, ultimately, notice the homing signal he was sending out. His heart sank, however, as he realized they would have had to do that within four hours of activating the device before the battery on the bracelet wore out. He cursed himself for not having thought of upgrading it to the Rolex style, known for its ability to use a person's kinetic energy of movement to self-charge.

While he tried to keep hope, his logical brain reminded him that he didn't even know how long he'd been out the last time and, for all he knew, four hours had already come and gone.

His thoughts were interrupted abruptly as a single light popped on over his head sending his eyes into a frenzy as they attempted to adjust to the stark change. In the meantime, he heard a door open and close, immediately followed by the hard sound of what he imagined to be dress shoes walking toward him. He could have mistaken them for heels but the debate was quickly settled when the man's voice came at him from the darkness.

"Mr. Jack Hawkins," the voice said with amusement.

Hawkins, not the mark of calm, frantically responded, "Who are you? What am I doing here? Let me go! Do you know the types of people that will be looking for me?"

To Jack's surprise and horror, the man merely returned an amused laugh at his rant.

He then cooly replied, "As a matter of fact, those people, Mr. Hawkins, are exactly why you are here."

Hawkins now noted a distinct Italian accent in the man's voice and then put a face with it as Armand Amici emerged into the radius of light around his chair. He stopped just as he came into view, and cocked his head slightly to assess his prisoner. Amici stood there waiting to see if Hawkins, albeit very unlikely, had any notion of who he was. After a few more seconds, he concluded that he did not.

"Mr. Hawkins, my name is Armand Amici. While you clearly do not know who I am, I most certainly know who you are."

Ever the social misfit with no filter on what comes out of his mouth, Hawkins said, "Congratulations. That means you are of average intelligence along with a million other people in the world who have picked up a Forbes Magazine in the last several years. As you probably noted, I am a genius and monumentally rich. I don't see what that has to do with me being here! Which, by the way, do you mind telling me where the hell here is?!"

Rather than getting angry, Amici merely laughed again, clearly amused by the famed computer geek's personality.

"You are quite right Mr. Hawkins. If I were merely to have seen you on the cover of Forbes, Fortune or Tech World Magazine and remembered your name and face, I would indeed be, as you say, merely of moderate intelligence. I would also be only moderately informed as well."

There was something in the way Amici had said it all that sent a chill down Jack's spine.

Amici continued, seeming to enjoy the process, "But what I believe puts me in a very small minority," he sneered a bit at that. "What makes my particular position very unique is that I am one of a very select few who know exactly how you *became* famous, Mr. Hawkins."

Though few people matched Jack's technical wit, most surpassed him in the way of common sense and awareness. "Again, I don't understand what is remotely distinguishable about that. I am a computer developer and analyst. I'm the best in the world actually. I'm not being arrogant, just honest. You can ask anyone in my field and they'll agree with that statement. After all, when I was only 15, I was hired by every bank you can think of after I broke into every single one of their supposedly 'secure' databases. Not like I wanted the money. I didn't want to go to jail and who's going to put me in jail merely for doing them a favor. Instead, I posted a message on every teller's computer that said 'Jack Hawkins was here and you're lucky your money is too.'"

Jack laughed awkwardly, even snorting a bit as he recalled the story.

Amici, of course, knew all of this already. He also knew that the FBI had raided Hawkins' home immediately following the incident. Despite Jack's apparent innocent view on the act, no bank institution is going to take lightly to a teenage hacker commandeering their financial systems with carte blanch control. Ultimately, they only levied a probation charge on him in the end. After all, by putting his damn name on the screen, he clearly wasn't on a covert mission to steal all of their money.

As it turned out, the courts came up with a rare and productive solution to the matter. In the form of community service, Hawkins was mandated to work not only for the corporate banks he'd threatened but for the likes of various government divisions. Jack Hawkins was the only person in history to issue himself the highest level of security clearance, albeit an act by request of the CIA as a test and one that was immediately removed. As a result, they were able to correct the security hole that Hawkins had exposed.

Amici also knew that after, and even during, his probationary period, various government agencies and defense contractors alike began paying Hawkins generous sums of money for his knowledge and assistance. He developed ironclad algorithms for the firewalls that were supposed to protect intrusions from the world's best hackers that were trying to break into America's national databases. Information that, if compromised, would provide details about troops' locations, weapons information, air and sea travel plans of the various armed forces divisions and a number of other vulnerabilities that could leave America exposed to any number of possible attacks.

But while all of that was a nice American success story to Armand Amici, what piqued his interest was a piece of intellectual property that did not end up in any of the magazines. At least not with Hawkins' named tied to it.

"Your accolades with the American government and banks are of no interest to me," Amici said flatly and then stared at him with a glimmer in his eye. "You are here because of your QTS Tek project. I believe you called it Project Hawkins' Gates?"

At that, Jack Hawkins' mouth dropped and the blood disappeared from his face. Nobody but he and a select few had even known the name of the project let alone his involvement in it. For this complete stranger to know and have kidnapped him put an earth-shattering level of fear into him. This Armand Amici clearly had some very powerful connections. While Jack wasn't sure exactly what the man wanted, he was fairly certain he wasn't going to like it.

Chapter 44

Dr. Ethan Goldman had not slept particularly well the previous night, as was the case on many nights as the director of the Central Intelligence Agency. He had been particularly put off by the call from Ian Collins regarding Ellen Stratton and was not, and hadn't been since the news broke, comfortable with her connection to a defense contractor that they worked so closely with. He couldn't be certain that she was purely a victim in the incident, though all signs thus far had pointed in that direction. Even if she was impervious to any intentional wrongdoing, her case of amnesia coupled with her highly sensitive knowledge that accompanied her occupation could be equally damaging.

It was those concerns that spurred him to return the favor of an off-hours call back to Collins; a five o'clock wake-up call to request a meeting first thing in the morning at Langley. He needed to assess QTS Tek as whole now. Needed to question everything. His instructions to his agent last night to use all means necessary to find what he could on Stratton would settle the story on her but his sleepless night was due in part to his overwhelming need to clear the defense contractor as a whole before he continued to use their resources in this increasingly confusing mission.

Like Goldman the night before, Collins was not exactly pleased about the disturbance and was even less enthusiastic about making the drive from Maryland into McLean for a seven o'clock sit-down with the director. The reality, however, was that at the end of the day, it was Goldman and a select few other clients that accounted for his considerable paycheck leaving him little choice in the matter.

When Collins had asked for more details on the meeting, Goldman remained vague expressing concerns about some information they had uncovered on Ellen Stratton.

The good doctor had gotten into his office around six that morning, delivered his ass-chewing to Kyler before their arrival to Villa Santini, gave them their marching orders and then proceeded to review the files he had on Ellen Stratton, Camille Blanche, Jacques Francois, Jack Hawkins and now, as he'd recently learned, Ferdinand Martin. The body count was piling up and he had very little idea who was doing the stockpiling.

They all wanted to believe Dimarco was at the center of it all. It sort of fit with the statement on the message sent to Andrei. *Mass chaos.* On the flip side, Goldman knew that a few deaths and a couple kidnappings, despite their ties to government agencies, in and of themselves did not equate to *mass chaos.* But it was the coincidental timing of *when* the incidents began. Stratton's story broke less than twenty-four hours after they'd received the message. Add the fact that there were certainly truths these individuals could produce and it made even more sense to tie them to Dimarco.

Playing devil's advocate, as Goldman re-read the message, it clearly indicated that it was *Andrei* who was specifically aiding this so-called truth. There had also been no indications of any activity out of the North Koreans other than the regular rumble of unrest, though they had certainly increased their surveillance since the message arrived.

Goldman decided to focus in on the victims. There were certainly connections between them and he tried to put together what little he had. Ellen Stratton and Jacques Francois both had a peculiar case of amnesia in the face of violent acts. They were similar in their affiliations to government employment, specifically the intelligence branch. But then there was the big piece that didn't match. Francois was dead and Stratton was not. Not yet, at least. All the more reason to justify his surveillance of

Stratton. It was for her protection. Sounded good at least, Goldman decided. Both did have access to military secrets and their respective controlling parties were keeping both of their identities under wraps. Enter the real reason he was trailing her. Was there more to know? Maybe.

Then there was Camille Blanche and Ferdinand Martin who seemed, at least for the moment, to be casualties by association. Reasonably, Goldman could only ascertain that someone had discovered the relationship between Blanche and Francois, as Goldman's team had easily done, and had murdered her for the same reasons they'd beaten and eventually killed him. Clearly Francois had information that someone deemed worth eliminating him for. Considering the free flowing nature of pillow talk between two new lovers, Ethan feared that he'd shared that same information with Blanche. Hence, she had to die as well. The only one Goldman didn't have a theory on yet was Officer Martin. His only connection was his investigation of the murders, which was enough to consider more than just a coincidence. He just wasn't sure what it might be. What had he uncovered about Francois or Blanche that was worth killing for? Had he uncovered the killer? He filed that in the category of possible.

Hawkins' similarities were the obvious. He, like Stratton, was affiliated to QTS. Like Stratton and Francois, he had access to more secrets then Goldman wanted to think about. The fear factor with Hawkins was exponential in comparison because of what he'd invented and Goldman suddenly thought back to the message from Andrei and paled. *Andrei aiding truth.* Hawkins's invention could certainly give access to "truths". The iris scanner itself wasn't exactly a threat though because its value was in the databases it accessed. Hawkins did not have access to those databases. It had been a clause that Jack had agreed to as part of his invention. QTS as well as Goldman knew that Hawkins could easily find his way into the databases but had convinced him that, for his own protection, it was in his best interest to silo himself from that information so he could avoid being a target. So much for that, Goldman huffed. Goldman's only explanation for his kidnapping, which was also unique in its modus operandi of both Stratton's and Francois's incidents, was that someone believed Hawkins did have access to those databases and viewed him as their way in.

That mounted a new level of fear in Goldman. What would his kidnappers do to him when they found out he couldn't get them what they wanted? On a global scale, Goldman asked the real question driving the whole mission. What did they want to do with that information if they got to it?

Gianni Dimarco had been on any number of watchlists over the years. Not just for the United States, but for several of its Allies, including Dimarco's own country of Italy. There were many stories, though they were never fully corroborated, suggesting his potential dealings with high-level officials in China, Iraq, Afghanistan and, yes, North Korea. Not exactly countries any of the allies wanted a man with that much power, wealth and influence to be strategizing with. With his reputation of ruthlessness and an appetite for power, he was a dangerous man. Plain and simple.

Even before Andrei had sent his now-infamous wine bottle, Dimarco had been elevated on Goldman and the agency's radar when he opened a large warehouse facility on the outskirts of Florence. When questioned by the Italian government of its purpose, he explained that his clothing business was planning expansion and he needed a larger facility to accommodate the demand. At the same time, he began hiring more known ex-military from Italy's Special Forces divisions for seemingly innocuous jobs. Valets, warehouse managers, waiters and employees of his winery. Then comes the message and cue in the domino effect of the rest.

Just then, his phone rang and Goldman noted it was from Debbie Ratner, his secretary. Thanks to Goldman and his propensity for long hours, she had been forced to come in early. It was something he knew she'd grown accustomed to when working for a man like him, but he still felt guilty for it nonetheless. Government workers worked a lot harder than the stereotypes would lead people to believe.

"Hello Debbie," Goldman said into the handset after hitting the speakerphone button. "I'm assuming Mr. Collins has arrived?"

"Yes sir, just a moment ago. Shall I send him in?"

"Yes but please offer Mr. Collins some coffee. I'm sure I don't have to tell you that it's an early one for us all," Goldman said.

Debbie responded with a small laugh and said, "I will be sure to offer him some of the agency's finest coffee."

Goldman cringed at the thought. Starbucks they were not.

"On second thought, maybe not," Goldman joked.

Debbie offered up another laugh and said, "Mr. Collins is on his way in sir."

"Thank you Debbie."

With that, he hit the button once more on the phone and organized some of the files he'd scattered on his desk. No need to give Collins a free glance at anything that was above his pay grade.

Goldman's door opened to first reveal a fiftyish sprite of a woman with short graying hair that was styled in what Ethan described as spiky. Debbie had worked for Goldman for the last ten years and, while she seemed to continually shrink in height, she grew in vigor as she was tasked with protecting the hundreds of people constantly vying for his time on a daily basis. You did not get to Ethan Goldman without going through Debbie. That she made sure of. And you did not get through Debbie without a damn good reason.

Having a life partner named Phyllis, there was absolutely no romantic connection between Debbie and Ethan but one thing was sure. Ethan loved the woman. She was his rock far more than his ex-wife had ever been and he trusted her implicitly.

All five foot two inches of Debbie turned to the side to allow a man, who was not much taller, to enter. Ethan could only assume it to be Ian Collins.

"Dr. Goldman. Ian Collins," he said as he stuck out an extremely thick hand towards Ethan. As he took it, Ethan thought that man could crush every bone in his own with just a slight squeeze and he was glad that the handshake was brief.

"Pleasure to meet you Mr. Collins. Thank you for coming out at this early hour. Please have a seat," Goldman gestured toward the two chairs angled in front of his desk.

He then turned to Debbie, "Thanks Debbie. Please hold my calls."

"Yes sir," and with that, she was gone.

The thickness of Ian Collins' hands extended into the rest of his build. What the man lacked in height, pushing five foot five inches tall on a good day, he made up for in bulk. Everything about him was thick. His arms looked like they were going to bust through his dress shirt and he wondered how he had found a collar wide enough to accommodate his tree trunk of a neck. The man was one wide solid muscle and, for a moment, Ethan wondered if he would even fit into what he thought was a fairly normal sized chair.

Goldman's concerns were put to rest as Collins miraculously melded into the chair with seemingly little difficulty.

Still mesmerized by the man, he was a bit startled when Ian asked, "So what is this about? I don't mean to be frank but you weren't exactly forthcoming on the phone Dr. Goldman."

"Please, it's early enough, call me Ethan."

"Fair enough. Well, Ethan, can you tell me a little more about why I dragged my ass across the beltway from Maryland to Virginia at the wee hours of the morning?"

The man got to the point in a way that seemed to correspond perfectly with his physique. Aggressive and strong.

Temporarily avoiding the question, Goldman asked, "Did you want any coffee Ian? I recognize it's a bit early and I know you didn't sleep a great deal."

"Dr. Goldman, let's just cut to the chase here, why don't we?" Ian was clearly annoyed and quite possibly a bit cranky. "We are both incredibly busy men and so I'd prefer to skirt the niceties and talk about whatever it was you couldn't ask me over the phone. You and I both know that I wouldn't even be here right now if it wasn't for the fact that your agency is largely responsible for the reasonably substantial paycheck I receive. However, that also means I am responsible for the security within QTS Tek that directly corresponds to your agency as well as the other agencies we support. I don't have time to talk about the weather over coffee."

Goldman held a face that gave away nothing but was amused by the fact that he had gotten under the man's skin so quickly. He realized he'd read Collins correctly. He figured that, if he could continue to stall a bit longer, the man would soon become impatient and more willing to offer up information that would end their meeting and allow Goldman to continue putting the pieces together on this puzzle.

At that, Goldman said, "It's interesting that you bring that up Mr. Collins. I'd like to know how much information you are sharing with other agencies and, more specifically, how certain I can be that information gathered for the CIA isn't also disseminated to our friends over at the NSA, Homeland Securities and the FBI. The public would like to believe we're always working together as one big happy family but, let's not be coy. We still hold a certain amount close to the vest. What the public doesn't understand is that there is also security in compartmentalizing. When the same information traverses multiple groups, it can increase the opportunity for leaks."

Goldman knew that, for reasons of their own reputation, QTS Tek would treat all information gathered with ultimate discretion. He also knew that Ian Collins would hold this information as sacred more than any other employee and that a challenge to the integrity of that information would be a direct strike against his responsibilities as the Director of Security for the company.

As expected, Collins' face grew a fiery red with anger but his words that came in response were of practiced control.

"I can assure you, Ethan, that QTS Tek treats *all* information gathered from all of the organizations we deal with the utmost discretion. I would challenge you to find any other company that takes as much pride in its integrity as ours. Furthermore, I have personal responsibility to ensure that that continues."

Right where he wanted him, Goldman thought to himself.

"If that's the case, then what interest would some of our perceived enemies have in people like Ellen Stratton and Jack Hawkins? Both conveniently treated as independent contractors for your organization? How would anyone outside our circles even know what information they hold to deem them as a viable path of access into our secrets?"

Goldman could tell that this took him by surprise. He may have expected something like that in relation to Stratton but he undoubtedly hadn't expected Hawkins' name to come out. Primarily because Goldman had made sure that very few knew that Hawkins had disappeared. With Jack's lack of personal ties, this was relatively easy to do. He wanted to use the element of surprise to rule out the possibility that QTS may be double-dealing information, particularly considering the level of sensitive material they were dealing with. This concern was at a maximum since QTS was aware of the operation Kyler and Alani were currently undertaking. The last thing he needed was for his best agents to be ambushed by a capitalistic defense contractor selling information to the highest bidder…particularly if that bidder was Gianni Dimarco.

"Jack Hawkins? He is not in the employment of QTS Tek. As a matter of fact, I understand he is on your payroll if anything."

Collins had shifted his crossed legs while he said this, which didn't go unnoticed by Goldman in the least.

"Cut the shit Ian. Do you think I'm a fucking idiot? Really. I want to know the answer to that question. Do you think I, Ethan Goldman, Director of the Central Intelligence Agency for this country am a complete fucking moron?"

Collins' tough exterior wavered a bit. Goldman had that affect on just about anyone. There were previous presidents who feared the man to such an extent that they avoided dealing with him whenever possible.

Collins replied, "No Ethan. Sir. Of course not."

"Excellent. I'm glad. So," Goldman continued, "by the assumption that I'm not an imbecile, we should then assume that I am fully aware of the background of those individuals that the CIA elects to employ. Correct again?"

"I would expect you to fully vet those individuals. Yes, I certainly agree with that assumption," Collins answered.

At that, Goldman stopped pacing, put both hands down on his desk and leaned into Collins to look him squarely in the eyes.

"I'm thrilled you agree. Then don't you think I am fully aware of the fact that your IriMetric product, one you've made millions selling to the collective agencies of our Counter Terrorism Center group, was in fact *not* a homegrown invention of QTS Tek but rather a *purchased* technology from our mutual friend Jack Hawkins? As a matter of fact, don't you think that not only was I privy to this exchange but was also involved in the details of what went into said agreement?"

Collins' mouth opened to speak but he then shut it again, seemingly not sure how to answer.

"Hmm," Goldman huffed. "Speechless? Well I will continue then." Goldman sat back down but continued his lean and gaze on Collins.

"While we are on that line of thinking, I am also aware that for that invention, QTS Tek has continued to pay Hawkins a generous cut of the profits from those sales as long as he maintains the façade that he had nothing to do with its creation. Instead, we as a community are to believe that he made his money as a paid hacker for banks and government groups. Alas, nothing pays nearly as much as a groundbreaking tool like an Iris scanner that makes biometric fingerprint scanning look like child's play. A tool that has changed the game for our agencies who've struggled to keep tabs on terrorists that may be on any number of our international Watchlists."

Collins admitted to himself that he shouldn't be but, despite that, was amazed with how much Goldman knew. It was his job to keep this type of intel within a very small circle and he was certain he had not provided this information to Goldman or anyone in close proximity to the director.

With no better response, he asked, "How?"

"Again. I am the director of the fucking Central Intelligence Agency. I have to know everything that has anything to do with security, safety, threats, terrorism...you name it. I can't afford surprises and this is not my first rodeo Ian."

Collins could only nod his understanding, realizing he wasn't going to get his question answered directly.

"So yes, I vet my people. I know what Jack Hawkins is all about and therefore know that he is not going to be sharing secrets with anyone, particularly since he doesn't have access to those secrets in the first place, so long as he maintains his part of the agreement. Which brings me back to my original question. How can I be sure that QTS isn't double dealing information to outside parties...particularly those outside the United States? I'm sure you understand the severity of exposure."

Collins regained his composure a bit as he went into Security Director mode again.

"Sir. Ethan. First of all, yes, Hawkins is on the payroll and I would hope that you would view my attempt to protect that information, even from you, as an indication of my intent to keep all information confidential and secure."

"Furthermore, what benefit would it be to QTS Tek if we put our relationship in jeopardy with the same people that are paying our bills and keeping our doors open?"

Goldman had to admit that it was a valid point. Reputation could make or break a defense contractor.

"Fair enough, Ian, but I still fear you have a mole in your employ. Despite my best efforts, I'm ashamed to admit that the CIA has not always been immune to leaks so I encourage you to acknowledge that it's possible you may have the same."

Collins considered the statement and said, "I concede that it's possible. So what is it that you would like me to look do? I assume that's why I'm here."

Goldman nodded, pleased with the common ground, "I need you to tell me if there is any way that knowledge of either Hawkins' invention or Ms. Stratton's level of clearance would have made its way to any outsiders. Check the communication history of outgoing Intel. Emails, Mail, encrypted messages. Everything."

"I will sir but if they were smart enough to get past me and my team, then we are going to have a tough time tracing it."

"It's there Ian. Find it."

"I'll do what I can."

"Fair enough," Goldman said and stood indicating the meeting was over. He added, "And Ian"

Standing as well, Ian replied, "Yes?"

"Check Stratton too. I want to make sure the victim wasn't the culprit."

"I can assure you…"

Goldman put his hand up, "Save it. Just check. Also, I need you to send me a full report detailing what Ms. Stratton's roles, responsibilities and level of clearance at your QTS Tek is. I want to know what information she sees."

Ian was going to argue but then thought better of it, "I'll have a report to you by the end of the day."

Collins and Goldman shook hands again and Ian opened the door to leave.

"Thank you again for coming down on short notice and at an early hour," Goldman said. "I appreciate the relationship we have with QTS and can assure you that I want to make sure we keep it in tact."

For Collins, message delivered: Don't give the CIA any reason to spread the word that QTS Tek wasn't who they should be spending their millions with.

With that, Ian nodded and left, closing the door behind him.

Goldman watched him leave and felt some level of relief at least in the belief that QTS wasn't intentionally involved. His concern of finding the original leak was more of due diligence for the future but, for the mission at hand, it was too late to care how the information got out. Hawkins was missing, Stratton had been grabbed and people had been killed. The damage was done. They needed to uncover the endgame and get ahead of it before the end came. Goldman's head began to throb.

Chapter 45

Another impressively built employee of Villa Santini guided Kyler and Alani to the large oak slat door that arched to a peak and stood about eight feet tall. It was consistent with the style of the building's castle décor. Kyler had thoughts of the door from Robin Hood Prince of Thieves that Kevin Costner and Morgan Freeman attempted to break down to save Lady Marion from disaster inside. The door shared the same sturdiness of English oak that prevented them from breaking the door down and Kyler imagined how old it must have been.

The bellman stopped before the door and inserted a classically-styled iron key into the keyhole, unlocked the door and pushed hard on the heavy structure to reveal the room's glorious interior.

The first site that caught Kyler's eye was the ornate bed frame. It was of the four-post variety and each post started with a thick dark wood base and stemmed up into an ornately carved design that carried to a solid wood overhang. The overhang displayed designed carvings that appeared to have been etched many years, likely centuries, ago. It was large and grand and instantly made Kyler and Alani feel anxious by its interpretation of their stay together. Kyler felt Alani tense up.

As they stepped into the room, they noted that the grandiosity of the bed was equally reflected in the décor of the rest of the room. Much like the lobby, the ceilings were extremely tall and supported by large oak beams that peaked at the center of the room. The walls were stone and decorated with sconces of candles throughout.

There was, as to be expected, a beautiful fireplace on one side of the room along with two beautiful wingback chairs angled perfectly in front of it, a table placed between the chairs and two empty glasses of wine with an un-opened bottle placed between them. Romance was certainly the room's intent.

Along another wall were several large arched windows that opened outward. They looked out the back of the hotel revealing what they had not yet seen; Rolling hills of vineyard fields as far as their eyes could see backed, in the distance, by mountains that tightly hugged the landscape. To the right of the vineyards, they could see what their eventual target would be. It was the building they had seen on the satellite image. Kyler made note of it immediately and then continued touring the room for the bellman's sake.

They continue along the same wall to find doors opening out to a beautiful terrace that overlooked the same back view the windows had shown. Again, in typical romantic style, it was set up with two chairs and a table hoisting another bottle of wine and two glasses. Kyler almost groaned but managed to stifle it.

To complete the misery for them both, they were shown a beautiful bathroom complete with a bathtub large enough for two and surrounded by more sconces for candles and, naturally, a bottle of wine and two more glasses.

Kyler was relieved when the bellman made a quick exit, guessing he probably wanted to leave the two love birds to themselves as quickly as possible. His sense was correct but for completely different reasoning.

As the door closed behind him, Kyler awkwardly said to Alani, "One hell of a room, huh?"

Doing her best to prevent the conversation from heading in the wrong direction, she replied.

"We definitely have a good view of our targeted building, that's for sure," indicating her gaze toward the terrace.

Kyler thankfully took the cue of being focused on the task at hand and began surveying the room.

"We need to see if this room is clean."

While he spoke, he lifted his bag that he'd been protecting so carefully onto the bed and began extracting a few items. He found the one he'd been looking for.

He pulled out what looked like a miniature attaché case that was made of reinforced magnesium alloy. The front of the case had an iris scanner. Kyler lined his eyes up to the device and, after a moment, heard a clicking inside the unit indicating that the case was unlocked. He undid its latches to reveal about a half dozen items. It was the CMS-11A, which was basically the government-issued version of a product that could be purchased by anyone online if they knew where to look. The iris scanner and a couple other modifications were made for the CIA, variations that wouldn't be showing up on any Home Shopping Network advertisement.

He began to extract the first item, which was an advanced transmitter detector that reminded him of an old school transmitter radio complete with a long extendable antenna, when Alani chimed in, looking at him with amusement.

"We both know tech is not your cup of tea so why don't you let me handle that."

Kyler thought about arguing, his machismo defenses brewing, but he quickly acknowledged she was right. He'd only been half paying attention when the techies were training him on the gear and he became even more grateful than ever that she was there. Instead of arguing, he smiled sheepishly and stepped aside for her to work with the equipment.

The transmitter device had an input for headphones that she inserted her iPod set into. As Kyler watched, he laughed at the intermingling of technology between two worlds. The device was relatively simplistic in its operation. As she walked around the entirety of the room, she was listening for a clicking noise that would indicate an audio listening device, or "bug," that may have been installed.

There were a number of different types of bugs that could be installed in a room. Some were battery powered which would be more temporary but easily concealed in picture frames, desk sets or even an ashtray. For those, Alani swept the probe in an up and down position while she canvassed the room.

The other forms of transmitters were more permanent and operated through electrical power sources to maintain their life span. Kyler knew that and made sure to turn on all electronic devices throughout the room including the lamps, radio, television and alarm clocks. If the device picked anything up, the clicking feed through the headphones would increase rapidly as Alani got closer to the device, ultimately leading to a high-pitched squeal if she was right on top of it.

After sweeping through the bedroom, living area, veranda, closets and finally the bathroom, she appeared satisfied that the room was clean and gave Kyler the thumbs up. She then took the device over to the phone. Alani angled the probe toward the phone and then nodded for Kyler to pick it up and dial down to the concierge desk.

Kyler listened as the woman said, "Bonjorno Signore Scott. Come posso aiutare??"

Kyler responded, "Grazie, Signora. We were hoping to have a couple extra towels sent up to the room."

The woman picked up the language cue and responded in perfectly accented English.

"Of course Mr. Scott. I will have that delivered immediately. Is there anything else we can provide for you?"

"No, Signora, that will be all for now. Grazie mille."

He hung up the phone and looked up at Alani.

"Clean," she said with a smile.

"So far so good," he replied. "But we should probably finish up quickly before they get up here with the towels and see your Inspector Gadget equipment sprawled out all over the place.

"Good point," Alani replied and grabbed another probe to insert into the device he was holding.

This tool was LED-based and was supposed to pick up the signal of any video surveillance devices. On Alani's cue, Kyler turned off the television this time since the frequency used by a TV was the same used by the video surveillance units.   She repeated her sweep listening through the headphones yet again. After making the same rounds of the room, it once again came up clean.

Sufficiently satisfied that they were clear of any devices for the time being, she put the toys back in the case and clicked the lid closed. Kyler returned the box to his bag just as they heard a knock at the door.

Alani opened it, took the towels from yet another beefy employee of the hotel they hadn't seen yet, and then closed the door.

"Assessment thus far," Alani asked him as she carried the towels into the bathroom and set them down with the rest.

"Obviously, even though the phone isn't tapped now, we don't use it for anything sensitive," Kyler began his countdown.

"Common sense," Alani agreed. "Although just for good measure, it may be a smart play to make some calls to your agent and Jon Christenson. Keep up the ruse in case anyone does start listening."

"Good idea," Kyler nodded. "We're also best suited to keep our communication to Langley and anywhere else to email. I know the boys back home say our wireless is secure but if we have brains on our side, they may have some as well."

"What about that gear?" Alani asked while pointing toward the bag he had closed up.

Kyler looked around and then spotted the safe on one side of the room.

"That looks big enough if we pull everything out of it."

As he said this, he walked over toward the safe and found the key sitting on top. He began pulling the gear out of the bag and filled up the safe, which was just big enough to hold all of the items. He closed the door and then locked it away. He admitted to himself that it wasn't the most secure method in the world but if someone in the hotel went far enough to break in, it was safe to assume their cover was blown and they'd have bigger problems on their hands.

"Ok, what else?" Alani asked after he'd completed that task.

"Clearly there are intelligent and, we can assume, skilled employees working here. We're going to begin digging around this weekend. I think we'd be wise to do the sweep every time we get back in the room. You never know whose antennas we might set off."

"Agreed," Alani replied satisfied with the plan. "Shall we play the part and make our way down to enjoy some of the wine this place has to offer?"

Kyler smiled for the first time in a while and said, "I believe that you have a great idea there Ms. Gannon. Best one of the day, as a matter of fact."

With that he stuck out his arm, she looped hers through his, he opened the massive door and they made their way down the hallway and back toward the lobby.

Had they both not been packing 9mm Glocks cleverly hid underneath a couple layers of clothing, one would think they were the prototypical picture of a romantic couple enjoying their first evening in one of Italy's finest establishments. Kyler only hoped they wouldn't need them.

Chapter 46

Noelle Broussard left the office of the Prefect of Police and sank down into the chair at his desk. To say he was distraught would have been a gross understatement. Having been on the other end of the phone with not only his partner but his best friend while he helplessly listened to his killer end his life, he wasn't sure what he felt other then numbness. Ferdinand Martin had definitely been the more motivated of the two of them, always looking to go out and get the bad guys, enforce justice, get to the bottom of the story. While Broussard had started out with similar intensity, he ended up settling into complacency as most of his fellow officers do after years of unsolved cases, ridiculous bureaucracy and a few brushes with death.

He'd seen other guys in the Prefect get killed in the line of duty and it usually just reinforced how he felt. Stay away from danger if you can. Do your best to solve the cases, but be smart.

His long-time friend and partner didn't share that feeling and now he was dead. But rather than further reinforcing that sense of protection, this time was different. Broussard wasn't married, had no kids and little family left to speak of so Martin was pretty much all he'd had. That man was just killed and there had been nothing Noelle could do about it.

He sat with the Prefect and delivered the news. That immediately prompted a call to send a team to Camille Blanche's place to begin dissecting any possible leads. Noelle then debriefed him on everything he knew about Blanche's case.

The Prefect of Police, Alexander Rousseau, gently prodded Noelle, "Take it back to the beginning for me Broussard. What was Officer Martin doing at Camille Blanche's apartment in the first place?"

Noelle took Rousseau through the story, beginning with Martin reviewing Blanche's file, storming out of the station, the call from Martin on the cuff links and, finally, the eerie voice of the killer that Broussard would never forget.

"Anything significant or distinguishing about the voice?" Rousseau asked.

Broussard tried to focus his brain, which was presently racing in a hundred different directions.

He responded saying, "Yes, sir. From what I could tell, he was definitely not French and, if I had to guess, although the conversation was brief, I would peg him as either Spanish or Italian."

"And the cufflinks that Officer Martin sent you…any idea what significance those might carry?" Rousseau asked.

"To be honest sir, I haven't had a chance to look into that yet."

Rousseau nodded his head quickly, clearly sympathizing with Broussard's ordeal.

"Of course. Officer Broussard, I encourage you to take some time off. I know that you and Officer Martin were very close."

"Actually sir, I'd like to stay on and work the case," Noelle replied, his anger from the reality of what had taken place starting to come through.

"As you mentioned, Ferdinand was like a brother to me and I owe it to him not only to find out who killed him, but to see this case through to the end. I have a feeling that there's something bigger at play here and I'd like to help find out what that is sir."

Rousseau shared Broussard's hunch, particularly considering that he was in regular communication with the Director of Central Intelligence in America. For that reason, he didn't put up much of a fight to Broussard's request. He knew that emotion could bring results faster than anything.

"That's your decision and one that I support if you like. As it has been with this case thus far, I need continuous reports on what you find. I have people very interested in this mess of a case."

Broussard nodded his head in agreement and stood to leave. "Understood sir."

"And Officer Broussard," Rousseau added.

"Yes sir."

"Watch your back on this one."

"I will sir."

Noelle sat at his desk replaying the conversation with Rousseau, the file of Camille Blanche fresh in his mind and the phone call with the killer sitting at its forefront. He decided what his next move should be. The obvious answer would be investigating any possible source of the cufflinks Martin had sent him the picture of.

Broussard pulled out his cell phone and pulled up his most recent text messages. He clicked on the one from Martin and opened up the picture. He emailed the picture to himself as well as Rousseau as he had promised and then pulled up the image on his computer at his desk to get a better look.

Broussard noted that Martin had certainly been correct in saying that these were not any run of the mill cufflinks that you could pick up at Galeries Lafayette. These were, without a doubt, custom-made and far from cheap.

Unfortunately, the two-letter symbol wasn't exactly screaming out an answer to him. He opened up another internet page and went to Google, selecting the images icon and hoped to get lucky. He typed in the two letters and the site returned over two hundred million responses. The most common of these were for Alcoholics Anyomous groups and American Airlines.

He cursed to himself as he sat back and thought for a moment. He tried the same letters, adding *wealthy people* to the keyword search. This again produced a sparse amount of useful information. There were images of Almanacs with listings of the world's richest people and thousands of other pictures of random people, references to Forbes Magazine articles and companies referencing stellar credit ratings. Broussard cursed the internet and its free-wheeling nature of way too much information.

"Think, Noelle, think," he scolded himself.

Broussard analyzed possible connections and tried to make some deductions. If a man was wealthy and had a specific symbol engraved on his cufflinks, they were sure to be worn in a business environment. Therefore, it was reasonable to assume that the mystery man was associated with a successful company. He combined that logic with his assessment of the man's accent and entered *AA, Companies, Italy*.

Bingo.

The very first image had the identical symbol of intertwined letter A's. He clicked on it and it took him to the site of Amici Corporation, founded and run by Armand Amici.

The home page had the very same symbol, Broussard had to click on to enter the site. When he did, the letters separated, disappeared into the background of the page and the company's main website came into view. Broussard clicked on the icon of the French flag to convert the language for him and began reading.

Amici Corporation, led by its President and Founder, Armand Amici, provides world-class Global Logistics Solutions. We focus on serving the elite companies of the world who are looking for first-class quality shipping. Amici is the only logistics company of its kind, supported by advancements from an in-house Research and Development team dedicated to integrating new technologies into our logistics processes. This focus ensures that our customers have up-to-the-second status on each and every shipment coming in and out of its organization.

Noelle continued to read on through the main site but nothing of note stood out other than the fact that it was the same symbol. Of that, he had no doubt.

He clicked on the link titled *Our Executive Team*. The first picture to pop up on the page was of Armand Amici, classically dressed in his typical attire of a finely appointed, handmade suit. His salt and pepper hair was thick and combed back and his skin looked as if he had recently spent a week on his boat in the Mediterranean. To Broussard, he looked tan, fresh and…well…rich. Who said money can't buy happiness? He flashed a handsome smile that exuded the power, wealth and status he yielded.

While Noelle obviously couldn't be certain, he was guessing he was looking at either Martin's killer or, at minimum, the man responsible for his death.

Broussard continued to look around the site, taking note of the address of their corporate headquarters that was located in Florence. His mind began to go blank and the impact of the loss of his friend was settling in so he decided to take what he had and send it off to Prefect Rousseau as promised. He composed and email with his findings including the website and told Rousseau he was going to continue thumbing through Blanche's file to look for any possible connections between her, Amici and possibly even Jacques Francois. That, after all, seemed to be where this had all started. The death toll piled up as did the mysteries.

He hit the send button, grabbed his coat and decided he needed a drink.

Chapter 47

"How in the hell do you know about Project Hawkin's Gates?" Jack Hawkins barked at Armand Amici, who had now been joined by two other men most accurately described as *muscle*.

"Mr. Hawkins," Amici coolly replied. "A man of my wealth and position has many connections and even more ways to find out the information that I need. My business associates and I have not undergone this task without careful planning."

Jack again thought that, had he actually had any liquid in his system, he would presently be urinating down both pant legs.

"So, let's review, shall we?" Amici said as he circled Jack's chair.

"We've established that I know that QTS Tek is proudly selling the product you invented and developed, though claiming as their own, to the fine international government divisions of the CIA, DOD, MI6, Direction Generale de Securite Exterieure and AISE. I know that this IriMetric product is being commonly used by these governments' ground troops to scan the eyes of foreigners coming in and out of military camps. And I also know that it then thoroughly cross-references those individuals against a number of databases to determine if any of them are on any of your government's or your allied governments watchlists."

Amici stopped circling, "How am I doing so far Mr. Hawkins?"

Jack could only look at Amici in horror. Whoever had given him the information was incredibly informed. Jack had actually invented the technology for his home. Being the paranoid freak he was, he wanted to create something for his exterior gate that would not just verify who the person was. He wanted something more advanced than a typical call box that merely offered grainy video surveillance. What he really wanted was to be able to run an instant background check on any of his visitors to ensure that anyone he granted access to his home would not prove to be some common criminal posing as a pizza delivery man only to have free reign to come in and rob him. His paranoia resulted from his work with the government and was only intensified by the fact that he possessed hundreds of thousands of dollars in technology equipment that would be very enticing for an opportunistic thief.

That spurred his idea to have a retina check at his gate, prompting him to develop his best, not to mention most lucrative, invention. After initially developing the technology of the iris scanner with a computer that could communicate securely and wirelessly wherever he directed it to, he then went to a high-ranking official within Homeland Securities to ask them for a favor.

Using the excuse that he had been getting some threatening phone calls and feared that he may have potential stalkers, he asked the official to order the local Palo Alto Police Department as well as the FBI to allow him access into both of their databases with no questions asked. The truth of the matter was that the official knew if he didn't grant the access, Jack would find himself a way in anyway. More importantly, though he hated to admit it, he was afraid of the geeky little shit and what kind of information he might dig up as blackmail if he didn't agree to help him out. He appreciated Hawkins asking first, at least, and knew this was the cleaner and more legal route. With the cover of national security under the Patriot Act as the current excuse for just about anything, it was a request that didn't get questioned, especially considering where it was coming from.

With the technology built and access granted, Hawkins installed what could only be described as a home security system on steroids. Visitors now drove up to the call box at his gate and, after hitting the call button, Hawkins would instruct the visitor to line their eyes up against the LCD panel on the box. The device performs a retina scan, which is then streamed to his large bank of computers, more accurately describe as a secure data center. From there a program determines the visitor's identity and sends a series of complex sniffers out to the various agencies of law enforcement. Once identified, the program queries the agencies' criminal databases to determine if the visitor has a record and, if so, produces a detailed report of what that record entails. Hawkins' software takes it a step further, analyzing the report by taking what is in it, and assigning a perceived level of threat the person presents. Was he or she a small time criminal who got busted for smoking pot at a Dave Matthews concert or was he granting access to John Wayne Gacey? He had even patched himself into the IRS, a fact he conveniently left out of his conversation with his friend at HS, which produced an instant credit report.

This procedure, thanks to his self-built world-class data center, could process all of this information in a matter of seconds...an act that a typical home computer might need up to half an hour to work through.

It was only then that he would decide whether or not to let the person come up to the house. He had, on more than one occasion, instructed a delivery person to leave their package down at the gate for him to retrieve via the Segway he used to make the short trip down the hill of his driveway. Jack Hawkins was not the pinnacle of fitness.

Hawkins even denied Kyler access on his first visit to his house after his system pulled up his past arrest as a teenager. It wasn't until Goldman called and nearly reached through the phone and strangled him that he decided to make an exception.

With all of his paranoia, Jack Hawkins thought how ironic it was that he was now sitting a world away as a prisoner being questioned on the same technology whose sole purpose had been to keep him safe.

"Am I boring you Mr. Hawkins?" Amici snapped, noticing that Jack had drifted off into his own world.

"No." he said, quickly shaking his head back and forth.

"Good, I'm glad," Amici snarled seeming to lose his patience with the eccentric computer geek now just a bit.

"I still don't understand what it is you want from me."

"That's simple. I want you to show me how to reproduce it."

Jack looked at the man puzzled. "Why would I do that?"

"You have two choices. Either you do so willingly or I have these fine gentlemen here, who I think are beginning to get a little bored, beat it out of you."

At that, rather than the cliché cracking of the knuckles and rolling of the necks, Hawkins watched as identical, evil smiles crept onto each one of their worn faces, seemingly delighted at the thought of inflicting a bit of pain onto the annoying little man.

Trying to think of anything, Jack responded by saying, "Well even if I showed you how to make the device, which I won't, it wouldn't do you any good. You still won't have access into the database of information. And do you have the proper equipment to run my software? I doubt it!" Hawkins nearly scoffed as he said the words.

"It's not going to work on some regular run of them mill piece of junk computer. The DoD invested almost two million bucks to overhaul their database computers after their own gear nearly crashed when they took it for a test drive."

"I can assure you," Amici replied with an amusement that puzzled Hawkins, "if we don't have what we need, which I am going to allow *you* to help us determine, acquiring it will not be a problem. Our resources are limitless."

Jack had ceased doubting the truth in those words at this point. Still scrambling and stalling, he asked, "What do you want with that type of information anyway?"

"You ask questions that are not your concern. All you need to worry about is getting me what I need. We can take it from there."

In a surprisingly brazen response, though probably more in mode of protecting his own pet of a project than his country, Hawkins said, "Do what you want to me because I'm not helping you!"

"Are you sure you don't want to reconsider that decision Mr. Hawkins?" Amici asked. As he did, the two men took a couple of steps closer in anticipation for their opportunity to convince Jack otherwise.

Surprising himself yet again, he said, "Go to hell. All three of you."

The two men began to walk forward but Amici stopped them. He turned to the man on his left and said, in Italian, "Bring me the syringe."

Both men looked slightly disappointed but didn't question their boss. They left and returned quickly with the needle as requested.

Jack looked at the man as he approached him with absolute fear. Was this going to be the end for him? At the thought of it, he began to tremble fiercely and he felt as if he was going to convulse so violently that he would throw up. His mind began trying to think rationally to calm his nerves. They wouldn't kill him just like that when they still needed his help would they?

Being bound to the chair, he had no ability to try to fight. One of the men grabbed his arm with incredible strength and held it out straight as the other drove the needle deep into Hawkins' median cubital vein on the inside of his forearm and pushed the plunger down releasing the liquid into his system.

At that, Amici said, "Now we wait. Prepare the room."

Chapter 48

It had only been a couple hours since Ian Collins had left Ethan Goldman's office. To his credit, Ian not only kept his word but far surpassed it. Goldman had to admit that he was surprised to already be looking at the contents of an encrypted file that contained the complete electronic records of one Ms. Ellen Stratton.

Ethan had printed the fairly large file out and began reading its contents, working on his second cup of the vile sludge his office called coffee. He decided that he would have to invest into his own coffee maker, maybe even one of those fancy single shot gadgets that made different flavors. He was convinced that the putrid government-provided coffee, not the stress of his job, would be the end of him.

Ethan crossed his office to a brown leather chair positioned in the corner which affronted several rows of bookcases. Next to the chair stood a small round table equipped with a reading lamp. The spot was intended to emulate the office he had in his home. He'd had it redecorated from his predecessor, a man who'd spent all his time at his desk and had been an apparent fan of rows upon rows of file cabinets. Goldman considered himself more of the modern era. He kept his files under virtual lock and key in various locations of encrypted storage, rendering the sheet-metal eyesores useless. He quickly discovered it to be far more efficient to key in a couple passwords and a few key words in order to search for a file rather than getting up and thumbing through thousands of sheets of paper, praying the documents hadn't deteriorated over time. As he once again felt the pressure that his developing belly was putting on suit pants he bought merely six months ago, he began to question whether there had been a method behind his mentor's madness. Anything to get one up off one's keister was probably a good thing.

Goldman couldn't argue with efficiency though and would have to force himself to find exercise elsewhere. He did still carry a flair for the traditional, though, and the freed up space he'd created in the office allowed for the introduction of the ornate dark wood and finely appointed bookcases that encompassed the room. The designated reading area completed the picture. The ambiance he'd created helped him focus, particularly in times like the present where he sensed he was going to have to read between the lines of what he was digesting.

Goldman settled in and began reading through Ellen Stratton's history. Stratton attended Concordia University in Montreal. Goldman knew what the general populous didn't realize; simply, Canada was quickly becoming a hotbed of technology. Emerging technologies were booming and more universities and specific trade schools were popping up to train the masses. Concordia was known as one of the best amongst them and Ellen Stratton had apparently been its top student. The school was also one of two in the city whose primary language was English. Those factors, as well as its convenient proximity to Washington DC and Langley, made it a perfect breeding ground for various tentacles of the defense institution conglomerates representing the United States to pluck from. That convenience of location was exploited by those entities and Goldman had been at the apex of that decision.

Ethan had been relatively vocal about concerns he'd had when representatives from the DoD, NSA and the FBI began working aggressively with schools like Concordia to establish loosely monitored internship programs in order to attempt to recruit talent into America. Even his own CIA's Counterterrorism Center Special Operations unit, or CTC/SO, led by a man he hired as its director, Scott Flannigan, made moves to do the same. He recalled the conversation with Flannigan at the time.

*   *   *   *

"Scott, I know you are under the same pressures we all are to get our arms around Al-Qaida and North Korean threats, but we have to be careful that we don't get desperate." Goldman had told him.

Flannigan was a second-generation Irish Catholic from Boston who was tough as nails and even smarter when it came to strategic planning. But he also lived up to his heritage as a feisty and passionate son of a bitch. It had a tendency to get the better of him at times. He and Goldman had also known each other for over twenty years and he'd ceased pulling punches with him long ago.

"That's bullshit Doc and you know it. That's the same bureaucratic horseshit every administration has fed us since '86," Flannigan said, referring to the date when the CTC had been formed under Ronald Reagan.

"Reagan seems to be about the only talking bobble-headed politician that understood what needed to be done."

Flannigan. No punches. Goldman saw his old friend growing a nice shade of pink, which was common when he was either drunk or fired up about his country's national security. He wasn't sure which was more dangerous.

"Easy Scott," Goldman put his hands up trying to calm him a bit. "This isn't about politics nor is it coming from those folks in DC you so affectionately referred to…and ultimately answer to, by the way."

"Save the grandstanding Doc. About the only person I answer to is you and that's only because I respect the hell out of you. I'd rather quit this racket than kiss ass in Washington."

"Ok ok…forget about them then. I'm just saying, I don't like what's going on here."

Frustrated, Flannigan asked, "What's the big goddamned deal? We're just trying to get some talent in here that doesn't cost us an arm and a leg. Every boy genius here in the states we try to reign in thinks they deserve to be paid in gold right out of college. They're a bunch of entitled punks, not to mention dangerous ones.

Shit...if we don't hire half of these geeks, they'll flip the other way. Then we'll have some shits, way too smart and capable for their own good, spending their days hacking Bank of America and Capital One so they can go drop ten large on some computer they build in their garage and play pretend recon on Call of Duty twenty-four hours a day."

Goldman knew he was right and thought of Jack Hawkins as a prime example of that, though Jack's motivation hadn't been money, just the audacity to prove he could do it. Goldman couldn't play into Flannigan's rants though because he had larger concerns.

Flannigan continued on, "Canada has so many kids clamoring to get into tech because everyone's telling them it's the future but they haven't created enough industry to employ all of them. Win for us, Doc. Bring 'em on an internship, promise them a guaranteed job when they finish school and pay them half what we'd pay our own punks. Win win because the kids get a sure thing for a job which is a hell of a lot more than they'll get up North."

Goldman had been nodding his head. Flannigan wasn't the first to dish out the argument and wouldn't be the last. Of that, he was certain.

"Scotty, the problem is that we have a lot less control over these kids. Sure, we catch them doing something, we deport them outta here but we're also recruiting them for a reason. They're computer geniuses. These aren't dumb low-level criminals. If they want to do something that would threaten our national security, chances are, we won't know it."

"No different than our own people," Flannigan retorted.

"Wrong. We can vet those kids. Background checks, references, transcripts from schools...whatever we need. We can make an educated guess on them. Have some slip through the cracks? Yes. But I like our chances better there."

Flannigan sighed, paused and pointed a finger at his boss and friend, "You're a pain the arse sometimes Doc."

Goldman smiled. Few people were granted this level of freedom with him and Flannigan was one. And that was only because Goldman, in turn, respected the hell out of him too.

"All I'm saying, and all I've been telling everyone that's up on this is, let's simply take the extra time to coordinate with the countries we're plucking from. There's no reason we can't get the folks over at the DND to open their doors to us a bit on these kids," Goldman was referring to Canada's Department of National Defense.

Now it was Flannigan's turn to nod his head, "I hear you Doc. That's on your shoulders. You're the one who'll have to get the bunch of arses in the cabinet to get that done. I don't see it happening, but you know how to reach me if it does. I'd love to have the green light to go get some of those guys."

With that, Flannigan had bustled out of Goldman's office about as quickly as he'd entered.

As Goldman sat in his chair reviewing Stratton's file, he laughed ironically. Flannigan was still waiting for his phone call. As it happens all too often, the cabinet Scott had affectionately referred to found other political matters that were far more pressing and the entire initiative died just about as quickly as it started.

As he read through Stratton's file, he realized that was not an entirely accurate statement. It appears that, where the agencies had restricted themselves, bound by concerns of their responsibility to national security, the independent defense contractor community saw the green light and drove straight through. Goldman could imagine the lure was even stronger in a business where the salaries paid out to these engineers directly affected the profitability of the coveted bottom line. Furthermore, he was certain that QTS's competitors had done the same. They were getting the best of the best in engineers on a proverbial fire sale while worrying very little about things like comprehensive vetting and, as seen here, even legal citizenship.

His conversation with Flannigan rang truer now than ever and his antennae were turned up to full sensitivity. He suddenly felt more curious than ever about Ms. Ellen Stratton.

Chapter 49

Kyler and Alani made their way back down the elegant staircase and into the lobby they'd admired on the way in. Kyler noted that this time there was no musical accompaniment in his mind, though he could feel the theme music from Jaws being relevant, growing steadily as they descended the steps. They were entering into the waters of danger knowingly and willingly and neither of them knew where it would lead.

As he'd brought it into mind, the theme now started pounding in Kyler's head. The simple, yet strangely eerie, two-noted song picked up its pace. It grew faster and faster as they came to the bottom of the stairs and, just as it hit its peak of intensity, Carmen, the lead concierge they'd met earlier, greeted them with a smile. Or was it a probing sneer? Kyler wasn't sure. He guessed he'd created that last bit of drama in his mind and shook himself into reality again.

Yep. Get it together, he thought. He aligned his mind to the task and began a quick surveillance of the room deciding there was nothing of note yet.

"Buonasera, Signore. Signora," Carmen said with a smile.

Kyler couldn't help but notice the woman's beauty. He pegged her to be in her late twenties and had quintessentially dark olive skin that he often associated with Italian beauty. Her eyes, an almond brown, were large and somehow seductive in the way she looked at him. She wore a tight-fitting black dress that came down low at the top and seemed to hug her body perfectly, making no attempt to hide what Kyler noted to be an incredibly well-proportioned figure. He was sure that her allure did little to hurt her effectiveness in her position. Frankly, it was probably mostly why she held the title. Having met Vitale Baldacci, he also assumed the slick innkeeper took advantage of having such a beautiful woman around. Call him a chauvinist, but he'd bet the house he was right.

Snapping out of the trance he'd fallen into, Kyler replied, "Buonasera Carmen. Come stai questa sera?" He was more than a little proud to show off his Italian to the beautiful woman.

Clearly impressed, Carmen smiled warmly at Kyler with a little more than just the welcoming look of a greeting. The interaction wasn't lost on Alani but she stayed quiet. After all, what was she? Jealous?

Possibly attempting to show off a bit herself, Carmen replied in perfect English, "I'm doing very well Mr. Scott. Is your room to your liking? Do you have everything you need?"

Carmen had not yet acknowledged Alani. She'd also seemed to pose the last question with a slight double entendre. Although that could have just been Kyler's imagination. More likely, it was wishful thinking. Kyler Scott, Italian heartthrob? Probably not.

"I believe so. Grazie."

Finally turning to look at Alani, she asked, "Would you like to join us for our tasting and Hors d'oeuvres?"

Alani replied this time, "Assolutamente, grazie," I can play this game too, she thought.

"Excellent, then. Prego. Please come sit."

With that, Carmen turned and sauntered toward two open chairs that were positioned in front of one of the behemoth fireplaces. Kyler didn't do much to hide his appreciation for the other view of Carmen. That had been enough to earn a smack from Alani.

"You're an ass," she said, but added a smile so as to not reveal the truth behind her chide.

He wasn't buying it though, "Hmm…is someone jealous?" He gave her a wink as he said it.

"Embarrassed…for you…that's more like it," she retorted. "You do realize she probably hasn't seen any of your movies and therefore is probably *not* in love with you by default like most of the floozies you run across."

"Oh contraire. I think she's a big fan. I may even give her an autograph later if she's good."

He was enjoying himself now. He did actually plan on giving Carmen an autograph but not because of any assumption that she actually had a clue of who he was, which he guessed she didn't. He was also relatively certain that whatever flirtation had seemingly occurred just then had been Carmen's modus operandi for all her interactions with clientele, particularly that of the male variety. Despite that awareness, he wasn't about to pass up on the opportunity to enjoy tormenting Alani. Maybe even make her a little jealous. Though, just as Alani wasn't sure why she felt that way, he wasn't willing to query his own emotions either.

"And I take offense to the floozy accusation. Rest assured that only the most refined woman can truly appreciate the overwhelming talent and smoldering good looks of the legendary Scott Cruz."

"I'm starting to think I should have actually run you over with my car this morning."

They both followed Carmen to the spot she'd directed them to and took a seat in the oversized wingback chairs.

Carmen raised a slight hand and nodded toward a man who'd been idly walking through the room with a bottle of wine, ready to pour more for any of the still-thirsty guests. He quickly routed himself toward them while another man appeared from thin air with two empty wine glasses.

"This is our Chianti Riserve Ruffino from what I personally believe was our best year of harvest. It is ninety percent Sangiovese and very mature with flavors of spice, tobacco, vanilla and café."

Kyler and Alani took their glasses from the materialized man who'd held them while the wine nomad had poured. They followed the typical wine tasting protocol of engaging all of their senses, acting the part of true wine snobs. They held the glass by the stem, the only truly accepted method, and tipped their glasses slowly to the side.

Sounding like the perfect connoisseur, Kyler noted the rich and beautiful deep red hue of the liquid, "Il colore e bello."

Carmen nodded in appreciation, "Grazie."

Alani and Kyler then plunged their noses into the glass, mouth slightly open to isolate the smell, and inhaled deeply. In unison, they let out an appreciative "Ah!"

It was Alani's turn to comment, "I can definitely smell the spice and tobacco! That is amazing!" And with that, they both savored their first sip of the wine, having properly prepared for the grand finale.

There was no need for exaggeration. Kyler thought and said, "Incredible. Truly. It is most definitely the finest we've had in Italy...perhaps anywhere!" Alani was nodding emphatically in agreement.

"I am so pleased you like it," Carmen said. "Our chef will be by shortly with some cheese and other items. Please enjoy and let me know if you need anything from us."

"Grazie Signora," Kyler said. At that, she was gone, leaving them to relish in what was arguably the most elegant and beautiful setting either of them had been in.

When it seemed safe that all the staff of the hotel were out of ear shot, Kyler leaned back slightly in his chair and crossed his right leg over his left, wine glass still in hand and at the ready. He was the perfect image of a man soaking in his surroundings. A perfect image only because onlookers could not, of course, see the weapon he was concealing under his pant leg.

Alani followed Kyler's lead, bringing her chair closer to his. She leaned in towards him and laid one hand to rest on his arm while the other nursed the glass. They looked to be two people completely in love in the most romantic of settings.

Kyler quietly said, "So be sure to enjoy as much of that wine as you want. We're not driving anywhere." The plan was in motion and his cues would not be lost on her. They'd been in plenty of similar situations.

"I'll be sure to. I assume that you are going to hold true to your promise of autographing some pictures for the hotel and hitting on the staff?" Alani replied.

"Yep. As a matter of fact, I had the set photographer pull some shots from Fire in Firenze and print them out. Hot off the presses. Sort of a special sneak preview to return the gesture of such outstanding hospitality."

"That was nice of you honey," Alani replied. "Oh did you happen to grab my lighter from the room?" As she asked that, she pulled out a pack of menthol cigarettes.

Kyler reached into his pocket and pulled out a slender black lighter with a silver top and handed it to her. "Of course. There you go."

"Always thinking of me, sweetheart," She said and took it from him.

"I know it's your favorite lighter," he said with a wink. "Well I think I'm going to run up to the room and grab those pictures. I'll give them to Carmen and she can decide what to do with them."

Alani fought to keep the smile up. It was all part of the plan but she was having a hard time staving off her discomfort. She covered it well though. "I think while you do that, I'm going to roam the hotel. I'd like to find Signore Baldacci to thank him for making room for us this weekend."

"Great idea," as he said this, he rose from his chair and gave Alani a gentle kiss on the forehead. With that, he was off, bounding the stairs back to his room.

Alani was up seconds later, with wine glass still in tow. She found a saunter of her own and made her way toward the nomad that was still making his way around the room with what looked to be a freshly opened bottle of wine.

"Buonasera Signora. Would you like some more wine?" He asked, noticing her nearly empty glass as well as the sensuality she had approached him with.

Alani touched his arm, cocked her head to one side, smiled an incredibly seductive smile and nodded, "That would be fabulous. Grazie. I seemed to have made my way through the first glass very quickly."

The man fumbled a bit. She was used to it by now. It wasn't even that she was aware of her own looks. She was often surprised by how easy it was to affect most men. She had realized long ago that most men were easily manipulated by female attention. Put a remotely attractive woman who knows how to work a situation in front of a man and she can get whatever she wants from him. Men are driven by the attention of woman. It empowers their identity as a man and often deceives them to think that they are actually in control when it comes to a woman. If they only knew that it was the woman who held all the power. It was an age-old irony.

As the nomad refreshed Alani's glass, she asked, "What is back that way?"

She was pointing to the hallway that ran to the right of the staircase.

The man followed her gaze and said, "Mostly employee rooms. The chef is the first door on the right, then Ms. Carmen's office is on the left and then, all the way back on the right, is the…umm…" the man snapped his fingers as he searched for the English word for whatever he was about to say. "Study?"

Alani nodded her head to indicate he had found the right word but added, "Study? Like a library, but more personal, right?"

The man nodded emphatically and blurted, "Yes!" He snapped his fingers, proud of himself for giving her the proper term. He added, "It is also Mr. Baldacci's personal office."

Perfect, she thought and then said to him, "I would like to go thank him for accommodating us and I'd also like to compliment him on the fine service we have gotten here." As she added the last part, she gave him a smile.

The nomad flushed and stammered, "Grazie Signora. It is our pleasure to take care of our guests." He puffed his chest out a bit and added, "You are welcome to visit Mr. Baldacci's office and please let me know if there is anything else you need. Anything at all."

Alani gave him a small kiss on the cheek and thanked him, leaving him behind, frozen in place. She was off to find Vitale Baldacci and maybe share a cigarette with the man.

Chapter 50

Ethan Goldman had just been getting to the meat of Ellen Stratton's file when he heard his computer beep. He had assigned a particular noise, the sound of a car horn, for emails that came in with high priority. It was meant for times like these when he wasn't anchored in front of his computer but still wanted to address urgent matters. As he rose from his chair he remarked on how much times had changed that urgent messages were emailed rather than phoned. Sure, the extremely urgent items came as a phone call. If there was a threat on the president, for example, he was damned sure to get a call, if not a dozen of them. The truth was, and he was a guilty party in the trend, people had become attached to technology to such an extent that it actually became the most efficient form of communication. The personal touch to his business, which was already so cold and blunt, was truly a way of the past. He had adapted but he wondered how long it would be until his generation was obsolete.

Goldman swiped his finger on the biometric finger pad connected to the computer. The computer automatically locked out after five minutes of inactivity. He looked at the screen as it came back to life, clearly agreeing that the finger was indeed its owner's.

The message was flagged as urgent and sat at the top of the list of emails. He noted that the sender was Alexander Rousseau, the Prefect of Police in Paris. It was a forwarded message and began with.

Ethan...hoping this email finds you well. As promised, I am keeping you apprised of any developments we uncover on the Camille Blanche and Jacques Francois cases. This email came from one of my officers, Noelle Broussard. He was the partner of Ferdinand Martin who, as I mentioned, was killed at Blanche's apartment by who we think was her killer as well.

The email detailed how the cufflinks had been found and sent to Broussard as well as the account of the phone conversation prior to the murder. Rousseau finished with promises to continue forwarding more information as he received it.

Goldman scrolled down to the forwarded message from Broussard and read about the Amici Corporation and, more specifically, Armand Amici. Ethan decided to look at ARCINS, or the Agency Records and Information System, to see what he could find on Amici. ARCINS houses thirty-four million records and counting and is frequently called upon, particularly in light of the Freedom of Information Act, to obtain any information on a wide variety of topics. It operates in that strange limbo of public but private. It isn't openly accessible by the general public, but if a citizen contacts the CIA with a request for information, ARCINS' plethora of records is available to them. That is, of course, assuming that what they are asking for isn't classified. JFK's assassination mysteries remain safe.

With that many records, a specific search is almost necessary otherwise the search will return hundreds of thousands of possibilities. It would be about as specific as going to Google and entering a search for pizza places in Italy which would likely render over ten million results. However, a search such as "Pizza, Florence, accepts American Express" would bring it down to the thousands. Naturally, the more specific the criteria, the more relevant the results.

Ethan typed in what he thought to be the most obvious. *Armand Amici, Amici Corporation, Italy, arrests.* Several hundred results returned but none of them actually referenced records of Amici being arrested.

He pinched the bridge of his nose and lightly tapped his fingers on his desk, trying to think of another search query. He tried the same search but instead of *arrests* he typed *lawsuits.* That spawned surprisingly few results for such a large company. Goldman attributed that to the fact that suing wasn't quite as popular in Italy as it had become in the states. He was beginning to get frustrated, particularly because the name was definitely familiar to him but he couldn't figure out why. Goldman did so much reading on a daily basis, between security briefs, statements released by the President, emails and general news upkeep, that all of the information began blending together. He used to be able to retain it all with amazing accuracy and attributed the skill deterioration to aging.

Goldman sat back and closed his eyes, trying to recall the information. He had just about given up when it hit him. He leaned forward again and furiously moved the mouse around the screen. After a few clicks, he located the file he was looking for. It was the transcript of the conversation Kyler had recorded from Gianni Dimarco's restaurant. He scanned the account of what was translated.

"Bingo," he said aloud. Near the beginning of the conversation, when Dimarco had approached the table, it read:

Armand, would you and the lovely Signora Amici like to give our Riserva a try this evening?

It was a concrete connection. As simple as it was, it was a link. Armand Amici was an acquaintance of Dimarco, a man they were certain was involved in a threat to national security, and now Amici appeared to be directly involved in, if not personally responsible for, the murder of a French officer. The same officer who was investigating the mysterious murder of a woman who'd run a story on Jacques Francois who, in his own right, had plenty of mystery surrounding his amnesia and death as well. Goldman stopped to think about what this finding meant. They now had physical evidence that corresponded to three of the five victims in their docket. First, a taped conversation tying Amici to Dimarco and now, a discovered article of Amici's clothing, which would be run for prints for confirmation, found at the scene of the murder of Martin and Blanche, Blanche having a known relationship with Francois. It did not draw any connections to Hawkins or Stratton but, now that three of the pieces fit together, he felt certain the other two would find their way into the web. Goldman just couldn't see it at the moment. He had enough to have the Italian Police pick Amici up. Maybe they could get something out of him then to complete the puzzle.

Trying to put more pieces together, he went back to the email Rousseau forwarded him from Broussard. He clicked on the web link for Amici's Corporation and it took him to the home page. He then selected the hyperlink at the top that was labeled *About Us*. The site jumped to a description of the company, starting with its history and general overview. Goldman scanned until he noted a reference to the company's overwhelming pride in technological advancements in shipping. There was an entire paragraph highlighting their research and development groups that created homegrown software and hardware to improve shipping efficiencies, high-tech GPS advancements and auto-populating information to their customers from a dynamically updated database. Goldman paused and thought about that. Stratton and Hawkins certainly had associations with technology. Could that be the final link back to Amici?

He decided to respond to Rousseau. He needed to confirm the evidence. Goldman thanked Rousseau for the information and updates and asked the Prefect to do his best to fast track a prints analysis on the cufflinks found at Blanche's apartment. He'd take the prints and send them along to his contacts at the Italian Police along with the audiotape from the restaurant and see if they'd be willing to pick Amici up.

Deciding that he needed eyes on this that were out in the field, Goldman crafted an email to Kyler and Alani with the key bullet points. He outlined the connections he'd gone through in his head thus far and finished by telling them to dig around for anything that might point back to Amici as well.

Goldman wondered what intel Francois could have at this point, having been removed from the military for several years now. What could be worth killing him over?

He looked through the information he had on Francois. The only address on file for him had been in the 20th Arrondissement of Paris and his address of record dated back to 1991. There were a couple pieces of that he didn't like. First, the mere fact that there was no other address on record before then begged the question...why? The other factor was that, having spent more than his fair share of time over the years in Paris, he was familiar with the 20th Arrondissement, direct English translation *District*.

Goldman knew that Arrondissements were how many countries separated larger cities into self-contained subdivisions. They usually, at least in larger cities like Paris, Marseille and Lyon in France, had their own mayor as well. Goldman knew that the 20th Arrondissement in Paris, which included the districts of Menilmontant and Belleville, was inhabited primarily by immigrants dating back to the middle of the 19th century. As a matter of fact, Belleville touted the second largest Chinatown in Paris.

Goldman leaned back in his chair again. He could feel that the answers were so close but knew he was missing a few vital pieces. He hoped that Kyler and Alani would have a breakthrough and, actually, was confident they would so long as they didn't have their covers blown. In order to make the best use of their time there, he knew he needed more information on Francois, Stratton, Amici and Blanche.

He picked up the phone and hit the speed dial.

After two rings, he heard a voice muffled by what sounded like a significant amount of food, "QTS. You got Barnes." It was Matt Barnes over at QTS Tek.

"Matt, it's Ethan Goldman," he responded while pulling the phone away from his ear to stave off the disgusting sound of Barnes's chewing.

"Yep, I know. Got caller ID on ya. What's up Doc?"

That surprised Goldman seeing as he knew for sure that his number was blocked. He decided he didn't want to know how Barnes circumvented that nor did he have time to get into it.

Instead Goldman asked, "Is Bob there with you too? I have a request that needs double time and so I need you both working on it."

"He's around here. Just went to the vending machine to snag a Snickers and a Red Bull. What's up? How can we be of excellent service?" Thankfully Barnes had swallowed at this point.

"Tell him to grab you a Red Bull too. You're gonna need it," Goldman replied. "I need as much information on three individuals as you can dig up. I don't care how or where you find it or what you have to do to get it. Just get it. Understand?"

Barnes smiled. He'd just been given the green light by the Director of the Central Intelligence Agency to do what he loved most. Hack into computers systems.

"I read you loud and clear Doc." He slid his chair over to his computer and opened up a new window. His hands hovered over the keyboard as he said, "Ok. Shoot me those names. I'm ready."

Goldman gave Barnes all the names except Stratton and as much information as he had to get him started on the search. He couldn't ask Barnes to dig into details on one of QTS's own employees nor did he want to set off any unnecessary red flags while he and Ian were playing so nice with each other for the time being. He also couldn't rule out QTS as having some connection entirely, though he knew he could trust Barnes. Besides, he had another group looking into Stratton anyway. Goldman always had a backup, something he'd learned years ago.

Then he added, "I am getting the feeling that, at the least, Jacques Francois is not who he says he is. May not even be a French native. I need absolutely everything you can find and I need it faster than ever. See what you can find out about his education and work history too."

"You got it Doc. We're on it," Barnes replied. He had already started hitting keys to start a variety of searches.

"Barnes. Remember. I don't care what you have to do to get it. Just get it." With that he hung up without waiting for a response. He didn't need to elaborate on a conversation in which he gave a computer hacker free reign to break the law.

Just then, his phone rang again. He thought it may be Barnes again but, when he looked down at the caller ID, he snatched it up right away.

"Goldman," Ethan clipped.

It was one of the agents that had been on the search for Jack Hawkins.

"Sir, I think we may have located Hawkins."

Chapter 51

Kyler had just entered his room and made his way over to his luggage to grab the pictures of Fire in Firenze. He rummaged through the bag until his hands found the manila envelope he'd been looking for.

He zipped the bag back up and was about to head out of the room when he decided he ought to check in on the computer. He popped open the other bag, his sack of toys, and grabbed the case that housed the laptop. Kyler walked over to the desk, slid the laptop out, set it down and fired it up.

While he waited for the machine to stretch its technology legs and come to life, he went back to his tools of the trade, having nearly forgotten the other reason he'd come up to the room. He found a smaller case that had a couple items he thought he'd take with him. One was a second pen, much like the one he'd used at Gianni Dimarco's restaurant to take a picture of the phone.

The second gadget was what appeared to be prescription eyeglasses. Being the famed Scott Cruz though, they couldn't be just any glasses. The boys back home had fashioned them with a customized frame from Dior Dior, glasses that typically went for at least five hundred dollars. The lenses were embedded with an invisible optical video camera near the top where the lens met the frame. This camera had circuitry wired into the frame itself. The frame, by design was thicker in order to hide its electronics as well as the fact that a proprietary storage card was housed within the temples of the frame which ran over the ear. At the spot of the frame where it began to bend around the ear, there was a nearly indistinguishable line where the piece pulled out in order to remove the storage disk. That disk is then inserted into a USB converter that could easily connect to any computer in order to upload images and video. The device was truly astonishing in that the frame even hid a well-placed microphone in order to pick up and record audio.

All Kyler could do was shake his head in amazement as he looked at the sheer ingenuity of what he held in his hand. He laughed a bit as he imagined what would happen if members of the paparazzi got their hands on such a device. If people thought they weren't safe now with the advent of camera phones and YouTube, what would happen if they could be recorded and have absolutely no idea? Mel Gibson might just have to sequester himself to his home and avoid the public altogether.

Kyler sat back down in front of the laptop and swiped his finger on the pad near the keyboard, initiating the process of logging him onto the computer, internet and, ultimately, his email. It ripped through the process quickly and, within a few short seconds, he was staring at his inbox. A high priority message from Goldman popped up front and center, being pushed to the top of the email. He clicked it open and read through what Ethan had sent about the recent connections Armand Amici had to the murders.

Kyler remembered the dinner and had already filed the thought in his mind that there was something of interest there but the Amici connection to the murders was an entirely new element. Kyler started trying to piece together possible ties for it all in his mind. Just as he was sorting through this new information, he saw the little window pop up for his secure instant messenger. It was Goldman.

"Scott. Perfect goddamn timing." Goldman typed. "Don't want to risk calling but I've got news."

Kyler responded, "Was just reading the email. Thinking as we speak."

"Yeah…got bigger news," Goldman replied.

Kyler was about to reply but noted the top of the dialogue box told him Ethan was typing so he waited.

"We are almost certain that Hawkins is in Florence."

Kyler stared at the words for a second before they fully registered.

"What? How do you know? Where?"

"The techs decided to ransack Hawkins' computer room at his house. Took forever just to get into the damn place. Talk about lock and key…" Goldman kept typing and Kyler nearly picked up the phone but thought better of it. Even though he'd swept the room, they couldn't risk taking any chances.

"Anyway, when they got in, they noticed an alert flashing on one of the computers. Clicked it, map launched with a blinking light…like a beacon."

"It was in Florence?" Kyler asked.

"Not exactly," Goldman replied and then said, "Tracking over the North Atlantic just east of Greenland."

"Airborne?" Kyler asked

"Yes."

"They watched it land in Florence?"

"Not exactly," Goldman replied.

"What do you mean?" Kyler was utterly confused now and frustrated by the form of communication.

"Lost the signal about an hour later. Whatever he was transmitting with must've been battery powered because it never came back."

"So how do you know he's in Florence?" Kyler asked.

"Deduction. Short version is the flight path put it landing in the UK, France or Italy. Assumed it left an airport near Palo Alto where Hawkins was picked up. The boys checked airports. Found San Carlos Airport had a match."

"Commercial jet?" Kyler asked.

"Private. Flight plan filed with the airport had it bound for Peretola Airport in Florence."

Kyler was pretty sure he knew the answer but asked, "Whose jet?"

"Registered to Amici Corporation."

Kyler had expected the answer but was still jolted when it was confirmed.

"Florence is a big place, Scott. You're gonna have to find him."

"Don't worry. I'll get it out of someone. Trust me."

"I don't doubt it agent."

Kyler was about to sign off but noted Goldman was typing something else.

"Something else just came in a few minutes ago. Look at this."

Kyler saw a link to a website pop up and clicked on it. It didn't direct him to the public Internet but rather to the CIA's *Intranet* which was a private website only accessible to authorized vistors. A report had just been filed and shared internally from an analyst out of the Los Angeles FBI office. It had today's date and read:

Agent filing report: Martino Scuzziano – Stationed in Lombardy Region of Italy

Scuzziano:

Acting on an anonymous tip coming to the Milan field office late last night, agents joined local police when they were dispatched to the Quadrilatero d'Oro. The caller stated she heard what sounded like another woman in a nearby building being beaten by a man with a Slovak accent, possibly Ukrainian.

Kyler knew that that area of Milan was where the concentration of the city's finest clothing stores are located. Translated, it meant *rectangle of gold.* Unlike Paris, whose fashion districts were spread all over the city, Milan's were all packed into one dense area. If you were a traveler looking for the latest trends that seemed to fall off the catwalk and onto a store rack, this was where you went to shop. Only the highest of high-end shops were located here and immediately a bell went off in Kyler's head, remembering that Dimarco owned a clothing store in Milan. He was willing to bet where it was located.

He continued reading:

A team of two FBI agents and four Polizia officers descended on the address provided by the caller. The address was a warehouse located in a small street/alleyway off of Via Alessandro Manzoni. The victim and her attacker were no longer present but, acting on suspicion, our group of six men raided the warehouse. Four armed men were inside the building. Two were killed, one detained and one fled. One member of the Polizia was killed in the raid. Other five were not injured. The main level of the warehouse contained racks and boxes of clothing. Coerced detained guard to lead us to the true purpose of this warehouse. A hidden door in the floor of the warehouse led to a dug out basement. Investigation into the basement revealed forty-two women of varying ethnicities with their feet shackled together, huddled up with each other in the corner of the roughly 20' x 28' space. All of the women are very attractive, model-types.

Officers and agents have begun questioning the women who are willing and able to talk. Discovered that many were picked up in nearby Croatia. They were all trying to make their way to Milan with aspirations of becoming high-fashion runway models. Men, claiming to be modeling agents delivering promises to take them across the water to help launch their careers, put them on boats and brought them to this warehouse. The women stated that more women had been here before them but had since been taken away. Interrogations of the detained guard confirmed our suspicions that these women are being sold as sex slaves. Some of the women are placed into underground brothels in the Lombardy region while others are shipped to locations around the world to the highest bidders.

Detainee has yet to give up the names of those running the operation but should break with further interrogation.

Details currently confirmed:

1) *Warehouse and corresponding clothing store is listed for ownership under the name of Mr. Gianni Dimarco.*
2) *Vessels used for transfer of women from Croatia to Venice owned by Amici Corporation.*

> *3) Amici Corporation also owns commercial vehicles that transport women from Venice to Milan.*

Sending this report to Mr. Director, Dr. Ethan Goldman per cross-referenced name of Dimarco on high-priority Watchlist.

Kyler tried to take it all in. It wasn't what he expected but, as he put the pieces together in his mind, it started to fit. He decided he needed to talk this out and launched the secure video call, hoping it was as secure as it claimed to be.

Goldman answered on the first ring and his image appeared.

"That's our man."

Kyler nodded, "Our men, really. So let's get this straight."

"Fire it out."

"Dimarco's using Amici's company and his employment of Italian ex-military personnel to freight women in to Milan for evaluation, let's call it 'inventory' and then an open-market sale to the presumably wealthy men of Milan and other countries."

"Apparently."

"And while the facts haven't confirmed it, we should assume that Amici's also facilitating the delivery of these women to their respective buyers."

"I concur with that as well."

Goldman had drawn his own theories but wanted to see what Kyler had in mind, "Assuming this to be true, where do the recent events fit in all of this?"

Kyler had already begun working through this question. His theory was a reach but it was all that made sense at the moment.

"Dimarco is a capitalist. That much we know."

"Without a shadow of a doubt."

"Maybe he started the sex trade with selling to his circle of contacts. No doubt wealthy men with questionable morals and an appetite for the typical desires that accompany men of that mold."

Goldman shook his head, "Money, cars, power and beautiful women."

"Right," Kyler said and continued. "But Dimarco is greedy. He may have decided that to truly capitalize on his venture, he needed to prepare a little incentive to these men to continue paying more for his services, particularly if he selected men who had risen to their respective positions of power and wealth through predominantly public means."

"Politics mostly."

"Exactly," Kyler was up pacing slightly now. "And what better way to squeeze a man that would do anything to maintain his position of power than to dig up their political secrets?"

"I follow you agent but you're forgetting that Dimarco already holds something over these men and that is the sex trade itself. Why not just threaten to expose them that way?"

Kyler shook his head.

"They would just stop using Dimarco's services and chalk the accusation up to an opportunist trying to exploit a political leader for money. Not to mention, that politician would then merely shut Dimarco's operation down and mark it down as a victory against sexual crime in Europe. The politician would be applauded for his fight against sexual deviants."

Kyler continued, not waiting for an agreement from Goldman now.

"No. He wanted to use political leverage. Proof. Acts of backdoor deals with perceived enemies, arms dealings with the other side, handshake agreements with influential but controversial groups. All the juicy details that if shared with the right people, could ruin the victim and take away the one thing he loves most. His power."

Goldman chimed in now.

"And in order to find this information, he had to find sources that could provide a database that obviously can't provide these details, otherwise the respective agencies would have arrested those involved already, but *can* list who their known associates are believed to be."

"And then Dimarco sends his ex-military muscle out to get the information he needs."

Kyler finished the thought and then continued.

"Francois and Stratton represent both access and skills to obtain that information. Blanche finds out what Francois was feeding Dimarco and gets killed through association. Francois is killed when he no longer agrees to cooperate once he finds out that his girlfriend had been killed."

"The timeline of events would support that theory," Goldman said.

"Meanwhile, Stratton is kept alive as long as she continues to feed them the data. The French officer was likely just a victim of circumstance. Snooping around and stumbled on Amici or one of his men who went back to Blanche's apartment when Amici discovered he'd left evidence behind."

"Logical as well."

"And Hawkins," Kyler stopped pacing and paused to think for a moment, "It's possible that they want to step up their game by using his invention to scan their clients at the time of transaction to confirm their identity. Higher stakes call for greater precautions. They could have grabbed Hawkins to force him to recreate the device for their use and plan to continue to leverage Stratton for access to the database."

Goldman was nodding. In truth, his theory had touched on Kyler's reasoning but he hadn't pieced it all together yet.

Then Kyler stopped, "But one thing doesn't make sense. What about the message Andrei sent to Jason Palmer? How could he be *aiding truth*? And what would it have to do with mass chaos in North Korea?"

"I think I can help you there," Goldman said. "I dug into Andrei's file and discovered what he'd done in his military days."

"And?"

"The guy's a chemist. His claim to fame was the development of a drug coded as SP-117. A truth serum that has no taste, smell, color or immediate side effects. Most importantly, the drugged victim has no recollection of what takes place while they're under its influence. The S directorate used it back then to check the trustworthiness of their own agents operating overseas to make sure they hadn't been turned."

"How's that any different than other truth serums the psychiatric field administers to patients? Doesn't sound very groundbreaking."

"They didn't have much of that back then for starters and even now, the current strains are administered intravenously and aren't nearly as effective because the victim tends to fall asleep or not go completely under. They also have memories of their incident. Even if that doesn't happen, there's rampant skepticism regarding its effectiveness after cases proving that information provided under current strains have been rendered false."

"So Andrei created a *real* truth serum and then cases of amnesia pop up from Stratton and Francois."

Goldman added, though felt his theory was weak.

"And it's possible that Dimarco's men are looking for information to specifically implicate his clients with the North Koreans which, if released, could cause mass chaos."

Kyler knew it was a reach but it was the best running theory they had.

"I think Andrei is there agent. Find him, grab him and then go find Hawkins. If we do that, we can start piecing this together. In the meantime, I'm going to check on our Stratton surveillance team. She could lead us to Dimarco's men here."

"Copy that sir."

With that, Kyler closed the computer, grabbed the envelope, pen and glasses and began to hurry out of the room. He stopped short of the door and doubled back to his bag. He decided to ditch the .38 and go for the Glock, adding a couple spare magazines into the pockets of his loose-fitting jeans. He was getting the sense that the nineteen rounds the Glock fired versus six on the pistol would come in handy.

He decided to stick to his original plan as far as Alani was concerned. She might turn something up in her search that could point to Hawkins or some additional details that could tie this all together.

Time was ticking though and he was certain of one thing. If Andrei was here, he needed to find him and get the hell out of here. He felt the walls beginning to close in around them and suspected their window of opportunity before getting discovered was closing.

With that, he closed the door behind him and headed back downstairs to find Carmen. He needed to find out when shipments left this place and was pretty sure she'd be able to help him find out, even if it took some creative massaging of the information. He passed the mirror and gave himself a once over.

Time to put on the Scott Cruz charm. He almost laughed aloud and then hurried out the door.

Chapter 52

Alani strolled down the hallway that the nomad wine pourer had directed her toward. It was not a typical claustrophobic corridor found in any Holiday Inn or Marriott. She noted that, in fact, there was nothing in this place that was done in a small or modest manner.

More sconces lit candles that lined the hall similar to the lobby she had left. The ceilings were at least fifteen feet tall at the point of its arched peak and were constructed in centuries-old stone. Under her feet ran a long, runner-style rug that followed the length of the hallway. Alani was certain it was made of nothing short of the finest material judging by its appearance. Between the candles, large tapestries hovered from floor to ceiling against the walls. Many looked to be of the surrounding areas including a castle that clearly dated back to its days of inception, judging by the men in armor positioned at its towers.

Alani slowly made her way to the end of the hall, which stopped at a large door that was nearly the height of the ceiling. It bore a large iron caste handle on it. She knew it was not the door to the library, seeing the classic double door entry to her right, which she was sure was it. Out of curiosity, she tugged on the handle only to find it locked. No surprise there, she thought.

Back to the mission at hand, Alani lightly rapped on one of the double doors.

"Si, entrare," she heard a voice say inside that she recognized to be Baldacci's from their earlier introduction.

She pushed hard on the heavy oak door, revealing an expansive and luxurious library. Dark oak lined the walls, ceiling, railing and bookshelves. She noted a spiral staircase to the left that seemed inset into the wall and traversed up to a second level. It was more of an all-encompassing balcony that encircled the room and gave way to more bookshelves. Alani noted a somewhat hidden door on that level and wondered where it would lead. Before she had too much time to take in more of the surroundings, she was brought to attention by Baldacci.

"Mi scusi signora Gannon," Baldacci said as he rose from his oversized brown leather chair that sat behind the desk. He crossed the room to greet her.

"I apologize for being so rude. I did not realize it was you, Signora Gannon. I thought it was merely one of the staff."

Despite his smooth approach, Alani didn't miss the swift hands of Baldacci as he had closed the lid of the laptop that was sitting atop his desk. He had done it as he stood and, she had to admit, would probably have done so without notice had she not been scrutinizing every detail.

"Oh no, Signore, excuse me for just barging in like this," she still held the glass of wine in her hand.

She'd made sure she left the top couple buttons undone on her shirt revealing a healthy amount of cleavage. Vitale hadn't failed to notice the signs Alani was giving off and he took a few steps forward to admire her beauty up close.

"It is of no inconvenience to me of course," then he stopped to look around her and when he found no one, asked, "Signore Scott is not with you?"

She shook her head, "No. He went up to the room to take care of some work. I decided to roam around and admire your beautiful hotel. I also wanted to thank you personally for making room for us on such short notice. I know you are booked months in advance so you must have made special arrangements to accommodate us."

Alani lightly grabbed his arm and continued, "It was very gracious of you. Grazie."

Baldacci actually flushed slightly, "It was nothing. Signore Scott's presence is important for our hotel," he paused and gave her a knowing look.

"Of course, had I known he would be bringing such a donna bellissima, I would have prepared our finest room!" With that he leaned down, grabbed her free hand and kissed it gently, lingering just a bit longer than normal.

Alani replied, "You are too kind but there's nothing to worry about. Our room is beautiful."

Alani knew she had his guard down a bit and began looking around. She didn't need the hassle of letting him take his attraction too far.

She said, "You have a beautiful library. Is this your office?"

Stepping back to follow her admiring gaze as she encompassed the room, Baldacci nodded, "Si, grazie. I have been here many years taking care of this wonderful winery and hotel. We have been very lucky to have such success."

She nodded and then reached into her clutch purse, opened it and pulled out the pack of cigarettes and lighter Kyler had given her.

"Would you mind if I smoke?" Alani asked.

"Of course not," he nodded taking her lighter from her to light the cigarette she'd pulled out. After having lit hers, he said, "I will join you."

She handed him a cigarette and he lit his as well and then made a move to hand the lighter back to her but she put her hands up to stop him. "No, that is my gift to you. I know it isn't much but consider it a token of my gratitude."

The zippo-style lighter was quite ornate and she hoped he wouldn't see it as a weak gesture. Though, in truth, she knew he wouldn't slight a woman whose interest he was trying to win over. He'd be the consummate gentleman.

True to form, he smiled and said, "Grazie. That is very kind. You do not have to do that. Like I say, it is my pleasure to have you here."

"Still, please take it. It's the least I can do."

"Grazie. It's beautiful. It belongs on my desk so I can be reminded of such loveliness," Baldacci set the lighter right where Alani hoped he would. It had a perfect line of sight to the laptop.

"Prego, please sit," Vitale said, gesturing toward two brown leather chairs that were positioned in front of another exquisite fireplace.

Alani obliged and set her glass down on the table, which was close to empty.

"Can I offer you some of our Riserva vino?" Vitale asked holding up a bottle and an opener. "I keep this only for my very special guests. We only bottled eighty of these. It is my personal favorite Chianti that we have made."

"That would be lovely," She replied.

Baldacci began opening the bottle and asked, "So what kind of music do you play?"

Alani shook her head back and forth as if deciding how to describe her supposed style, ultimately settling on, "Well I don't know if this will mean anything to you but I would say it is a combination of Alani Morissette and Nora Jones.   Sort of tormented, yet soft."

Baldacci shook his head while he poured the wine into two fresh glasses, "Si, si I believe I understand."

Alani almost laughed and thought, glad you do because I know I don't. She suspected, though, that he actually didn't have a clue.

Vitale handed her the glass and took the seat beside her, holding his glass up to her for a toast. "To the most beautiful woman I have ever met," he said and lightly clinked her glass.

Alani took an appreciative sip from the glass. It was nothing short of amazing and she decided that she would have to agree with his account of it being a favorite. She was sure she'd never had anything quite like it.

"Grazie Signore Baldacci. That's sweet of you to say."

"Please, call me Vitale. And I say this because it is true," Vitale took a gentle pull from his glass, not taking his eyes off of her as he did.

"You said that this has been your office for a long time? How long have you been working for its owner?"

"More than twenty years. This beautiful place is owned by my long-time friend, Gianni Dimarco. I'm sure you've heard of him. He's a great man. Very well-respected in Italy."

"Yes of course. We came from Florence and I heard great things about his restaurant…what is it called?" She had chosen to keep the fact that they'd visited the place a few nights ago a secret. No need to give Vitale the chance to start making connections.

"Via Di Santo Spirito," Vitale responded. "It is, without a doubt, the finest in Florence and possibly all of Italy."

Alani found that difficult to disagree with but, yet again, kept that to herself.

Vitale went on to say, "Gianni is also very well-respected in the clothing design community. He owns numerous high-end boutiques. He does not do anything…how would you say in America…half-assed?"

Alani laughed and said, "That's right. Well there is nothing half-assed about this winery. How did you and Signore Dimarco meet? Where you friends before you started working here?"

"Si. We were friends since childhood. We followed very different paths in our teenage years. Early on, he possessed a strong entrepreneurial spirit. He began starting his own businesses, the restaurant being his first."

Baldacci took another drink of his wine and went on.

"I was a bit of a rebel, I suppose, and went off join the Italian Army. After a short time, I was injured and had to leave the army. Gianni was very wonderful to ask me to help start his next business, this winery." He said the last part with a grand gesture of his surroundings, wine glass still in hand. "The rest is history."

He leaned forward to pick up the cigarette that had been sitting in the ashtray on the table and took a long drag from it.

Alani took the opportunity to speak, "I'm sure that Mr. Dimarco only offered the opportunity to you because he knew you would do well."

Baldacci smiled appreciatively, "Si, Gianni selects his entrusted partners in business very carefully. That is why we have only used the Amici Corporation for deliveries. No one else. Gianni has known Armand since his teenage years as well and would trust no one else to take care of his deliveries."

Alani was a bit surprised by how little coaxing she had to do with the man.

Baldacci leaned forward then and said in a much lower voice, "I will let you in on a little secret Signora Gannon. We are a few days away from taking Gianni's successes to new heights."

"Oh? What do you mean by that?" Alani asked, trying her best to appear nonchalant and even seduced by the mystery.

"I would tell you…but I would have to kill you," Vitale was looking at her with an intensity she hadn't seen from him yet and admitted to herself that she believed him.

Then Vitale laughed heartily, "You were so scared, Signora. I was only making a joke. But it is true that I cannot tell you more than that. But I can tell you that I will no longer need to run this hotel. I can leave it to Carmen to do most of the work."

"You're quite the tease," Alani replied, hoping he may reconsider elaborating.

Vitale took a drag from his cigarette but didn't take his eyes off Alani. The silence seemed to be minutes rather than seconds as Alani waited for his response.

As he exhaled, he narrowed his eyes at her and said, "So tell me why you are really here Signora."

The turn of conversation took Alani off guard but she did her best to keep her appearance neutral. *Does he know?* She wondered. She tried to think of everything they'd done since they arrived. Had they tipped him off somehow? She decided that it wasn't possible. They'd been extremely cautious. They'd played the part and had been discreet in their conversations. No, she decided, he couldn't possibly know so she played coy.

Alani leaned forward, drawing him, "What do you mean, Vitale?"

Vitale didn't hide his interest, giving her a long once over as he took another drag from the cigarette. He brought his eyes up to meet hers, his stare piercing into her. She fought to return the look while sticking to her sultry temptress act.

Just when she thought she'd look away, he responded.

"I believe you know exactly what I mean, Signora," as he said this, he leaned forward and she could feel his intensity as he did.

This time she fumbled a bit, her strength wavering only slightly and she prayed he didn't notice. She decided two could play at this game of coaxing the other to bite.

She leaned in and put her hand on his and said, "Why don't *you* tell *me* what I'm doing here, Vitale."

Baldacci did not move an inch except for his head, which slowly cocked to one side as he kept his eyes zeroed in on hers. She could feel his breath and she began assessing her ability to defend herself. She'd put herself in a vulnerable spot having one hand on his and the other holding the glass of wine, making a grab for her gun a split second delayed if she had to go for it. Alani kicked herself. She knew better than that.

She stayed calm and thought of her exit in her mind knowing that it would be the better bet. She was fairly certain he wasn't armed meaning any move he made toward her would be of his own physical ability rather than a weapon. *Stay still* she thought. *Let him make the first move.*

"You are not really who you say you are, Signora."

Shit. Despite her fear, she continued her ruse, running her hand up and slowly onto Vitale's arm.

"If I am not, then who am I?" It was the last question she would ask before making a move, she decided. His answer would decide the fate of her.

He kept his gaze on her, never looking away and then finally moved his hand to her leg.

"You, Signora, are Helen of Troy looking to wage war," as he said it, his lips curled up into his own devilish smile.

"You, a donna bellisima, arrive as the lover and guest of Signore Scott but here you sit…with me."

Alani relaxed slightly, relieved, but didn't respond as Baldacci continued on.

"So I say you are indeed Helen as it would only be waging war against my business to carry on with…this" as he said this he looked down to her hand on his arm. He added, "Although I would like nothing more, you understand. However, you arrived with a very important guest to me and I would be a fool to do anything to anger Mr. Scott."

Alani, truly relieved by the turn of events, pulled her hand back slowly.

"I understand Vitale. You're a true gentleman."

"Please don't misunderstand me, Signora. Maybe you can return soon…by yourself…and we can have another drink under different circumstances."

She smiled coyly, "I'll have to take you up on that offer. Soon."

That was her window to leave so she rose and said, "Grazie. Il vino e eccellente."

Vitale rose with her, took her hand and kissed it softly. "Please do return Signora and I will show you much more than my finest bottles of vino."

She smiled and said, "I will. It is a promise." Then she added, "I guess I should return to Mr. Scott. Wouldn't want him getting any crazy ideas, would we?"

"No we certainly would not," Vitale answered, releasing her hand. "Buona Sera Signora."

"Buona Sera."

With that, Alani turned and left, leaving him a healthy last look.

When she made it out into the hallway, she nearly collapsed as she finally fully relaxed. She'd been ready for a fight, which she wasn't sure she could handle knowing Baldacci's history. And more importantly, she didn't want their cover blown seeing as they had learned very little aside from confirming connections they already knew.

She decided she needed to get back to the room if nothing else than to collect herself. She'd wait for Kyler there, hoping he had a bit more luck. Alani's only solace being that she'd at least placed the lighter in a spot that could capture what they were looking for. Now it was up to Vitale to give them what they wanted.

Chapter 53

Kyler landed at the bottom of the stairs and, after a brief survey of the room, found Carmen chatting up a few guests sitting by the fireplace. He watched her as he waited for her to finish, not wanting to interrupt the exchange. He couldn't help but admit that she was quite beautiful and could understand why Vitale probably kept her in such close confidences.

Carmen and the two guests shared a laugh and she said something that Kyler guessed was an encouragement for the couple to let her know if they needed anything. She turned to walk back toward the front desk and spotted Kyler eyeing her. He didn't take his gaze away but, instead, smiled.

"Buona Sera Signore Scott," Carmen said as she made her way over to him, returning his smile with a polite one of her own. "Come stai questa sera?"

"Wonderful, grazie."

"Is everything to your liking in your room?"

"Absolutely. It's great. Grazie." He added, "Ms. Gannon is just getting some rest so I decided to roam a bit. See some of your beautiful hotel."

"Of course! Prego! Would you like a fresh glass of wine while you walk?"

Kyler paused and gave her his best bravado, "Yes. But only if you join me in a glass. Maybe you could show me around?"

Kyler Scott, a.k.a. Don Juan…or in this case, Don Giovanni.

He'd like to think that it was his charm that quickly persuaded her but knew it was more likely her duty as a hostess. Whatever the reason, mission accomplished. He could tend to his ego later.

"Si, it would be my pleasure. Solo un momento per favore."

She left him standing there to look around while she went to retrieve a couple glasses of wine. The opportunity to take more of the hotel in wasn't wasted on him. Admittedly, the first time they'd come into the lobby, he had been so overwhelmed by its grandeur that he failed to look around through investigative eyes. Now, as he did so, he noticed a few subtleties.

First to catch his attention were the "eyes in the sky," as Las Vegas called them. They were cameras that were effectively hidden in the dark ceiling that helped blend the black dome that encased them. Kyler surmised that the camera was positioned to one side of the actual mount with enough distance to pan in all directions if necessary while using the dome lens to create space for the camera to move about without its line of site being infringed upon by the ceiling.

As he looked around the large space, he counted four cameras covering all corners of the lobby. By their positioning, they could also pan down each of the hallways and up the stairs to the second level. The end result was full coverage of every visible inch. Kyler would bet his Enzo that the method was replicated throughout the hotel, taking advantage of the interior design and its necessity for elaborate lighting fixtures.

Why the need for such surveillance, Signore Baldacci? Kyler mused, though knowing the question was a bit rhetorical.

"Beautiful, isn't it?" Kyler heard Carmen say, somewhat startling him. He hadn't heard her approach, which was a surprise.

He recovered efficiently, "The most beautiful I've seen," he agreed and added, "And I've seen my fair share of amazing hotels."

Kyler Scott, King of Modesty.

"I'm sure you have. Thank you," she handed him the glass of wine and turned toward a hallway to the left of the stairs.

"Shall we?"

"Lead the way, Signora," as he said this he offered her his arm which she took as they made their way down the hall.

As they entered, he did a quick scan noting that there didn't seem to be cameras anywhere. Nothing to protect, he imagined. He assumed that the lobby was an initial point of evaluation of sorts to determine who came and went, not to mention keeping a record of it. Kyler made a mental note to look for access to such records. Seeing who frequented the establishment could provide additional clues if necessary.

"This piece was donated by a descendent of Paul Letarouilly," Kyler heard Carmen say while pointing to a tapestry that hung from the wall to his left.

"Do you know the history?"

Kyler actually did, thankful she didn't notice he hadn't been paying attention.

"Si. He published the folio, The Buildings of Modern Rome, to show the Italian representations of architecture in the Renaissance Era, correct?"

Clearly impressed, Carmen nodded, "Bravissimo, Signore Scott, you know your Italian history very well."

Kyler couldn't help feeling a bit proud.

"I have what you might call a bit of a love affair with your country." He shot her his best seductive look, which he hoped didn't look like he was constipated. He couldn't be sure.

He added, "I've found its people to be quite alluring as well"

Go on with your bad self, Don Giovanni. Kyler Scott, Renaissance Man.

To his surprise, his ruse worked and she pulled in a bit closer to him as they continued down the hallway. She pointed out a few other tapestries, some of which Kyler also knew the history of, further dazzling her with his brilliance.

As they neared the end of the stretch of hallway, which broke off into two directions, he decided to test his success in the art of swooning the fair Carmen. He and Alani couldn't afford to wait until tomorrow's tour to see the winery in light of the fact that

Hawkins was in danger, assuming he was still alive, and now they had a possible connection with the sex trade news. They needed answers tonight and they needed to get out of here as soon as they had them.

"Signore Baldacci promised me a private tour of your winery, particularly where the wine is made. I'd like to take him up on his offer but would much prefer you as my guide if you don't mind." He glanced at his empty glass, adding, "Maybe even sample some of the latest batch from a barrel if it wouldn't be too much trouble?"

Carmen eyed him curiously, obviously making her own assumptions of what he was intimating. The production operations were shut down for the day meaning that he wouldn't see much. As a matter of fact, there would be nobody back there at all.

"It would be my pleasure," she answered with a coy smile.

Chapter 54

"When did they arrive?" Gianni Dimarco asked in Italian as he spoke into the phone. The restaurant was closed and empty, having said goodnight to its last guest about twenty minutes earlier.

"How sure are you?" he asked, listening to the reply.

"Our cameras scanned the images and compared it to the database as we do for all guests. The man's name is indeed Kyler Scott, the actor. I remembered you mentioning he was at the restaurant a couple of days ago." Vitale Baldacci answered.

Dimarco had mentioned the visit offhandedly when the two were idly chatting the day before. He hadn't thought anything of it at the time.

"Are you sure it's not just a coincidence?"

"That they would visit both of your establishments within a couple days of each other?"

"It's possible. We could just be paranoid since we are so close to the end," Dimarco didn't believe it but he needed confirmation from his entrusted partner.

"Possible. But it's not the case here. I can't be sure about Mr. Scott. He's not directly listed in the database our men looked at. The only connection is through his father who spent several decades in the United States Army. The woman...a beauty...came back with a hit. She is not, as she claims, a famous musician by the name of Grace Gannon. Her name is Alani Langdon. According to our sources, assuming they are correct, Ms. Langdon is with the CIA."

"What do we make of Mr. Scott then?"

"Covert agent? Black ops? Maybe he's nothing at all and she's just using his fame to get reservations where she needs it. Who knows? Either way, he is involved."

"Well you know what to do Vitale, keep them there and under close watch. Do you have an eye on them?"

"The woman just went back to the room. Scott is getting a tour from Carmen."

"Don't lose them and do not let them know you know who they are unless you have to," then Dimarco added, "Keep them inside the hotel. Do you understand?"

"Completely. I'll pull up the video of the room and monitor them."

"Good. Call me if anything changes."

Dimarco didn't wait for Vitale's reply. He hung up the phone and immediately picked it up off the receiver again, dialing a number he'd committed to memory long ago.

When the other end answered, he said, "Armand, our suspicions were correct. At least one of the Americans works for the CIA. Maybe both of them. They seem to know nothing at the moment but get what you need out of Hawkins immediately."

"Are you sure they don't suspect anything?" Armand asked calmly.

"Arrogant Americans. They are underestimating us. Vitale will take care of them if necessary."

"Understood. We are on schedule." At that, Gianni's line went dead and he hung up the phone. Dimarco smiled as he hoped Vitale would indeed have to…take care of the Americans.

Chapter 55

Vitale Baldacci hung up the phone, opened the lid of his laptop and hit a few buttons. He reached under the desk, pressed a button and waited as a piece of the top of the desk just beyond where his laptop sat slid to the side. When it was done, a thirty-inch monitor rose seemingly out of nowhere and settled into place. Baldacci hit another key and the image from the laptop was now showing on the high-resolution monitor.

On screen were over fifty thumbnail images of live video feed representing where each camera in the hotel was installed. He scanned the images and found the one he was looking for. He double-clicked on it and the image immediately morphed to encompass the large screen. To his surprise, the room was empty. He swore aloud. Kyler Scott was not in his room. Surprise surprise...Ms. Gannon, or more accurately, Alani Langdon, had lied.

He minimized the image into half the size, selected the search area, typed his query and pulled up a still image from the lobby. It was time-stamped an hour ago and had the symbol synonymous with *play* at its center. He clicked the icon and the video launched. Vitale sped it up to three times normal speed until he saw Kyler Scott come into frame where he returned it to normal speed.

He watched as it replayed the interaction with Carmen and then Scott's subtle scan of the lobby, at which point he looked directly at one of the cameras trained on his face. It was a great angle to freeze-frame the high-resolution image, run the identity analyzer and confirm his identity. That is, if he hadn't already done that an hour ago when they arrived.

Vitale watched closely as Carmen returned with two glasses of wine and they made their way down the western hallway. Vitale hadn't brought Carmen in on the information he'd discovered on the two Americans. He wasn't big on trust and she didn't rank high enough on his list. Though at the moment, he was wishing he had given that a second thought. There were no cameras down that hall though they'd be picked up if they went anywhere vital.

Vitale pulled open the drawer and pulled out a walkie, clicking onto the desired channel.

"Position four, report in," he said in Italian as he pressed on the button of the walkie.

"Copy position four. Go ahead," he heard in response.

"Target Alpha is on the move with Carmen through Pisa. Surround the channels lightly," Vitale said. Pisa was what they called the western hallway. He wanted his men to watch Carmen and Kyler's travels without tipping Scott off so he could see where they were headed.

"Copy that. Soft surveillance in motion."

"And position teams on the perimeter of Venice," Vitale added, Venice being the wine production building on the grounds.

"Copy. Over and out."

Vitale put the walkie down and returned his attention to the screen. Just as he did so, he saw Alani enter her room. She scanned the room, looking for Scott he guessed, and then watched her make her way to the desk. She stopped short of it though and turned her attention to the duffel bag sitting on the bed.

Alani pulled out the same bug detection tools she and Kyler had used before to sweep the room and Vitale laughed out loud.

"You won't find anything Signora but please…carry on. This is quite entertaining," Baldacci said to the image.

The cameras installed were created by Armand Amici and his company of engineers. They had found a communication method that operated on a frequency not yet recognized by any of the most advanced bug detection systems, including those used by military units around the world.

Vitale watched as Alani settled on her false sense of satisfaction when her tools set off no warnings of bugs. She then walked over to the desk where the laptop sat and hit a few buttons to boot it up. She exited to the bathroom and Vitale cursed himself for not having line of site into it. While she was the enemy whose life he'd happily put an end to if need be, she was, without question, one of the most beautiful women he'd ever encountered. What a waste it would be to have to kill her.

She returned to view in jeans that flattered her long legs and a tank top that did little to hide the rest of her. To his disappointment, she pulled on a sweatshirt and zipped it up tight.

Sitting back at the desk, Baldacci watched as she swiped her finger on the machine to gain access. He knew from watching Kyler earlier that he'd see nothing on the screen. Though the display was slightly in view and, in most cases, he could zoom into get a glimpse, this laptop had been installed with an advanced privacy screen. It was a film that prevented overly curious bystanders from viewing what was on the screen unless sitting directly in front of it. While most merely prevented others from seeing from any angle, this filter required the viewer to be seated within two feet of the screen. It used the laptop's camera to first authenticate the individual as authorized to access the computer through facial recognition. After that initial confirmation, it continuously monitored the person's distance from the camera, putting the laptop into standby mode after two minutes of someone being out of its range.

Vitale mused that they were probably invented by someone who got tired of nosy airplane neighbors catching glimpses of family photos and using it as an excuse to talk your ear off for an entire six-hour plane ride.

Baldacci watched Alani's face closely as she read something on the screen. He could only assume it had been left there previously from when Scott last looked since she hadn't clicked on anything new when she logged in.

Whatever she was reading registered something on her face. Was it concern? Fear? He wasn't sure and, apparently she wasn't sure how to react either because she stayed in the chair after finishing reading. She looked to be debating her next move. Making up her mind, she went back into the bedroom, returned seconds later with the sweatshirt off again, another in hand and was sticking a pistol into the back of her jeans. He watched her pull on the sweatshirt, which appeared to be looser fitting as to conceal the weapon. She scanned the room once more, closed the lid of the laptop and hurried out.

Vitale shook his head sadly. "We could have been a beautiful couple," he said aloud. "But now you have to die."

Chapter 56

Kyler walked alongside Carmen as they exited the rear end of the hotel onto a stone walkway. The air was brisk as they stopped to take in their surroundings, which, despite the dark night, were lit up just enough by a nearly full moon to reveal acres upon acres of rolling hills of vines.

Carmen began pointing to various patches.

"That row," she said, pointing to the far left side where the vines started, "Those are the Chianti Riserva vines. We will bottle maybe a hundred with those grapes and sell them to our VIP guests."

"Maybe yours truly?" Kyler inquired.

"But of course," she smiled and continued on, pointing to a much larger section in the middle.

"And that group is for the Chianti that we will sell to the restaurants all over Italy. It is...how would you say...common wine?"

"Ah...the poor man's Chianti," Kyler chided.

"I don't think I understand."

"Never mind," Kyler waved it off. "And where does this path lead to?"

"Our destination," she replied, not hiding her undertone of intent. "That is what we call Venezia. It's where all the grapes are brought in, they are sorted through and only the best are chosen to be used for our wine. Then they are, as we like to say on our tours, made into flavors of love and seduction."

Kyler raised an eyebrow as he glanced back at her, "Love and seduction. Hmm."

"Si. Hence the name of Venezia, the city of lovers."

"Well it would seem appropriately named for more than one reason," he countered. "Shall we?"

She began to follow but then shivered violently as an icy breeze rushed through.

"Would you mind waiting while I grab a jacket?"

Kyler smiled from the inside out, "Oh not at all."

He watched as she turned and strode back inside. When she was clearly inside and out of view, he turned and made his way toward the building. At first in a walk as to not draw any attention and then breaking into a full out run when he was completely out of the light of the hotel.

It was now or never. As he ran, he knew he was starting the domino effect. Carmen would return and wonder where he went. If he were lucky, she'd assume she was rudely deserted. More likely, she would send someone to come looking for him. Judging by the security he'd already seen, not to mention the staff, his bet was on the latter. He picked up his pace. He had about fifty yards to go and he was at max speed now. His eyes were darting around every which way, ready for someone to pounce from the perimeter of the building or the dark rows of vines.

He made it to the door of the building, checked it and was not surprised to find it locked. He couldn't afford the noise of shooting the door open so he opted to pick the lock despite the extra time it'd take.

From his pocket, he pulled out a small pouch that looked like a mini vanity kit. He pulled out two pieces; a wrench and thin wire that had five prongs sticking upward at a ninety-degree angle and evenly spaced out in order to simultaneously push up the pins of most locks. Kyler could pick a lock in three seconds with the kit and, true to form, was turning the lock and entering the building in under five.

He closed the door behind him and extracted glasses from inside his jacket pocket. In addition to being an ingeniously designed camera, they also had the added benefit of night vision. He put them on and quickly took in his surroundings.

What he saw were the green hues of rows and rows of oak barrels that ran down man-made tunnels of caves intended to create the desired climate ideal for the wine to mature over periods of two and three years until they were ready for bottling. While it was ideal for wine development, Kyler was more concerned with it being an incredibly convenient place for an attacker to hide. He needed to get out of the line of sight. He doubted anyone saw him enter but couldn't be sure Baldacci hadn't stationed men inside the building at all times either.

Kyler ran toward the wall that ran along the backside of the building and flattened his body against it. Once he was sure he was in a relatively safe position, he pulled his phone from his other pocket, hit a couple buttons and pulled up the image of the heat zone map of the building that he'd reviewed earlier. He needed to identify the hot zone, get there, grab a sample of whatever the hell was in it and get the hell out.

Kyler got his bearings and identified his current location. He saw that he needed to enter a door that was to his right which would lead to a hallway that ran clear to the back of the building.

He tried the handle and found it locked yet again.

"Screw it," he said as he pulled out the Glock. He didn't have time to fumble in the dark again for the kit and hoped that being indoors would be enough to quiet the noise of firing the weapon. He cursed himself for leaving the silencing tube behind.

He stepped back, aimed at the bolt and fired a single round with success. Scott gave the door a kick and it flew open. He actually laughed to himself at the many times he'd purely kicked the door down without the gunshot in his own movies knowing it'd never work on most doors assuming they weren't made of paper. Crazy, he thought, the things that come to mind in times like these.

Kyler was already racing down the hall and doing his best to see ahead of him. His eyes had, as many in his profession, become adapt to adjusting to the dark quickly and the aid of the glasses was about as good as daylight to him at this point.

There was one last door in front of him leading to the room he knew he needed. He raised the gun once more after stopping short, fired and kicked again. He was in.

After a quick assessment of the room, he saw boxes of what he could only assume were wine bottles on one side. On the other side, there was a smattering of lab equipment mixed with machinery that he guessed were used to bottle and seal the wine.

He sprinted over to the table with the boxes and pulled out his phone again. One of the many tools he'd been given included an application the techs installed on his phone that used the camera lens to shoot out an infrared beam. It was similar to the ones used to uncover the truth beneath the sheets of the most popular hotel chains across the country…the same ones that suddenly made staying at home in a trusted bed a lot more appealing.

Kyler reached in and grabbed a bottle. He couldn't afford any wasted time and opted to slam the top skinny opening of the bottle against the edge of the counter. The effect was a messy one but it did the trick. He poured the contents out on the counter, hit a couple keys on the phone to activate the program and waved the back end of the device over the spilled liquid.

After getting what was apparently a sufficient sample of the substance, he saw the hourglass icon appear on the screen indicating the program was beginning to process and save the sample. When the operation was complete, he clicked a couple more buttons, pulled up the option to email the sample, entered Goldman's address and hit send.

Task completed, he began making his way back when he remembered what else Goldman asked. He needed to find a delivery vehicle. His internal clock of time until he believed he'd have company ticked away quickly. He pulled up the image of the building again on his phone and located where the garage would be that housed the trucks.

Scott looked around the room once more and found a door that he was certain, judging by the image, would take him deeper into the building and back to the garage. He arrived at the door and was glad to find it locked from the inside out, obviously not caring who got out to the garage as long as they couldn't get in this room. He unlatched the door, flew down the hallway, took a slight turn to the left and hit the door he was looking for.

This one, gladly, was also unlocked. He swung it open and smiled. *Bingo*. There were two trucks, both with five glorious letters etched along the side. A...M...I...C...I.

He ran over to the truck and circled it, looking for an ideal space. Taking the truck in again, he realized that the rear of it was a removable cargo carrier. He quickly ascertained that to be the best option to follow the delivery to its final destination even if it went air or sea-bound.

Having sent off the sample, he no longer needed the phone, not to mention he had two more in the bag sitting in his room just like it. The cell signal was also ideal for GPS triangulation and the spare battery would give them over eight hours of tracking, more than enough for wherever it was headed.

On the back of the phone, he peeled off an exterior layer revealing one of the strongest adhesive materials produced. It would easily attach to the metal surface and could withstand a pounding from all elements that would hit the underside of the carrier. The phone itself emulated his laptop. It consisted of military-grade ruggedized material, ensuring it, too, would last the trip and would continue to communicate its location back to the team at QTS Tek who'd be tracking the vehicle.

Just as he set the phone in place, tugging on it several times to make sure it was secure, he heard a noise. It was faint but he knew the sound well. It was the squeak of rubber soles on the garage surface. It was a mistake by its owner, not accounting for the type of surface usually associated with garages. A mistake he was grateful for, springing him into defensive action.

In a flash, his gun was drawn and he was crouched low in an attempt to scan the floor under the truck for the feet of his assailant...*or assailants*, he thought, was more probable. Scott was sure his attackers wouldn't assume he'd have night vision and were probably waiting for him to walk right out in front of them for an easy kill.

As expected, as Kyler panned the room, he found not one but six sets of legs staggered around the perimeter. They all seemed to be momentarily frozen, collectively establishing a strategy, he was certain. Kyler quickly calculated his options and decided getting to high ground was going to be his best point of attack.

Not looking to give the half-dozen trained opposition more time than necessary to pounce, he silently scaled the front side of the truck. He used the step on the passenger side to mount onto the hood, reached up to the topside of the truck and, using his upper body strength, quickly and quietly pulled his body up to the roof where he lay still for a second. He held his breath momentarily and listened. They didn't seem to hear him and, for their part, weren't offering up any sounds of their own.

Kyler slowly crawled to the edge of the roof just enough to see the outlines of the men. He pulled back and cursed silently again as he noted they too all had night vision goggles of their own. None had been looking upward, to his amazing good fortune, and he'd had enough time to mentally mark where each were positioned. He needed accuracy more than ever and gripped the Glock firmly with his finger trained just over the trigger.

Here goes nothin' he said as he slid out again with the gun aimed. Going right to left in marksman-like accuracy, he took the first three men out in sequence with well-trained head shots before they could even react. Anticipating their reaction time, he pulled back after the third shot, just in time to feel the first bullet whiz past the spot his head had been not a split second before.

He rolled three times to the left with blazing speed and popped out once more. Starting left to right this time, Kyler fired headshots into the first two, dropping them instantly, and then a shoulder shot on the shooting arm of the third. The last man dropped his gun and hollered in pain. For good measure, Kyler unloaded another bullet into the man's kneecap. The shooter collapsed in what he imagined was a fire of agony as the knee exploded. Again, unlike the movies, most people, even the most badass individuals, weren't going to keep going strong after having a 9mm bullet rip through their flesh. The shots may not be fatal but were definitely debilitating.

After the last shot, Kyler leapt down from the roof, landing softly on the balls of his feet like a cat, preventing his knees from exploding right out from underneath him. He kept the gun trained on the man who was now writhing, in obvious pain. Kyler guessed he had a few minutes until the man would likely pass out as the body went into self-preservation mode.

"Parli inglese?" Kyler asked the man.

"Yeah," the man winced. "I can say fuck you!"

Kyler shook his head in disappointment and stepped a foot down onto the man's injured shoulder. A loud cry filled the room and sweat was beginning to pour out of the guard's face as his body desperately fought the effects of the pain. Kyler knew if he pushed too hard, he would pass out from shock. He released his foot.

"I'd say your English is fine."

Kyler leaned down to face him, positioning the gun just over the wound as the man, despite his best attempts, began convulsing from his fear of the additional pain.

"I just need to know where Armand Amici's office is. That's it. If you tell me that, I promise not to shoot your other arm and knee cap and leave you for dead."

"I know nothing! Go fuck yourself you fucking American asshole!"

Kyler again shook his head, making the *tsk tsk tsk* sound as he did so. He then pushed the muzzle of the gun hard into the spot where the bullet head entered the man's shoulder. The man let out a blood-curdling scream and Scott pushed a little harder.

He tried to struggle away but Kyler mounted him, pinning his knees against the man's legs and just above the injured knee as his free hand went to his neck. It didn't take a great deal of force since the man was quickly losing strength from the pain and loss of blood.

Without taking the gun off but releasing a little of the pressure so as to be heard, Kyler said, "Just an address. That's all and this will all be over. Or you can end up like your friends...i tuoi amici, here." He said nodding his head to the bodies strewn around them.

Just when Kyler thought the man was going to pass out, he gasped, "Via Del Giglio...13."

Kyler wasn't sure he heard the man right. "In Florence?"

"Si! Si!"

"You're lying. That's a hotel, I've seen it," Kyler said, pushing down on the shoulder again.

The man howled louder and Kyler released it a bit again.

"That's the fucking point! Amici owns the fucking place you ignorant asshole. First three floors for guests, the rest for Amici!"

At that, he finally released the man.

"Grazie." And with that, he slammed the butt of the gun against the man's head, knocking him unconscious.

Kyler couldn't believe it. The address for Armand Amici was on the same damn block as his own hotel, Boscolo Astoria. This morning, he and Alani had been twenty yards from where he suspected Hawkins was currently being kept and they didn't even know it. There had been no way they could have suspected it but he couldn't help wishing somehow they had seen some kind of clue. Now he could only hope they weren't too late.

Looking around at the bodies strewn around him, he decided his stay at Villa Santini had run its course. Time to find Alani and get to Hawkins.

With that he raced back the way he entered. He arrived back in the lab he had just been in and was about to hit the door that led back into the warehouse when, out of the corner of his eye, he saw light peeking out on the floor from a door to his left. He put the brakes on and looked closer. The door was at the end of the rows of tables that housed the lab equipment and Kyler wondered how he'd missed it moments ago. He supposed he had been so fixated on gathering the sample from the bottles that he hadn't taken the time to look around.

Kyler knew he was both short on time and probably on the verge of being faced with another wave of attackers but he felt the pull of curiosity to see what was behind the door. As he took a few steps towards it, his interest escalated when the light suddenly went out.

You can't hide in the dark, whoever you are. Kyler thought to himself and quickly arrived at the door. He lightly checked the knob and was surprised to find that the lock for the door was oddly on *his* side. *Designed to lock something in instead of keep others out?* he questioned. Strange.

Kyler readied his weapon and, in a swift motion, turned the knob and rushed the room, gun trained on whatever was on the other side.

A frightened man who looked to be in his sixties shot his arms high into the air and screamed "Vi prego di non mandarmi!"

Kyler kept his gun aimed at the old man and asked, in English, "What is your name?"

"Please don't shoot me!" the man repeated in English.

"I'm not going to shoot you. What is your name?"

"I am Andrei Ivanova."

Chapter 57

Alani tried to keep her pace normal as she walked down the hallway. She recalled the words she'd read on the screen from the conversation Kyler had had with Goldman. Hawkins was in Florence. She also read the article Goldman had sent over and, though she didn't have time to fully process it, she was starting to put pieces together. Kyler had obviously left that behind for her in case she returned to the room before he did and she could imagine he'd picked up the pace of their plan as a result. It was time for her to do the same.

She had a feeling that there was something either behind the locked door at the end of the hallway by Baldacci's office or in the room on the second tier of the office itself. Whatever it was, she wasn't going to find it sitting around in her room waiting for Kyler to get back. The other concern that haunted her more was the possibility that he wouldn't come back at all.

Alani needed a distraction, something to pull Baldacci out his office so she could be free to explore both rooms without getting caught. She tried to think quickly. She, like Kyler, had noticed the surveillance cameras in the lobby and needed to carefully plot her next move. Though it was an old trick she decided it was the best way.

Alani found a man walking around with trays of wine and asked, "Dove il bagno, per favore?"

The man smiled and pointed her toward a small hallway.

"Grazie," she said and followed the man's signal. She pushed down on the handle of the door marked *Donne*, or Ladies, and entered. She scanned the ceiling and found the fire detector just above the countertop. She hopped up, reached into her purse and then remembered she'd given her lighter to Baldacci. She examined the device and decided she had no idea how to trip the alarm manually. She guessed she should have learned how to steal cars in her youth.

Hopping down from the counter she had to come up with a different plan. She couldn't simply have him summoned to the front desk. It wouldn't give her enough time, for one, and it would raise too much curiosity when he got there only to find her not there waiting for him.

The only idea that came to her was not one she loved but it was sure to be effective. She pulled out her own Glock that she'd stowed away in her jeans and reached inside for her silencer, which she, unlike Kyler, had remembered to grab.

She screwed the tube on the end of the muzzle, popped out the magazine to make sure it was loaded, slammed the magazine back in and clicked off the safety on the weapon. She then pressed her ear up against the door and listened silently. After only about a minute, she got lucky and heard the footsteps of what sounded like a man's dress shoe.

She waited a few seconds longer and knew she was right when the sound passed by her door toward the men's room that she knew to be another twenty feet down the hall. In silence and amazing grace, she slipped out through the barely-cracked door, stepped lightly into the hall and took aim, apologizing silently as she did so. Just as the man began to slow, she fired and hit her mark. The bullet struck with perfect precision, skimming the side of the man's foot as he'd paused to enter the bathroom. The shot was intended to pierce his skin, hurt like hell but do no permanent damage.

In the short time that it took for the pain to register with the innocent and oblivious victim, Alani had turned, slipped out of the hallway, around the corner, down the next passageway and out of sight just as the man began to scream. She had watched carefully as she passed, confident that nobody saw her as she did, and then heard the mass rush of staff and guests coming to the man's aid.

From her position, she was effectively hidden but still had a line of sight to the front desk. She watched as a staffer, whom she noted was not Carmen, picked up the phone and hit a button. She hoped that it was an internal call to Baldacci requesting his assistance and direction. The woman hung up the phone quickly, picked it up again and dialed a longer number this time. Alani assumed it was the medic and guiltily hoped, for the victim's sake, he or she was close by.

For what seemed like an eternity, she waited, eyeing the alcove that she knew Vitale would have to emerge from, assuming he hadn't left his office since the time she left.

A few more excruciatingly long seconds passed and then she saw him, half walking, half running toward the front desk. The staffer who'd called it in, pointed toward the spot where the man had gone down. He jogged toward it while Alani held her breath hoping not to be spotted. He passed and she waited another beat and made her move. She swiftly made her way back to the point he'd exited from and hurried down the hall, confident that ninety-nine percent of the hotel was entirely focused on a man suffering from what she hoped they would determine to be a mysterious wound. The desire for mystery, not the attempt to minimize pain, was the primary reason she'd tried to merely graze him.

No bullet hole, no bullet. At least not one that would be discovered quickly. That left the question…What had the man viciously injured himself on in this fine, upstanding hotel? She couldn't help but smile at how perfectly she executed the shot. The simple pleasures of the profession.

She picked up the pace, running toward the first locked door. As she ran, she pulled out the tools she'd stowed away in her purse, which looked quite similar to the ones Kyler had been carrying. She had both in hand by the time she hit the door and was quickly going to work on the lock. In a matter of a few seconds, she was pulling the door open.

"You gotta be kidding me," she said aloud with more than a bit of disappointment. The room was full of spare toiletries, towels and sheets for the guests. Not something she deemed worthy of high security.

Not having time to dwell on it, she quickly made her way into the library. Turning immediately to her left, she bounded the spiral staircase as quickly as possible, arriving onto the landing of the second floor. She crossed the ten steps over to where she'd spied the concealed door earlier. It was hidden well, surrounded by rows of shelves on its exterior paneling so as to blend in, but she had clearly seen the narrow gap that ran from floor to ceiling earlier. She moved some books aside on the level she assumed the door handle to be, hoping it wasn't some crazy trick door that she'd need to find a latch for.

She breathed a sigh of relief, exposing the handle she'd been hoping for. She went back to her tools once again after checking and confirming the door was locked. In even quicker time than the first, she freed the nob and pulled the door open slowly, hoping to keep the books relatively intact.

As she opened the door her jaw dropped as she took in the room. She could not believe what she was looking at.

Chapter 58

Kyler stared back at Andrei Ivanova, a small, shriveled man who looked like the stereotypical image of a mad scientist. He had long, grey, disheveled hair that hadn't seen a comb or a shower in months and an unkempt beard. His fearful eyes were cloudy blue and the skin not covered with hair was worn and wrinkled.

Seeing how scared Ivanova was, Kyler lowered his gun.

"You can put your hands down, Andrei. I'm not going to shoot you."

Andrei slowly lowered his hands and relaxed, but only slightly. He eyed Kyler with skepticism.

"It's ok," Kyler said, seeing the look.

Kyler took a moment to scan the room, which contained a small twin-sized bed, a card table pushed up against the wall with a utilitarian-style lamp on it, a metal chair positioned in front of the table and about two dozen medical books stacked in the corner next to the table. The room was windowless and had the odor of the man who likely hadn't showered for an excruciatingly long time.

Kyler thought quickly. He suspected that he didn't have long before more men were going to be all over him. More importantly, his thoughts went to Alani. She likely didn't know that she was exposed and that meant she was a sitting duck. He needed to get to her and quickly.

Worried that Andrei might take off, he pointed to the metal chair.

"Sit," he caught himself. "Please…sit."

He looked around and saw the pillow on the bed. He grabbed it and pulled the pillowcase off of it. Pulling a knife out, he made quick work of cutting the material into four slits of cloth. He put the knife back and swiftly secured Ivanova's hands and feet to the metal chair.

Checking the knots once more, he said, "I'll be back. Don't go anywhere."

He closed the door behind him to maintain the appearance that nothing was awry, rounded the corner and raced down the last hallway of the building and away from the lab.

Kyler skidded to a stop at the door that led back into the first room, pausing to listen momentarily while remembering the rows of wine barrels that provided ideal cover for those potentially waiting in the wings.

He concluded that there was no fully protected path he could take toward the exit. At the very least, he'd have to be exposed for brief gaps of time as he passed the faux cave entrances and needed to minimize that time as much as possible through speed. He was quietly hoping that this wouldn't be necessary. Maybe he'd taken out the entire protection squad. Logically, he knew there was a fat chance of that though. Baldacci was likely to have employed an army of disciplined men. Even if they'd heard the firefight through walls and multiple sets of doors, they would be trained to keep their position. If the first team wasn't successful in their mission, they were to stand their ground to prepare for their opportunity to do so. It was textbook military tactics and he, of all people, knew it.

Standing behind the door, his nerves flared up briefly like a teenage boy going in for his first kiss with his high school crush. He took a moment to center himself, focusing on his breathing as his years of Tai Chi training had taught him. He felt the world around him slow down, including the pounding in his chest. In his mind's eye, he saw the layout of the room and saw himself go through the stages of his exit, preparing for the worst. Right about now would have been a great time to be fully stocked with grenades or even some flash bangs but he'd have to make do without.

Here we go again he said as he quickly and quietly shoved the door open with his left hand, gun poised at the ready in his right, and peeled himself to the same wall that the door was on. With the entrances to the caves being along that same line, Kyler ran quickly along it toward the first opening, running in tip-toe style on the balls of his feet to avoid making any noise as he went along. He ran in a semi-crouched position to keep his profile as low as possible until he arrived at the first opening. There was a barrel in front of it that served as a shield for him to hide behind and take in the layout.

Kyler reached into his pocket and grabbed a spare clip of ammunition so he'd be ready to reload. He had a choice to make. Either run like hell across, opting for the element of surprise, or fire a warning shot in the cave and let anybody that was there fire back to show him their positions.

Gambling on the off chance that this pack of enemies may not be sporting night gear, he decided on option one. With gun and clip in hand he took off across the opening. He got about halfway when he heard the first shot and felt the breeze as it narrowly missed his head. *Guess I lost that bet* he thought. Seeing the end of the opening just ten feet ahead, he launched his body like a torpedo through the air, tucked his head inward and used the heels of both palms to brace his fall, curling into a perfectly executed dive roll. As he did, he heard a torrent of gunfire follow the initial missed shot, their sounds even more deafening as they ricocheted off the walls of the hollowed out cave.

Kyler needed to keep the shooters at bay so he quickly wrapped around the other side of a barrel for protection and looked back into the opening as the spurts of semi-automatic shots continued to spray in his direction. He was able to spot the areas of origins and took quick aim.

He squeezed off half a dozen rapid-fire shots in as many different locations. He wasn't aiming for targets, knowing there was a slim chance his bullets would find flesh, but rather at the barrels closest to each. With each shot, the oak exploded into the air, with an eruption of liquid to follow. The attackers weren't going to die from wine exposure but the well placed explosions and spray of shards of wood and liquid would buy him enough time to make a break for the door, assuming there weren't more units stationed at each cave.

He was off and running in full sprint now. No need for tip toeing anymore. The jig was up. He didn't bother pausing at the next opening but jetted right through. The minute he hit the opening he held his breath for a split second and closed his eyes in preparation for another firing onslaught. It never came and he exhaled in relief. He'd assumed there wouldn't be more troops otherwise they would have likely emerged after the initial gunfire erupted but he couldn't be sure.

His relief was brief as he heard a shot hit a barrel a few feet to his left. The group had recovered, were out of the cave and in pursuit.

He began a zig zag run while he calculated the distance to the door. He decided he wouldn't make it and changed his plan. Gunfire was exploding to all sides of him, several which were close enough for him to feel as they skimmed past his head. Ten yards ahead of him was a window and he picked up the pace. When he was five yards away, he pulled his jacket up over his head and launched his body in the air head-first toward the window. Leading with the metal of the clip and gun in each hand, he exploded through the pane of glass. The first half of his body made it through relatively unscathed but he felt a hot sharp pain as his calves and ankles took the brunt of the shattered glass raining down on him. He dropped the gun and clip, felt his feet clear the opening, stuck his hands out and tucked aggressively into a roll just in time for his hands to find grass. He rolled quickly, surprised by how little impact he took through the fall and silently thanked his recent parcore training.

His flesh was on fire from the glass but he didn't have time to worry about it. Thankfully his glasses had miraculously stayed in place through the dive and he was able to spot his gun and clip quickly. He snatched both up and made a mad dash for the rows of vines.

Just as he hit the first patch and flattened himself to the ground, he heard the door to the building swing open and the men shouting orders to each other. Kyler now had the advantage of position and he calmed his breathing while he waited for his opportunity. He counted five men standing at the corner of the building, one of them clearly the leader as he pointed and barked orders to the other four. The ring leader directed two of the men to follow along the wall that Kyler had exited through, clearly betting on the chance that he may have ran around to the back side of the building. The other three were headed directly for him, surprising him since that left them completely exposed with no cover while he had plenty.

Before he could understand what was happening, he saw two men wind back and hurtle two objects in the air. *Shit* he said aloud as he caught a glimpse of the objects as they propelled in his general direction. Flash bangs.

He sprang to action running a few steps and then dove in the opposite direction of the trajectory of the objects. He felt the scrape of the branches as he slashed through the bushes of vines, hit the ground, ducked his head and covered his ears just in time for the explosion. He felt the jolt of the devices going off, feeling like an intense, short earthquake, but he'd gotten clear in time to avoid the desired effect of being knocked unconscious.

Taking his hands off his ears, he heard the sound of running boots on the ground as the three men came toward him. Kyler was sure they heard his movement and they probably assumed the objects hit their mark. Now they were coming in for the easy kill.

Kyler lay still, pulling himself forward on the ground just enough to see their advance. The three were approaching on a line to enter the patch on the row next to him. They were all bunched together. *Advantage, Scott.*

The men slowed their pace as they neared the vines. Kyler calculated his next moves in his mind. The branches had dislodged the Glock from him and sent it flying so he'd have to rely on his hands. A problem for some but not Kyler. He could feel the adrenaline surging through every fiber of his body, calmly harnessing its power, ready to strike.

Scott shifted his body to the left and aligned himself with a gap between two of the bushes. He silently pulled his feet into a runner's stance and held his hands up in a fighting position. He remembered that he still had another clip in his pocket, which he whipped out quickly and gripped in his left hand.

As Kyler centered his focus, time slowed down again as he'd heard great athletes describe moments when they were in the *zone*. This was his zone. His element.

Five more seconds passed and then he saw the first pair of feet pass his line of sight. When he saw the leg of the third line up, he sprang into action driving the base of his right palm hard into the man's right knee as he planted in the ground. Kyler felt the knee explode as it bent opposite its natural direction.

In the same fluid motion Kyler was rising and driving his left hand upward with the metal of the clip exposed toward the second man who'd turned in his direction at the sound. He felt the impact of the metal as it found its target, crushing the man's larynx before he could even process what happened, effectively destroying his airflow instantly. As the man dropped to the ground, he released his weapon and clutched at his throat, desperately searching for air. Kyler saw the weapon falling, snatched it in mid-air, turned and delivered a fatal blow to the head of the fallen man whose knee he'd shattered. With lightening speed, Kyler spun back to the leader, who'd had no time to process what had just happened, and trained the stolen weapon squarely on the guard's forehead.

Kyler barked, "Cadere la pistola!"

When the man didn't respond immediately, Kyler pulled the gun away from his head and fired a shot to the side as a warning.

"Drop it now!" Maybe English would work for the man.

It worked and the man released his gun. It looked to be a semi-automatic AR-15 assault rifle. Knowing that it could spurt off 100 rounds in less than ten seconds, Kyler couldn't believe he'd gotten out of the building without a knick. Truth was, running and shooting at a moving target was far from a sure thing.

"Hands up asshole," Kyler barked and the man obeyed, likely decided by the fates of his two comrades behind him.

"Sei un uomo morto," the man spat.

"*I'm* a dead man? Who has the gun pointed at his head, moron?"

"You can kill me. Fine. But you are still dead. You don't think we know who you are? Who you work for?"

That shook Kyler and he tried to process what the man told him. How the hell had they figured it out?

"What the hell are you talking about?"

"You and the woman. You are CIA, yes?"

"You don't know what you're talking about. I'm a goddamn actor and you all come attack me?"

"Bullshit. We have your file. Baldacci does. He knows who you are. We've been watching you since you arrived, waiting to see what you know. And now you're a dead man. The lady is probably already dead." The last part was said with a smirk.

Kyler had more questions, wanted to know how they'd blown their cover, but the possibility of him being right about Alani took precedence. He wrapped his arm around the man's neck, pressed the rifle against his head and spun him back in the direction of the castle.

"Walk….and don't be stupid or I'll blow your goddamned head off."

Kyler's puppet, now his shield, obeyed. There were still two more men to contend with who, Kyler had no doubt, had heard the gun shot and screams and would come investigate.

As if on cue, the men yelled "Alto!"

Kyler simply said, "No."

He turned the man's body so he was directly in their line of fire, protecting himself from having a clean shot at him.

"Alto!" they tried once more. This time Kyler didn't bother responding but kept a side shuffle with his puppet in step toward the castle.

The two men took Kyler off guard and opened fire into their leader. Kyler felt the man's body lurched backwards repeatedly as the bullets pelted into his chest, arms and legs. Wasting no time, Kyler dropped the man and rolled quickly to his left, coming up onto his elbows face down with the gun poised. He lined up the first assailant and pulled back on the trigger. Holding down the trigger, the rifle continued to fire off rapid rounds. The first man went down and Scott swung the rifle to the right while keeping his finger on the trigger as at least five rounds exploded into the second man's chest before he finally fell backwards.

Kyler stood up slowly and observed the wreckage. Twenty minutes time and eleven bodies to count. Not exactly the way he had planned the evening to go but he was just thankful he wasn't the one on the ground.

With nothing left to salvage at the scene, he made a break for the castle, hearing the man's words ringing in his head. He had to find Alani. He only hoped Baldacci hadn't beaten him to it.

Chapter 59

As Alani stood at the door's entrance, she stared back at a familiar face. Her own. Correction...*several* familiar faces.

The room was a command center of sorts and on the wall opposite her hung four flat-panel monitors. From left to right, in addition to her own face, she noted those of Kyler, Jack Hawkins and Dr. Ethan Goldman. The pictures themselves were also unique and even more alarming. They had not been taken via surveillance but rather pulled directly off of the CIA's database. Alani recognized the image of herself as the one she looked down at on her badge every time she visited Langley.

Even more frightening was the text underneath each photo. It was each person's full personnel file including records that could only have been pulled from internal resources. Listed were dates of birth, birthplace, height, eye color, hair color, educational history, training history, dates of their start of employment and assignment history. There were bios, performance rankings, strengths and weakness assessments and even a list of personal hobbies.

"What the hell..." she muttered in disbelief.

"Beautiful photo...Ms. Langdon," she heard a voice say, startling her.

She turned slowly and was looking back at the face of Vitale Baldacci.

"It was a good plan, really. The shot to the man's foot. You are quite the markswoman really. It just grazed him leaving nothing but a flesh wound. That's going to cost me, you know.

I'm not about to tell him that one of my guests opened fire on him in the middle of this beautiful establishment so the hotel must take responsibility for it. Some unknown object, maybe glass, tripped him up...who knows? The only problem was that I saw you leave your room a few minutes before. When I found the bullet lodged into the floorboard, it was easy to know what happened. I came back here to check the playback, see if you went back to your room, only to find you standing here. How convenient for me, actually." As he spoke, he had a skinny-barreled pistol aimed directly at her chest.

He saw her eyes dart to the weapon and turned it for her to see.

"Ah...you like?" He asked proudly. "It is a .45 ACP Luger, you know. There was less than half a dozen made and this was the first. Many believed it was lost...possibly damaged or deemed ineffective being the first attempt to produce the gun...but they were wrong. The story of how it came to me is a long one. After a bit of restoration, it has become my most prized possession. It is worth well over a million of your American dollars. It's serial number...1." His lips curled into a smile that sent ice through Alani's veins.

"You see, Alani...may I call you Alani?"

He paused but she didn't respond so he continued on, "I have a way of acquiring things. Information, objects, people..."

"How did you get those files?" She asked, cutting him off.

"Impressive, isn't it?"

"How did you get it?!" she scowled, simultaneously frustrated and frightened. Alani wanted to know but, more importantly, she needed to buy time to figure a way out.

"You shouldn't get so upset, mi amore. It isn't becoming of you."

"That is classified information from a United States government agency. How in the hell did it end up here? With you?"

Baldacci was clearly enjoying this as he smiled and stared back at her before continuing.

"Classified information is only as strong as those who protect it, Signora."

"Are you saying we have a mole in the Central Intelligence Agency?"

Baldacci lightly rocked his head to each side, "Not exactly accurate but close."

Seeming to have made a decision, he paused and then said, "I suppose it cannot hurt to tell you now and, really, I'm even impressed myself on how easy it has all been."

He motioned the gun to the wall on his left, which housed additional monitors, "I believe you are familiar with at least a couple of those individuals, si?"

Alani turned slowly and found the faces of who she knew to be Jacques Francois, Ellen Stratton and a third man she didn't recognize but whose name read as Oliver Bailey.

"These are...how you did you put it? Your moles?"

Alani was confused, "I don't understand. Francois is dead and Ellen Stratton works for one of our subcontractors."

"Si...and all three actually had a very similar case of amnesia, do you agree?"

"Yes but they were also both physically tortured...Francois beaten and Stratton raped."

"Correction...Ms. Stratton was never raped. She came to that conclusion by her own deductive reasoning. She was quite unharmed."

"Still, I don't see why that makes them candidates for being an infiltrator of government databases," Alani retorted.

"Have you ever heard of a substance called SP-117?"

Alani shook her head no.

"Fascinating substance really. It is completely odorless and tasteless in its liquid form. I believe you Americans have made attempts at similar substances and call it a *truth serum.*"

Baldacci explained the drug, reviewing much of the same information that Goldman had detailed for Kyler in their earlier conversation.

Alani concluded, "So you could get your victims to do whatever you wanted while they were stoned out of their mind and then they wouldn't remember a damn thing when they came to?"

"Bravissimo, Signora! Beauty and brains! I really wish we had met under different circumstances."

Ignoring the comment, Alani asked, "Why them? Why did you choose these three?"

"That is simple. Access and skill. They had it for information we need."

Alani looked back at the screen and processed what she'd just learned. Obviously Stratton provided them with data on the United States' databases, Francois for the French and then she read underneath the image for Bailey. Great Britain. She wondered if there were others.

"What about those men," she asked pointing to screens that had pictures of men that she didn't recognize and names that didn't register either.

"Let's call them valuable assets. Wealthy men willing to part with money if one possesses the right information about them."

"Blackmail."

"That's one way to put it."

"So this is all about money? The murders, kidnappings, all of it?"

"I can think of no better reason, mi amore," Baldacci's sneer was back.

Alani wasn't actually passing judgment but knew the longer she kept him talking, the more time she'd have to figure a way out. So far, she had found none. It was a room with one way in, one way out and if she made a move for her weapon, she was certain Baldacci would put a bullet in her head.

Alani opened her mouth to ask another question but Baldacci stopped her with his hand to quiet her.

"Enough questions. This has been fun but I have business to complete. You see, access to the database is only the first step of the plan. The culmination is about to take place and I don't have time to let you continue your attempt to distract me so you can find a way out of here. There is no way out. I'm afraid this is the end for you."

This was it, Alani thought. This is how I'm going to die. Her thoughts went immediately to Kyler. Was he safe? Did they get to him too? Sadness crossed over her an in overwhelming tidal wave at the thought of not being able to say goodbye.

Baldacci spoke again, almost with sadness, "I spoke the truth earlier tonight when I said if I told you, I would have to kill you. You should have listened, signora. But you leave me no choice."

Baldacci took a step closer to her, moved a strand of hair away from her forehead and aimed the pistol's end in the center, just inches away.

A tear streamed from her eye as Alani realized she was going to die.

As she heard Vitale click off the safety of the gun, kicking herself for not noticing he hadn't done so earlier. She took a breath and closed her eyes for the last time.

BANG!

She'd heard the crack of the gun but felt no pain and wondered for a moment if this was what death felt like. She quickly realized that she was alive as she first felt the warm liquid on her face and, a split second later, felt the weight of almost two hundred pounds collapse forward onto her.

Alani hit the ground hard, her head slamming against the wood floor as she landed with immense force. Vitale Baldacci's dead body lay heavily on top of hers and she was dazed from the blow to the ground. Her eyes began to go out of focus.

Just before she blacked out she saw the concerned but smiling face of Kyler standing over her, gun in hand. Moments later, the lights went out.

Chapter 60

Alani felt the throbbing in her head first. She was sure that she could have actually taken her own pulse by the constant pounding.

She slowly opened her eyes, which had difficulty focusing at first but, when she did, she saw a hilly countryside flying by at blazing speed. The edges of dawn seemed to be emerging with a golden light protruding on the horizon though the sun had not quite made its appearance yet.

Alani's eyes continued to focus more and she took in the rest of her surroundings. The first thing she noticed was the red leather on the glove compartment in front of her. Before she could open her mouth, she heard a voice.

"Good morning sunshine."

It was Kyler's.

"How's your noggin?"

The sound of his voice nearly made her cry as her memories of the most recent events began rushing back in. She fought back the tears welling up in her eyes and smiled a bit.

"It feels like Babe Ruth took a Louisville slugger and swung for the fences against it."

"Ruth, huh? Kicking it back waaaaaay old school. Not Barry Bonds or A-Rod but a guy who hit his last homerun when FDR was in office?" He laughed though inside Kyler was relieved she was ok.

"Cut me some slack alright? I went from thinking I was dead to nearly cracking my skull open as a two hundred-pound dead-man tackled me NFL style."

"Sorry…there's some Advil in the glove box waiting for you and a coke I snagged from the hotel. I'd take at least four if I were you."

"Thanks," Alani replied gratefully. "What is this thing anyway?" Alani was referring to the vehicle that was clearly not the Audi they'd arrived at Villa Santini in.

"First car I saw. Didn't exactly have time to give our valet our ticket and wait around. It's a Maserati. Kind of a score, actually. The damn thing gives my Enzo a run for its money and it's a sedan."

"The red isn't doing much for my headache. I feel like I'm back in college after a night of one too many Tequila ice luge shots."

"Well ma'am…red's the only color they had on the lot. They weren't taking special orders at the time. Take it or leave it."

She finally smiled, "Take it." And then, "Thanks."

"Forget it," he waved it off. "Besides, we're far from out of the woods yet. We gotta get to Hawkins and, more specifically, Amici."

Alani had been so groggy, she hadn't noticed the old man in the back seat. He was buckled in and had his hands and feet bound to each other. She actually didn't *see* him first. The man's odor engulfed her. It didn't do much for the way she felt at the moment and she debated on whether to have Kyler pull the car over. She opted to open the window and pulled herself together.

She gave Kyler a look that said, *are you going to explain that?*

"Alani Langdon, meet Andrei Ivanova."

Alani opened her mouth in surprise but said nothing.

Kyler took her silence as an opportunity to fill her in on how he had come upon Ivanova, left him behind to come to her aid, took her to nab a car, went back to the warehouse and threw him in the backseat.

"And there you have it."

The questions came pouring out of her.

"What was he doing there? What does he know? Did he tell you where Hawkins is?"

Kyler put his hand up, "Slow down, Rain Man. We haven't gotten to that yet. I had a few things on my plate...namely getting out there before having to fight off any more of Baldacci's goons."

He looked at her now. "By the way, I'm glad you're ok. I was worried about you."

She had a million things she wanted to say but instead opted for, "Thanks."

"Now that you're up though, I was counting on you to do the handy work," he said, with his eyes shooting back towards Ivanova. "I can't do everything, you know."

"Yes, yes, yes...Mr. Hero...come down a few notches, would you?"

Before she started on Andrei, Kyler filled her in on the conversation he'd had with Goldman, including the deductions that had made about the sex slave trade activity, Dimarco, the truth serum and the incidents that were loosely linked to it all.

Alani then turned her attention back to Ivanova.

"Mr. Ivanova," she started, opting to seduce the answers out of him, as was her uncanny skill.

"What were you doing for Mr. Dimarco and Mr. Baldacci?"

Her seductions didn't resonate with the old man, though. Fatigue, and more specifically, fear was the look that he returned to Alani.

"I cannot say," he said, shaking his head.

Alani and Kyler exchanged a surprised look. She turned to him again and opted for the soothing approach.

"Mr. Ivanova, whatever it is you're afraid of, we can protect you. You are in the protection of the United States government." She then added, "I'll also remind you that you are an assumed associate to some pretty serious crimes. I suggest you cooperate with us. Helping us now could buy you some forgiveness when we put you in front of those that will decide your future."

Andrei's look was lifeless.

"You cannot help me."

Alani decided to take a different route since they were running out of time.

"Let's try this another way. Why don't I tell you what we *believe* is happening and you can tell us if we are on the right track? That way you are not revealing anything."

When Andrei didn't disagree, Alani pressed on.

"Where you producing SR-117 for Dimarco and Baldacci?"

Ivanova relaxed a bit at the question.

"Yes I was."

"Is Dimarco running an elaborate sex trade out of his clothing warehouse in Milan?"

A glimmer of hope shone on Andrei's face.

"Yes," he then added, "I heard Vitale talking to Dimarco on the phone about women that were coming from Croatia into Milan about a month ago."

"Good, Andrei. Now we are getting somewhere."

She continued, "Was Baldacci using SP-117 to gather intel out of Ellen Stratton, Jacques Francois and Oliver Bailey?"

"I don't know those names, but I know he was using it for information, yes."

"Fair enough Mr. Ivanova. And was a shipment of your chemicals scheduled to make a major delivery by way of the trucks parked in the back of that warehouse?"

Andrei paused but then answered, "Yes. Yes it was."

"Where is it going?"

"I don't know."

"Mr. Ivanova, if you are lying to me…"

"I don't know these things!" He burst, suddenly. "They told me nothing! They stick me in lab for months with little food, no light, no shower…nothing. They tell me to work and nothing else. I only know little from what I heard."

The outburst surprised Alani but she then looked closer at the man. He wasn't a military goon. He wasn't a conniving conman. He was a man that looked like he could have been her grandfather who had been mentally tortured for god knows how long. Her compassionate heart broke and she believed him.

"Ok, Mr. Ivanova. Take it easy. Just a couple more questions. Do you know a man named Jack Hawkins?"

Andrei seemed on the verge of tears. He was having a full-fledged breakdown. He shook his head. No.

"What about Armand Amici?"

He nodded. "Yes, of course. It is his trucks that handles the deliveries."

"Can you confirm that his office is in Florence at this address?" She lifted a sheet of paper that she'd written on when Kyler had recounted the address he'd gotten from the man in the warehouse of Amici's address in Florence.

"I am not certain but I think that is correct." He was exhausted, that was clear.

Alani turned back to Kyler.

"Where do you think the trucks are headed?" She popped the can of the soda, realizing she'd forgotten to take the Advil and she could feel the veins pulsing in her head.

"Assuming this is a complex sex trade we're looking at, my best guess would be to Milan. Load up the women and ship them around the world. It explains the maps at least in Baldacci's office."

"Maps?"

"Yeah, there were some maps on the third wall of that room. Didn't you see them?"

"I was a little preoccupied."

"Right. Well anyway, there were two world maps hung on the other wall. The map had a mark in Long Beach in California, one on Le Havre in France and a third in London. All major shipping ports and all dated within a day of each other at the most."

"Interesting locations. I would have thought they'd be going to Asia or some Czech countries where prostitution and this type of trade is more common."

"Men of power are located in our 'sophisticated' civilizations too."

Alani nodded, "I'm not naïve. You can't say you weren't a bit surprised by that too."

"Well the second map had a spot in Korea marked."

"North or South?"

"South."

That made Alani think of something they'd forgotten to ask and she turned back to their passenger in tow.

"Mr. Ivanova. What did you mean in the message you sent your nephew when you said you were aiding truth and that there was mass chaos tied to the North Koreans? How does a sex slave trade tie to mass chaos?"

Ivanova responded quickly, "I don't know what message you are talking about."

Alani stared back at the man and was kicking herself for feeling sympathy for him a second ago. She needed to remember what branch of the KGB the man had been affiliated with. He was a trained liar. She pulled her gun from her ankle holster and turned back to Andrei.

"Let's try this again," she pressed the gun hard against the old man's kneecap. "Tell me what you meant when you wrote that message."

"I told you! I don't know what you're talking about!" his eyes shot open wide with fear.

"We don't have time for this Andrei. I'll count to three and if you don't start talking before then, I'm going to regrettably make it very difficult for you to walk for the foreseeable future."

"I'm telling you! I don't know what you're talking about! I never wrote such message!"

"One…"

"I haven't talked to my nephew in twenty years!"

"Two…" Alani removed the safety and pressed a little harder for emphasis.

"Please!" tears began to flow freely down the man's face.

"Three!"

Andrei shut his eyes and screamed out.

But Alani hadn't pulled the trigger. They may not know why he didn't write the note but the exercise was enough for her to believe he was telling the truth.

She faced forward again.

Kyler said aloud, "What the hell?"

"I don't know but we need to get to Hawkins," she then added, "assuming he's still alive."

Kyler said nothing. He'd uttered the same words to himself.

"I still don't see what they need Hawkins for?"

Kyler was about to venture an answer when his phone rang. The noise was actually coming from behind them. It was from the bag that had been in their room earlier.

"Can you grab that?" Kyler asked.

Alani reached into the back seat and pulled the duffel bag onto her lap. Unzipping the top, she fumbled around until finally locating the source of the ring. She pulled it out and checked the caller ID.

"It's Ethan," she said.

"Put him on speakerphone."

"What's up Doc?" Kyler answered.

"Christ, there you are…is Langdon with you? Are you both safe?"

"I'm right here sir," Alani answered for herself. "Safe…yes, aside from a helluva headache."

"Scott, I got the sample you sent last night and then when I tried calling and you didn't answer and then didn't log in to the computer to check in last night, I assumed plans were altered slightly."

"You could say that, sir," Kyler replied.

He then took Goldman through everything that had happened between Alani and Kyler in the last several hours leading up to them hijacking the car, Ivanova and speeding away from Villa Santini.

"Ivanova is there with you?" Goldman asked, surprised.

"In the back seat. Alani just scared the shit out of the poor old guy. She's so mean." He gave her a smirk and she returned a smile. It was the first in a while.

Goldman was not in the joking mood.

"Where are you headed now?" Goldman asked though he was pretty sure he knew.

"Florence…time to grab Hawkins and eliminate Amici."

"We're tracking your phone, by the way," Goldman said, changing gears slightly. "It hasn't moved since the time you planted it on the truck."

"It won't. I have a hunch that they're waiting for Amici now…and Hawkins."

"Ok…I'll take that for now," Goldman replied. "We're sending in a team to arrest Dimarco as we speak. I just got off the phone with Interpol and they've got a dozen cars on their way to pick him up."

"Doc, I can't explain why but hold off on that. Let us grab Hawkins and take care of Amici at least. I just have a feeling on this."

Goldman paused for a long moment.

Kyler added, "Trust me sir."

Goldman was silent a few moments longer, not sure he could bite down on possibly letting Dimarco get away now that they finally had something on him.

Kyler read his mind, "There's too much money at stake here…whatever is going on. He's not walking away until it's done even if his men are dropping like flies. I know this guy sir."

"Will do Agent but it's a short leash on him."

Before hanging up, Goldman added, "Be safe."

"Safe? I'll just opt for smart." Kyler didn't wait for Goldman's response before hitting end on the call.

Alani stared at him for a second and then asked, "Are you going to tell me the rest?"

"No time now. We're five minutes out and we still need a plan for how we're going to get Hawkins out of there."

Alani's curiosity was burning but she knew he was right. She saw the city in the distance so they began formulating their plan of attack. With the surge of adrenaline, Alani all but forgot about the throb in her head as they zeroed in on the task at hand.

Chapter 61

Armand Amici stood staring out the window of the sixth floor of the building that had been his personal ground zero for the elaborate plan he, Baldacci and Dimarco had begun nearly two years ago. He stared out at the dome of the Cathedral in the distance and smiled realizing that, once they were done, he could literally buy the building and anything within the city limits if he so desired.

He turned back from the window and stared at the man that was going to give them the last piece of the puzzle. Jack Hawkins stared back at him with eyes showing no recognition of what was going on.

Amici's goons had given the computer nerd too much of the sedative the first time around and he'd passed out for several hours. The cocktail, as he affectionately referred to it, when delivered intravenously as they had earlier, couldn't exceed a certain potency or else it would have the affect akin to one too many shots of tequila…incredibly potent Tequila, that is. It was the stark difference between dancing naked on a table-top in a bar without a care in the world for who was watching versus laying face down, passed out on the bathroom floor in a trance that nothing short of a nuclear bomb could disturb.

So here Amici stood, just ten minutes after giving Hawkins the second dose of SP-117, having done so himself this time to make sure it was administered correctly. He sent tweedle dee and tweedle dumb off to fetch him some pizza. Preparing for infinite wealth had given him one hell of an appetite. Besides, Lord knows he wasn't going to need help defending himself against an out of shape computer geek who was bound to a chair.

Amici checked his watch, deciding he'd wait five more minutes for the drug to hit its desired level of effectiveness.

As he waited, he looked at the plump American sitting in front of him. He had to admire this Jack Hawkins, recalling the man's earlier refusal to recreate his device even in the face of what appeared to be imminent death. Amici was a killer, always had been, and admittedly enjoyed the act with no hesitation or guilt. His favorite part of killing had always been to see how each person responded in the face of death. Over the years he had often been surprised. Men who could bench press cars resorted to tears and, often, self-defecation more times than he could count. Other physically weak, perceivably feeble men stood firm and accepted their death in peace. Amici had no comment on the subject but was merely intrigued by it.

Amici said to a stoned Hawkins, "After you give me what I need, we'll see how *you* respond before I turn off the lights of your pathetic life. Will you cry? My bet is no."

Just then, he heard the ding of the elevator, looked up and saw his two muscle men standing there empty-handed and staring back at him.

"How fucking difficult was it to get a goddamned pizza!" Amici screamed.

At that moment, he watched as the bodies of the two men fell forward, limp as…dead weight.

"For two dead men, I'd say pretty damn difficult," Kyler said as he released the man he'd been holding up alongside Alani who'd held up the lighter of the two.

The three stared at each other, waiting for someone to make a move. Recognition registered quickly on Amici's face, identifying his intruders almost instantly, and he reached for his weapon.

Before Armand could even get the gun from its holster, two crimson dots emerged side by side on his forehead. A moment later, with his hand still on his gun, Amici's limp body crashed to the floor.

Kyler looked to Alani, "Hell of a shot, agent."

"Not too bad yourself," she replied.

Meanwhile, Hawkins remained unmoved, staring straight ahead, clearly oblivious to the action that had just gone on around him.

"I sort of liked our plan of coming through the window and all but I have to say, these guys coming back from their delivery was a helluva lot easier."

"After the last 12 hours, I'll take easy," Alani replied.

They stepped over the bodies of the hired muscle and made their way to Hawkins. Kyler got directly in front of him and snapped his fingers. When he didn't flinch he gave him a healthy smack on the face. Nothing.

"Jackie boy's in la la land," Kyler said.

"It's probably better that way. I doubt he's going to want to remember much. Lord only knows what the poor guy was awake for and what he wasn't."

"Let's get him out of here."

"What about them?" Alani asked pointing to Amici and his two thugs.

"Leave 'em. We'll call Interpol…let them clean up their own mess. You call for an ambulance, tell them to pick us up outside the hotel while I cut Jack loose."

With that, Kyler flicked out a switchblade, slicing easily through the rope tied to Hawkins' wrists. After Alani hung up the phone, she helped Kyler lift Jack up and onto his shoulder, the weight of his limbs bearing heavily down on Kyler. He made a mental note to advise Jack to go on a diet when he came to.

Kyler, with Jack on his shoulder and Alani at his side, walked back to the still-open elevator kept ajar by the dead men's bodies. They both entered and Alani gingerly pushed the men clear of the opening and hit the button for the ground floor. As the doors closed and Kyler watched more wreckage he'd created disappear, he felt the sense of exhaustion from the last several days. Still he smiled. He was glad to be alive and relieved that they'd gotten to Jack when they did.

Chapter 62

An exhausted Kyler and Alani entered room 512 of Boscola Astoria and Kyler realized it was the first time she had been inside of his room. She stopped short as she looked across at the view out the balcony that Kyler had become so accustomed to seeing. Kyler stopped with her and took in the view again as if for the first time. They both stood there quietly for a moment, not sure if it was fatigue or something else that lingered.

They silently made their way across the room, dropped their gear on the table on the way and descended on to the balcony. Their eyes were fixed on the city before them and then, at the same moment, they turned to face each other. Kyler was four or five inches taller than her and she looked up at him with a searching gaze.

Not sure what to say, Kyler blurted, "Quite a night. Couple of nights, I guess."

Alani nodded. "Thanks again."

"For what?"

"Oh I don't know…saving my life."

"That? That was nothing. All in a day's work," Kyler Scott with a fresh slice of humble pie.

"Well I'd prefer to not make *that* a daily occurrence."

They then ran out of things to say and an uncomfortable silence fell between them. They searched each other's eyes, each looking for a sign to forge ahead. Kyler thought he saw one and began moving toward her. He could feel the cool air of her breath and closed his eyes as he prepared for their lips to engage.

Riiiiiiing!

Both of them jumped slightly at the sound and immediately looked at each other with a bit of embarrassment for what had nearly happened.

Kyler's computer on the table rang again.

Riiiiiiing!

He ran back into the room, popped open the lid, hit a key to bring the screen to life and hit the answer key to launch the video call. Goldman's weary but smiling face looked back at Kyler, Alani arriving at his side to share the call a moment later.

"Congratulations to you both," Goldman started.

"Thank you sir," Kyler replied. He became aware of the fact that he was feeling self-conscious, wondering if their boss could sense the tension between his two agents. He cast the worry aside as paranoia.

"Interpol is cleaning up the mess you left of Amici, Andrei is in holding and Hawkins is recovering nicely at the hospital. He should be ready to talk to you both soon to debrief whatever he may know."

"He's doing ok?" Alani asked.

"Seems to be fine. They drew his blood but couldn't identify the substance in his system. I asked them to send it to me. I've got a pretty good guess that it'll match up against the sample of the SP-117 you sent over, Agent Scott. Good work on that, by the way."

"Thank you sir."

"So let's talk about Dimarco."

"Right, sir."

"You mind elaborating on what we are waiting for with him agent? What are you holding back from me?"

"I'm not holding back sir. Something just doesn't feel right about this."

"Details agent."

"I haven't put my finger on it completely yet but here's what I'm thinking." Kyler was up pacing again and Alani eyed him as he did so, shrugging to Goldman who shot her a look as if to say *he hasn't clued me in yet.*

"Dimarco has obviously been running this sex trade for some time now. His store and warehouse have been there for…what…five years?"

Goldman thumbed through the file, "Yes…that's correct. Opened in 2007. What's your point?"

"So why is it all of a sudden such a big deal now? So much so that it prompts all of the risks that he has taken with kidnappings and murders of people that he had to have known would warrant significant attention."

Alani chimed in, "You said it yourself. He wanted the big pay-off and needed to step up his game to bank on it."

Kyler wobbled his head back and forth, "Maybe. But it just doesn't feel right. And that's not all."

"What?" Goldman asked.

"Ivanova is bothering me. His story…" Kyler trailed off, trying to forms his thoughts.

"What about it? It checks out with all the details," Goldman looked confused.

Kyler remembered what they hadn't shared with their boss yet so he filled him in.

"He claims to know nothing about the message he sent to Palmer."

Goldman was confused, "He what? It had his damn name on it. It came from a bottle from the winery *you* found him at. A winery that's clearly tied to Dimarco. How is that possible?"

Alani cut in, "We pressured him on it sir. Very hard. Either he's telling the truth or he's the most amazing liar I've ever seen."

Kyler broke in now, "That's just the thing. I saw his face when you asked him about the note. Saw it in the rear view mirror. When you first mentioned it, there was recognition there. I think he is lying. I thought it then but we had Hawkins as a priority at the time."

"He'd rather get a bullet in his knee then admit to writing it?"

Goldman rounded the thought process, "Meaning that whatever is keeping him from telling you information is more important to him than pain and, quite possibly, his own life."

Kyler was nodding. Then he stopped dead.

Goldman and Alani saw it and asked, simultaneously, "What is it?"

Rather than answering, Kyler was rifling through the bag that he took to set the other day, looking for something. He finally found it and pulled a newspaper out, flipping through pages until he found what he was looking for.

"There it is." Alani looked down at the story he was pointing to and, after a moment, her face registered horror. It was a story Kyler had read but thought little of when he was on set the other day but now it took a whole new spin. He held the article up to the camera so that Goldman could see. It was the story of the town in Vietnam with a mysterious outbreak of illness.

Goldman understood and said, "Looks like you need to have another little chat with our friend, Mr. Ivanova."

Chapter 63

Kyler and Alani stepped into the holding room and saw a weary Andrei Ivanova sitting at a table with his hands free but his feet chained to the floor. He was drinking a cup of coffee, holding it with both hands as if he feared he would lose handle of it. Judging by the shaking of his hands, he was probably right. He looked up and back at them with dead eyes as they entered.

"Leave us," Kyler said to the Interpol officer that had escorted them in. Kyler scanned the room and then barked to the man as he left, "And turn off the cameras."

The man hesitated.

"Did you not understand me? Spegnere la fotocamera, ora!"

"Si signore," the man replied sheepishly and quickly left.

Kyler looked back at Ivanova who looked a little more concerned now. *Good,* Kyler thought. He pulled up a chair and sat opposite Ivanova. Alani stayed standing back in the corner, her arms folded across her chest and her gaze fixed on the old man's eyes. She cursed herself for letting him off so easy earlier.

"Mr. Ivanova," Kyler started. "We got started off on the wrong foot back at the winery. You see, I told you then that I wasn't going to hurt you and I feel bad about that because that's actually not completely true. So, I lied to you and then, in turn, you lied to my lovely partner back there." Kyler cast his eyes back toward Alani who gave him a little wave.

"But I'll take the fall for that. My bad…as we Americans like to say."

Andrei stared back at him with little change to his expression.

"The truth is, Mr. Ivanova, that I *will* have to hurt you… a lot, as a matter of fact…if you don't start being honest with us. And, the thing is, I'm pretty sure we don't have a lot of time here so this could get ugly pretty quickly."

Ivanova still showed no change. He was unfazed by the threat. Either that, or too defeated and exhausted to show it.

Kyler had expected the reaction. He reached down into the briefcase he'd brought, pulled the article out, set it on the table facing the man and slid it toward him so he could see for himself. Ivanova paused a moment, looked down at the newspaper and read the headline. Kyler saw it again. It was quick but a moment of recognition and even surprise crossed the man's face before he quickly recovered and returned to the same blank look.

"Does that mean anything to you, Mr. Ivanova?" Kyler asked, knowing what answer he'd get.

"Nothing," was all the man said in response.

"Nothing? Nothing at all, huh?"

Andrei did not respond but, instead, continued to stare back at Kyler.

Kyler hit him with it, "We know where your family is, Mr. Ivanova."

That rocked Ivanova to the core and he stared back at Kyler with considerable surprise, fear and hope all at the same time. *Gotcha,* Kyler thought.

Ivanova opened his mouth to say something but couldn't form the words. He then finally just asked, "How?"

Kyler paused a moment, letting the news fester a bit further in the man before he continued.

"That's not important. What *is* important is that I am your only hope of getting them back alive but, if you ever want see them again, your memory had better start improving pretty damn quickly here or I won't be able to do much to help you."

"How do I know you're telling the truth?" Ivanova blurted.

"You don't. You're just going to have to take my word for it. Then again, you could take the chance that I am lying and throw away the one potential opportunity you had to save them. It's up to you."

Ivanova looked utterly panicked, "No! What do you want to know?!"

"Let's start by setting the record straight first. Were you really being held to help Dimarco execute the final stages of an elaborate sex trade?"

Andrei slowly shook his head no.

"Didn't think so," Kyler nodded, satisfied. "Then let's just have it from the beginning. Sound good to you Alani?"

"Sounds good to me," she agreed and pulled up a chair next to Kyler now.

Kyler then waved his hand at Andrei as if to say, *proceed.*

Ivanova sighed deeply and then began.

"I began working for Signore Dimarco a few years ago when I moved to Italy to start a new life. I had a new identity and, after being in Florence for just a few months, met Gabriella. We married after two months and she got pregnant a month later. I needed work and Signore Dimarco hired me at his restaurant."

"Doing what exactly?" Kyler interrupted.

"Bus boy. At first, at least." Andrei took a drink of the coffee as if to give him courage to continue.

"We then were talking over wine late one night after we closed. I got too drunk and told him too much about my past and what I did at the KGB."

"Your chemicals work," Alani finished.

"Yes," Andrei nodded, seemingly not surprised that they too knew his history.

"Dimarco then asked if I wanted to make some more money? I had a wife with a new baby so of course I said yes. He told me of his drug dealings and asked if I could help him in his lab to make cocaine. I joked that I could not only make cocaine, but I could make something for him that would make people tell him all their secrets and never remember ever saying a word. I told him that I could make a chemical for just about anything a man could imagine."

Andrei looked sheepish now as he recalled the memory.

"Like I said…too much wine. When I drink, I talk too much. Gabriella always said it would be the death of me."

Kyler was getting impatient now and they needed to get to the point soon.

"So you told him about SP-117?"

Ivanova looked a little surprised at the sound of the name but quickly nodded his head.

"Yes."

"Did he ask you to make it?"

"Not that night but the next day he came to me and did. I was sober then and said I wouldn't. I told him if my former government ever found out I'd produced SP-117 again that they'd bring me back to Russia and throw me in jail for the rest of my life. I would never see Gabriella or my baby again. He seemed to understand at the time and dropped the subject immediately."

"And then he kidnapped your wife and baby," Kyler interjected.

Tears began to fall down the man's face now and he nodded again.

He continued, "Dimarco told me he was sending me to Villa Santini. I was to produce SP-117 and, once I'd made enough, he'd pay me a lot of money and let my wife and baby go free."

"But the plan changed, didn't it?" Alani now chimed in.

Andrei looked at them in horror, "It is too late now. I'll never see my wife and baby again and now I'm going to be responsible for such terrible things!" He started to cry again.

Kyler slammed his fist down on the table, "Get it together. Enough. We can help you but we need more information. Tell us about this story." Kyler pointed to the article again.

Andrei wiped his face and composed himself, "Dimarco had created a new plan. He had talked to his contacts in North Korea and promised them that he could produce a deadly chemical like none they'd ever seen before. A liquid that was sealed in an air-tight container that, once opened, the oxygen acted as an accelerant, releasing a deadly chemical that had range to kill everyone within a five-mile radius."

"Did such a chemical exist?" Kyler asked.

"Not yet. Dimarco came to me and told me what he wanted and said that if I didn't make it, he would kill my family."

Alani was afraid to ask, "And did you finish it?"

Andrei nodded his head slowly.

Silence filled the room.

"So where does this fit in?" Kyler asked, pointing to the article again.

"The North Koreans were going to pay $2.5 billion in advance and the other $2.5 billion when they received the final shipment of the package. They said, before they agreed to pay the first installment, there needed to be a test run but one that was scaled back so as not to draw too much attention. So I created a slightly milder version of the chemical and they shipped it out to this village." He pointed down to the article. "It was supposed to make those in its vicinity violently ill but not kill them. It worked."

"That doesn't make sense though," Kyler said. "Even if the North Koreans got their hands on this, what are they going to do with it? They could release it in civilian areas but they could never get close enough to military to do any damage there." He was talking more to himself than to Andrei now. Then a thought occurred to him.

"Did Dimarco ask you to produce SP-117 as well?"

Andrei looked back at him and nodded.

"That's it then."

"What?" Alani asked.

Instead of answering her, he asked Andrei, "When did you finish the chemical weapon?"

"The final sample…three days ago. Then we packaged it into two hundred bottles. The shipment is supposed to go out tomorrow."

"Shit. Where?"

"I don't know."

Kyler turned to Alani, "We need to get out of here and on the phone with Goldman. We need to get ahead of this now. We need a plan."

Choosing not to ask Kyler to elaborate on what he'd left out, Alani stood with him and they both left the room quickly.

Andrei yelled out to them, "What about my family?!" but they were already gone.

As they raced down the hallway, Alani asked Kyler, "How did you know Dimarco had his family."

"I didn't."

Alani shook her head as they bolted toward the exit.

Chapter 64

It was dark inside of Via di Santo Spirito except for a light that shone out of the small office in the back. Gianni Dimarco paced impatiently back and forth in front of the phone trying to sort out all that had happened in the last few hours. Baldacci had failed him and so had his men. He lost too many good soldiers tonight and two good friends. At the end of the day though, he only cared about finishing the mission. In truth, he didn't need them anymore. They'd accomplished what he'd needed them to and now he just needed to complete the delivery. They'd fallen a bit short with Hawkins but they'd have to do without. Most of the package was still in tact and it would at least be enough for him to collect the other half of his money. The fucking North Koreans could figure out the rest. He'd done enough for them as it was.

At least I don't have to split up the five billion, he realized as he thought about the deaths of his two primary partners. Where the hell was his fucking team? He'd sent a small crew out to Villa Santini to make sure the delivery was still in tact. Once he got the call, he'd let his contact know they were a go.

Finally the phone rang.

The man on the other end said, "The vehicle was not entered. Its contents are untouched."

Dimarco breathed a sigh of relief and then said, "Good. You will leave tonight."

"Yes sir."

He depressed the release of the phone and then let it up as he dialed a number he had committed to memory long ago. The man on the other end picked up on the second ring.

Dimarco spoke, "The vehicle is leaving tonight. It will be in Yeosu on as scheduled."

"Good," the man replied. "We will be waiting for it in the morning."

"What about my money?" Dimarco barked, a little too frantic for his own liking.

"You will have it once the package arrives and it is deemed to be to our satisfaction. No sooner. I will call you when it arrives."

Dimarco wanted to argue but, instead, settled on, "Fine. I will be here."

"I know you will Gianni."

With that, the man hung up.

*   *   *   *

Ten blocks away, Kyler and Alani were parked in the Maserati listening to every word that had been said on both calls. When Dimarco hung up, Kyler called Goldman and filled him in on the details.

Goldman said, "There is a port in Yeosu."

Kyler nodded. He knew the region of South Korea well, particularly the multitude of military bases positioned all over the country.

"I want the SEALs deployed on this one," Kyler said. "Subtle will be the key word here. We can't have whoever's waiting for that shipment sniffing us out before it has a chance to arrive."

"They'll be on a plane to Commander Fleet Activities Chinhae in thirty minutes or less."

Kyler knew that to be the US Naval installation in Busan, South Korea...only about fifty miles from the Port of Yeosu. The SEALs could load up with whatever they needed for the mission and be at the site of extraction with plenty of time to await the arrival of Dimarco's precious cargo.

"Thank you sir. Anything we can do?"

"Wait for our call. We'll let you know when it's done."

*   *   *   *

Bob Buckney sat in the QTS Tek command station and watched his screen with ferocious intensity. He'd been sitting in front of the screen for the last six hours, monitoring the movements of a blinking dot that made its way all over the world, occasionally checking in with Dr. Goldman to keep him apprised of its progress.

He watched as the dot slowly crossed the Italian countryside and made the short trip northeast from Rufina to Luigi Ridolfi Airport. It then sat there for about forty-five minutes, enough time for the cargo unit that sat on the back of the truck to be lifted from the flat-bed and into what Bob presumed to be a cargo plane. He reported each of these activities to Goldman once complete.

The dot then moved at a quicker pace as it went airborne. He followed it as it went over Bosnia, down through Turkey and leveled itself as it made its way over the hotbeds of middle-eastern activity. It passed over Pakistan and then Bob went and grabbed a Red Bull as it made the lengthy journey over China. He contacted Goldman again when the moving bulls eye reached Shanghai. Close now. Goldman redirected his communications to the Naval base in Busan now having confirmed that the team of SEALs made their arrival there a short time ago.

The target finally rested again, landing at Ishigaki Airport, which sat on the tiny Okinawan island of Ishigaki. There was another hand-off there again as the cargo now made its way onto a freighter at the Ishigaki Port. When Bob saw the freighter begin its final journey towards the Southern coast of South Korea, he reported to the team one last time. It was their turn. Bob could go home but he felt transfixed to the screen, wanting to watch the blinking icon complete its long journey. When he saw the dot stop at the Port of Yeosu, Bob made a gun with his hand, pointed it at the screen and made a BANG! noise as he pretended to shoot the dot. He knew the people around it were as good as dead.

*   *   *   *

Dimarco was still in his restaurant, pacing in front of the phone. It was light outside now and the sun broke brightly through the windows of his beautiful place of business. Dimarco, however, did not notice its splendor. He could not focus on anything but the silent phone that he been trying to coax to ring for the last hour. One phone call and he would be $2.5 billion richer. Five billion dollars in total. More money then even he, the most powerful man in Italy, could have ever dreamed of.

His thoughts of all that money had overshadowed his remorse over the loss of his fallen comrades and friends. He was already spending the riches in his mind, having picked out several boats, a G5 and castle in the Swiss Alps. He'd keep the restaurant going as well as his other businesses just to maintain the façade that he was still the up-standing Italian business mogul. He laughed at the thought. Eventually he'd close the businesses. Then again, maybe not. Who cared though? He could truly do whatever he wanted.

If only that damn phone would just ring.

"They're not going to call Gianni."

Dimarco spun around to see Kyler Scott standing in the front door of the restaurant. He hadn't even heard anyone unlock, let alone open, the door. But yet there the man stood looking back at him with a look of sheer cockiness.

"What are you talking about? And how did you get in here?"

Kyler held up his handy dandy lock pick kit.

"You really should invest into some better locks. That one was just too easy."

Dimarco said nothing.

"Like I said," Kyler took a few steps toward the confused restaurateur, "that phone will not be ringing."

Less confident now, Dimarco feigned a reply, "I don't know what you're talking about. I'm just…getting ready to open the restaurant for the day. Paperwork, orders…typical business duties."

Kyler saw that Dimarco was still trying to keep his poise but the arrogant man who'd greeted him and Alani at his restaurant just days earlier was replaced with a confused and terrified version now.

Kyler walked over to the bar and grabbed a bottle of wine labeled as having originated from Villa Santini. He peeled back the covering that protected the cork of the bottle.

"Amazing process, isn't it? The bottling of wine. The way that it manages to seal down the bottle, preventing that terrible enemy, oxygen, from sneaking in and spoiling the masterpiece inside until the drinker is absolutely ready to enjoy its delicacies."

He shook his head, "Amazing."

"What are you doing here? Do you want to buy something? Is that it? Some wine? Fine…which one?" Dimarco was absolutely frantic now.

Ignoring Dimarco's rambling, Kyler said, "Speaking of seals…"

He took the last final steps to close the gap between the two men and pulled out his phone.

"I have something to show you."

Kyler held the phone up to Gianni. The color drained instantly from the man's face as he stared in horror at the image. It showed a dozen North Korean men on their knees lined up in front of a large cargo container that looked all too familiar to Dimarco. It had the letters A..M..I..C..I along its side. The men had their hands behind their heads as several gunmen had their assault rifles trained on their prisoners.

"I asked them to take this picture just for you," Kyler said as he watched the man search for words.

Kyler then reached around the phone and slid his finger across the screen to reveal the next picture. Dimarco stumbled back at the sight of the dozen men now face down on the ground, splayed in various arrangements. It was the result of the randomness with which they fell after the gunmen put a single bullet in each of their heads.

"It's over and I wanted you to know we are serious Signore Dimarco."

The man was shaking as he squealed, "Are you going to kill me?"

Kyler sneered, "If you don't tell me what I want to know, yes I most certainly will."

"Anything," he blurted.

"You will write down the exact location of Mr. Andrei Ivanova's wife and child. I will then have you join an escort as we go to that address and retrieve the two innocent victims you have terrorized for the last two months. If they are not there, my agent will shoot you. If they are harmed in any way, my agent will shoot you. If you try to escape at any time, my agent will shoot you." Kyler retrieved his trusty .38 Special then…no need for heavy artillery for an unarmed pansy of a man.

"And if you don't write the address down in the next ten seconds, *I* will shoot you."

Kyler slapped a pen and paper on the counter of the bar. It only took Dimarco two seconds to begin scribbling furiously onto the pad. While he did so, Kyler grabbed the mic attached to his vest and said, "Come on in. He's ready to go."

A few minutes later, a junior agent came through the front door with a Glock trained on Dimarco. He nodded to Kyler in acknowledgement.

"He's all yours," Kyler then turned to look at Dimarco once more. "Grazie Signore Dimarco. My meal here really was one of the finest I've ever had. I'll be sad to see the place go."

With that, Kyler Scott turned and walked out of Via Di Santo Spirito for the last time.

Prologue

"I don't think I ever thanked you properly for saving my life," she said, giving him a look that told him everything he needed to know about her intentions.

They stood on the terrace of the fifth floor of the Boscolo Astoria just outside his room. The sun was nearly set and put off an explosion of reds, oranges and yellows. The dome of the Cathedral seemed to illuminate from the dusk light and the lights of the city below had just begun to come to life. The sounds of the city were constant but he loved them; voices from the pedestrians below, the feeble horn of scooters as they announced their approach to intersections, avoiding what was otherwise certain death from the cars that flew by with reckless abandon. This was his city and he loved every piece of it. He then turned his attention back to the one woman who had even more effect on him than this great city he loved so deeply. He recognized the desire in her eyes as the same that he felt in the depths of his soul.

"Well I have some thoughts on how you could repay me," he replied.

"Is that right? Care to share?"

Instead of responding, he pulled her in close and pressed his lips hard against hers. She kissed him back, both feeling the passion finally pour out of their bodies after what had seemed like an eternity of ignoring their impulses.

He lifted her up onto his hips and she wrapped her legs around his waist, their lips still locked in a kiss of pure passion. He carried her into the room and, once clearing the threshold, used a foot to close the single open door to the terrace.

As the door slowly came to a close, the last light of the day disappeared from the sky and the lights of the city fully illuminated the golden dome of the cathedral before the picturesque view completely disappeared from frame. The night was theirs.

"CUT!" Kyler heard Jon Christenson say. "And that's a wrap! That's it people. Check the gate but I think that's it. Fire in Firenze is officially wrapped!"

Kyler set his female costar, Veronica Stone, down on the ground gently and joined the rest of the cast and crew in a round of applause as they celebrated wrapping what they hoped was another successful blockbuster smash for Kyler Scott, a.k.a. Scott Cruz. It had actually been his idea to use his hotel room for the final shot, deciding there was no better view of the city than what shone from room 512 of the Boscolo Astoria.

Kyler couldn't help but consider the irony that both he and Armand Amici had shared the same view for a month of his time in Florence, albeit with completely different minds behind it. He was taken aback by how interesting perspective truly was.

After giving hugs to Jon, Veronica and a few other cast and crew members, Kyler made his way back out to the terrace for what would be his last night in Florence, at least for now. As he looked out over the city, much like the movies he had created so many times, it didn't seem real. The beauty of such a place just didn't make sense. Kyler felt like there was no way his eyes could truly take in the sight...truly appreciate what he was looking at. But he would certainly try.

He heard soft footsteps approach behind him and turned to find Alani approaching him.

"Thanks for letting me watch the last scene," Alani started.

"I'm glad you could stay the extra day to see it."

"You and Ms. Stone seem to have some great chemistry," Alani said, trying to hide her obvious jealousy.

"It's just a job. Nothing more," he responded. "I mean...I suppose I could try and make a move...but...she's actually a lesbian."

"Really?" Alani couldn't hide her joy at the news.

"No, not really." He laughed, seeing her cheeks turn a pretty shade of red in embarrassment. "Why, were you interested?" He added.

With that, Alani wound up and delivered a shot to his arm with what felt like everything she had, which Kyler had to admit, was a lot.

"Ouch!" He said but laughed, knowing he'd had it coming.

"You're an ass, you know that?"

"Let me make it up to you. Cup of Florence's finest cappuccino?"

Alani considered it, then said, "Fine but you're buying."

"Fair enough," he replied and turned and offered her his arm. She took it and they made their way past the mess of a movie set that had previously been his hotel room.

The two continued arm in arm as they exited the hotel and strode down Via del Giglio. They passed the hotel that had been Armand Amici's demise just 48 hours earlier, neither of them giving it a sideways glance. The ability to move on from the emotions of a mission was crucial in their line of work. Stopping to take in the hotel, or even acknowledging it for that matter, would also mean reliving what they'd done. For, when it was all said and done, they'd both ended a man's life, regardless of the threat he posed to the world. For Kyler's part, he'd been responsible for not one but fourteen men's lives. The majority of those were likely just following orders, no doubt enticed by the promise of fortunes when it was all done. The true villains were Baldacci, Amici and Dimarco, not to mention the group of North Koreans. Dwelling on the role he played in deciding these men's lives' fate could torment Kyler's psyche if he allowed it. In truth, the idea of it always sat back in the recesses of his mind and he wondered when it would catch up with him. When he'd have the rushing realization of all the lives he'd ended and, more importantly, how it would affect him when it came. It was all the more reason to just keep walking by.

Kyler hit the end of the block and led them to the right down Via del Conti. They walked in silence for several minutes, both enjoying the first bit of peace and quiet in a while. Kyler wondered if Alani was thinking what he was. How nice it would be if this, in another world, was their life. What if they were just a couple, living in this beautiful city, heading out for a nightly stroll? No enemies sticking assault rifles and pistols to their heads, no diving through windows to avoid certain death, no blood on their hands.

Even as he tried to picture it, the image never fully materialized. He had found a purpose in this world and it wasn't his filmmaking. At the end of the day, his actions saved hundreds, maybe thousands of lives and he could never bring himself to be selfish enough to turn his back on those innocents. So instead, he strolled and enjoyed the moment.

After several blocks and a couple more turns, they arrived at a café that sat directly across from the Cattedrale di Santa Maria del Fiore that they had been staring at just ten minutes earlier from Kyler's terrace.

They took a seat and the waiter came by to take their order.

"Due cappuccini, per favore," Kyler said to the man.

"Si, Signore. Grazie."

"Have you ever climbed it?" Alani asked him as they waited for the man to return with their drinks.

Kyler followed her gaze to the tower that rose adjacent to the church.

"The Giotto Campanile. Yes. All four hundred and fourteen steps. The view is spectacular from the top. It's a complete panoramic view of the city. Have you?"

Alani shook her head no.

"Well it's closed now but I'll have to take you sometime."

They both looked at each other a bit more without saying anything, knowing the promise would likely be one he wouldn't keep.

Breaking the silence, the waiter returned with two beautiful works of art that were their cappuccinos. They thanked the man and, when he was out of earshot, Alani leaned in and said,

"So what was your big aha moment with Andrei anyway? Fill me in."

Kyler had debriefed Goldman but Alani had been visiting Andrei to give him the good news and the bad news. The good news being that they had recovered his wife and baby, unharmed, and they had been returned to the safety of their own home. The bad news was that they wouldn't see Andrei on the outside world for the foreseeable future as he was being convicted of acts of terrorism with a sentence of life in prison. Andrei, for his part, seemed to barely hear the latter though, being so overwhelmed with relief and joy that his family was safe. He had not been the cause of their deaths.

"Like I said to Andrei," Kyler began, "the chemical weapon was only going to be as good as the opportunity that would present itself for the North Koreans to use it.

"I got that part Kyler," Alani said with more than a bit of impatience.

"It was the thought of Andrei producing SP-117 that made it come together."

Alani looked at him as if to say, *get on with it already!*

"The package that Dimarco was selling the North Koreans was a combination of the physical and the intellectual. The physical being the chemical weapon, obviously, but also Hawkins's IreMetric device."

"What about SP-117?" Alani asked.

"That was for Dimarco and his crew to continue to use. We're still confirming the details but this is the way I think it played out."

He took a sip of his cappuccino and started in.

"Dimarco and his cronies kidnapped Stratton, Francois and, as we found out in Baldacci's office, Bailey. He drugged them with SP-117 and, while they were under the influence of the drug, used the opportunity to have these coders give them access to a multitude of watchlist databases. As we all know, those databases are the key to identifying who's good and who's bad in the collective eyes of those trying to keep the peace."

Alani was picking it up quickly. "So you think they used those three to make alterations to the lists? Say…change someone on the list coded as a threat to now be a friendly?"

"That's my theory," Kyler nodded and continued. "Then they grabbed Hawkins with the intention to make him reproduce his device. The North Koreans get it in their possession and use it as a safety precaution."

"What do you mean?"

"They needed to make sure that the changes Dimarco's kidnapped victims made actually took. They wanted to test it themselves and planned to use the IriMetric device to scan their terrorist mates to make sure they wouldn't be flagged as a threat."

Alani added, "Smart on Dimarco's part to keep the intelligence side of it on his end so he can keep squeezing the North Koreans for money."

"Exactly. And they would have probably continued using Stratton or anyone else that had access to pop in whenever they needed a few names changed. Once they had clearance, they would have free reign to enter any military base, assuming they thought of a good excuse to be invited…say, special delivery of some fine wine for the troops courtesy of some rich donors somewhere back in the states?"

Alani finished the plot, "And with access to the base, they could release the chemical and literally take out an entire camp full of US military personnel, one base at a time."

They both paused in silence for a moment as the gravity of what had come so close to being a reality settled in.

"Jesus," Alani said under her breath.

She then held her cup up in a toast.

"Well here's to you agent for saving the world, though the world will never know it."

"No," Kyler said, "here's to us."

Alani clinked her cup with his and said, "To us…Defenders of the free world."

"And to Scott Cruz, defender of bad-asses of the silver screen."

"Since you saved my life, I'll let you have that one."

With that, they clinked their cups, took a savory sip of the finest cappuccino Florence had to offer, sat back and enjoyed the view of one of the world's most beautiful cities.

Firenze, Italia.

# # #

ABOUT THE AUTHOR

Anthony Joseph was born and raised in Chicago and moved to Los Angeles at the ripe age of 18 to pursue illusions of grandeur as an actor and singer/songwriter, playing guitar and piano since his early teenage years. He had mild success, appearing in commercials for McDonald's and Reece's Peanut Butter cups, a stint on The Young and the Restless as well as writing music for and performing with singer Chioke Dmachi (songs can be presently found on iTunes). In 2001, he met his beautiful wife-to-be Shanti Lowry, a talented and beautiful Actress and Dancer, marrying her 3 years later. Ultimately, Joseph found his true passion in writing, combining his life's experience with his love of travel to bring Kyler Scott's adventures to the page. He still lives in Southern California, surrounded by his wife, family and friends.

Fun facts:
Florence, Italy is Anthony's favorite city in the world and his favorite food, like Kyler Scott, is gnocchi. He, also like Scott, has a weakness for red wine and is an avid runner of marathons.

Thank you for reading...Identity.

Connect with Anthony Joseph Online:

Website: http://anthonyjosephbooks.com

Facebook: http://facebook.com/anthonyjosephbooks

Follow on Twitter @AJwritesbooks

Smashwords: Anthony Joseph Smashwords

Email: anthonyjosephbooks@gmail.com

www.ingramcontent.com/pod-product-compliance
Lightning Source LLC
Chambersburg PA
CBHW060008180626
46817CB00015B/62